Marc Alexander had his first short stories published when he was fifteen, and became a full-time writer in 1972 of both fiction and non-fiction. He is an established writer of horror novels under a pseudonym. He is at present working on the fourth title in the fantasy quartet *The Wells of Ythan*.

Shadow Realm

Part the Third of
The Wells of Ythan

Marc Alexander

First published in 1991
by HEADLINE BOOK PUBLISHING PLC

A HEADLINE FEATURE paperback

10 9 8 7 6 5 4 3 2 1

ISBN 0 7472 3027 7

Typeset by Medcalf Type Ltd, Bicester, Oxon
Printed and bound by
Collins Manufacturing, Glasgow

HEADLINE BOOK PUBLISHING PLC
Headline House
79 Great Titchfield Street
London W1P 7FN

For my sons
Simon and Paul

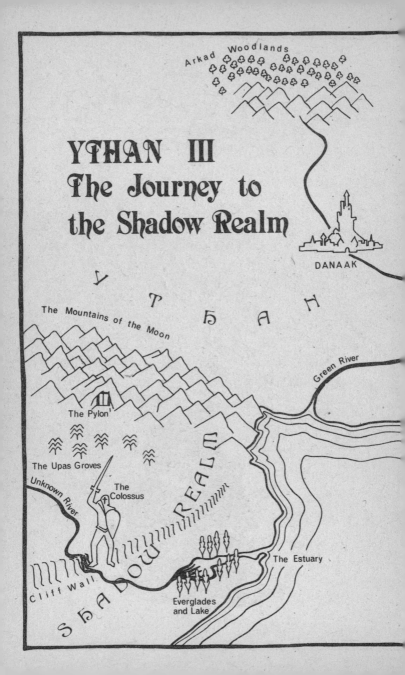

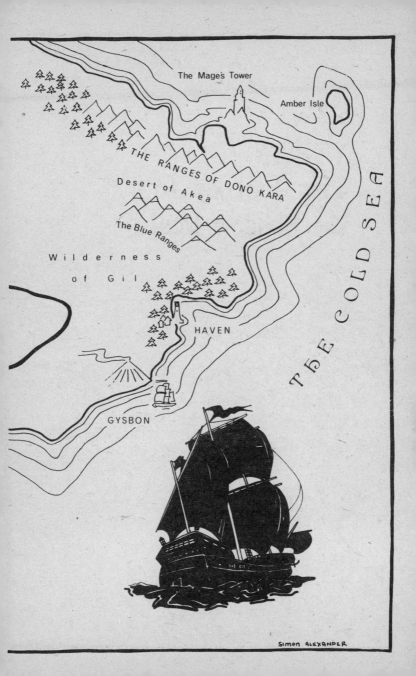

The Mage's Tower

Amber Isle

THE RANGES OF DONO KARA

Desert of Akea

The Blue Ranges

Wilderness

of Gil

HAVEN

GYSBON

THE COLD SEA

SIMON ALEXANDER

Book One

Passing strange was the way I learned the dire news of Thaan's fall, not by force of arms but the foul tactic of catapulting plagued bodies into the city.

On a recent Night of Scents, a band of strangers appeared at the gate, claiming to have reached my Domain by the Varah River. This subterranean waterway flows through the chasm above which my great-grandsire built this palace as a refuge at the time of The Enchantment. Fantastical as their story sounded, I found it to be true, for there was no deception about my unexpected guests; indeed, they carried a curious innocence despite the travails they had suffered, and innocence is a tender plant that withers under the cold blast of hardship. It appeared that they had undertaken a quest . . . but, before I touch on that, I shall describe them, for their diverse characters were a great intriguement to us all.

The leader was a young man whose fair appearance bespoke noble blood, the scion of a family of Marcher Lords on the far side of Ythan.

3

Alwald was his name and he had been dispossessed when the Wald was invaded by the Wolf Horde from the Outlands. Like his murdered sire, he was a follower of the Pilgrim Path.

On this journeying he was squired by Krispin, a youth who had been an apprentice toymaker until his mountain village was razed by the same barbarians. A comely lad, if somewhat simple by nature, time proved there was more to him than appearance showed when he became the saviour of my realm.

City-bred Gambal was Revel Master at the Regent's Court until, for some private reason, he found it necessary to flee Danaak. This he did in company with the other three after rescuing them from the dungeons of the Citadel.

With them was the guide who had led the way to Thaan across the Wilderness of Gil, a crouch-backed fellow of few words but reckoned to be a peerless pilot of caravans. He was named The Hump.

The other male of the party was Ognam, a member of the Guild of Jongleurs whose sallies against the Regent had won him prison lodgings with Lord Alwald and Master Krispin. I must confess that he delighted me the most. His antics at our feasts brought laughter till tears drowned our cheeks. Would that he had accepted my offer to stay in the Domain as my jester, for I verily believe that mirth is a panacea for most worldly ills.

The other two of the group were young women though, to be pedantic, one was only partly so. She was known as Silvermane – one only had

4

to see her beautiful hair cascading down her back to know why. Ere long I discovered that she was a horsemaid, from the far Woodlands of Arkad, whose lower limbs were equine. She was a beautiful, delicate-seeming creature whom I observed with fascination, as the study of fabulous beings has been the preoccupation of my line. The odd thing was that she adored the misshapen guide, and soon the servants nicknamed them 'Beauty and the Beast' from the folktale.

The other maiden was a novice from the heretic priesthood of Thaan, a girl of solemn beauty who now, alas, lies in our most tranquil grove beneath a stone incised 'Lorelle the Lily Maid'.

Such were the first wanderers to arrive here by chance in my long memory.

I learned from Lord Alwald that they were following the Pilgrim Path in search of Princess Livia who, it is believed by many, lies yet entranced in some secret place. Because of my ancestors' connection with Ythan's royal line I know it to be true that Livia, the only child of good King Johan, disappeared as a result of The Enchantment, and that he died heart-broken without recovering her.

Much fable and legend was spawned by The Enchantment for it was followed by a time of chaos during which the Guild of Witchfinders put torch to manuscripts without number in their cause against gramarye. Since those terrible days Ythan has suffered the yoke of tyrannical Regents and, from what I have gleaned from the outside

5

world, the shadow of despair grows ever darker over the land.

In Ythan it is still a hope that if the Princess be found, freed from her glamour and restored to the Empty Throne, the Age of Gold will return.

As to the truth of this I am unable to remark, this forgotten enclave being far from the world of men; yet do I honour those who down the generations have quested for Livia – and usually perished in the attempt.

Thus, when Alwald and Krispin told me that the next step of their journey was to consult The Mage, an ancient sorcerer whom they believed held the answer to their quest, I willingly agreed to help them find the location of his legendary abode. We achieved this by means of star charts devised by my scholarly father, but this gave no satisfaction to my friends as The Mage's tower stood on an islet in the Cold Sea – an impossible place to reach by normal means as it would entail transversing Akea's deathful desert and scaling the forbidden ranges of Dono Kara.

At this point the possibility of continuing the quest became secondary to the monstrous event which threatened the existence of the Domain. I must explain that in the desert, where it is our pleasure to hunt sandharts, there stood great stone statues known as the Circle of Giants who, according to myth, were once real giants petrified by the Mage Ysldon. Now, through some unguessed agency, these colossi regained power of movement and marched on the Domain. Today the palace would be rubble and we all dead, or near to death in the wilderness, had not the toymaker lured them to their own destruction in the chasm.

Alas, it was on this woeful night that the novice Lorelle was slain by a giant, though why she ran into his path will always remain a mystery.

For Krispin's reward I revealed to him and his companions the secret of the great griffins that is known only to the head of our House, his heir and one or two most trusted servants such as my huntmaster Brund. These fabled creatures, survivors from a more majestic age, spend the summer preying on kraken in the Cold Sea and when it turns to ice they winter in a desert valley a day's ride from here.

As time was nigh for them to return to hunting, I arranged for the Pilgrims to fly to The Mage's isle upon their backs.

It was with regret that I watched the griffins soar away with these adventurers whom I had come to regard in the light of friendship and gratitude. How fared they after I lost them to sight I cannot tell. Whether they did reach their destination, or were deluded by their ancient dream to die in parlous lands beyond the ken of men, I may never know. But I pray sincerely that somewhere they still follow their quest . . . and that in some farahead time I might even laugh again at the merry quips of Master Jongleur.

As for the Hump and Silvermane? The quest held naught for them; it was their desire to journey to her Arkad homeland and to this end I provided food and the best drongs in my stable. As with the others, I have no knowledge of their

7

fate. Perhaps, with the Hump's wayfinding instinct, they crossed the wastes and found a route through the unpathed forests beyond.

May it be so.

        – from the Chronicle of Mesire Florizan,
                Lord of the Domain of Olam.

ONE

Magic Clouds and Werewolves

With wine-soaked veils masking their features instead of their usual visors, two armour-clad figures led a small cavalcade through the silent streets of the heretic city of Thaan. The black emblem on their scarlet surcoats proclaimed them to be Companions of the Rose, the elite guards whose dedication to the Regent of Ythan was expressed in the motto 'Fealty Unto Death'. Behind them, on skittering drongs, rode a small body of shot-bowmen and two apprehensive scholars. There would have been something comical about the pair – one beanpole thin, one dumpling fat – had it not been for the scene of horror through which they rode.

Thaan had fallen to the Red Death.

Wherever the intruders glanced, the sight of corpses met their sickened eyes. Some stared at them incuriously from doorways, crimson pest marks still visible on their faces; others lay bloated on the cobbles where they had fallen. As the riders

9

advanced further through the narrow thoroughfares, swarms of black flies rose in murmurous clouds. And rats – the inevitable camp-followers of the plague – paused from feasting and watched the intruders with defiant eyes.

'Serene Mother, Gorfic, I have known more than one battlefield after days of slaughter but nothing to compare with this,' muttered Captain Drogo to the Companion beside him. He wrenched the reins of his drong to prevent it sliding on a huddle of bodies in a street so narrow the gables of its timber-framed houses almost met overhead.

'It has been a foul venture,' Gorfic agreed. 'When the Commander of the Host shot plague-carriers over the walls he never dreamed the heretics would march out and throw themselves on his spears.'

'In days to come sagamen will call it a noble gesture,' said Drogo. 'The heretics have managed to infect most of the army and if the Commander has any sense he will fall on his sword rather than face the Regent's anger in Danaak. As long as I live I shall not forget the women of Thaan, women kissing our fellows, spreading death even as they died upon our swords.'

'Whether Commander Mandal falls on his sword or not, I doubt if any of his troops will be permitted to get within twenty leagues of the capital. Remember when plague broke out in the old Fire Spear Legion? Archers picked off every survivor when they entered the Dolorous Pass.'

'At least you and I will be safe from such a fate.'

'Providing the scholars find what the master wants in the Great Library. At the moment they look too sick to seek scrolls.'

'They will look a lot more sick if they fail,' grunted Drogo. 'But I wonder what it can be that he desires so desperately?'

'Sometimes it is wise to be ignorant when it comes to the master's business, but it is said that he ails.'

'More than ails . . . *Look out!*'

With this warning Drogo wrenched his rein and drove the spike of his goad into his drong's flank causing the animal to lunge sideways. Gorfic followed suit. He looked up to see a figure leaning over the parapet of a shrine above them. Seconds later a block of masonry shattered cobbles a pace ahead of them.

Without pausing for orders, the shot-bowmen raised their weapons and a volley of leaden balls struck fragments from the stonework over which the would-be assassin had been bending, but he had vanished with a heartbeat to spare.

'The Dark Maid has not yet collected all the heretics,' said Drogo. 'Reload, bowmen, and keep your eyes on the housetops.'

The men were regular soldiers and, like all their kind, regarded the Regent's elite Companions of the Rose with the same mistrust in which they held Witchfinders and spies with authority outside the army's discipline.

Now they made no reply but their ironical glances said much. As a matter of course they had reloaded immediately after firing and did not need these potton turds from Danaak to tell them what to do! If the Companions had not demanded the taking of Thaan in a matter of days, the siege would have proceeded in the approved manner with mine and battering ram, and Pillage Permission at the end. Instead, plague warfare had not only infected the enemy but their comrades as well. They would not have been averse to lining their sights on the Companions had it not been for the promise of a hundred crowns each to carry out this mission.

'Sir, according to prisoners questioned before . . . before the Red Death . . . the Great Library is across yonder square,' called the tall scholar whose name Quillon had been playfully shortened by his colleagues.

Drogo grunted and gazed up at the ivied tower which soared above them. Like all the buildings in Thaan, its outlines had been softened by time and weather; from a distance the ancient city appeared to grow out of the plain as naturally as the Drankenfel mountain which reared behind it.

'Are you the conquering army?'

The voice, weak but mocking, came from the doorway of a small shrine above which was carved the golden eye symbol of the All Father. Drogo held up his hand to restrain the shot-bowmen and saw the woman wore the green robe of the heretic priesthood which, unlike the True Faith, was open to both sexes. Although her hood covered much of her face, he could see that once she had been handsome.

'Woman, do you know the penalty for heresy?' Gorfic demanded.

'I know there are no Witchfinders to carry it out. Is it not true that they were the first to flee the Red Death?'

'Why did you remain here when the rest of your people marched out against us?' Drogo asked in a reasonable tone.

She shrugged beneath her robe and left the doorway.

'I have a question for you,' she said. 'Why have you destroyed us? We lived far from Danaak and harmed no one, and our riches were not worth the expense of such an army.'

'Because heresy is an abomination.'

The priest came closer to the captain until she was looking up into his face.

'Come, sir,' she said with a slight smile on her haggard features. 'Is the fact that we worship the Father and you His daughter worth all this slaughter?'

'It was orders,' said Drogo. 'We were commanded to root out heresy.'

She nodded. 'The All Father works in mysterious ways. Perhaps this is his way of rooting out your heresy, for now the army is infected, the Red Death will march across the Regent's lands. As for you, what is your chance of leaving Thaan alive?'

With a sudden leap she tried to throw her arms about the Companion, but he was mounted too high and her hands – whose palms bore the crimson plague mark – merely left bloody smears on his surcoat.

With a curse Drogo sent her reeling with a gauntleted blow. Triggers clicked and under the impact of the shot the priest was plucked from her feet in a reddish haze, a discarded marionette. For a moment the only sounds were the tearing of cloth as the captain ripped away his defiled surcoat, and the retching of the fat scholar. Then the cavalcade moved briskly across the square to the tower.

At the entrance the soldiers were left on guard while the Companions and the scholars ascended a spiral staircase to a vast chamber lined with leather-cased tomes, muniment chests and scroll jars. Light flooded in through high windows which gave views of the city's roofs and the plain beyond, and under one of these an old man sprawled across a table surrounded by charred parchments.

'Lucky the Dark Maid took him before he set the place afire,' said Drogo. He turned to the awed scholars, their fear of the dying city replaced by admiration for the last great library in Ythan.

'You know what to do.'

Papen, the stout one, said, 'There are many hundreds of manuscripts here. The work may take a considerable time.'

'Work fast then,' said Drogo. 'Do not forget the Red Death is in the very air about us.' He gestured to the body of the old man.

Gorfic nodded and crossed to the open casement. With his veiled face averted, he lifted the corpse and heaved it over the sill. Drogo looked curiously at the burnt parchment on the table and, sweeping the ashes away, saw lettering scored on the wooden surface.

'Quill, what has he written?' he demanded.

The tall scribe looked at the erratic characters.

''Tis Old Ythan,' he said. 'Luckily I happen to know the rudiments . . . Let me see. It reads "Lorelle, my love."'

Drogo roared with laughter.

'Randy old dotard!' he cried. 'Right, you two, get to work for your Regent. Come, Gorfic.'

The two Companions went to the far end of the library and, sweeping a pile of manuscripts from a table, began to roll dice.

' . . . and Tico the Clever Cat waited until the wicked witch had turned herself into a mouse, and then he pounced and in a moment all that was left of the wicked witch was a smile on Tico's face. After that he and his master lived happily ever after in the silver palace.'

The slender, blue-veined hands of the Lady Eloira, Reeve of the High Wald, gently closed the jewelled volume on her knees.

'And that, Jennet, is the end of the story of Tico the Clever Cat,' she said with a smile. 'My father used to read it to me when I was very small, and this book has not been opened since.'

Sitting on a stool beside her was a young woman of remarkable beauty whose spun-gold hair fell to her waist, yet despite the pleasing picture she presented in a dress of blue that matched her eyes, there was something disquieting in her rapt expression – the suggestion

15

of a child rather than someone approaching her eighteenth season.

'Was the Clever Cat anything like Smoke?' she asked, stroking the large grey cat asleep on her lap.

'I am sure he was very like Smoke,' replied the old woman whose features, framed with silver hair, had gained a delicate beauty with her long years. Although it was now late spring in the High Wald, a fragrant fire danced in the solar's fireplace and on Jennet's knee Smoke rasped his contentment. The doll beside her feet added a pleasing touch of domesticity.

Eloira sighed at the thought of Jennet's malady – the regression of her mind to childhood to escape the horror of being the only one to escape the destruction of her village by the invading nomads.

The Reeve reached for a crystal goblet of her favourite wine, telling herself that at her age she deserved the comfort that the sparkling liquid gave her. With the Wolf Horde in control of the Wald, anyone in her position needed a stimulant from time to time.

'You should rest, my dear,' she said to Jennet.

'Oh, do I have to? I always wake up feeling unhappy.'

'Perhaps not this time. If you promise to be good I shall take you to watch the pretty colours.'

Jennet smiled her pleasure at the idea. 'All right, I promise.'

Taking her by the hand, Eloira led the young woman up a circular staircase to the flat roof of the tower. Jennet aptly called it the garden-in-the-sky; trailing vines fell from lichened urns, aromatic herbs grew in wide-mouthed pots, and in the centre stood a large astrolabe-like object constructed in copper greened with age.

The couple crossed to the parapet and gazed across what appeared to be a plain of white vapour rolling to a distant range of snow-capped mountains. This was the cloud the old woman had conjured to protect the Peak Tower after the Wolf King's warriors had crossed the River of Night, and as long as its clammy shroud covered the forest of the High Wald, no enemy could find his way through. The westering sun gilded the feather clouds drifting high on the wind that for ever blew from the Outlands. On the horizon the ranges became mauve beneath their snow mantles which in turn blushed in the sunset. The two highest peaks – the White Virgins who guarded the pass leading from Wald to the outside world – glowed magnificently as they reflected the orange sun before she plunged over the edge of the world.

'If only Krispin were here,' Jennet said.

'He will come,' said the Lady Eloira softly. 'He will come.'

At the same time as the Lady Eloira and Jennet were admiring the play of colour over the High Wald, the young Witchfinder Mordan cursed the pain in his buttock as his mule struggled resentfully up the narrow track towards the pass between the White Virgins. Accustomed to travelling in the black coaches of his guild in

Danaak, he blamed the hard saddle for the boil that tortured him

Behind him rode Master-at-Arms Yanos, and following the two mounted men toiled a dozen veterans from the dreaded Nightwatch Company who traditionally provided Witchfinders with armed support. This honour was testified by the iron symbol of a cauldron worn on a chain over the men's mail tunics.

As the path widened, Yanos urged his mount abreast of the young man whose black cowl was thrown back to reveal an open, almost boyish, face which he had found to be a powerful asset when gaining the confidence of suspects.

'With luck we will reach the outpost by duskfall,' said the soldier. 'My lads will be glad to drop their packs, though what we will find there the Mother only knows.'

'At least it was commanded by Companions of the Rose.'

'With a good detachment of our spearmen and archers. But a number of nomads are also encamped in the pass, as was agreed with the Wolf King through Affleck.'

The Witchfinder winced as it seemed a red-hot skewer entered his tender nether flesh. 'Affleck is the Regent's spy who opened the gate of River Garde to the barbarians?' he said when his eyes had ceased to water.

'The same, Master Finder,' replied Yanos. 'He is high in favour with the Wolf King, which is lucky for us as I no more trust those wolf-worshippers than I can shit silver pieces.'

'Though they are pagans we must accept them while they are of use to our Lord Regent,' said Mordan, and he made the Circle of the Mother at the thought of their idolatry. 'The time will come when they have served their purpose aaand . . .!'

'Do you ail?' asked the Master-at-Arms as the Witchfinder gave a sudden cry of agony – his boil had burst.

Soon the little band reached the entrance of the pass, a defile between two walls of rock on whose higher ledges layers of winter snow still gleamed. Ahead a fire flickered and the troops muttered when they saw its dancing light reflected on steel. They did not need the order of their master-at-arms to be on the alert; their shield straps were loosened, and so were their packs – ready to be flung down at a moment's notice should they have to defend themselves.

The Witchfinder, euphoric since the pressure had been relieved from his rump, was reminded of the realities of the situation when Yanos, conveniently conscious of protocol, fell behind to allow him to take the lead. Suddenly he sensed strangers poised on rocks and hidden in shadows but determined to act as befitted his caste – feared by all and supported by both Regent and Archpriest. He forced his mule to trot up the final slope into the circle of firelight. Before it lounged a number of short, sturdy men, faces tanned by steppe wind and yellow-eyed beneath coarse hair. Long-handled war axes were slung across their backs in the way archers carried bows.

'I am Brother Mordan of the Guild of

Witchfinders,' Mordan declared in the voice of authority which had been an essential part of the training at his seminary, 'and I come on official business of the Lord Regent of Ythan.'

Normally his tone commanded immediate respect, but on this occasion the barbarians only stared at him with insolent eyes and several spat into the fire.

'I fear these fellows do not understand your speech.'

A figure moved into the fire glow, a head taller than the nomads and wearing a red surcoat over his armour.

Mordan masked his relief at the sight of a Companion of the Rose. 'My credentials,' he said, proffering a vellum scroll.

The Companion gave it a cursory glance. 'You are far from home, Witchfinder,' he said with an amused note in his voice. 'You must have pressing business to come on such a dangerous route.'

'I have a warrant for the arrest of Lady Eloira, Reeve of the High Wald, on the charge of practising sorcery as attested by Lord Odo in the Citadel of Danaak,' replied Mordan.

'That carries no surprise,' said the Companion. 'But before we discuss the matter I suggest we retire to my camp – if these gentlemen will give us leave,' he added drily.

After addressing the nomads in their guttural tongue, he led the way to where the defile widened above a track sloping steeply into the shadows of the High Wald. Here a small pavilion and several tents had been erected, and a number of regular troops kept guard. Within minutes Mordan was raising a cup of wine in the pavilion while outside, the men of the Nightwatch Company huddled round their fire pots and grumbled at their rations.

'I do not envy your errand, Witchfinder,' said the Companion.

'It should be straightforward,' Mordan replied. 'A charge of sorcery has been laid against the Reeve and it is my duty to arrest her.'

'You may find it an impossible duty to perform.'

'Impossible? That word is alien to our guild.'

'I mean that it is impossible to reach the Peak Tower. You are right about the sorcery, that beldame's family have played with it for generations, and she has magicked a cloud over the forest that surrounds her castle.'

'Weather magic is very low-grade stuff,' said Mordan. 'I do not see that it is beyond our ability to find a way through mist.'

'This is no ordinary mist. It confuses all who enter it so they wander enchanted and can never reach its centre.'

'I can hardly return to Danaak and report that I failed because I was afraid of getting lost. At dawn we will set out for the Peak Tower, mist or no mist.'

The Companion shrugged. 'As you will. A band of nomads will escort you, not only because such is part of the agreement since the Wolf King became master of the Wald, but you will need them to guide you as far as is possible.'

'Tell me about these nomads.'

'They are murderous fighters with their long-handled axes but have little discipline. I believe they hunger for their Outlands over which they roamed in sailed wagons. After the freedom of the steppe they are uneasy amid forest and hill.'

'They deny the Serene Mother?'

'They have probably never heard of her. Their deity is the Wolf-in-the-Sky who prowls along the Star Bridge.'

'And they conjure magic?'

'I know nothing of that except some of them are shape-changers. It was in the likeness of a wolf that their leader tore out the throat of Grimwald VII.'

'Magic clouds and werewolves,' exclaimed the Witchfinder contemptuously. 'Is there aught else?'

'Perhaps you will find out tomorrow,' said the Companion and reached for the wine flask.

TWO

The Tower Restored

A grey wind shrilled over the desolate deeps of the Cold Sea. A demonic hunter, it chased tatters of panicked cloud across the dim sky and drove ranks of spume-streaming waves westward until they burst against cliffs of wetly gleaming basalt. As though inspired by a spirit of malice, it tore at the towers of the hoary castle rising out of a rocky islet close to the barren mainland, its banshee voice keening among conical-roofed turrets and its invisible fingers drumming on diamond-paned casements.

Yet within, all was unnaturally still. No errant airs disturbed the dust of ages in this kingdom of decay and silence. Only in one chamber was it possible to imagine how the castle might have been before it became the domain of woodworm and spider. Here the furniture was whole, ancient tapestries retained something of their once vivid colours, and in a grotesquely sculpted fireplace blazing logs defeated the salty damp which pervaded the rest of the tower.

Here, too, was life. Three travel-stained young

men stood before a four-poster bed on which lay an old man whose frail hands were folded over his fleece covering. His head rested on a samite bolster; locks of silver hair lay tangled on either side of a face which time had etched into a mask of venerable tranquillity. He lay as still as a statue carved on a sarcophagus.

Equally still were the intruders who gazed upon him in dismay, the auburn-haired toymaker Krispin, the fair aristocrat Alwald, and Gambal, the innocent-faced young man who until recently had been the Regent's Revel Master in far-distant Danaak. Now it was he who muttered, 'He has gone with the Dark Maid. We are too late.'

'Too late!' Alwald echoed bitterly. 'To reach The Mage we travel through the Land of Blight, escape the Citadel's dungeons, cross the Wilderness of Gil, survive the siege of Thaan, sail the underground river and fly over the Dono Kara Ranges on the backs of griffins only to find him dead! Serene Mother! I curse the day I let that witch-hag Eloira persuade me to follow the accursed Pilgrim Path!'

His normally handsome features were suffused with ruddy anger and for a moment Krispin thought that in his rage Alwald would strike the still figure on the bed.

In contrast, the blood had drained from Gambal's face and an unusual look of defeat appeared in his dark eyes.

'Mayhap he is not dead . . . ' Krispin began.

Alwald turned to him, eager to vent the rage which was coiling within him. 'Have you learned nothing since you left Toyheim? Have you not seen

24

enough death to know when you are looking at a corpse?'

Roughly he thrust his hand under the bed covering and laid his fingers on the skeletal breast.

'There is no movement of the heart.'

'I remember Master Hobin of my village,' said Krispin mildly. 'Some distemper struck him down and all thought he was dead, indeed he looked just as *he* looks now, at rest but without movement, yet he recovered and many a rocking horse he carved before he was killed by the Wolf Horde.'

'Rocking horses!' exclaimed Alwald in disgust. 'Face it, man. The quest for Princess Livia has failed here in this chamber.'

'Yet he may have some glamour upon him,' Krispin persisted, willing himself not to answer Alwald in the same vein. 'If Princess Livia was entranced as we believe a hundred seasons ago, she would most like be lying thus, no heartbeat yet not dead . . . '

'He cannot have been long without life,' Gambal mused. 'The fire still burns high.'

'The Mage must have had servants,' Alwald said. 'Such an ancient creature would not have had the strength to carry logs.'

'But ours are the only footprints outside this chamber,' Krispin pointed out. 'It seems to me that there is sorcery in the air. You, Alwald, said when we entered the tower that you did not feel it was real, that there was something of a dream mixed with it.'

'True,' agreed Alwald in a calmer tone. 'Would

that I could wake up from a dream and find myself back in River Garde.'

As he spoke, Gambal took a small leather case from within his doublet and extracted a mirror which he held gently to the old man's bluish lips. A moment later he held it up in triumph – on the silvered glass was a slight haze of vapour.

'He is not dead!' he cried. 'The Mage is not dead.' In his excitement he shook the old man's almost fleshless shoulder. 'Awake, Mesire Mage, awake!'

There was no response and when Alwald laid his hand on his breast again he shook his head. 'I still feel no beat.'

'Perhaps Ognam could rouse him with that pipe of his,' said Alwald. 'His music has a strange power, as I recall.'

'Aye, where is the buffoon?' Gambal asked.

'He must have wandered off by himself while we were exploring.'

'I shall fetch him,' said Gambal quickly and before another word could be said he quit the room.

He passed through the cobwebbed antechamber and into a gallery whose air of neglect came as a shock after the warm bedchamber. Dust lay everywhere, musty wall hangings drooped in tatters and mice had long robbed the scattered chairs of their upholstery. Through grimed panes Gambal saw vast combers speeding like watery avalanches towards the tower, giving the illusion that it was about to be engulfed, though in fact the waves crashed far below on the islet's cliffs and only sheets of icy spray enveloped the dismal walls.

26

'Ognam,' he called softly, and then repeated the name a little louder.

When there was no response, he smiled grimly at some inward satisfaction and, seating himself in an alcove, brought forth the mirror with which he had tested the old man's breath. Holding it at arm's length, he watched as it clouded and coils of grey smoke appeared to writhe behind its surface. When this blended into the semblance of a face, a face that continually melted and re-formed just as the smoke had done, Gambal's lips began to move.

Several minutes later he drew his sleeve across his face, which was beaded with sweat despite the coldness of his surroundings, replaced the mirror in its case and returned to his companions.

'No sign of Ognam,' he reported. 'The fool must have lost himself in the passages.'

'Then we must seek him,' said Krispin rising to his feet from where he had been sitting before the fire.

'First I have an idea which may rouse the old one.'

'Say on,' said Alwald who was also luxuriating in the heat of the logs after the cold of the aerial journey to the tower.

'As I understand it, Master Krispin, you carry a special stone which you gained in the City Without a Name – a marvellous gem you showed to Brother Mias in Thaan.'

'The Esav.'

'Yes, the Esav, the jewel from the stars, Brother Mias called it. I believe it has great and strange properties.'

27

'So?'

'Lay it on the heart of the old man. If there is a spark of life in him, the Esav will surely bestow strength and wakefulness.'

'What makes you so certain?' demanded Alwald. 'And why did you not think of it immediately?'

Gambal looked at the young noble with a slight smile on his thin lips. 'My lord, the idea only just entered my head. Perhaps it is the fatigue of the journey that has slowed my wits. As to being certain, I merely though that mayhap—'

'Let us try,' interjected Krispin. From inside his shirt he produced a purse of soft leather on a thong – such purses had been worn by most of Toyheim's inhabitants – and from this he took a heart-shaped crystal in which colours constantly mingled and changed as though the essence of a rainbow were trapped within.

Eagerly Gambal pulled back the fleece to allow Krispin to place the opalescent stone on the old man's breast. He could not be sure but it seemed as though its swirling colours waned briefly the moment it touched the parchment-like skin.

For a long moment the three held their breath, then the faintest of tremors passed through the floor of the chamber and the air was filled with whispers, the words of which remained tantalisingly just beyond the reach of their ears. They looked wildly about them, half expecting to see the whisperers materialise out of the air, but the chamber remained empty. The sibilation grew more urgent until a deep voice cut through it with startling effect.

28

'Beware! Death is the greatest mercy for those who wake The Mage for no worthy reason.'

As the words resounded through the chamber, Krispin snatched away the Esav, thrust it into his pouch, and with his two companions backed towards the door. As the disembodied voice repeated the warning, Alwald felt for his sword grip but the moment his hand brushed against its jewelled hilt he gave a cry of pain and gazed at his hand. He was amazed to see that there was no mark on it though the sword had felt white hot.

'Serene Mother, protect thy child,' he muttered.

The whispering died. The three felt no more tremors beneath their feet and in the fire basket logs crackled as cheerfully as ever. Then, from the bed came the faintest of sighs, and the veined lids of the old man slowly opened. They revealed eyes as black as jet which were in startling contrast to the bloodless pallor of his face. For a moment they gazed upwards at the four-poster's canopy, then turned towards the young men by the door. No expression of surprise crossed the ancient features though the bluish lips twisted into the hint of an ironic smile. Then, as though from a great distance, came the voice of The Mage.

'Wine.'

They looked about them in vain, then a hand raised and a white finger pointed to a massive chest on which had been carved grinning woodwose faces. Gambal immediately crossed the room and, pulling open a door, found a flagon of the black wine of Ronimar. He poured some into a pearl-hued glass, which he calculated would

29

have been worth a hundred crowns in Danaak, and took it to the old man.

'Drink, my lord,' he said in the courtly tone he had learned in the Regent's Citadel.

'Fine wine . . . is the best gramarye I know,' The Mage murmured. 'Another glass . . . young sir.'

The black liquid was certainly having an effect. A faint flush replaced the sickly hue of The Mage's skin, his lips lost their bluish tinge and his chest rose and fell with normal breathing. After a minute he was able to sit up and regard them.

'Forgive . . . my not giving you a welcome you deserved . . . on . . . reaching this far shore but your . . . arrival was unheralded and I . . . was far away . . . when I was recalled,' he said in a voice that was little more than a whisper. 'You are from . . . Ythan?'

'That is true,' said Gambal. 'May I present Lord Alwald, Hereditary Lord of the River March of the Wald . . . '

When the introductions were concluded, The Mage merely nodded and said, 'You must have business of . . . great import to undertake such a journey . . . but that can wait until we sit at table. No doubt . . . you are as hungry as I, so we will dine shortly. Let us . . . meet in the banquet hall in an hour. Meanwhile you can bathe, rest and dress in fresh garments in the guest chambers . . .'

'My lord,' began Alwald, 'your castle does not appear to have the necessary amenities—'

'We shall be honoured to accept your mage-ship's hospitality,' interjected Gambal and taking Alwald by the arm he led him quickly from the chamber with a bewildered Krispin following.

'The pottons take you!' cried Alwald, shrugging off Gambal's hand as the door closed behind them. 'You forget your manners.'

'Perhaps, but I think it unwise to be critical of a sorcerer or of his abode.'

'But what sort of sorcerer must he be to live in such a dismal ruin. You only have to look around you . . .'

His words faltered. The other two were gazing in awed silence at the gallery ahead of them. The floor was no longer covered with dust; sumptuous rugs scattered on polished wood glowed richly in the soft light which suddenly flooded from amber lamps suspended on silver chains.

'The walls,' muttered Krispin.

Mouldering hangings appeared to writhe against the walls they covered: threadbare patches regained their original sheen, rents healed, broken threads joined and embroidered scenes – long faded into obscurity – regained their subtle hues and exquisite forms. Everywhere glass lost its patina of grime; corroded metal gleamed again and woodwork revealed its grain once more. Warm perfumed air carrying strains of gentle music replaced the dank atmosphere which had pervaded the edifice.

'The Mage must have been lying entranced for a long time for the tower to become so neglected,' said Krispin. 'Strange that he did not have servants to look after it.'

'Why have servants when you can work magic?'

31

said Gambal. 'It is as though the whole place has come back to life with him.'

'To me it seems even more unreal,' said Alwald.

Ahead of them a globe of golden light appeared and remained suspended as though held by an invisible hand.

'I think we are meant to follow,' said Krispin.

When they stepped forward, the globe glided ahead of them, down a flight of stairs whose balustrades shone with new gilding, and along more corridors until it bobbed before a curtained archway. When the companions reached it, the curtain slid back to reveal a chamber with a floor of rare marble in which was set a pool from which steam drifted.

'A bath,' cried Alwald in delight.

The globe remained hovering while they removed their clothing and threw themselves into the circular pool whose sides were fashioned from white-crystalled porphyry. As the heat of the scented water soothed the weariness from their limbs, they lay back and came close to dozing. Then Krispin said suddenly, 'Ognam! We have forgotten Ognam.'

'Fear not,' said Alwald lazily. 'He will turn up, bad jokes and all. No harm could come to the likes of him.'

'Do not be too sure. One should always be watchful when there is sorcery in the air,' said Gambal. 'With sorcery nothing is ever what it seems and there is truth in children's tales of Fey money turning into dry leaves.'

When they finally left the bath, the globe led

them to three guest chambers where coverlets of spider silk were folded back for them to rest on ivory couches.

'Mayhap we are near the end of the quest at last,' said Alwald. 'I pray the Mother it be so, for the time draws on to the Lady Demara's birthing of my father's child, and I—' He stopped abruptly.

'We are a long way from the Vale of Mabalon,' said Krispin gently.

'We are a long way from anywhere,' Gambal exclaimed, 'and we are stranded at the edge of the Cold Sea without any means of returning to Ythan let alone continuing our quest.'

THREE

The Alchemist

The long gallery in the oldest part of Danaak's Citadel was a mystery of shadows. Shrouded shapes stood eerily along the walls, shapes that suggested figures petrified in a moment of action and veiled with white fabric. The only illumination came from a lantern held by a small man with rounded shoulders in grey tunic and hose who, with pebble spectacles gleaming in the yellow glow, moved slowly along the line of his mechanical charges. At each one he paused, pulled away its dust sheet and with a cloth of finest white samite polished already burnished metal and dusted wax features that were dustless.

Sometimes he spoke in a sibilant voice to a favoured automaton.

'Good even, Executioner,' he said as he unveiled a mechanical man with the haft of a crescent-shaped axe gripped in his iron fingers. He towered above the curator, his face concealed by a mask such as was prescribed by the Guild of Executioners. Only two eyeholes pierced the black leather shaped to fit the human visage, and these allowed the light to reflect on a pair of eyes fashioned from blue crystal.

The little man bent to run his finger along the blade of the axe.

'Finely honed as ever. Oh yes, finely honed,' he murmured and replaced the cover to move to the next swathed form.

He had his favourites among his charges. These he would talk to for minutes at a time; others – such as the winged lion or the erotic dancer – would be dismissed with a grumbled sentence, though all received the same attention from oiled feather and duster. On reaching the end of the row a smile lit up his sun-starved features. Here, beneath a drape of finer weave than the rest, was his favourite of favourites. Not only were her hidden mechanisms more cunning than those of the fencers – or even the lute player – but she was an aristocrat, that is to say she had been modelled on one.

'Good even, my lady,' he said with a bow as the covering rustled to the floor revealing the replica of a young woman dressed in a gown of spider silk that sometimes shone green and sometimes blue in the lantern light. The coils of her soft hair were held in place by a comb of jet inlaid with river pearls; moonstones glimmered at her throat and garnets glowed on her fingers. Her eyelids were down but there was a hint of a smile on her delicately painted mouth.

'Perfect!' breathed the curator. 'Perfect as ever, my lady, and so you should be, for you were inspired by the most beautiful girl in Danaak, the mistress of the Lord Regent. And though he tired of her, he did not tire of you because you surpassed she who was your model. Oh yes, you surpassed her. And though you, too, have to wait like the others for the master to return to his family – a family more loyal than one of flesh and blood and deceit – your beauty still shines brighter than the rest.'

Stretching up, he slipped his hand into a slit in the back of her gown and touched a lever. There was an almost inaudible whirr of lovingly-oiled gears and the eyelids snapped open to reveal large lustrous eyes, while her breast rose and fell in perfect imitation of breathing. To the never-failing delight of the curator she performed a graceful curtsy, held out her arm for him to take and together they promenaded the length of the gallery.

'What a delightful stroll,' he said. 'May I say, my lady, how becoming your new gown looks this evening.'

The human-sized doll turned her head to him in acknowledgement. He knew exactly how to time his speeches to fit her movements.

'Shall we take another turn, Merlinda . . . '

His voice died. His ears, so acute that he could hear the squeak of new-born mice through the massive walls, caught the sound of distant footfalls; one pair the heavy tread of a full-grown man, the other pair as light as a child's.

'The master!' the curator almost screamed. 'Oh, my dears, he returns to us at last. We must be ready, oh yes . . . '

The dwarf Fozo had trembled as he waited outside the Regent's chamber; of late he had dreaded the call to light his master to the oldest part of the Citadel. Never had he known him to have such black moods and the lamp-bearer did not doubt that the rumours that he was suffering from a mysterious malady were true.

'Trim your lamp, manikin, I hear his footfall,' muttered the sentinel who stood, visor down and with naked sword gleaming, beside the massive door.

'How is his humour, sir?' Fozo asked in his rasping voice as he adjusted the wick in his silver lantern.

'Hush. You will know soon enough.'

The door swung open and the burly figure of the Regent appeared. His entire body was hidden in a voluminous cloak of dark red velvet which swept the ground. Fozo risked an anxious glance at his master's features and was shocked at what he saw. Until recently the Regent's face had been ruddy-hued which gave an illusion of geniality; now it was gaunt and colourless. Only his eyes burned with the same cold intensity as before. The dwarf felt as though the Regent's glance raked his inner being and laid bare his miserable sins.

'Light me to Leodore's tower.'

'As my master wills,' responded the dwarf ritually. He hoisted the lamp high on its silver pole and led the way along passages and through galleries until they reached a small door guarded by another Companion of the Rose. The Regent brought forth a key, awkwardly fitted it in the lock, then followed his lamp-bearer into the gallery where his collection of automata stood ready to jerk into life.

The curator scuttled forward.

'You have come to see your toys?' he hissed. 'The executioner still waits to swing his new axe for you . . . '

'Keep them oiled and ready, Prince,' the Regent answered. 'Mayhap someday . . . ' His voice faded wearily and Fozo knew to continue.

'Oiled they are, ready they are, oh yes, but they fear you forget them.' The sibilant complaint drifted after them.

The Regent followed Fozo to the end of the hall and up a flight of steps to where a mechanical sentry in plate armour guarded the way with a raised mace. In the past it had been the humour of the Regent to make the dwarf brave the swinging weapon but tonight he merely touched a hidden spring and the automaton remained a statue.

'Wait,' he ordered and unlocked another door. Taking the silver lamp he left Fozo in darkness and ascended a spiral staircase to the octagonal room built beneath one of the tallest of the Citadel's spires where the alchemist Leodore worked amidst a confusion of retorts, crucibles, scales and other instruments of his esoteric craft.

The old man was sitting in a stained robe on a stool by the huge fireplace in which a blazing log filled the chamber with stifling heat.

'My lord . . . ' He climbed to his feet while the

Regent, his face bedewed from the effort of climbing the stairs, lowered himself into a heavy wooden chair with a grimace of pain.

'Wine, my lord?' Leodore asked.

The Regent nodded and when a goblet was handed to him he drank greedily, then turned his cold gaze to the alchemist.

'I need more than wine, Master Leodore,' he said slowly. 'I need a cure. The poison from the bite of the monster spreads through my body.'

'Night and day I work on the elixir, distilling and distilling again to obtain the very spiritual element of the blood.'

'Aye, the blood,' growled the Regent. 'No longer is the garrotter's cord used in the Hall of Execution but the headsman's axe to get you blood. There are rumours in the city that I have become a vampire.' He laughed without humour. 'If my devoted subjects only knew the real truth . . . It is better they believe something fantastical. Now it is the night of the full moon. You promised that by this night you would have my cure prepared.'

'It is a problem of quantity,' said Leodore hurriedly. 'Your cure lies in the same elixir with which the homunculi were created. It took me months to prepare the small amount to animate them but you, my lord, are many times the size of those tiny manikins and therefore much more is required if it is to be effective.'

'You have not had enough blood? Serene Mother! I have emptied half the dungeons to keep you supplied.'

The alchemist said nothing.

The Regent threw back his cloak and tore away the bandages that bound his arm, flinging them with disgust into the fire. Then he held out a hand swollen to twice its normal size and with talons for fingernails. Above the wrist the arm was bloated and the veins stood out like purple cords.

'See, I am turning into one of those abominations! Soon I shall appear like the creature that bit me before I threw it in the fire. Where is my cure, Leodore?'

'Soon,' said the old man. 'Soon it will be ready.'

'The pain is beyond belief. Only Mandraga's potions can ease it when I need to make an appearance. Where is my cure, Leodore?'

'My lord, I . . . '

The Regent rose to his full height, his pallid face ghastly in the firelight.

'Show me the elixir you have made.'

Leodore turned to a bench on which stood an object draped with a cloth. He carefully lifted the covering away to reveal a flask of milky liquid.

'Is that all? You told me how much would be needful and there is not a quarter of it there.'

'My lord, the distillation is a lengthy process . . .'

A spasm crossed the face of the Regent, whether of pain or fury the alchemist could not tell.

'I smell something wrong here,' the Regent said. 'Treachery is afoot. I know it. The Hall of Execution has become a slaughterhouse for your requirements, yet you dare show me this pitiable flask after all this time, while I – who saved you from the Witchfinders – am turning into a monstrosity. Tell me the truth, old man, what has happened to the rest of the elixir?'

Leodore tried to answer but in his fear he could only shake his head.

'You need prompting, Leodore,' hissed the Regent, and stepping forward he raised his huge deformed hand and closed his fingers round the old man's scrawny neck, the horny spikes which had once been well-tended nails digging into flesh. Then, seemingly without effort, the Regent raised his inflamed arm so that the feet of his victim were lifted off the acid-holed carpet.

'Admit your — '

A cry filled the chamber, a gurgling, slobbering wail which was so unexpected that the Regent released the alchemist and spun round. From a curtained alcove in the far corner emerged a nightmarish creature, a pallid nude female the size of a half-grown child. The round head was without hair, as was the rest of the body which was a cruel parody of the human form: the mouth a lipless slit above which two holes served as nostrils, the eyes protuberant and gleaming with ferocity. By normal standards the creature's feet and hands were grotesquely over-sized in relation to the rest of her body. Breasts without nipples sagged to the bloated stomach, yet there was a suggestion of unnatural strength about the homunculus. For a moment the Regent, thought accustomed to the freakish beings in his private menagerie, stood as one paralysed.

Then in a voice of mixed anguish and fury he cried, 'You have been feeding her the elixir! You have let me suffer for the sake of that . . . that . . .'

He turned towards Leodore whose body was shivering as though in a fever — a fever of fear — and again he raised his terrible hand. At that moment the creature waddled across the floor and, leaping with unexpected agility, threw herself upon the Regent.

He felt the dead weight of her body, felt her talons clawing at his cloak and saw her face a handspan from his. The slash of a mouth was now wide, and needle-like teeth — teeth that would not have been out of place in the mouth of some monstrous fish — glittered in the firelight.

With a tremendous buffet the Regent hurled the creature from him. She reeled against the bench on which the flask of white fluid stood, and her flailing arm sent it rolling over the edge to smash into fragments on the floor. The homunculus howled in despair and threw her stump arms round the thighs of the alchemist while he and the Regent gazed helplessly as the pool of white liquid soaked away into the filthy carpet.

At last the Regent said in his normal voice, 'Thus it ends. Even if you were true to me and started again there would not be time to distil the needful amount. Why did you give what was rightfully mine to that travesty?'

Aware that there was no hope for him, the old man drew upon himself the dignity that was occasionally witnessed in the Hall of Execution.

'It took my lifetime to create the two homunculi — the male of which you burned through your perversity in this very fire,' he declared. 'It was like seeing my own child destroyed and it determined me that come what might, the female would survive. I found that the only substance which would nourish her was the elixir through which she was made quick and, as she grew from the size of a doll to the size of a child in such a short time, I had to feed her increasing quantities of the distillation. I could not let my own creation starve, for never forget, Lord Regent, that what I have achieved has been the quest of alchemy down the generations.'

'So you allowed me to suffer, to watch myself become loathsome, that your . . . your *daughter* might live,' said the Regent. 'It was misjudged loyalty, my old friend, and now there is nothing more to be said.'

For a moment he gazed at the two contrasting figures in front of the fireplace, the tall old man who returned his look with defiance and the stunted homunculus clinging to him like a frightened child. Then the Regent left.

Below, in the antechamber leading to the stairwell, Fozo – dreaming he was a giant – was kicked back into his diminutive reality.

'Bring Captain Bors to me,' shouted the Regent.

The dwarf fled while his master sank into a chair and regarded the mace-wielding automaton who guarded the door.

'I must needs find new work for you,' he murmured and passed his healthy hand over his face in weariness. Within minutes Bors, Captain of the Companions of the Rose, stood to attention in the soft glow of Fozo's lamp while the Regent gave him his orders.

'Choose a man without kin, one who will not be missed when his task is finished. And hurry, for this work I will see completed before I leave,' he concluded.

Within a short time a small procession crossed the hall to the antechamber under the unseeing gaze of the Regent's mechanical figures. Beside Captain Bors walked a young mason still rubbing his eyes, and behind them several Companions of the Rose incongruously pushed a handcart on which were bricks and a tub of mortar.

'Seal it,' ordered the Regent, pointing to the doorway leading to the spiral staircase. 'Seal it so that none will ever enter again – or leave.'

The mason nodded. He could not understand why he should be called at such an hour but he did understand his craft and within minutes the first row of bricks was in place and he was laying the mortar for the second.

When the task was finished, when a blank wall obscured the only entrance to the alchemist's tower, the Regent grunted with satisfaction.

'Have the brickwork draped with a tapestry, one with a pleasant scene – such as a father playing with his child,' he said. The companions came to attention and the mason tugged his forelock respectfully as the Regent followed Fozo into the hall beyond.

Here the dwarf heard him mutter aloud, 'I wonder who will eat whom first.'

FOUR

The Star Captain

'Awake, awake! A feast awaits!'

The voice was soft. It came to Krispin through a dream in which he was running across a flower-starred meadow beside a girl in a blue ninon gown, whose waist-long hair floated behind her like spun sunbeams. There was such joy in his heart . . .

The dream faded. He was lying on a couch covered with soft furs and he opened his eyes to see a globe of golden light hovering an arm's length from his face.

For a moment he gazed at it in stupefaction, then reality returned – the flight on the griffins from the Domain of Olam, the arrival at the desolate tower and the awakening of The Mage. Since then the tower had magically returned to its former glory, the travellers had bathed luxuriously and fallen into exhausted slumber.

'Awake, awake! A feast awaits!' repeated the globe.

Krispin pushed aside the cover and swung his feet down onto the silken rug beside his couch, and then for a moment his face reddened with embarrassment. He had thrown aside his travelling clothes to sleep naked beneath the furs – supposing the globe was female! There was a feminine timbre about its voice.

'My clothes,' he muttered, hastily pulling back the cover. 'They seem to have gone.'

'Look down – there's your gown.'

Krispin looked. Folded on an ivory stool was a robe of dark green spider silk on which had been embroidered silver arabesques. Beside it was a pair of shoes of softest green leather.

'Dress fast – or you'll be last.'

'All right, all right,' murmured Krispin, reaching for the clothing which had been magically provided for him while he slept.

A few minutes later he followed the globe into a tapestry-hung hall where a long table had been laid as though for a banquet. At the head of the table, on a elaborately carved chair whose high back gave the impression of a throne, sat The Mage in a black robe decorated with silver stars. Colour had returned to his face and his thin lips curved into a smile as Krispin entered the chamber.

Alwald and Gambal – attired like Krispin except that each had a robe of a different colour – were already seated and, after bowing politely to his host, Krispin sat opposite them. One chair remained empty at the table.

'Where is Ognam?' he whispered.

Alwald shrugged and Gambal said scathingly, 'Our jongleur friend seems to have got himself lost. He will turn up sooner or later, for there is no way he could leave the island – unfortunately.'

'Welcome to my table,' said The Mage in a voice barely above a whisper. 'Eat what you will and then tell how you came here to disturb my dreams.'

The three travellers looked down at their empty platters. There was no sign of food.

The Mage smiled. 'You, young lord,' he said to Alwald. 'What is your favourite dish?'

'When my father was still Hereditary Lord of the River March, on high days he had the kitchen prepare venison in a rare red wine and served with forest mushrooms and petals of a certain mountain flower which added an exquisite flavour . . .'

As he spoke a number of globes hanging in the air at the far end of the chamber, like servants awaiting their master's bidding, began to move as though following the pattern of a saraband. Alwald became aware of a delicious aroma in his nostrils, and looking down he saw dark meat and white mushrooms exactly as they had been prepared by the master cooks of River Garde.

His smile of boyish delight was followed by a doubtful frown. The food looked delicious but it was the product of sorcery . . . Then hunger overcame caution and he raised a sliver of venison to his lips.

'What a sauce,' he murmured. 'It is exactly as I remember it.'

'Of course,' said The Mage. 'And fear not for, in a sense, it is your own creation and therefore could be of no harm to you. You will learn that much of my home is the fabric of dreams.'

His words found an echo of understanding in all their ears. Everything around them was solid, the wine tasted as pure and cool as though it had just been brought up from the cellars of the Citadel, and yet there was a feeling of being on a brink beyond which everything could dissolve, transform, melt without warning.

These uneasy thoughts were soon dispelled by the food. When Gambal looked down he saw a magnificent river fish steaming on a bed of herbs. His favourite dish! The air might be filled with gramarye but he was hungry! He raised his knife and parted the rainbow skin.

'What is that before you, Krispin?' Alwald demanded.

'A pie,' replied Krispin simply, but he did not add that it was just such a pie that his beloved Jennet used to bake on special occasions in Toyheim.

Alwald smiled, amused that a peasant dish should be chosen when such gastronomic delights were available.

'Now that you have meats before you and wine in your cups – I see one of you prefers apple ale, very good! – I would be interested to hear how you came and why you are here,' said The Mage. 'Visitors are rare on this remote shore, and usually far from welcome. But I know that you are no danger to me. If you had been, you would have been blasted by my unseen guardians while I still slumbered. I think, young lord, that you should begin.'

'Then I shall begin by admitting that we follow the Pilgrim Path.'

'You mean the quest for Princess Livia still

continues?' said The Mage. 'You must forgive my surprise but I have been so long from the world of men that I know little of what now transpires.'

'The secret search continues,' said Alwald. 'And we are here to prove it. It was that which led us to your island.'

'Tell from the beginning.'

Alwald began by describing the fall of River Garde to the Wolf Horde, of how his wounds had been nursed by the Lady Eloira, the Reeve of the High Wald, and how she had set him upon the quest for the Sleeping Princess.

The Mage smiled at his words and raised a goblet of dark wine in his emaciated hands.

'The Lady Eloira appointed Master Krispin – an excellent toymaker – as my esquire,' Alwald continued. 'And she instructed him into becoming the wayfinder.'

'And why did Eloira think that you might succeed after so much time had passed since The Enchantment and all other attempts have failed?'

'She told me that it was because of portents foretold in ancient prophecy. A crystal bird had been seen.'

'That is indeed true,' Krispin could not help adding. 'I saw the bird myself at rest on a forest mere.'

'So the bird has left its silvern tree,' mused The Mage. 'Pray continue with your tale.'

Alwald described how they had set out along the River of Night. The Mage lay back in his throne-like chair with drooping eyelids; he could have been sleeping but for the fact that he held his wine goblet childlike in both hands and raised its rim to his lips from time to time.

Alwald found this lack of response disconcerting but when his voice wavered, The Mage encouraged him with a slight nod and once said, 'I am so very old and there is a weariness within me that you in lusty youth could not guess at, but I listen.'

His interest visibly quickened when Alwald spoke of their arrival in the City Without a Name.

'You survived the Land of Blight – you saw the city?' he said, sitting forward with his eyes intent on Alwald. 'Few men can claim to have done that. Ruins now, empty thoroughfares choked with weed, wrecked causeways once highways through the air, and death brooding over all.' He sighed. 'Do you know the history of its bane?'

'In Ythan the name of the city is beyond memory,' said Gambal.

'Once, when Ythan was just a tiny kingdom among many tiny kingdoms, the Land of Blight had another name – a name in a language long forgotten but which means the Fair Garden, and many generations of men dwelt there in contentment,' whispered The Mage. 'But this changed when a ship arrived from the stars.'

'A ship from the stars!' Krispin exclaimed.

'Truly. A ship of bright metal came down from the night sky, a strange sealed vessel which trailed white fire, and when it rested on the earth by the river it stood like a tower, and those who lived there knelt before it.

'And from it appeared a being in armour who by gesture told them that he had travelled from the

50

Constellation of the Griffin, and the men who knelt before the ship revered him as a god and from then on he dwelt among them.'

Krispin, pigeon pie forgotten, leaned forward to catch every word as in his mind he once more saw the great figure enthroned like an idol in the heart of the City Without a Name.

'The star captain soon learned the tongue of men and taught them knowledge that had never been known before in this world, or since. And as they learned from him over the years, the men of that happy region built a great city around the star ship where the captain continued to dwell, and when he walked forth among them he walked in his armour. Generation after generation passed and, by following the words of their god, men made great machineries and engines.

'Then one day he seated himself upon the throne in the hall of audience and never stirred again. But they went on worshipping him under a priestly caste, and as more generations passed, they became so in love with worship that they forgot the words of their god when he walked among them, and they no longer remembered how properly to tend the machineries he had taught them to build. But the priests told them it was of no matter because if they had faith and worshipped their god, one day he would awake and repair the machineries.

'But the machineries began to fail, and none knew how to make them whole, and despite the prayers of the priests and great sacrifices the god never awoke. The dying machineries went out of

control and from them flowed poison which
turned the river into a channel of dead water
bringing distempers to all who drank from it and
deformity to all plants whose roots it had
nourished. And from the dying machineries there
flowed a glowing fume which killed all who
breathed. Those who lived many leagues away
from the machineries saw great flashes between
the earth and the heavens as though lightning was
celebrating the end of the world. In terror they
fled but great winds pursued them bearing the
fume and few escaped, and those who did were
scarred and wretched and their women bore
monsters.

'When the machineries died, a great silence
fell on the land, for there was no bird to sing.
And a great silence fell on the city, for no man
walked its streets and decay was king. At night
the sky was lit with strange lights which glowed
above the dead machineries, and there was light
also in the tower where the star captain still
sat in his armour. Strange creatures guarded him
on his throne, and the treasure which he had
brought from the stars.'

'The Esav!' whispered Krispin.

'The Esav.' agreed The Mage. 'And how is it that
such a name is known to a . . . toymaker?'

'It was the Lady Eloira, I believe, who put it into
my mind,' said Krispin. 'Much ancient lore was
known to her.'

The Mage looked at him sharply. 'And did your
Reeve of the High Wald know the fate of the Esav,
the jewel that brought magic from the stars?'

'She must have had an inkling,' said Alwald, 'for we found it in the City Without a Name.'

'You found it?'

'Not me exactly,' admitted Alwald. 'I was ailing at that time and it was Krispin who ventured into the ruined city and actually collected it.'

'I find your words hard to believe.'

'Then see for yourself, my Lord Mage.' Alwald said. 'We used it to restore you to wakefulness.' He nodded to Krispin who felt under his robe and from his purse he brought out the heart-shaped crystal which he laid on the table before The Mage. As before, its myriad colours seethed within it, their light reflecting ever-changing hues on the worn face of the enchanter. For a long while silence hung over the table.

'Put it away, Toymaker,' The Mage said at length. 'I have seen enough for the moment. Say why have you brought it here?'

'To trade,' said Alwald simply.

A strange, soft sound came from The Mage. For a moment the three travellers looked at him in alarm and then realised that he was laughing.

'Trade?' he said. 'You have the jewel from the stars and yet would trade it? For what, pray? The secret of transforming lead into silver? A cloak of invisibility? Seven-league boots? What magician's boon is it that you require in return for that pretty bauble?'

'Knowledge,' said Alwald quietly.

The Mage's eyelids drooped and a tremor ran through his hands as he raised his goblet.

'You ask for what is of the most value in the world. What in particular is it that you seek?'

'The secret of where Princess Livia lies enspelled.'

The Mage sighed.

Krispin was aware of the beating of his heart. Were they about to learn the secret for which they had travelled across Ythan? Like the others, he leaned forward, wine and viands forgotten; all eager for The Mage's next word.

'Serene Mother be thanked – I have found you!'

At the sound of the familiar, over-modulated voice they turned to see a strange figure in the doorway, its jester's motley of red and green grimed and in part swathed with cobwebs.

'Ognam!' cried Krispin in relief at seeing their companion again.

'Ognam!' said Alwald irritated at the interruption.

'Ognam!' muttered Gambal in disgust.

'The final guest has arrived at last,' said The Mage. 'You are welcome, Master Jongleur, for that I take by your garb is your profession.'

Ognam limped forward and Krispin and Alwald saw there was a look of shock in his eyes that had never shown before; the habitual grin had gone from his face, even the bells sewn to his cockscomb hood ceased to jingle as though in sympathy with his mood.

'I shall leave you to entertain your companion,' said The Mage. 'Fatigue falls quickly upon me and I needs must rest and ponder your words.'

He rose and walked slowly away, the globes dancing after him in a dutiful line.

'The pottons take you!' cried Alwald when they were alone. 'Of all the times to make an appearance, just when I had brought up the question of the Princess.'

His words had little effect on Ognam who seized a cup of wine and drank like one in desperation.

FIVE

The Wish Maiden

Night. True, palpable night unknown to city-dwellers.

Above the High Wald the stars glittered like crushed crystal; high in the east the Constellation of the Griffin blazed in cold glory. Also to the east a faint luminosity – the harbinger of a waxing moon – turned the twin peaks of the White Virgins into black silhouettes. Such was the stillness over slope and valley that it was possible to sense the forest's slow secret breath, and when a distant wolf gave voice, his lament sundered the silence like a desecration.

Wolf – or a man whose totem is a wolf? Wode wondered as he sat cross-legged on the edge of a high woodland clearing. He was conscious of others waiting quietly like himself, curious to see the Wish Maiden and yet cautious enough not to speak. The men of the river and forest had become as wary as hunted animals. Indeed, they were the hunted.

Wode's thoughts turned to the Wish Maiden. *Why 'Wish'?* Many and strange were the stories that had spread about her but none suggested that she was more than mortal. Perhaps it was because she called her meetings in this unhallowed place, a place avoided by foresters before the nomads brought terror to the Wald.

The moon rose, transforming the snow-capped White Virgins from black to silver and illuminating the forest clearing and its ring of waist-high hoarstones. Who had placed them there originally or why was long-forgotten; all Wode knew about them was that as a child he had heard that each time they were counted, a different figure was reached. He and his brother had left the hut of their woodcutter father one day to see if this was true – and had scuffled as to who had counted right, though both agreed that the number was over three score.

He remembered now that the tall megalith – twice the height of a tall man – which stood in the centre was known as the Wish Stone and the circle surrounding her the Coven.

He looked around as the lunar light showed the men who were ranged round the glade. Some lounged against the trunks of the encircling evergreens, others crouched beyond the silvered stones. They clutched a variety of weapons, some converted from domestic implements; all were ragged and their drawn faces reflected hunger and fatigue. Wode decided that, like him, they had learned of this gathering through chance meetings in the forest with fellow fugitives. Hardly a word was said as they waited.

Suddenly there was a universal gasp of surprise as a figure in a simple kirtle materialised out of the shadow cast by the Wish Stone. As with everything else, she was drained of colour by the moonlight; her youthful face appeared chalk-white framed between two thick braids of black hair which hung to her waist.

For a moment she gazed about the glade with shadowed eyes, then raised both bare arms high above her head in a gesture of welcome.

'Men of the Wald, come out of the dark.' Her voice carried easily across the hoarstones. 'Come within this ancient ring. There is naught that will harm you here. The spirits that men once worshipped here hold no harm for forest folk. Come within the ring so that for a while we shall be a company of companions rather than lonely men who start at shadows.'

'It is more than shadows that afright us, Wish Maiden, or whatever you are,' a man growled.

'Then come within the ring that you may see each other and listen to what I must tell you.'

For a moment none of the watchers round the glade stirred; mistrust had grown strong within them and was a habit hard to break.

What does a lass like her think she can do with men who live like animals, once cheerful lads and fathers who now would cut a throat for a bag of meal! thought Wode as he gazed at her slender form dwarfed by the megalith rearing above her. As he watched her, it seemed that she turned and looked straight at him, and without thought he found himself rising to his feet and walking into the circle to stand before her. There was a murmur behind him, a rustle of soft deerskin shoes on coarse mountain grass, until most of the others had followed his example.

For a second the girl's lips quirked a slight smile in his direction, a sign of thanks or recognition perhaps. Whatever lay behind it, he found it pleasing – and that in itself was strange for he was no longer a youth with an eager heart. He was old enough to have fathered the Wish Maiden, old enough to have a family, though the only family he had known were his fellow soldiers in a once fair castle known as River Garde.

'There is no need to stand to hear my words,' the girl said. 'Take your ease. Here we are all friends and equals.'

The semicircle of men sat down, some with their legs stretched out in comfort, others on their heels. Wode, whose eyes had not left the Maiden, found that he alone was still standing and with a laugh at himself he sank to his knees and tilted back, supporting himself on his brawny arms.

'I thank you for coming this night,' said the Wish Maiden. 'Perhaps you have come out of curiosity to see this strange creature, this unknown maid who talks in wild places. Perhaps you have heard something of my message and would know more. Perhaps you have come out of hope.'

She paused on the last word to give it full meaning, and somewhere on the other side of the valley the howl of a wolf filled the silence.

'Hear me!' she said, almost in the manner of a minstrel about to recite a romance. 'The moon has waxed and waned but thrice since the Wolf Horde came in their wagons from the Outlands to camp on the shore of the River of Night. Those in River Garde were unafraid despite the wolfmen's numbers, for no nomad could swim the great river, and Lord Grimwald, Lord of the River March, set out with confidence to parley with their leader whom they call the Wolf King.

'But Grimwald was murdered by the King who, it is said, can change his shape, and the nomads crossed the river in their wagons which had been built to float like boats, and River Garde was taken, not by force of arms but by treachery from within.'

She stopped. Wode found her silences as effective as her words.

'We all know what has happened since that time,' she resumed quietly. 'The villages of the river folk were pillaged, forest hamlets put to the torch, even Toyheim in the High Wald was destroyed and all the toymakers and their families slaughtered. And there was none to help us. Lord Grimwald's guards are dead, the old dame Eloira, the Reeve of the High Wald, stays in her tower safe within an enchanted mist, and no help has come to us from the outside world. Each day our enemies spread further through the forest seeking plunder. Barbarians, they rejoice in destruction, in killing all but the young whom they enslave.'

Her words brought a mutter from the men, a mixture of anger and shame.

'I saw my home burn,' she continued in a softer tone, 'but I escaped into the forest where, being forest bred, I lived as you have lived, fearful of the bands of wolfmen, heart-broken at the passing of the happy life, weeping for my dead dears.'

Again she paused and all could see a tear glitter like a diamond beneath her eye, a tear which she angrily rubbed away with the back of her hand.

'I have not come here to weep before you. Each of you has his own grief. I have come to tell you of a dream I had – a vision if you like – in which it seemed I stood within a circle of standing stones, this very ring, and I heard a voice, a whispering voice as old as the Wald itself, telling that it is my destiny to lead men against those that despoil the forest land, to gather together fugitives and weld them into a band of comrades who could strike back against the enemy.'

A burly man, his beard flowing over his chest, stood up. 'Whose was this voice you heard?' he demanded.

'I know not for sure, yet I believe it was the spirit that has presided over the forest since the time these stones were raised.'

'That sounds like blasphemy,' someone murmured.

'And what is there about you, a young maid, who can teach men about fighting?' the burly man continued. 'It is easy to talk of striking back at the enemy – the woods are full of men who have tried that and all dangle from halters.'

There was a mutter of agreement.

'Our only chance is to wait for the pass to clear and leave the Wald while we are still whole,' the man went on, 'or for the Regent to send an army.'

'As for that,' said the Wish Maiden, 'you must know it will never happen. Companions of the Rose have been seen in company with wolfmen

61

and the man who opened the gate of River Garde to the horde was a spy for the Regent. It was in his interest to have Lord Grimwald destroyed and his emissaries taught the nomads how to cross the River of Night.

'I tell you, men of the Wald, our only hope lies within ourselves. You may say, what can a maid know about warfare, and once I would have agreed with you but I have been granted a vision and through me inspiration will flow. Do you think I would be standing here on account of some girlish whim? Do you think that those who already follow me are fools? Hark to me, your messenger, and show your love of your homeland by joining us. Revenge your dead ones by taking up sword and slingbow. Follow me until the head of that werewolf king is spiked upon the topmost turret of River Garde and once more the Wald is ours.'

As she spoke her words took on a thrilling tone and Wode had no doubt of her sincerity. He could not take his eyes off her face which now appeared animated by the memory of her vision. But the burly bearded man was once more on his feet.

'Fine words,' he sneered, 'but words will not bewitch men like us who, while we may not have been granted visions by ancient spirits, know that to fight the horde is like trying to kill a wolf bare-handed.'

Many men chorused agreement and rose to their feet.

'I speak true. I can give you victory.'

'You may as well expect us to believe in the

Sleeping Princess!' There was laughter. 'Let us leave this maid to her stones and voices while we can. You have heard the wolfcalls, mayhap a band of nomads may soon be upon us.'

At these words many looked at the surrounding pines with apprehension and began to leave the Coven.

'Go if you must, and may the Mother protect you,' cried the Wish Maiden, 'but to those who have enough courage and faith in my message to remain I give welcome.'

Wode leaned against a stone until most of the men had melted into the trees. A dozen other men – half of them already the Wish Maiden's followers he later learned – remained within the circle.

The Maiden left the Wish Stone and approached him.

'I knew you would stay,' she said. 'From the moment you entered the ring I knew you would follow me.'

Wode smiled at her confidence. 'How did you know that?'

'Since my vision I seem to know things without asking. I have a power that as yet I hardly understand.'

The wolf howled again.

'Fear not, it is a real wolf. I have my sentinels posted in the forest and there is not a nomad within two leagues of us.' She turned to the others who had remained behind and with a sudden easy smile she said, 'Let us go and sup and become friends.'

She motioned Wode to walk beside her and led

the way along a deer path through the trees; behind, the new recruits were shepherded by the Wish Maiden's followers, answering their whispered questions in low voices.

'You believed my words?' she asked.

'I am here.'

'Good. Do you have faith in me?'

'Ah, faith! For some it has to be earned if it is not just wishful thought.'

She remained quiet for a minute. 'You have the bearing of a soldier.'

'That I am, or was. I was second-in-command to Master-at-Arms Emon at River Garde.'

'It was told that the whole garrison was killed or wounded when the castle was overrun.'

'A few may have escaped, as did Lord Grimwald's son after being badly hurt, but I was far from River Garde when the nomads came: I had leave to tend my old father through his last days, may the Serene Mother bless his spirit.'

'My followers are river fishers, charcoal burners and such. I need a man like you to teach them weapon skills.'

An hour later the party was seated at a long, rough-hewn table in a warm cavern deep in a tree-covered hillside. Bowls of game stew steamed before them and a precious cask of wine had been opened to welcome the new arrivals.

'While your words may inspire some,' Wode said to the girl, 'you need a victory over the enemy to convince—.

A large man appeared in the torchlight, grinning good-naturedly through his luxuriant beard. With an oath of surprise Wode recognised him as the fellow who had sneered at the Wish Maiden.

'Meet Brindal,' she said, smiling at the newcomers' astonishment. 'It is his task to lead away those who would never be heart-whole for our campaign. Such can be of more danger than one's true foes.'

Wode grinned at her with added respect. Yet while he had no doubt of her passionate conviction that it was her fate to deliver the Wald he, as a professional soldier, was aware of the odds against a band of dispossessed peasants having the slightest success over the ferocious nomads who handled toy battle axes before they could walk. He had not followed her with the thought of heroic deeds but because, from the moment she emerged from the shadow of the megalith, his heart was caught in the spell of her beauty.

'Tell me how to win this victory over our foes,' she said.

'We must be more terrible than they,' Wode replied.

SIX

The Cage

Ivory trumpets sent a fanfare ringing through the Great Hall of the Citadel. As its echoes died under the vaulted roof, the voice of the herald tolled, 'My Lord Mandal, Commander of the Host.'

Mandal drew a deep breath and strode forward, a stocky figure in a travel-soiled uniform, who nevertheless retained the confident air of one who had risen from the ranks through ruthless effort. He looked neither right nor left as he passed through broad shafts of mauve light cast by the windows set high in the ancient walls. In the days of King Johan XXXIII these had been set with cunningly cut panes of crystal which filled the hall with brilliant light and rainbows, but since the rule of the Regency, sombre stained glass has been substituted. Likewise the bright tapestries depicting charming sylvan scenes were replaced with funereal drapes depressing to men's spirits − as the Regent intended.

The only bright light allowed into the hall shone on the dais at the far end, on which stood the Throne of Kingship, empty for the last century. To the right of this sat the Regent, while behind him towered six members of his bodyguard, the Companions of the Rose, as motionless as graven images with their gauntlets locked on the hafts of halberds.

In the minstrels' gallery stood the Regent's avenger whose cocked crossbow was loaded with a terrible triple-barbed bolt. Behind his silver mask – his identity was one of the closely guarded secrets of the Citadel – his eyes surveyed the crowd of officials, burghers and governors of far-distant provinces. In the event of his master's assassination, his duty was to slay the person present who had most to gain by the Regent's demise.

As Mandal neared the dais he looked up at the Regent. He had heard a strange rumour about his health and the sight of his appearance seemed to confirm it. He wore a voluminous cloak concealing his large frame, a new fashion for the Regent, and while his hair was as glossy black as ever, his face was no longer inflamed with rich living but gaunt and – could it be? – toned with cosmetic. Only his adamantine eyes sustained the sense of power which surrounded him like an aura.

'My Lord Regent,' cried Mandal coming to attention before the dais. The bluff soldierly manner was something which he had cultivated and which had often stood him in good stead.

'Welcome back to Danaak, Commander,' said the Regent in his unexpectedly high voice. 'Come up and sit by me. We are old friends who do not need to shout to each other, and needs must speak in confidence. A stool for the Commander.'

A page with long fair hair – the Regent had a penchant for female pages – brought a delicate stool and placed it on the step below the Regent's chair. The Commander seated himself upon it uneasily, unaware that it had been carved from rare Upas wood and would not crack beneath his weight.

'And wine. Our friend must be weary unto death after riding by day and night.'

'My thanks,' said Mandal. 'I wore out three drongs on the road.'

A second page brought a cup fashioned from electrum.

'What of Thaan, Commander?'

'Thaan is fallen, my lord.'

'And the army?'

'Destroyed, my lord.'

'So I heard. The Witchfinder General arrived a day ago, but I want the story from your lips as he is not a military man.'

'We saw that from the way he quit the battlefield,' said Mandal.

'No doubt, but how went the siege?'

'We encircled Thaan and despite the supplication of the Witchfinder for the heretics to abandon their blasphemy that the All Father never fell from grace, the people defended their city like the fanatics they were.

'Added to this was the fact that they had a sun mirror, the like of which has not been known since ancient times. It threw a searing beam which set our siege engines afire and shrivelled troops like ants on a stove top. It meant waiting for overcast skies before an attack could be mounted, something rare in those parts at this time of year, but I saw no harm in this. I knew starvation would come to our aid before too long.'

'The sun does not shine at night.'

'True, my lord, but I found it impossible to breach the great walls of the city after dark.'

'Continue.'

'Then two Companions of the Rose arrived with your message that Thaan must be taken immediately so they could search the Great Library.'

'They are doing that?' asked the Regent, his voice still soft but eager.

'They entered the city before I left to report to you.'

'Continue.'

'As it was impossible to follow out your order by usual tactics on account of the speculum, it was decided to use the method which you had devised, my lord, and make the Red Death our ally. At night, carriers of the pestilence were catapulted over the city ramparts and by morning their corpses had infected the city. You know the speed with which the Red Death strikes. It seemed that we had but to wait a few days for those caught in the rain of contaminated blood to succumb.

'Then the unexpected happened. The city gates opened and out came every man, woman and child who could still walk, to advance upon our camp. All had the stamp of the Red Death upon them, and many fell dead before they reached our spears.

Yet those who did, kissed those who struck them down!

'As soon as my men saw the heretics had come forth to pass them pestilence, they fled. They would have faced overwhelming human odds without flinching but the Red Death makes cowards of heroes. Within hours, hundreds of them had the bloody mark of the Death upon them. Companies who were not involved were ordered to leave the camp before the contagion reached them, but some who had faced the citizens followed.

'Where is this rabble now?'

'The survivors will be halfway from Thaan, my lord.'

'Tell me, Commander, does not the road from Thaan wind through a steep ravine?'

'The Pass of Amos, my lord.'

'Excellent. Not one of your men must come beyond it. A company of archers on the heights will ensure that.'

'My Lord Regent! They are faithful fighting men, splendid—'

'Faithful they may be but they could never be relied upon in the field after this; splendid they may be but they carry plague. Imagine if the Red Death reached Danaak! And imagine how it would spread along the highways and caravan routes!'

The Regent winced as under his cloak his bandaged hand began to burn, warning that the draught he had taken to dull the pain was wearing off.

'If you had conducted the campaign properly you would have still had an army,' he hissed.

Mandal felt the tension within him coil yet tighter. 'My lord, whatever the Witchfinder General may have said, there was no other way. At least Thaan is a ghost city, and the heretics are dead.'

The Regent signalled for wine and when he had swallowed some his voice became soft again, almost friendly, as he said, 'Yes. Of course. You are right. Extra taxation in the provinces will enable us to replace the army. And if I have the new Archpriest proclaim a week of thanksgiving, it might be seen as a triumph. You will be quite a hero.'

Mandal allowed himself to relax slightly. Was it possible that after all he might retain his rank? This hope eclipsed the thought of what was going to happen in the Pass of Amos.

'Now I suggest you rest, and later we can decide what your next command will be,' said the Regent. 'An apartment has been prepared, and these gentlemen will escort you to it.' He raised his hand and two Companions of the Rose stepped forward.

As they led the Commander from the hall he remembered how, when he had seen his army disintegrate before the screaming, plague-marked heretics, he had drawn his sword and was ready to fall upon it, yet something had held him back. Now he believed it was the intervention of the Serene Mother for his punishment of those who denied her.

The Companions led Mandal through a maze of passages and up staircases, the haphazard architecture testimony to the different hands that

71

had added to the Citadel down the centuries since Ythan was a fledgling kingdom. And as he walked, his stride still brisk despite his fatigue, he felt an unusual need to speak to his guides. After all, they were military men like himself.

'Well, that did not go too badly,' he hazarded.

'There are times when our master is not as hard as we think,' one responded.

The other laughed. 'On occasion he can even be amusing.'

They entered a dim corridor lit only by small oil lamps and halted before a bronze-studded door at the end. Here one of the Companions produced a massive key.

'I hope you will find everything to your satisfaction, Commander,' he said as he turned it in an antiquated lock. 'Your apartment is airy and has an excellent view.'

'I am sure . . . began Mandal.

The door swung open. Brilliant sunlight dazzled them. The Commander had an impression of the roofs of the city divided by slender lines, then gauntleted hands thrust him forward. The door crashed behind him. He sprawled forward on a grating of rusting rods.

'Serene Mother!' he cried. 'The Cage! *The Cage!*'

Sunset over Danaak.

The city's multitude of spires were transmuted to gold; the steep-pitched roofs of the old timber-framed houses gleamed in the roseate light and the river curving through the city took on the appearance of burnished brass. In the caravanserai, drongs were unharnessed by weary men with trail-mazed eyes, merchants put away their abaci, innkeepers scolded servants in preparation for the night's hospitality, and yawning girls appeared at the pleasure-house windows with their powdered breasts resting on the sills.

It was the Regent's favourite hour. Reclining on a couch on the balcony that opened from his apartments high in the main tower of the Citadel, he gazed down upon the city – *his* city – briefly touched with glory. Up here the air was fresh and he could see beyond the walls to the verdant plains. *His* plains, and beyond them, for hundreds of leagues in every direction, *his* kingdom. He was undisputed master of Ythan, yet what was the worth of such power when his own body was in revolt?

Kneeling beside his couch a lady in a robe of emerald damask poured wine and proffered the cup as though she was one of his pages.

'Drink this, my lord,' she said. 'It will ease your discomfort.'

A sudden breeze teased strands of fiery hair across her face, whose pale-skinned beauty had been the downfall of more than one ardent suitor.

'Urwen, queen of spies, my discomfort requires more than wine to allay it,' the Regent answered with a bitter laugh, but he took the wine and sipped it while his eyes stayed on the slender figure before him.

'Would that I could do something to ease you,' she said.

'With your special talents you have served me well,' he said. 'Thanks to you Lord Odo was entrapped, and once he was housed among my sharp-toothed pets below he could not reveal his fellow conspirators fast enough, from Archpriest Gregon – may his spirit rest – to a follower of the Pilgrim Path in such a distant place as the High Wald. Ah yes, it was an unlucky night for many when Odo whispered his plans to his lover. Was it a moonlit night and did nightingales sing outside your chamber window, and did His Lordship try to win your heart as well as your body by boasting he would be the next Regent?'

Urwen said nothing.

'And the Lady Merlinda. It was thanks to you she was arrested with those two young Pilgrims. I knew her once, when she was young and before she became a whore.'

'My lord, 'tis said you have your loves made into dolls. Is it true that you had an automaton made in her likeness?'

'Such was my fancy.'

'Do you have all your mistresses copied thus?'

'Some.'

'Then, my lord, would that I could see myself as such a toy.'

The Regent gave a bark of laughter. 'Surely if you want a lover you should find a lusty young noble who would kiss your footprints.'

She looked at him full in the face. 'That is not the love I crave, Lord Regent. To me young men are callow . . .'

'. . . but vigorous.'

74

She made an impatient gesture. 'The only thing that quickens me is power. When I heard that you sent the Commander of the Host to the Cage this day I felt my pulse race.'

'You speak pretty but if you knew the truth of my affliction you would be sickened.'

'Put me to the test.'

Leaning forward she pulled aside the cloak which hid his swathed hand and began to unwind the bandage. The Regent made no move to stop her urgent fingers, but he watched with a touch of amusement in his usually bleak eyes.

'You risk much in doing this, Urwen. You will be filled with disgust. Worse, you will have the burden of my secret.'

'I care not.'

The bandage came away in coils. Urwen gave a cry as in the fading light she saw the Regent's hand. Pallid, bloated to twice its normal size, fingers swollen and disfigured and tipped with spikes of horn, it was no longer the hand of a man.

'So that is it,' she whispered while he held it still before her face, ready to sneer at any attempt to hide her revulsion.

'You see the hand of a homunculus . . . ' he began, but before he could say another word she seized the inflamed wrist and pressed her soft lips against the ghastly fingers, ran her tongue over the distended palm.

'I care not, I care not,' she murmured and continued to caress the corpse-like skin.

The Regent watched her with a mixture of curiosity and fascination. His whole arm throbbed

75

with pain, yet through the pain the touch of those perfect lips on his malformity caused a rare ripple of pleasure to course through him.

'Enough, you have proved your words,' he said.

'Not enough, my lord,' she replied and rose to her feet. A moment later her gown fell to the marble floor and she stood before him naked.

'Touch me,' she whispered and drew the homunculus hand towards her while her eyes closed in seeming ecstasy.

SEVEN

Tana

'Master Krispin, I would talk with you.'

At Ognam's words, Krispin looked up from the couch where he lay in his chamber. Like the others, he had drunk too much after The Mage had left them. The liquor in his cup had been apple ale, which he had not tasted since Toyheim, and its old familiar fragrance filled him with a longing for the High Wald.

'Come in and sit down,' he said kindly. The jongleur sank into a chair and sighed. 'I am sorry that Gambal was short with you,' Krispin continued, 'but he has not been himself since the death of Lorelle. It is my belief that he really loved her. But what is it that ails you? You look to have been through an ordeal since we arrived here.'

Ognam gazed moodily at the carved jester's head, a replica of his own, on his staff of office. 'As a strolling player, as a buffoon cheered by the mob one day and ordered out of town the next, I have had my share of experiences,' he declared. 'But here is much beyond my understanding.'

'It seems to me that our ancient host spends long

periods like one entranced, and while he slumbers everything falls into decay and is transformed again when he wakes. It is as though he and the tower are part of each other.'

'He must sleep for years for it to get into the state in which we found it,' muttered Ognam. 'I tell you, Krispin, I fear for us here.'

'Yet what else could we expect? We arrived knowing he was a great sorcerer from the days of High Magic, and we should not be surprised if his home is strange.'

'Strange!' cried Ognam. 'Strange is commonplace to what this tower is!' For a moment he revolved his staff in agitation, then said, 'I would take it as a favour if you would listen to my story. I must tell someone, and I find Lord Alwald a little too grand for confidences, and Master Gambal has never liked me since I forced him to take me with you from Danaak.'

'There has been much on my mind that would have laid more easy had I been able to speak about it,' said Krispin, 'so I understand your need. Speak on, Master Jongleur.'

'After we began to explore The Mage's tower we seemed to get separated,' began Ognam. 'I remember we came to the top of a staircase and I saw you walk into a gallery with a row of draped windows rising from floor to ceiling . . .'

'The magic casements,' Krispin murmured thoughtfully.

'. . . and Lord Alwald and Gambal went off in a different direction. I passed through a doorway and found myself in passages that led into other passages so that after several minutes it was like being in a maze again. Then I came to a stairwell and I thought that if it descended to the great hall I could start again from there and catch you up. It was very dim, so I took a candle from my pouch and lit it with my flint and steel, and this lighted my way down the steps. I went down and down . . .'

Down and down the spiral steps went the jongleur with the candlelight flickering on the damp wall. He had thought it would only take him a minute or two to reach the ground floor but the steps continued to dissolve into the heavy darkness below without break or exit.

Several times he paused, wondering whether to turn back – progress down the stairway was uncomfortably reminiscent of his unwilling descent to the dungeons below the Citadel – yet Ognam had more than his share of curiosity and he continued downwards. He comforted himself with the thought that the castle was little more than a ruin and a long time had passed since it had been inhabited by anything other than spiders.

At length he reached the bottom, and passed through a dark archway into a series of narrow galleries. As he walked along them, his curl-toed shoes raising clouds of dust at every step, the feeble light of his candle reflected on statuary sheeted with cobwebs and strands of nitre festooning vaulted stonework. He tried to whistle to encourage himself but the thin sound only emphasised the tomb-like atmosphere. He continued in silence.

Entering yet another gallery, it occurred to him that he could see further than the rays of his candle should allow, and when he shielded the tiny flame with his hand he saw there was pale light beyond an archway.

Curiosity heightened, he hurried on past cobwebbed lumber which lined the walls on either side – ancient chests from which flowed dusty scrolls and mysterious instruments, barrels whose contents had hardened into sediment, weapons and armour stained by verdigris and, incongruously, a child's toy cart. On reaching the archway he exclaimed in astonishment, for instead of another gallery he was looking into a cavern whose roof and walls were lost in shadows, and whose floor was not of stone but still water. He was on the shore of a subterranean lake and the light which had attracted him came from a silver lantern suspended from the graceful prow of a white boat.

It had been fashioned in the shape of a swan, the swan's neck being arched over the bow to form the figurehead. A silken cord moored it to a ring set in the rock wall.

As Ognam stared, hot wax burned his knuckles and he blew the candle out. The light from the lamp held in the swan's beak provided enough illumination for him to appreciate the craftsmanship which had gone into the construction of the boat. Intrigued, he stepped aboard and seated himself gratefully on the cushioned seat in the stern. It was the sort of craft in which a wealthy prince might go midnight sailing with his mistress. What puzzled Ognam was that there was not a speck of dirt or strand of cobweb on its enamelled woodwork. And from whence came the oil for the lantern if The Mage's tower had been so long deserted?

Gramarye! thought Ognam, and involuntarily made the Circle of the Mother.

He stood to leave, but as he did so the knot of the mooring untied itself and slid from the ring. Before the jongleur could move, the boat glided away as gracefully as the creature it represented.

Ognam reseated himself, undismayed by this magical manifestation. The truth was that he was beginning to enjoy the experience. He told himself if harm had been intended, there was no need for such elaboration; he could have been struck down in the dismal passages.

No. For some unknown reason he was privileged to witness something of rare beauty. The lantern light cast shifting patterns of silver over the black water, glittered on crystal veins in the rock roof and surrounded the swan-boat with a halo. Minutes passed and the only sound was the occasional murmur of water beneath the stately bows as it continued on its serene course without oar or sail, and from the depths of his memory Ognam recalled folktales about a swan princess. For a moment a smile creased his face – he was like as not becoming a folktale character himself.

He became aware of a glow ahead like moonlight which increased in strength until it appeared brighter than that of the lantern, and he could make out white marble steps rising from the water. Beyond them were low trees with silver foliage.

Anything is possible — even trees so far below the tower — because I am sailing through an enchantment, or I have fallen asleep and am in a dream, Ognam thought. But everything was too solid for a dream. The swan-boat rocked gently beside the steps and for a long moment Ognam remained with his back against the silken cushions. Then he disembarked and the boat remained as though held by unseen moorings.

Beneath the high roof of the cavern stood groves of graceful trees bearing brilliant fruit, their branches and leaves glittering silver in the pervading light. Ognam stretched out his hand to touch a leaf and found that it really was silver, like the work of a dedicated silversmith. He looked closely at the fruits which hung from the branches and with a gasp realised that they were fashioned from jewels.

It was wealth beyond a poor man's dream, but Ognam remembered too much folklore to risk picking even one bright berry. As he walked forward, the leaves rustled musically and suddenly a jewelled bird trilled a song from its silver throat.

Wonderland! Ognam thought. After making sure that the swan-boat was still in place, he hurried forward to see what further marvels lay ahead. Beneath his feet grass was pleasantly soft but he knew it was as unreal as the trees. No natural grass was ever such a vivid green and no meadow plants ever held such dazzling colours as these begemmed flowers of the underworld. Yet, if they were not natural, where did such fresh perfumes waft from?

He pushed his way through a bank of tinkling shrubs and halted yet more amazed.

He saw what appeared to be a courtyard lit by seeming moonlight so bright every tiny detail was as clear as though it had been etched. It was paved with tiles of black and white like a chequerboard; massive terracotta jars were draped with flowering vines, a fountain ceaselessly splashed into a jasper basin, and seated on a couch of samite was the most striking girl Ognam had ever seen.

Her shoulder-length hair was raven-black and equally black were her eyebrows arched over violet eyes; her skin in this sunless abode was unnaturally pale yet her crimson lips belied any suggestion of ailment. Her simple fur-trimmed gown lozenged with silver and blue did nothing to hide the fullness of her breasts or the graceful curve of her hips. On the couch beside her sat a cat whose fur was as black and glossy as her hair.

She dropped the scroll she had been reading and looked eagerly at the stranger in the jester's motley emerging from the trembling foliage.

'You have come for me?' she asked in a voice that had unexpected depth.

For a mad moment Ognam thought he had stumbled upon the object of the quest, that here was the Princess Livia hidden away underground. Then he remembered the portrait of Livia he had seen in the Domain of Olam; the Princess with her spun-gold hair and blue eyes was an exact opposite of the girl on the couch. Again a folktale came to Ognam's mind, this time about a Snow Maiden.

'Lady, I know not why I am here . . . by accident I found the way . . . but if I can be of service,' he stammered. As he spoke he moved forward, and then halted as a line of silver rods materialised to bar his way. They had not been there a second ago, yet when he grasped one in his strong hands it was solid and unyielding.

'As you see, I am a prisoner,' said the girl in her sweet, deep voice.

'You must have been here for a long time,' he said, 'for we found the place desolated.'

'It is long,' she sighed, 'but how long I cannot say for time in The Mage's tower has strange qualities, as you may well learn.'

Summoning his strength, Ognam tried to force two of the bars apart but neither moved a fraction and he gave up when the pain of them cutting into his palms became unbearable.

The girl smiled slightly at his efforts.

'Only a power more powerful than that which caged me will prevail against that barrier,' she said. 'For a moment I had hoped that you were a champion who, having heard of my plight, had come to my rescue.'

'Alas, I am no champion but member of the Guild of Jongleurs at present unemployed, Ognam by name,' he said and bowed.

'And I am Tana.'

She rose to her feet and walked to the bars and, putting her hand between them, gently laid it upon Ognam's wrist.

'You may be a jongleur instead of a knight errant but I know your heart is steadfast and it is a joy to meet you. For so long have I had no other companion than Samkin.'

Her fingers were cool yet Ognam felt a rush of warmth at her touch. He had seen her before in dreams, the image of the ideal lover-friend that so many men cherish in secret and so few ever meet. Perhaps Ognam's dream lover had not looked exactly like Tana, but now it seemed to him she did.

'How came you to be here?' he asked.

'My father was a princeling and in some manner I do not understand he offended The Mage who in revenge had me stolen to this enchanted prison. I remember little of it for I was much younger then and, as I told you, time is different here, and passes like a dream.'

'But did not your father try to find you?'

'I know nothing of the outside world since I was brought here. I sleep and eat, and pass the time reading scrolls and working at my embroidery frame . . . and oftimes wondering what it must be like to be young in the world of men. Tell me of it, Ognam. Tell me of the perils you must have braved to reach this woeful place. Oh, tell me anything just let me listen to a human voice. . .'

At these last words, tears coursed down her white cheeks. Ognam took her hand in his and spoke gently to her. Unmeasured time passed as they stood together with only bars between them.

It seemed to Ognam that never in his life had he been encouraged to speak so much about himself. There were moments when Tana smiled into his eyes at what he said, and sometimes she was grave, and several times she actually laughed. It was this that filled his heart with joy because he valued laughter above all else. But it was not a one-sided monologue, for when he had won her confidence he brought his talk round to herself and began to learn about her, not so much her history which was vague but about her thoughts and imaginings, and above all her yearning for life which she feared was slipping further and further away.

On and on they talked, now sitting side by side with his arm round her shoulders through the bars and her glossy head just able to rest against his shoulder. Samkin's eyes glowed with jealousy, and it was his growling which finally drew them back to the reality of the situation.

'Serene Mother! My companions will be searching for me high and low. It seems we have been talking for days,' he exclaimed.

Tana smiled at him, and the beauty of her mouth added to the ache which he felt in his heart when he looked at her.

'Perhaps,' she said. 'But remember my words about time. You must leave now?'

He stood up, forcing determination upon himself.

'I should . . . my companions . . . but I shall come back and somehow I shall . . .'

Putting her arms through the bars she pulled him against them, and he felt the warm softness of her lips against his cheek.

'Do not forget me,' she murmured as he turned away. 'And beware The Mage. He is doubly dangerous because great age makes his mind forgetful and inspires strange fancies.'

'I shall return,' he promised and hurried through the trees to where the swan-boat waited at the steps. Once he was seated, it glided away across the black water . . .

' . . . and it glided across the black water to the place where I had found it,' Ognam told Krispin. 'I relit my candle and returned through those dreadful galleries and finally I found you at table with our host. I must say no one seemed very upset at my absence . . .'

'We knew that you would turn up,' said Krispin soothingly. 'After all, you were not away for very long.'

'Not very long! It seems I was a day and a night – more! – with Tana.'

'It is strange that The Mage should keep a captive,' mused Krispin. 'Everything we heard about him suggested he was a great enchanter but not an evil one.'

'I am only a Fool and have no understanding of enchantments but, by the Serene Mother, I shall find a way to free Tana.'

'She said you needed a greater power than that which caged her,' said Krispin.

'I know such a power,' said the jongleur simply. 'It is called love.'

EIGHT

'The Wald!
The Wald!'

As the boom of the gate gong reverberated through
the Peak Tower, elderly servants looked at each
other in surprise and some in dismay. Serene
Mother! The wolfmen had penetrated the mist
which protected the castle!

'If it were the nomads, they would not be
sounding the gong,' the Lady Eloira chided them.
'There is only one who could come through the
mist, and he I count as a friend.'

Some of the servants still looked distrustful; fear
of the Fey folk was something inherent in them.
Meanwhile the old chatelaine hurried to the
gateman and ordered him to open the main gate
and winch up the portcullis.

As the massive blue door slowly swung back she
beheld a slight grey figure standing in the archway,
and then with a start of alarm saw that another
figure was lying at his feet. Nevertheless, as the
iron portcullis creaked upwards on protesting
rollers, she intoned the ritual welcome taught to

her by her father, who was proud of being a Fey friend: 'You are welcome by dayshine or starshine. No iron will harm you, no spell will charm you.'

The figure, whose face was mostly hidden by the brim of his high-crowned hat, advanced and said in a voice that was little louder than the sigh of the wind through summer trees, 'I bring greetings from the forest folk. I also bring a poor wretch I found wandering in the mist.' He pointed with his bone pipe to the figure sprawled on the cobbles in front of the gateway. 'He is too sorely hurt to harm you.'

'Carry him in, bed him and call the chirurgeon,' Eloira commanded. 'I fear he has been the victim of the horde. Do you have knowledge of him, Piper?'

The grey man shook his head as he followed the old woman up the great staircase to her solar. The fire burned brightly, filling the chamber with a pungent odour of herbs, before which sat a young woman with a grey cat on her lap.

'See, we have a guest, Jennet,' said Eloira.

Jennet put the cat aside, rose to her feet and, bobbing a childish curtsy, asked in a voice equally childish, 'Do you play a pipe? I saw you once, by the mere . . . and there was a wonderful bird, and Kris . . . have you seen Kris? Why does he not come?'

'Jennet, take your doll out to play in the courtyard,' Eloira said kindly.

Holding a beautifully dressed doll in the crook of one arm, and with the struggling cat under the other, Jennet left the solar.

'So she still hides in her childhood after what she saw in Toyheim,' said Piper, sitting opposite the old woman who poured out two goblets of white wine which took on a slightly greenish tinge when raised to the light.

'She has not changed since her brother Krispin – if he is her brother – brought her here,' She sighed and raised her goblet, and as the fragrance of her favourite wine reached her, the colours of the wall hangings became brighter and the flames in the fireplace flared with greater warmth. 'The chirurgeon says he can do nothing, but she may become her proper self again with the passage of time, or suddenly as the result of a shock equal to that which she suffered.'

Piper raised his glass appreciatively. 'Your wine refreshes man and Fey alike.'

'It warms my old blood,' said Eloira. 'What news do you bring me?'

'Word has reached the High Wald that Thaan has fallen to the Regent.'

'I wonder if my brave lads reached the city before the siege, and if they were able to journey on.'

'Few would know of that,' said Piper. 'Our interest lies only in the forest. There, at least, some men are fighting against the invaders. Have you heard of she whom they call the Wish Maiden?'

Eloira shook her head. 'Since I laid the mist about the tower you are the only one who can bring me news from the outside world.'

'She is a simple woodcutter's daughter, yet she gained the power to inspire men to follow her against the Wolf Horde. Just a few forest fugitives at first but more and more are joining her now, for her band has had success against nomads. They say her men are trained by a veteran from River Garde, and that side by side they lead the attacks.'

'And where does this simple maid get her inspiration to lead warriors?'

'She believes it comes from the ancient spirit of the forest.'

'Or is it a gift from the Fey?'

Piper smiled a gentle smile but made no reply.

'I know not if Krispin will ever return from the quest,' said Eloira, 'but I promised I would discover if he and Jennet really are brother and sister or not – whether it would be possible for them to marry. As I told you, they were found wandering in the forest by old Tammas the Toymaker – may his spirit rest – when they were very small and they have little memory of how they got there or who they were.'

Piper nodded and said, 'I sought the cottage where you said they might have stayed in the dark heart of the forest.'

'And you found it?'

'I found the ruin of it. It had been abandoned for years. The shingles had peeled from the roof, the furniture was rotten, the big stove was rust red, the climbing roses outside had turned to thorn.'

'So there was no sign of Mistress Goodheart who once lived alone there?'

'Not unless some of the bones scattered there were hers,' said Piper. 'Even the Fey avoided that part of the forest because of her. You know, of course, what she was.'

'I heard many stories over the years,' said Eloira. 'And all were equally horrible. Poor Krispin! But I must still find out the truth as I promised.'

'And I will go on seeking for you,' said Piper.

Mordan opened his eyes and for a long moment it seemed that he was in his bedroom in his mother's house. The ceiling sloped in a way that was familiar, the rose pattern on the curtains glowed as the sunlight shone through them, just as his curtains used to glow, and the old furniture was as highly polished as his had been. There was even the same evocative smell of wax in the air.

He lay still, not even moving his head which rested on a pillow filled with sleep-inducing herbs. First he must remember . . . But the images that came into his mind were chaotic: playing kick-bladder as a little boy, the journey to Danaak where he had entered the College of Witchfinders, a girl whose name he had forgotten but whose caresses still taunted his celibacy in shameful dreams, a looming mountain pass, men who wore wolf skulls as helmets, a march along a forest track . . .

'And how are we this fine morning?'

The voice was high and birdlike, and in Mordan's line of vision appeared a face as wrinkled as a last-season apple beneath a brush of grey hair. Mordan had enough self-control not to reply. He let his eyelids droop over his eyes. The coverlet was pulled back and he was aware of the touch of dry fingers.

'Well, Master Whoever-you-are, you heal well,' trilled the chirurgeon as he retied the bandages which bound the young man's chest. 'That blow to the head may have done more damage than the stab wounds.'

Mordan fought an impulse to cry out, to demand the nature of his hurt, but he reassured himself that as he felt no pain, it was unlikely that the Dark Maid would be approaching him.

'If you can hear me, young sir, I beg you to have no fear,' continued the chirurgeon. 'Narcotics from my herbarium have kept you sleeping while your body has been healing, and soon you will be whole again – as whole as Lord Alwald after I had treated him. And he had been brought to the Lady Eloira sore wounded like you. What parlous times! What parlous times!'

There was the sound of a door closing and Mordan opened his eyes again.

The Lady Eloira!

The name induced a trickle of recollection which soon swelled to a torrent.

It was to arrest a woman called Eloira on a charge of sorcery that he had travelled from Danaak. Lord Odo had given her name to the Witchfinder General himself, and now it was he who was in the power of the witch.

Thank the Mother they seem not to have guessed my calling, he thought. *I remember throwing away my robe of office, but . . . But what happened before that?*

Concentration was an effort but with the determination that was the hallmark of his vocation he sifted through the random images now crowding before his mental eye.

He remembered arriving with his men at the pass between the White Virgins which was guarded both by Companions of the Rose and those shaggy barbarians with hostile yellow eyes.

That night they had camped on the Wald side of the pass, and he remembered the tension of his men at being so close to the nomads.

The Companions had told him how the witch had surrounded herself with a magical cloud but in the morning he had set out with his men and an escort of wolfmen. They followed a trail leading through forested valleys towards a mountain hidden by cloud. As they slowly approached the bank of mist which crept down the wooded slopes he became aware of a guttural litany being chanted by the nomads who regarded the vapour with superstitious awe. Even his own men were surly and without heart for the task. He put it down to the presence of the barbarians with their long-hafted axes and their obvious hostility to strangers.

The attack came at noon when the track was about to disappear into a vaporous wall a hundred strides ahead. There was the soft hiss of an arrow flight. Master-at-Arms Yanos screamed and died trying to tug a shaft from his chest; a wolfman pitched forward with an arrow protruding from his throat; several others dropped to their knees in agony or reached for low branches to stop themselves from falling.

The men of the Nightwatch Company raised

their shields and stared about them in a bewildered fashion, but the nomads flung themselves towards the underbrush from where the volley had been fired.

A line of ragged figures rose to meet them, armed with an assortment of weapons, some of which were no more than woodmen's choppers or scythe blades turned into makeshift halberds.

There was a thunderous cry of 'The Wald! The Wald!' and Mordan turned to see more tattered warriors racing up the track behind him.

To his astonishment the attack was led by a girl with dark braids streaming behind her, a battle-light glittering in her eyes and a sword flashing in her hand. Beside her ran a tall man in a patched military uniform whose stentorian voice urged on those behind them. A brief memory remained with Mordan – the free hands of the man and the girl were locked together as they ran, and they were laughing at the prospect of slaughter.

Soldier and wolfman alike were unprepared for the ferocity of the ambush. Before they could group to defend themselves the Waldmen were among them, weapons swinging, their voices raised in shouts of rage.

'The Wald! The Wald!' shrieked the girl and plunged the point of her blade into Mordan's chest. He reeled to one side and she darted into the fray.

A man of Mordan's office did not carry arms so there was no question of his fighting back. His hope of survival lay in flight, but for a moment the pain of his wound paralysed him. He clutched the branch of an overhanging tree for support and an ex-charcoal burner armed only with a cudgel dealt him a blow on the side of the head. Stunned, he collapsed into a patch of tall ferns. At that stage none of the combatants was interested in the fallen, and later Mordan realised that he owed his life to the blow to his head.

When he regained his senses, the fighting had moved further along the track as his men sought to retreat, and gave him the opportunity to crawl into the trees. Then, with a supreme effort, he managed to climb to his feet and stagger in the direction of the mist which blanketed the forest ahead of him.

Only once did he look back, and between the dark trunks he saw that the guerrillas were victorious. Some were holding wolf-skull helmets high on the points of their spears, others bent over the bodies of his soldiers and quick movements of their arms told him that they were cutting the throats of those who were still alive. But most memorable of all was the sight of the girl. A couple of her followers had hoisted her onto their shoulders and she threw up her arms in a sign that was both a benediction and a gesture of triumph. In the fighting her tunic had been torn and her young breasts were spattered with blood.

Mordan turned in terror and a minute later breathed a prayer of gratitude as the clammy mist swallowed him.

For a while he forced himself on until the shouts of triumph and the occasional scream, as another victim was found and dispatched faded behind him. He slumped down and tearing material from his robe he folded a pad which he pressed against the wound from which blood welled in time to his heartbeat. Thus he sat for a long time, fighting the impulse to cry out as spasms of pain racked his head.

At last the pain ebbed and he looked up – and this time a cry did escape him. A few paces away a man floated in the mist.

It took Mordan several seconds to realise that it was not an apparition but a victim of the Wolf Horde. He had heard that their favoured way of dealing with captured foresters was to hang them and leave them hanging as ghastly reminders of who now ruled the Wald.

For several minutes Mordan sat with his back to a tree trunk, his hand pressed to his wound and an idea just out of reach in his throbbing head. It was as though the victim of the wolfmen held a special significance for him and if only he could think clearly it would become evident. It could be that the riddle of his survival was held by the silent shape hovering in the mist.

Then it came to him. As long as he wore a Witchfinder's robe, he would be regarded as an enemy by all. He could at least expect succour from the fugitive Wald folk if they thought he was one of them. He would have to discard the robe and dress like one of them. In this guise he might even be welcomed in the castle of the old woman he had been sent to arrest.

Conquering his revulsion at having to handle a corpse, he stripped off its outer garments and dressed himself in them, concealing his own garb in a rabbit hole. The exertion made his wound bleed again and he was conscious of the warmth of his own blood as it seeped beneath the dead forester's jerkin of undyed wool. He pressed his hand against it and began to walk further into the mist. Somewhere within it was the Peak Tower and his only hope. On and on he stumbled, his head paining him more and more until suddenly the opacity about him changed to whirling motes of dusk and he pitched forward to lie oblivious until he opened his eyes in the pleasant little bedchamber.

Now he lay in contentment. His head no longer pained him and he had the satisfaction of knowing that, despite the shock of the attack and his hurts, his wits had not deserted him. Thanks to the dead forester's clothing he had been taken in as a fellow Waldman, a role he would be happy to play as long as it suited him.

A soft mew drew his gaze to the door. A huge grey cat stalked in, tail erect, eyes glowing with curiosity.

'Oh, Smoke, you are naughty to go in there.'

Before Mordan could feign slumber a young woman walked in after the cat.

Serene Mother! The lost Princess!

A moment later logic told Mordan that it could not be *the* entranced Livia whose portrait he had seen when studying at his seminary. But this girl was identical to that portrait. A paean of joy filled Mordan's ambitious heart. Here was the key to the power he had always dreamed of.

NINE

Beyond the Casement

A languor lay upon the four travellers in The Mage's tower. The accumulated fatigue of the quest had suddenly overwhelmed them, and they spent most of their time reclining on couches in the guest chambers waiting for the glowing globes, which appeared to be the only visible servants in the castle, to summon them to The Mage's presence.

Several times they had dined with him. In a weary voice, he had questioned them in detail about their adventures but each time Alwald had raised the question of Princess Livia he had announced that he needed to rest and had retired.

'I do believe he is senile,' said Alwald moodily as he sat opposite Krispin in a chair carved in the fanciful likeness of a crouching beast.

'He is certainly ancient,' Krispin said. 'But there is more to it than that. There is gramarye all about us and did not The Mage say it is only possible to understand Magic when one understands Time. I can understand neither, but it occurs to me that time might move at a different pace within these walls, that we may have been here for only a few minutes or mayhap a full season by the reckoning of time in the outside world. There is much here that makes me feel as though I am living in a dr—'

'You show too much imagination for a toymaker,' interrupted Alwald. 'I do not know what has come over you all. The jongleur has given up trying to make jokes and looks as though he has had a holy vision, Gambal broods on his bed and has hardly spoken since that girl he bedded in the Domain of Olam was killed by the stone giant . . .'

'That is surely understandable.'

' . . . and you spend your time either snoring or thinking you are dreaming. Serene Mother! Surely The Mage should be able to tell us the whereabouts of the Princess in return for the Esav – did you see the look on his face when you brought it out? He wants it, without doubt, but I begin to think he has lost his memory and has no more idea than we do.'

'I should be careful what you say,' said Krispin, nodding to the open doorway through which they could see a globe floating past. 'Has it occurred to you, Alwald, that if he so wished he could take the Esav from us and give nothing in return?'

'That old dotard? You talk like a fool.'

'It is not me that talks foolish. What chance has swordplay against magic.'

'Pottons take you!' Alwald grumbled. 'You have lost your spirit. Understandable, I suppose . . . '

100

He did not finish his sentence but his meaning was clear.

'You are probably right, my lord,' Krispin said angrily. 'Spirit is an aristocratic virtue.'

'Krispin, there are times when you become tedious.'

'A thousand pardons, your lordship.'

For a while the two young men sat in moody silence.

'Come,' Krispin said at length. 'I shall show you something – something that has been on my mind ever since we arrived here.' He stood up. 'I think I can still find the way. From time to time the castle seems to change.'

Behind Krispin's back Alwald said nothing but rolled his eyes to the ceiling of blue panels decorated with tiny silver stars.

They entered a dim gallery with a row of floor-to-ceiling windows set in one wall, each of which was covered with damask drapes.

'What would you see if I pulled back the curtains?' Krispin asked.

'The same dreary view we see from the other windows – grey skies and grey seas crashing against grey rocks.'

'Then look.'

Krispin pulled back the first curtain. The diamond-shaped panes of the casement showed the same pleasant scene that he had beheld when he had newly arrived at the tower, a river winding through smiling countryside along which a white barge was being pulled by a horse on a towpath.

'It is a painting,' Alwald exclaimed after his

initial surprise. 'Very lifelike, I admit, but what is so special about it?'

'Touch it.'

Dutifully Alwald drew the tips of his fingers across it; it was not painted canvas they felt but cold glass and lead strips.

'It is a window but . . .'

'These are magic casements,' Krispin said. 'Each looks out on to a different scene.'

He tugged aside the damask covering the next window. The first time he had done that, Krispin had seen a great spiral of stars glittering against a background of endless night but now the view had changed – a dark river flowed oil-smooth in the foreground, and on its bank rose a castle with black pennants fluttering from its towers. Behind it a carpet of forest stretched away to distant snow-peaked mountains.

'River Garde!' gasped Alwald. 'It is my home but . . . but as it was before the Wolf Horde came. The flags are flying and our guards patrol the ramparts.'

He stood for a long time gazing through the window, watching the movement of the sentries and straining his eyes in the hope of seeing others – his father Grimwald VII and his lovely young wife the Lady Demara who had inspired a guilty love in Alwald's heart. Oh, for a glimpse! Yet he knew that the castle had been overrun and the Lady Demara was close to bearing her dead husband's child in the remote Vale of Mabalon.

'It is a vile deception,' he muttered, turning away with his eyes close to overflowing. 'Some cruel trick of that accursed old man.'

'I think not,' said Krispin quietly. 'I came here before we roused The Mage, and the third casement I looked through showed my village of Toyheim, before it was destroyed. I could not help wondering what would happen if I unlatched the window and walked through.'

Alwald shuddered. To go back to the high days of River Garde, to be dazzled by Demara's beauty again . . .

'No!' he said. 'It would be wrong to go back, an unholy thing, like recalling the spirits of the dead.' He turned and almost ran from the gallery.

Krispin watched him go and then regarded the curtains which hid the other windows. He felt drawn to gaze through the next casement at the neat village which had been his home since Tammas had found himself and Jennet wandering in the forest, unable to give a proper account of themselves. He reached for the rich material that curtained Toyheim, and then stopped himself, resisting the temptation.

He moved on to the next casement. The scene beyond the glass held no significance for him. It was a lonely lakeshore of white sand; against the glow of an approaching sunset moved a formless shadow which suddenly divided into the figures of a man and girl. They stood hand in hand gazing over the darkening water to the far shore which appeared no more than a line of purple. Then the man stood apart and, to Krispin's amazement, his silhouette lost its shape for a moment, to regain it with a great pair of wings spreading gracefully above his shoulders.

'Cursed gramarye!' muttered Krispin and he tugged the curtain back into place.

The next casement had a startling effect upon him. It was a forest path in winter, with a powdering of snow upon it and bordered by sere bracken. Cold bright sunlight shone down through the roof of leafless branches and sparkled on patches of hoarfrost. But what caught and held Krispin's attention were the figures of two children walking slowly down it. Their backs were to him but he could see by their dress they were male and female; the girl had long golden hair, the boy's was auburn. He held the girl by the hand and sometimes stopped patiently while she plucked crimson berries from scrawny bushes.

And he knew them.

Pale-faced, he reached for the window catch, then as a thought struck him he hurried from the gallery to his chamber where he pulled Woundflame from beneath his couch. Once its baldric was over his shoulder he raced back to the magic casements. The uncovered window still showed the winter scene but the children were further down the path now.

'Wait,' Krispin heard himself mutter in his anxiety. He turned the catch and chill air redolent of dormant woodland made his eyes water as the casement opened. Then he stepped through.

Krispin felt the cold of the snow reach him through the soft leather soles of his shoes as he stood on the track. He looked about at the stark trees in amazement – he had stepped through a window casement which by rights should have opened on to a bleak seascape but here he was in a forest perhaps a hundred leagues from The Mage's tower. But how far in years?

He looked behind him for the casement through which he had passed but no tower rose behind him; instead of a casement set in stone there was only the empty track vanishing among the trees whose tangled branches appeared like black lace against the winter sky. How would he ever return to his companions? Panic tugged at his heart and caught at his breath – would he have to remain here for ever in exile from his own world?

Then he saw a flicker above the path, a mere tremor in the air; as he gazed more intently he made out the palest suggestion of a large window – the ghost of the casement through which he passed. He turned back and saw that the two children had passed out of sight. He paused only to memorise the shape of a hornbeam close to the casement and then ran after them.

The ground was frost hard beneath his feet and the cold air brought blood to his cheeks, yet there was a disquieting hint of unreality – not of his surroundings but of himself. The sensation was too vague to put into words, but as he ran, the uneasy thought occurred to him that to others he might be as unsubstantial as the casement which was little more than a trick of the light above the path.

Krispin told himself that this was not the time for such questions. He was here and he had to catch up with the children; that was all that mattered. But the question returned when he found them sitting on a fallen log in the middle of a small glade. The boy had his arm round the girl's shoulder.

'Do not weep, Jennet,' he was saying. 'I shall look after you. Rest a little and then we will find a way out of the forest before dark.'

Krispin stood still, gazing at the boy he had once been, and at the little girl his beloved Jennet had once been. His heart ached for them in their loneliness; an echo of the fear that the boy was feeling returned and with it a stirring of things long forgotten.

'Be not afraid,' he said in a kindly voice and walked up to them. They did not seem to see or hear him. The child Jennet shivered, but that could have been due to the fact that her ragged cloak was not thick enough to keep her warm.

Of course they cannot see me, he thought. *If they could I would have remembered a man coming to comfort them. But that cannot be, for if I helped them, things would have been different. They — we! — might not have reached Toyheim, and if that had happened I would never have undertaken the quest or reached The Mage's tower and stepped through the magic casement, in which case . . .*

His mind reeled.

'I am hungry,' said the child Jennet, wiping her eyes with her fists.

'Eat some of the berries you picked,' said the child Krispin.

'I am tired of berries. Why did the woodcutter bring us into the forest and then lose us?'

You know the answer but you will not tell her, thought Krispin as more memories returned. *You will say 'He was silly and he is probably looking for us at this very minute.' And Jennet will say, 'I think he and his goodwife wanted to lose us because they have no food.'*

'He was silly,' said the boy. 'He is probably looking for us this very minute.'

'I think he and his goodwife wanted to lose us because they have no food. She never liked us. Why did my mother take us there?'

'People were sick in the town . . .'

Krispin strained to remember further back. His memory was clear at this point – he could remember the boy's present feelings, even what he was about to say – but beyond that the archive of his mind was closed to him. He could not add a single thing to the vague pictures he had always carried of people lying in doorways with red marks on their faces, of sulphurous fibres flaring at street corners and of holding Jennet's hand as some forgotten adult led them into the countryside.

They had been found exhausted and blank-minded in the forest, and it had been assumed that they were brother and sister. The possibility that they might not be related had become of overwhelming importance to Krispin, for they had fallen in love. Indeed it was the Lady Eloira's offer to seek the truth about their mysterious past that had made him agree to undertake the quest. Such knowledge might free them from the law of incest and allow them to marry.

If only he could ask the children one question,

their answer might tell him all that he needed to know.

He heard himself shouting to them, as though the strength of his voice might break through the barrier of time.

'Just tell me, tell me,' he implored.

'Come on, Jen,' said the child Krispin. 'We must keep walking if we want to get out of the forest.'

'My feet hurt.'

'So do mine.'

He took her hand in his and together they began to follow the path which led across the glade.

Krispin fell silent. He shivered as he saw a lead-hued bank of cloud rolling up from the east. Before long its dark edge obscured the white winter sun and a freezing shadow spread over the forest.

The children plodded on.

Once, after Jennet had announced that she was not going any further, the boy lost his temper and after telling her that she could do what she liked, he marched away.

Krispin, who had been walking behind them, was filled with remorse at the sight of the girl's tearful face as she stood among withered ferns with her arm round a frosted tree trunk. How could he have been so unfeeling?

If only he could reach out to her!

Then the boy came back, took her hand without a word and they continued through the trees. The only sound was the snapping of twigs beneath their feet; the tiny half-heard noises that fill a forest even in winter died to a brooding silence. The first flake floated down and kissed Jennet on the cheek, like a salutation from the snow that would mantle them in its soft and deadly caress. A few more fell and the children held out their palms to catch them. Soon the air was full of snowflakes and again Krispin recalled the boy's fear.

And then the trees, now silver-edged in the fading light, opened into a clearing and in the centre of it stood a delightful steep-gabled cottage with a cheerful column of smoke eddying from its chimney. Even though it was winter the rose bushes on either side of the door were in leaf, and roses, as white as the snow that fell about them, still bloomed.

The children stood amid the whirling flakes and watched with smiles of delight as the yellow door opened and a kindly-looking old dame appeared supporting herself with a crooked walking stick. She peered at the children through pebble glasses and called, 'Who be there?'

The boy led Jennet forward. 'If you please, I am Krispin and this is . . .'

The man Krispin strained his ears. Was he about to say 'this is my sister'? Serene Mother, no!

'. . . this is Jennet.'

'And we are lost,' said Jennet.

'And I am Goody Goodheart and I love little children. I am just going to take a tasty pie out of the oven so come in out of the cold, my dears, and share it with me.'

As they ran to her, sudden recognition filled Krispin with horror.

'No!' he screamed. 'Run away!'

But the children could not hear him and the

futility of trying to alter the past silenced him. It was he who ran away, racing back over the children's footprints and along the forest track with tears freezing on his face until he saw the hornbeam landmark. Beyond it the magic casement glimmered faintly luminous in the snowfall.

With a sob of relief he climbed through.

TEN

The Golden City

In the high days of King Johan, Danaak had been known as the Golden City, and a century later there were those who still knew it as Danaak the Golden. These were the citizens who prospered under the reign of the Regent: wealthy favourites whose tall houses lined the Green River; merchants who traded lucratively under warrant from the Citadel; burghers; the military elite – all, in fact, who accepted the regime.

The other aspect of Danaak the Golden was not so visible. Crooked alleys led to the sagging tenements which housed the wretches who toiled the daylight hours for just enough copper to keep spirit and body linked, the stews where boys and girls not only hired out their bodies but sold their youth, the grog-den refuges of the desperate, the necropolis where outcasts shared tombs with the dead, the slave workshops – especially the slave workshops! – and the quaking lime pits that were the final destination of the unnamed poor.

Yet the city did appear golden when beheld from the height of the Citadel; sunlight gilded the spires

111

of numerous shrines, flashed on the armour of sentinels and reflected off the river which carried an endless traffic of barges and gondolas between time-mellowed buildings.

Such was the prospect before the Commander of the Host after he was thrust into the Cage which, constructed of iron latticework, was mounted high above a square on an outer wall of the Citadel.

His first difficulty was to keep his footing on the thin rods which formed the floor of the aerial cell and allowed a view of its inmates from below. His foot had already slipped between them once, and with one leg protruding painfully between the bars, his shoe had plummeted to the jeers of spectators below.

The second difficulty was to comprehend the enormity of what had happened to him.

I am Mandal, Commander of the Host. I have subdued three provinces in my time, won eight great battles, repulsed barbarian hordes and built up the finest army Ythan has ever known. So why?

Then he thought further.

I was the Commander of the Host. I lost my army to the Red Death. Yet the use of plague in war was the Regent's idea. If I must bear the blame, at least he might have let me drink the banewort draught. But this way will amuse him more. So much for my loyal years . . .

Panic assailed him. It was not fear of death. He had seen so much of it during his career it had become commonplace, and he had long been reconciled to the fact that each man has his

112

appointed time for his meeting with the Dark Maid. No, it was the terror of indignity.

Would he be able to keep control of himself? Or would the coming torment transform him into a beggar snivelling for a crust?

He looked at the bars about him. There was not the slightest hope of pressing between them and plunging to a self-appointed end.

Why did I not turn my dagger on myself when the heretics brought the plague out of Thaan?

He looked about him – as hundreds had done before – in the hope of seeing something which would enable him to free his spirit. Apart from a bundle of rags in the far corner the Cage was bare, but he saw that set above the latticed roof there was a gargoyle with water trickling from its leaden jaws. Victims of the Cage died by slow starvation, not thirst.

The rags stirred and an emaciated woman sat up and regarded him with a broken-toothed grimace.

'Welcome, dearie,' she said in a cracked voice. 'Nice to have your company. If you lie flat the bars do not hurt so much. Spreads the weight, see?'

Mandal nodded. 'How long have you been here?'

'Five days, dearie. I hope to make the fortnight. Them down there respect you if you make the fortnight. Shows you have the right spirit, and of course they lay bets.'

Mandal looked down at the crowd gathering in the square. Word had spread that there was a new prisoner in the Cage.

'They will stay there until you have to relieve

113

yourself. That always gets a laugh,' the hag continued.

'Why are you here?' he asked.

'I am a witch, dearie.'

'A real witch?'

He had a wild impulse to laugh. Who would have thought half an hour ago that he would be displayed on the wall of the Citadel with a mad woman!

'Real enough for the Witchfinders, dearie. I was given a choice – cage or cauldron. Well, I thought, it would be a more peaceful way to go, up here. And the city does look lovely . . .'

'If you are a witch, why do you not magick yourself out of here?'

His irony escaped her.

'I am not good enough for that. Love potions, draughts for girls when they miss their moon, a bit of scrying, a bit of healing. But no high magic.'

'The Witchfinders must have thought otherwise.'

'They have their living to make, dearie. My big mistake was talking to my cat. That got around.'

'And did he talk back?'

'Of course he did. Why are you here, dearie?'

'I offended the Lord Regent.'

She nodded understandingly. 'At least we are lucky there have not been any others for a while. It would not be very nice with corpses for company.'

'The dead are left?'

'That door only opens one way, dearie. Here we stay until the birds feast and our bones drop through the bars. See that man in the corner of

114

the square? Very interested in you, he is. He's a flute carver. He will make sure he catches your thigh bones when they drop. And there is them that will fight over my skull,' she added with a macabre touch of pride. 'Witches' skulls fetch a good price when they are cleaned up nice.'

'You seem resigned to your fate, dame.'

The old woman lay back again. 'Nothing is for ever, dearie, and I have danced Gillartrypes in my day.'

Mandal turned his face from her, shamed by her calm acceptance of her fate. Now that his mind had cleared from the initial shock, a cold anger against himself began to grow. Thanksgiving for Thaan's defeat would not compensate for the loss of the army, and when the news of that swept Danaak, coupled with rumours of the destruction of the survivors, the square would fill with the bereaved cursing him for a traitor. Why had he not had the wit to realise the inevitability of this and thought of himself instead of his duty?

Lying full length on the criss-crossed bars, he gazed up to a turret above, in which a single window was cut beneath its candle-snuffer roof. Could a rope be lowered from it during the night? Perhaps a few old comrades who would risk it for past favours and future reward, but how to get word to them?

As he kept his eyes on the window he saw a movement above the sill. A pale face – the palest he had ever seen on a living man – surrounded by fluttering white locks appeared and looked down, the mouth working as though in speech.

The distance was too far, the breeze too strong for Mandal to hear the words, but he sensed the old man was not merely mouthing abuse. Mandal gestured to indicate that he could not hear. The face vanished, yet he was left with the impression that there was some significance in the incident.

He looked down between the bars to see if the spectators had taken notice of the brief appearance but at the moment they were more concerned with sweetmeat pedlars and a begging girl dancing to the beat of a tambourine.

The sun which gave the city is golden sheen was shut out by heavy curtains from the sanctum of the Lady Mandraga. Here the amber globe of a lamp burning scented oil shed soft light on Ythan's Lore Mistress as she sank into a cushioned chair opposite the mirror of silvern crystal which hung between two pillars wrought with intricate grotesquerie. As ever, its bright surface showed a youthful face of remarkable beauty, a cruel contrast to the time-wizened features of the crone gazing at it.

But Mandraga's blue lips tautened into a gap-toothed smile of pleasure at the sight of her *alter ego* and the thought of briefly returning to that stage of life which enabled her to taste again the earthy pleasures she had enjoyed so long ago.

'Spirit of the mirror, I command, show the secrets I demand,' she said ritually.

The false image wavered like water rippled by the breeze; pale smoke fumed within the magic crystal. Mandraga leaned forward in expectation,

116

her chin resting on the twisted fingers clasping the crosspiece of her crutch.

The smoke steadied, became a dark shadow out of which appeared the face of a young man that was not only pleasingly formed but held an expression of innocence which the majority of mortals lose with childhood. His lips began to move and Mandraga nodded with satisfaction.

Half an hour later she limped onto the balcony adjoining the Regent's private apartments. Since his sickening this had become his most favoured retreat. The clean airs cooled his fever and the view of his city brought comfort to his mind — there was not one ant-like person down in the widest avenue or meanest alley over whom he did not have the power of life and death. Now he reclined on a couch and on an ivory stool nearby the spy Urwen played attendant. The Lore Mistress gave her an enigmatic glance and then turned to the Regent.

'At last the mirror has shown me a message,' she announced and paused, but the Regent showed no sign of sending away his new handmaiden.

'Is that all you have come to tell me?' he demanded finally. Never before had he used such a brusque tone to Mandraga who was the only person in the Citadel whom he respected — some whispered *feared* — and it was a measure of the irritability besetting him.

'I had thought that the link with the Pilgrims was lost,' she said calmly. 'The last time, I saw the face of a girl within the glass. Mayhap she only took the mirror to comb her hair, mayhap she had seen its rightful owner using it and was filled with curiosity. Whatever the reason, she did that which was forbidden and she had to pay the penalty.'

'And that was?'

'To behold me – and the truth deep within her heart. Such truth is the destruction of all illusion and would be her death. Since then the mirror remained blank until now.'

'Perhaps our pilgrim had a dalliance with the owner of the face and resented her punishment,' suggested the Regent.

'He is too self-seeking to allow some moonstruck girl to hinder his ambition. His dreams are dreams of power, and such men are useful for a while.'

'Until they dream of becoming Regent,' said Urwen quietly.

'Then they too learn a truth,' said the Regent, 'and it does not reflect from a mirror. But tell me, lady, what has your mirror shown you?'

'The questers have reached The Mage's tower on the edge of the Cold Sea to learn the resting place of Livia. It seems The Mage lies like one cataleptic while his spirit roams the dream time, but the Esav will recall him.'

'They have had remarkable fortune or they are remarkable men to have survived so far on their venture,' said the Regent. 'I would I had more like them in my service.'

'They do serve you but without realising it.'

'True, lady. Did you learn from your glass how they reached The Mage.'

'From the Domain of Olam they were borne by griffins. Our pilgrim cannot tell where The Mage's

118

islet lies, all he knows is that it faces a barren coast.'

'No matter,' said the Regent. 'Such relics from the days of high sorcery are best left undisturbed. It is the domain that interests me. A small expedition to such a secret enclave might prove to be of profit. And griffins! Never have I had such a creature in my menagerie.'

'There is much more at stake than freaks, my son. I have been studying the prophecies of Omgarth anew and it is clear the fate of Ythan could go many diverse ways this year. We must ensure that it will be our way, no matter the cost.'

ELEVEN

The Grateful Guest

'My wound has healed well, my lady, but the blow to my head has cost me my wits. I cannot even remember my name.'

The Lady Eloira looked at the young man standing deferentially before her.

'Sit,' she said kindly. 'You are still pale and weakly.'

With a gesture of thanks Mordan seated himself in a wooden chair close to the aromatic fire which was never allowed to go out in the Reeve's solar. He looked with veiled curiosity at the old woman who, despite the weight of her years, had an inner beauty that shone through her fine wrinkled features. Her parchment fingers furrowed the fur of a car purring contentment on the rich brocade which clothed her frail body.

'You are not the only one here whose memory is lost,' said Eloira with a sigh.

He gave her a look of inquiry.

'There is a young woman in the tower who was shocked back into her childhood. You may have seen her from your window, playing with a doll.

120

Alas, she shows no sign of regaining her years, but you, I have no doubt, will recall your past life as the effects of your injury wear off. My chirurgeon is well pleased with your progress.'

'My progress is due to the tender care I have received under your roof for which I shall be ever grateful,' said Mordan.

Thanks to the rigorous training at his seminary, where those selected to become Witchfinders were taught to mask emotion, he betrayed no hint of the excitement that seethed within him at the old woman's description of the young woman whose appearance had so agitated him. If she had the understanding of only a child, his bold intention would be so much more feasible. Destiny had decreed that he would have to return to Danaak without the Reeve, but with a far greater prize.

'You remember nothing of the attack?' continued Eloira.

He shook his head, then raised his hand to his brow to suggest he still suffered from the cudgel blow.

'All I remember is waking up in the room you gave me,' he said.

'Your clothes were those of a forester, though none of my retainers recognised you so your home is unlikely to be in this part of the Wald. Probably you were a fugitive from afar, for I understand the Wolf King sends his raiding parties further and further afield.'

'Wolf King, my lady?'

Briefly Eloira told him of the invasion of the Wald.

121

'But you are safe here. The cloud that surrounds the Peak Tower keeps our enemies from reaching us.'

'Gramarye?' Mordan's voice was suitably alarmed.

'Fear not, young man, I am not a witch. But my ancestors delighted in the study of arcane lore and I was able to call upon it for protection. You will be welcome here until it is possible to travel in safety again.'

'How can I repay . . .'

Eloira dismissed his words with a wave of her hand. 'When you are strong enough you may help with daily work here. You will notice that my retainers have grown old with me and your strong young shoulders would ease their tasks.'

'Gladly.'

'Meanwhile you must rest. You may use the courtyards which, being above the mist, are open to the sun but if you encounter Jennet remember her mind is but that of a child and say naught that would distress her.'

Rising to his feet he acknowledged her words with a bow and left the chamber.

The Lady Eloira continued to stroke her cat.

The silver leaves of the silver trees rustled musically as Ognam brushed against them. For a moment he turned to make sure that the swan-boat which had brought him once again over the black water of the subterranean lake was in position for his return, then he pressed eagerly through the metallic foliage.

Before long he came in sight of the court where Tana sat by a splashing fountain while somewhere silver birds trilled magically. As before, a grille materialised across the cavern when he stepped out of the glittering shrubs. At the sound Tana looked up and ran to meet him, putting her hands between the bars which separated them.

'Ognam, what joy to see your faithful return.'

Smiling foolishly, the jongleur took her hands in his. 'And what joy to return to you.'

He was about to repeat the neat little speech he had rehearsed but she pulled his head forward and pressing her face between the bars kissed him on the lips.

'Forgive me but it means so much to be alone no more.'

To Ognam it seemed that the world had stood on its head for a dizzy moment. Those soft lips, bright in that pale but perfect face, sent a tide of warmth through his body; it felt as though his blood was bubbling in his pulses and the weight of his weary wandering years was dissolving to free the lively youth he once had been.

Without thought he stretched his arms past rods that formed her enchanted prison and held her as close to him as the accursed barrier would allow. She lifted her head to regard him with grave eyes.

And in a return of sanity Ognam recognised the reality of the situation. After such loneliness the captive would be delighted to see any fellow being; and the warmth of her greeting would reflect that – but no more. How could a creature so beautiful, high-born and obviously intelligent feel anything

123

deeper than passing companionship for a vagrant Fool such as he!

Fool I be and a fool I am – a fool of a Fool, he thought. *And a fool of a Fool no longer a young fool.*

He was conscious that the bars against which he stood pressed deeper into his belly than his chest and the cropped hair beneath his cockscomb hood had little of its one-time lustre.

Tana read his thoughts as his arms relaxed and he stepped back.

'I esteem your motley higher than the armour of an errant knight, Sir Jongleur,' she said, a smile warming her pallid features. 'Before my captivity I knew handsome blades who in folktales would have rescued distressed maidens and slain monsters, but despite their family trees and charming manners they filled me with boredom. But you are a man of the great world, a man of generosity who bestows the greatest gift of laughter, and a man of great heart, for who else would undertake such a parlous quest without thought of personal gain?'

Perhaps there is something in what she says, Ognam thought, *but such virtues are not enough to qualify me as the lover I would be.*

'Oh, Ognam,' she continued in her soft voice, 'each time you brave the wrath of The Mage to pay me a secret visit I feel my heart warm to you . . .'

Until that moment it had not occurred to Ognam that he was actually braving the wrath of The Mage. No restriction had been put on the pilgrims' movements in the castle, and The Mage had seemed quite a benign if somewhat vague old enchanter. But now Tana's words made him look hastily over his shoulder. How would even a benign enchanter react if he discovered that a guest was dedicated to freeing his chosen captive!

Ognam relegated this surge of apprehension to the back of his mind.

' . . . and each time you leave me,' Tana was saying, 'the loneliness is worse than before, because it reminds me that the quest still lies ahead of you and then I shall be left as I was before but with a broken heart. You understand my words, Ognam?'

Did he? Could it mean that she shared something of the emotion that had engulfed him?

He gasped at the possibility.

Once more her arms reached for him and once more her lips were on his and he could feel the warmth of her firm breasts pressing against him through the bars.

'Never have I hated these bars so much,' murmured Tana. 'Oh, my dear jongleur, if only we could break them down we could find each other properly as man should find maid, for there are times when a caressing hand tells more than a thousand words.'

Again Ognam had the sensation that the world had tipped over. It was as though her words were releasing new forces in his body and youth was returning with the sensation of excitement in his loins.

'Tana,' he murmured, his arms pressing her

painfully against the grille which allowed him to hold but not have.

She gently disengaged herself and walked towards the fountain where she stood with her back to him. When she turned he saw that tears glistened on her cheeks.

'Perhaps this is some trick of The Mage — you may be nought but an incubus sent to torment me.'

Ognam's natural humour surfaced through his whirlpool of thoughts and he laughed aloud.

'I am no incubus, my lady Tana,' he cried. 'Surely The Mage could do better than sending you a Fool in motley — a handsome troubadour to sing you songs of love more like. I am the most unlikely incubus you could conceive.'

'You were a poet once, of that I am sure.'

'Long ago. The world has taken its toll since those days. Instead of sonnets, I pen dirty ditties and petty parodies.'

'Oh, Ognam, if I were free I would have you writing sublime verse again,' she cried and now she was smiling at him through her tears.

'I brought this,' he said simply and produced a small saw. 'I found it in the castle kitchen. Perhaps when The Mage had flesh-and-blood cooks instead of balls of light that float like jack-o'-lanterns, it was used to cut up bones.'

He knelt down and drew it backwards and forwards against a silver bar with all his strength, but not a single filing fell and after some minutes he paused to regain his breath.

'Not a scratch on it, yet silver is a soft metal.'

'This is no ordinary silver, Ognam,' Tana said

sadly. 'No saw ever made will cut it for it is the work of sorcery that will only yield to stronger sorcery.'

'I am no sorcerer but Master Krispin carries a gem that holds sorcery from beyond the stars,' mused Ognam.

'That which you told me will be bargained with The Mage for help with your quest?' Tana asked, and for a moment there was a rare suggestion of cunning in her dark eyes.

'Yes, Tana. The Esav.'

'Bring it, O beloved, and set me free.'

Jennet, who had been laboriously knitting a small misshapen garment for her doll, sent her ball of wool rolling across the blue and white tiles that paved a courtyard high in the Peak Tower. Smoke danced after it.

'You have a good friend there,' came a gentle voice.

Jennet looked away from the cat to the nice young man who had come to the castle and who, so Cook told her, had forgotten his name.

'He and Dolly are my best friends – that is, the best friends I have here. Krispin is my bestest friend but he is not here.'

'And who is he?' asked Mordan. He sat on a bench against a wall of mellow brick up which a vine had climbed since the Lady Eloira was a child.

The Reeve had been touched by the gratitude shown by this stranger. He had made himself popular in the kitchen where he would take on any chore with the same cheerfulness as he mixed the

127

mortar for the old mason repairing stonework or fed the stabled kine who provided milk for the dairy. Most of all Eloira noticed his kindness to Jennet, ever ready to join her in some childish game. But the body of Jennet was not that of a child and the Reeve, mistrustful of all men, ensured that a trusted servant was always in the background when the two were together.

'And who is . . . your bestest friend?' said Mordan again, pulling a cord from his pocket to play cat's cradle.

'My brother . . . I think. We were always together, but now I do not know where he is. My Lady Eloira tells me he will come some day but she will not say when.'

She smiled at the pattern the young man was forming out of the cord.

'You are clever,' she said. 'Krispin used to do things like that.' She sighed. 'I do not suppose you know him?'

'Of course.'

'How could you? You do not even know your own name.'

'I did not forget everything when I was hit on the head.'

'Then why did you ask me who Krispin was?'

'Did I? I thought I just asked you who your best friend was?'

'Do you really know him? Does he have greeny eyes?'

'I told you I know him. He likes playing games and his eyes are a sort of green colour.'

Jennet clapped her hands. 'Then you do know

him. Please tell the Lady Eloira so he can be brought here.'

'I cannot,' said Mordan gravely.

'Why?'

'It is a secret.'

'Why is a secret?'

Mordan shrugged. 'If I told it would not be a secret.'

She looked thoughtful for a minute. 'Is it because of the old woman in the forest?'

Mordan had no idea what she meant but he nodded gravely.

'Would you take me to see him?'

'I told you, Jennet, it is a secret.'

'Please.'

'I shall think about it — if you promise not to tell a single living soul what I have told you.'

By way of promise she made the Circle of the Mother over her heart. 'You will think about it very hard?'

'Because it is a secret, we would have to go late at night when everyone is asleep.'

'What fun.'

Several nights later, when the moon transformed the mist surrounding the Peak Tower into a lake of pearl, Mordan led Jennet by the hand to the postern gate. On his back he carried a light pack filled with food filched from the kitchen. In his belt was a long cook's knife.

'Not a word until we are away in the forest,' he whispered and the girl nodded obediently. She was wearing a warm cloak, as he had instructed her, and in her free hand she carried the elegant doll which Eloira had given her on her arrival in the Peak Tower.

'Dolly must come too,' she had told Mordan when he had tapped lightly on the casement of her bedchamber. To his immense relief she was awake and ready, the thought of seeing Krispin again having kept sleep at bay after the lights of the tower had been extinguished. Only one window glowed high above them. In her solar Eloira pored over the vellum pages of a rune book penned by her great-grandsire before The Enchantment.

Now Mordan released Jennet's hand and heaved on the oaken crossbar which held the postern gate. It was heavier than he expected and it made him realise he had not fully regained his strength.

'Someone is coming,' Jennet whispered.

Turning from the gate he looked up the stepped path following the base of the castle wall and saw the yellow eye of the watchman's lantern.

'Wait while I go and tell him all is well,' he whispered back and then hurried towards the light.

'Why, Master No-name,' said the old man when he saw Mordan in the glow of the lamp. 'You be about late and no mistake.'

'Come, there is something you must see,' Mordan said with a note of urgency and he led the watchman behind one of the massive buttresses which reinforced the wall.

'Nothing here,' he said holding aloft the lantern. 'What do you expect me to see, young sir?'

'The Dark Maid,' hissed Mordan and drove the slim-bladed kitchen knife into his heart. Then he clapped one hand over the mouth of the dying man to stifle his final groan and lowered him to the ground with the other.

'I just said goodnight to old Dodkin,' he told Jennet as he returned and heaved against the crossbar with renewed urgency.

'There is blood on your hand.'

'I must have caught it on a splinter.'

A moment later the crossbar moved in its iron fastenings, the gate creaked open and Mordan led Jennet into the clammy mist which hung over the forest.

TWELVE

Return to Mabalon

Alwald slowly entered the narrow hall with its row of draped windows.

'Magic casements' Krispin had called them.

The thought of stepping through the second casement, approaching River Garde's castle and perhaps even seeing his beloved father on its ramparts, with the knowledge that soon he was destined to have his throat torn by a werewolf, was unbearable. And yet the knowledge that it was only the thickness of glass that separated him from his ancestral home and those he loved haunted him. The temptation to go back to the hall and draw the curtain once more for just a *look* at the graceful castle had been a torment.

If only we could get away from this accursed isle and its master who seems to be in his dotage, thought Alwald. *Every time we meet him he is more vague, more unable to come to a decision, more feeble.*

This day he had decided the only way to escape the burden of temptation was to yield to it. He came to a halt before the casement through which he had glimpsed River Garde and, bracing himself, pulled aside the dark curtain.

To a mixture of dismay and relief he saw no graceful castle with a background of forest green but instead a river curving through swampland towards a horizon hung with purple clouds, a dismal setting with skeletal trees reflected in stagnant water. Alwald believed he could smell the miasma rising from its bubbling surface. Hastily he replaced the hanging.

The thought that he had picked the wrong casement took him to the next, and though he saw no castle with black banners through the window, the scene which met his gaze held him spellbound. Lit by moonlight, houses with bright doors and shutters were grouped close to the bank of a river flowing through a broad valley whose gentle slopes were patchworked with the squares of vineyards. From the centre of the village a slender spire divided the low moon.

'Mabalon!' he breathed.

Mabalon, the hidden sanctuary that he and his companions had reached by river after crossing the Land of Blight; it was here that the Lady Demara, his father's young widow, had stayed behind to await the birthing of her child.

This time Alwald stepped up to the casement with no thought other than that of Demara in his mind. He turned the catch, pushed the window open and jumped over the low sill . . .

The air was filled with the soft scents of growing things and the tang of wood smoke. It was

133

suddenly so familiar that Alwald began to tramp towards the village as though he had never left it. Only once did he look back and see the faint shape of the casement glimmering above the path, but at that moment he doubted if he would return to it. He had given enough to the quest which seemed no nearer to being accomplished. Here, safe from the growing ugliness of the world, he could settle in peace and care for Demara.

He passed the first of the houses and entered the square with the shrine at one end and a half-timbered inn he remembered as the Rose and Vine at the other. How astonished the good landlord would be to see him walk in. Ahead of him he saw a figure in a flowing dress hurrying towards one of the houses where it seemed a small crowd of villagers had congregated. He recognised her as the Bailiff of the Vale of Mabalon and ran after her.

'Mistress Earth,' he cried. He drew alongside her and laid his hand on her arm, but she did not hear his voice and his hand passed through her flesh as though he were a phantom.

It was then he realised the truth about the magic casements. Although the world he had entered appeared substantial, he could not be a physical part of it.

He followed the bailiff to the house where he recognised many of those waiting quietly outside: Master Corn, Master Dew, Mistress Grape and Mistress Rain who held the old soldier Emon gently by the arm which told Alwald that blindness was now upon him.

'Emon!'

Without thought Alwald uttered his name, but none heard him though he could hear them.

'If it be a boy there will be free wine for all at the inn,' promised the landlord. 'And if it be a girl there will be free wine for all!'

There was muted laughter and Alwald realised that within the house Demara was about to give birth, a momentous occasion in the village, for childlessness was the bane of Mabalon, a bane brought by the river from the Land of Blight.

Unseen, Alwald followed Mistress Earth into the house but he halted in the kitchen as the sound of a woman gasping in pain came from a bedchamber upstairs.

Serene Mother, spare your child! he prayed and sank onto a wooden chair to sit with his elbows on a table and his head in his hands, trying to block out the moaning from above, trying not to imagine Demara in pain.

Suddenly there was a long-drawn cry, followed by muffled exclamations. Mistress Earth ran down the stairs to the open door.

'A boy,' she told the crowd. 'And he is whole.'

Cheers greeted her words.

Demara? thought Alwald in desperation. *What of Demara?*

Outside a voice demanded, 'How fares Mistress Star?' – the name bestowed on Demara in the custom of Mabalon.

'She is exhausted but well.'

Alwald heard no more. His shoulders shook and he was thankful that to those hurrying about the house he was invisible.

When he did look up he saw a pretty girl, whose bright cheeks had once earned her the nickname of Rose Red, hurry into the kitchen. Her face was wreathed in smiles as she collected a bowl of warm water to wash the newborn, and it was obvious that she was with child.

Alwald recognised her as Margan, Demara's maid, and he remembered his suspicion that after their farewell feast in the Rose and Vine she had spent the night with Krispin.

So I have a surprise for you, Toymaker, he thought.

How much longer he remained at the kitchen table Alwald did not know, for time had become difficult to gauge. But when the sound of celebration echoed from the inn, and many of the women who filled the house had gone, he rose, climbed the staircase and looked into the bedchamber. A rushlight was the only form of illumination. All he could see of Demara was a figure lying in a great carved bed with what appeared to be a bundle held in the crook of her arm. Then Margan, who was sitting beside the bed, moved and Demara's lovely but exhausted face appeared out of the shadow.

At the sight of her Alwald felt again the pain of guilty love, for he had adored his young stepmother ever since his widowed father had brought her as his bride to River Garde.

If only he could take her hand, tell her that somehow he would return to Mabalon . . . but there was nothing he could do and he turned away with a heavy heart until he heard Demara whisper.

'It is strange, Margan, but Alwald came to my mind as Grim was born. It is as though his presence is close to me.'

The Mage sank wearily into his throne-like chair at the head of the table and looked at his four guests with a ghost of a smile on his thin lips. Food appeared on the platters before them, but they took little notice of it. All were withdrawn and even Alwald, whose manners were such that he usually tried to engage his host in polite conversation, was silent.

'Despite the comfort of my tower there is much here to oppress the spirits of those unused to gramarye,' said The Mage. 'You, Master Jongleur, look as though you could never utter a jest again.'

Ognam, unusually pale, moved nervously in his chair.

'And you others look more like those condemned to the wheel in Danaak than hearty adventurers.' The Mage sighed and sipped his wine. 'Perhaps it is with me that the fault lies, for it seemed to me that you needed to rest after the rigours of your journey before continuing your quest.'

'What troubles us is not knowing whether we will be continuing it,' said Alwald gloomily.

'I think mayhap there may be more than that which weighs upon you, Lord Alwald,' said The Mage. 'But as to the quest, the time has arrived to banish your uncertainty.'

At his words they looked up with awakening interest in their eyes.

'By your judgement of time you think it has

taken me overlong to consider what you have told me,' he went on, 'but in late life decisions do not come quickly, and I am older than you would believe possible. It is because of the burden of my age that I spend much time with my body as dormant as a bear under the winter ice while my unencumbered spirit sojourns in realms beyond mortal ken. Were I to remain as I am now, the Dark Maid would soon beckon.'

'But surely, Mesire Mage, with your sorcery you could enjoy eternal youth?' said Alwald.

'For the uninitiated, the nature of magic is not easily understood,' The Mage said. 'You see it as a mighty power free from the rules of nature, that can be summoned by a magician's tricks, by incantation and ceremony. What is not realised is that the essence of magic is finite, that just as the All Father created so much water or air in the world, so there was only so much power for magicians to conjure. The more advanced the magician, the more power he or she commands, but whether a humble weather-charmer who can do no more than summon clouds or as great as Ysldon who could petrify giants, the reserve of power each may call upon is lessened every time an act of sorcery is performed.

'You would not know, but it was theurgy that ensured Ythan's golden age. If the harvest failed, sorcery replenished the grain towers; if plague was in the cities, sorcery supplied the cure; if enemies invaded, the king had only to ask his court magician to bespell them. It was the noontime of the enchanters and the land prospered through

138

their wizardry. But while the kingdom grew, the power of the magicians reduced accordingly.

'The last great magical act was The Enchantment. Not only did it end royal reign in Ythan but it was the swansong of the great mages. Some, such as myself, sought solace far from Ythan; others with lesser skills became the victims of the Witchfinders.'

'Yet there is still magic in the world,' protested Gambal. 'Your castle is filled with enchantments.'

'You are right that there is still some magic in the world. Some is a law unto itself and cannot be harnessed by magicians; some, instilled long ago into places and objects, still retains its potency. But you should understand that I have been talking of the demise of High Magic that could build or destroy kingdoms, the remnants of which are enough for the paltry conjuring that survives today. Yet even that is dying and ere long magic will be nothing more than the ingredient of folktales. Everything has its turn and the age of the magician must give way.'

'To what, mesire?' asked Gambal who had been following his words intently.

'To the age of the alchemist.' He gazed thoughtfully into the depths of his wine. 'As for myself, I retain enough sorcery for my wants though I must admit that I husband it and do not keep up appearances when my body sleeps – one dry room with a fire is all I need – but such power as I have left is nothing compared to that which I once commanded.'

'Then it would seem to me that the Esav, coming

as you told us from the stars, must carry a power for magic-working that has not yet been tapped,' said Krispin. 'With such a stone might High Magic be possible again?'

'You have a shrewd wit for a toymaker,' said The Mage. 'The Esav would be of use only to one who has the knowledge to work it.'

'In that case, mesire, the Esav must be of value to you,' said Alwald, 'for it is useless to such as we except as a payment for something we need desperately to know — the true resting place of Princess Livia.'

'I have given the matter much thought for it is not as straightforward as it may seem, as you may later learn. At the time of The Enchantment oaths were sworn . . . but no matter now. You tell me of portents and mayhap the time has come for Livia to awaken, though whether that be a good or evil thing even I cannot say.'

'Then you will accept the Esav and tell us the route to the Princess?' asked Alwald.

The Mage slowly lowered his snowy head in agreement and all four were filled with relief. Soon they would be out of the unreal atmosphere of the tower on a proper journey again and even if the way were rough, honest journeying was something they understood.

'A toast to your quest, my young friends,' said The Mage.

The light of beeswax candles shone ruby through their goblets as Alwald added, 'And a toast to Princess Livia, the hope of the kingdom.'

The old man's bloodless lips twisted in an ironical

smile. 'And may you not regret the knowledge I shall give you. It will take more courage than you realise to awaken her.'

'We have to find her first, mesire,' said Gambal. 'Will you give us a chart?'

'Where will the journey take us?' asked Alwald.

'The Princess's resting place is deep in the Shadow Realm.'

Alwald frowned. 'The Shadow Realm? I have never heard of it.'

'Few in Ythan have. It lies beyond the Mountains of the Moon which are the southern-most boundary of the kingdom. It is a savage place but if you have crossed the Land of Blight you may find it no worse.'

'Knowing where we must go is one thing, getting there is another,' said Krispin. 'Griffins brought us but—'

The Mage raised a trembling hand and they saw that his face had paled to ivory. The golden globes that had been suspended at the far end of the table streamed towards him in consternation.

'Forgive me, but the curse of the years is suddenly heavy and this frail body of mine must rest. Tomorrow I shall . . . tell you . . . all you need to know.'

Serene Mother! prayed Alwald. *Let him live until then!*

'Help me . . . to my . . . chamber.'

The voice was little more than the whisper of reeds stirred by the breeze.

Krispin leapt to his feet and took The Mage in his arms, and marvelled that he had no more weight than a child. Following the hovering globes, he carried the old man from the hall and along a passage to his bedchamber where flames danced above aromatic logs in the huge fireplace. Here he gently laid him on his four-poster bed and placed a light coverlet over him.

The veined eyelids opened.

'My thanks, Master Toymaker . . . show me again the Esav . . .'

'Yes, mesire.'

Krispin slid his hand inside his tunic, encountering the Disk of Livia he wore as a Pilgrim, and then the purse in which he kept the heart-shaped jewel . . .

But already The Mage slept.

THIRTEEN

Execution

'Welcome to my Gallery of Toys,' said the Regent. 'There are few in the Citadel who have ever crossed its threshold.'

'I recognise the honour,' said Urwen quietly. 'And my curiosity is burning to see what I have only vaguely heard of.'

'Forward, Fozo,' said the Regent and the lamp-bearer entered the long hall which housed his master's collection of automata. The dim glow from his lantern showed that the walls were lined with shadowy figures, most of which were shrouded in dust sheets.

'Ah, master, you have come at last,' came a sibilant voice from the shadows. 'We have waited so long, oh yes, so long, but all are ready to play before you as in the old days.'

Urwen saw the speaker was a fawning little man, not much taller than the dwarf, whose pebble glasses gave him a grotesque appearance as they reflected the light from the lantern.

'I have brought this lady to watch the antics of the family,' said the Regent. There was a rare note of good humour in his voice for he had recently swallowed a potion which gave him brief respite from the pain which surged into his body from his misshapen hand.

'Fozo, light the lamps and then wait in the usual place.'

The dwarf hurried down the centre of the gallery and one after another chandeliers burst into sparkling light. The Regent led Urwen to a damask-covered couch on a low dais while the custodian bobbed behind, twisting his duster in his breathless excitement.

'It will be like old times, oh yes, just like the happy old times,' he chuckled as his master and the beautiful lady seated themselves. 'What you like first, master? Timbal to play his lute or—'

'I shall leave the entertainment to you, Prince, and the refreshment.'

'Yes, oh yes, master.'

The little man squealed his delight and darted away.

'You called him Prince,' said Urwen reclining against a cloth-of-gold bolster filled with the down of cygnets.

'He is believed to be very remotely descended from the old kings of Ythan,' the Regent explained. 'If that be true he is the last alive with a few drops of royal blood in his veins – apart from the Princess Livia if she could be thought of as having life. It amuses me that the last of such an illustrious line should have toys as his subjects, yet none could do his work better. He has a flair for mechanisms and he is so devoted to the care of his

144

charges that I swear he thinks of them as living beings rather than collections of cog wheels and counterweights.'

At the end of the gallery the last chandelier was lit. Fozo disappeared through an archway to await his master's bidding. He sat with his back against the tapestry-hung brickwork which now blocked off the spiral staircase leading to the high chamber in which the alchemist Leodore had sought the secret of life.

The dwarf pressed his ear against the new wall but all he heard was the beat of his own pulse so, after his ritual imprecation against the cruel whim of the Mother in stunting him, he closed his eyes and as usual sought solace in sleep.

In the gallery the custodian raced along the walls to snatch away dust sheets and Urwen watched as the Regent's collection emerged into the bright light. She gave a gasp of alarm as a gleaming figure of brass suddenly appeared beside her and, with a whirring and clicking, proffered a tray on which were two crystal goblets filled with black wine.

'Prince has the servants well trained,' the Regent remarked as he and Urwen raised their goblets to each other. 'And, unlike those of flesh and blood, they are incapable of treason.'

'I am flesh and blood as you have found, my lord,' said Urwen. 'My heart would break if you ever thought . . .'

The Regent turned to her with an unusual smile on his wasted features. 'You have proved your loyalty. If it had not been for your spying I might have been forced to swallow Lord Odo's draught

145

of firewort. I suspect, however, that he would barter his spirit to drink such a draught in his present condition.'

He smiled again as he thought of his last visit to the dungeon world below the foundations of the Citadel to see 'his pets'. Caked with his own ordure, rat-bitten and mostly out of his mind, the once haughty Odo was paying a horrendous price for his dream of seizing the Regency for himself.

'Was he a good lover?' the Regent asked casually.

'He worshipped me.'

'Yet you betrayed him.'

'Betrayal was my work – and my pleasure, for such adoration breeds contempt. In me it bred more than contempt. He would have had the whole of Ythan kneel before him yet he knelt before me and made an offering of his secrets.'

'It might amuse you to see him now – he is still on his knees,' said the Regent. Urwen shivered but not with fear.

'We are ready, master and my lady, oh yes we are ready,' came the hissing voice. 'The executioner has been repaired and works very well, and Merlinda has new finery. May we begin?' The Regent nodded. There was a ticking of hidden mechanisms, a slight creaking, and the metal fingers of a handsome young automaton caressed the strings of his lute and several mechanical figures garbed in glittering costumes performed a pavan.

'They are amazing,' Urwen breathed.

'There are none better in the world,' said the Regent. 'See their eyes? They are cut from blue

146

quartz that is only found in the Crystal Ranges, a four-moon journey from Danaak. And their fingernails – they are fashioned from unicorn ivory that continues to grow.'

Urwen glanced at him in surprise. She had known him to be cold, sardonic, haughty, occasionally impassioned, but she had never seen him so enthusiastic.

The notes of the lute filled the long, brilliantly-lit gallery and the life-sized toys glided before them. Thanks to Prince's meticulous timing, it appeared that the rest of the company was watching the dancers, and when the last notes of the lute faded softly into silence many of the automatons applauded. The dancers bowed to the dais and walked – albeit somewhat jerkily as their springs were running down – back to their accustomed places.

They were followed by an acrobat and then a mock combat between a knight and the winged lion. At times there was a clumsiness about their movements as they lost synchronisation, causing Prince to rush to them in a fever of anxiety to adjust hidden levers. But Urwen was delighted with the performance and laughed aloud at the metallic roarings which issued from the lion's throat.

The brass servant brought more wine and she sat happily with her head against the Regent's shoulder, a goblet in one hand and the fingers of the other resting gently on the swathed shape of the Regent's monstrous hand concealed beneath his velvet cloak. Once she glanced up and was alarmed to see that his broad forehead glistened with perspiration.

'Do you ail, my love?' she asked.

'It is the heat of the chandeliers,' he answered gruffly, and then added as though to himself, 'Mandraga's potions are losing their potency. I am master of Ythan yet I am powerless against the poison of a creature that never knew the spark of true life.'

The spasm passed. He wiped his brow with his healthy hand and drank the dark wine.

'Merlinda would like to show you her new finery, oh yes, very much she would,' hissed Prince after a life-sized doll had performed a dance of such eroticism that Urwen glanced at the Regent's once-fleshy features with new interest. Could the stories be true that he found more satisfaction with his dolls than in natural coupling even though he could have any of the most beautiful women in the kingdom? The idea alarmed her and she tried to reassure herself with the thought that, despite his pain, it was with her that he had achieved satisfaction, the savagery of which had left her in a glow of sensual ease – and in love for the first time in her life.

'I want to see Merlinda,' Urwen said.

The Regent nodded and the custodian danced away to lead the beautiful automaton forward by the hand.

'The Lady Merlinda greets you, my lord,' he chuckled. She curtsied as he pressed a spring hidden in her palm.

'A good likeness?' said the Regent.

'Merlinda was older when I stayed with her,' Urwen replied, 'but the likeness is there. She must have been a great beauty when she was young.'

'She was when she resided in the Citadel,' said the Regent.

'You will think me foolish, my lord, but I confess to a feeling of jealousy.'

'Then I hope this will amuse you.'

The Regent bent forward and whispered in Prince's ear. His words appeared to shock the little man.

'Oh no, my lord,' he cried. 'Impossible! I could not! The family love you and . . .'

The Regent whispered again.

Prince bowed formally. 'It will be as you wish,' and he walked away ringing his hands.

A minute later a drummer marched into the centre of the gallery and began a steady beat on his drum. Next the Merlinda figure walked daintily forward and halted before the Regent to repeat her curtsy, her face set in an eternal smile, her crystal eyes reflecting the youthful hope that the real Merlinda had felt all those years ago. Then she stood still while the drummer continued his menacing rataplan.

'My lord, I beg you to think again,' began Prince.

'Be silent and do not hold up the play or mayhap I shall give you the main role.'

His spectacles flashed as Prince bobbed and turned back to the automatons. With a tramp of metal feet a huge figure marched forward holding a sickle-bladed axe. It halted beside Merlinda and raised the axe in salute to the Regent.

'Continue,' he commanded.

Suddenly Urwen felt a thrill of excitement mingled with fear as Prince moved about the three mute figures, adjusting hidden controls and muttering beneath his breath.

The drummer increased his tempo and with her fixed smile the Merlinda doll knelt down and threw her arms wing-like behind her back. The drum thundered, the executioner brought his axe down in an arc of bright steel, there was a metallic screech and Merlinda's head flew from her body – wires, springs and metal tubes burst from the severed neck.

Later Urwen was to wonder whether it had been her imagination but at that moment – as the eyelids of the severed head fluttered coquettishly – it seemed that a sigh rose from the mechanical spectators.

The Regent laughed.

'Well staged, Prince,' he cried. 'Now, Urwen, there is nothing to rival your beauty in the Citadel.'

She looked at him with shining eyes, then an expression of concern replaced her smile as she saw the Regent's face twist into a rictus of agony.

'My lord?'

'I am on fire,' he gasped. Sweat oozed over his pallid skin and his teeth clamped his bottom lip to stop himself shouting in his agony. With his free hand he tore at the bandages hiding his deformity.

'Fozo!' he roared.

The dwarf came at a stumbling run through the archway.

'Fetch my physician – run as you have never run or I shall have you spiked.'

With his lantern swinging wildly, the manikin trotted down the gallery.

'Prince, set up the executioner.'

Too terrified to demur, the custodian cranked the axe back into position.

The Regent's eyes closed as new waves of pain flooded his body.

'My chance of a cure was lost by that cursed alchemist,' he muttered. 'There is only one way to free myself of this abomination.'

The last of the bandage coiled away.

The Regent stood up. 'Prince, this must be cleaved from my arm.'

At the sight of his master's hand the little man swayed as though about to faint.

'My lord, there must be some other way.'

'If there was, do you not think I would know it? They said water from the Wells of Ythan but they are long lost . . . *Serene Mother!*'

Blood flowed from his bitten lip as another spasm gripped him and he sank back onto the couch. Urwen thought he had fainted and she and Prince exchanged helpless glances. From the floor came a faint ticking as the eyelids of the severed head continued to flutter. On the other side of the gallery the glassy eyes of the automata gazed at the tableau on the dais, while the executioner stood with his razor-edged axe poised.

'Urwen, take word to Captain Bors,' whispered the Regent. 'Only the Companions of the Rose . . . and Mandraga . . . must know of . . . of what is about to happen . . . treason lusts for such opportunity.'

'I cannot leave you yet, my lord.'

The Regent said nothing as he waited for the pain to ebb. There was a sound of rapid footfalls and Urwen looked up with relief to see the dwarf returning with a portly man puffing under the weight of a basket of bandages, salves and implements of his trade. He gave a grunt of disgust as he saw the Regent's hand with its bloated fingers scrabbling on the damask as though it had independent life.

'Then they are true – the rumours,' he said in an awed whisper. 'It is the bane of some man-created abomination. What can the likes of me do for that?'

'You know what to do for a severed limb?'

The physician looked from the Regent to the executioner and with shaking fingers began unpacking bandages and phials of medicated oils from his basket.

'On the battlefield we used boiling pitch to seal such wounds,' he muttered.

'We are not on the battlefield,' said the Regent, opening his eyes.

'My lord, I will give you a sleeping drug and then remove the canker, so you can escape the pain.'

The Regent shook his head. 'There are many who would like to hold a knife to me while I lay unconscious. I will not expose you to such temptation, Wibba. Your task will be merely to bind me.'

The Regent stood up and, with his healthy hand

resting on Urwen's shoulder to steady himself, he approached the executioner. He knelt with his arm outstretched on the marble floor so that his inflamed wrist lay directly in the path of the axe.

'Prince . . . *now!*'

The little man reached towards the back of the executioner for the lever which would release his mighty arms.

'No!'

It was more like the furious croak of a raven than the voice of a woman and all eyes turned to the gallery entrance where the Lady Mandraga appeared.

'The Lore Mistress,' murmured the physician.

'What foolishness is this?' she demanded coming forward with the aid of her crutch.

'Lady, there is no other way,' said the Regent wearily. 'Your potions are no longer powerful enough and I sense this toxin will soon be my death.'

'Then I have come not a moment too late,' she said. 'This hour the scholars have returned from Thaan. In the Great Library there they discovered the secret of Ythan's Wells.'

There was a crash as the executioner's axe shattered a marble tile close to the Regent's twitching hand.

FOURTEEN

The Amber Star

Lancet windows filled with blue lightning as Ognam walked fearfully along a passage adorned with clusters of barbaric weapons. It was past midnight and the storm sweeping the Cold Sea wailed round the turrets of The Mage's tower and sluiced its walls with freezing spray. But the elemental fury without was nothing compared to the turmoil within the jongleur.

Never before had he been so devious. The night before last he and his gloomy companions, still unaware of The Mage's intentions, had dined without their host and, under the pretext of trying to lift their spirits, he had entertained them with songs and stories until even Gambal could no longer repress a smile. And all the time he encouraged them to empty their cups which were magically refilled with heady wine. Then he had introduced them to a drinking game known as Archpriest Huff in which the penalty for a mistake was to swallow yet more wine.

When the evening ended he was the only one capable of walking steadily, though he cannily swayed the most as they sought their chambers. Once sure that all slept, he had walked softly into the room where Krispin lay, drunkenly snoring. With the deftness of one who included simple conjuring among his talents, Ognam felt for the peasant purse that hung from Krispin's neck by a thong. It had taken only a moment to extract the Esav, hide it in his own pouch and hurry away with a hammering heart.

He was about to continue to the staircase that led to the subterranean lake when he saw several glowing globes drift towards him like servants making the final rounds of their master's house. He staggered to his room adjusting his points as though he just visited the latrine and flung himself down.

After a while he ventured to his doorway, and was aghast to see that there was a globe hanging as though suspended by invisible thread at each end of the passage. Their immobility told him that they would be there for the rest of the night and he returned to his couch in agony of mind.

Through the following day he had lived in expectation of Krispin suddenly putting his hand in his tunic and shouting that they had been robbed of the jewel that was the key to the quest. He tried to reassure himself with the thought that the Esav was a flat stone and had little weight, and unless Krispin actually sought to remove it he was unlikely to miss it.

Each time he attempted to leave for the netherworld beneath the tower he was thwarted. If it was not one of the accursed globes following him about like a servant eager to do his bidding – 'I am here to grant your slightest wish, with garment, goblet, bath or dish' – it was Alwald who on this day of all days felt it necessary to reminisce about his homeland, describing in great detail characters who meant nothing to Ognam, especially his father's second wife.

Several times he had to resist a compulsion to seek Krispin and admit the theft – the *borrowing* – but he knew that the kindly youth, who had listened so sympathetically when he confided his tale of the beautiful captive, would never dare risk the hard-won Esav.

The worst moment had come last night after The Mage had been taken to his bed and asked to see it. He had watched in frozen panic as Krispin had reached for it, but – thanks be to the Mother! – the old man's eyes had closed and Krispin withdrew his hand. Yet was it his guilty imagination or had Krispin looked at him strangely?

Pleading a headache from the previous night's debauchery, Ognam had left his companions eagerly discussing The Mage's words at supper and hurried unhindered to the staircase that was like a well of night until he lit his candle.

The swan-boat bore him across the lake once more. As soon as it touched the far shore he raced through the silver trees to where Tana read her scroll and metal birds sang.

'Dear jongleur, how I have awaited your coming!' she greeted him.

'There is little time,' said Ognam. 'We will soon

be on the quest again – and somehow you are going to come with me.'

'Impossible!' She gestured to the grille which as usual had materialised between them.

'I have brought something which may out-magick them.'

'The Esav?'

'The Esav!'

Ognam took it from his pouch and raised it for her to see, then he held it against the nearest bar. For a moment he felt the crystal scorch his fingers and its colours flashed so brightly it seemed fragments of rainbow were reflected all about, on the silver leaves and on their faces so that they were transformed into the likeness of carnival masks. The rod the Esav touched shrivelled to mere wire as the magic that had been melded in it was absorbed by the unearthly jewel. Within minutes, more bars had been transformed to threads of blackened metal which Ognam easily parted with his hands.

'You are free,' he told Tana simply.

'Not yet,' she replied. 'Not until I quit the domain of the accursed Mage.'

'That you must leave to me, but now I must go.'

'Have you no time to step into my court? Come, let me hold the Esav for a moment. There must be no other jewel like it in the world.' She held out her hands to him.

'I must return it,' he said stubbornly. 'If the others guessed what I had done, there would be no more questing for me – and no escape for you.'

'Go then with my loving gratitude.'

For a moment their hands locked, then Ognam was hurrying to the swan-boat.

Now Ognam must creep into Krispin's darkened chamber and approach his couch . . . He was just drawing back the fur coverlet to replace the Esav in the toymaker's purse when a hand clamped his wrist.

'Ognam?'

'Yes, Krispin. I . . .'

Krispin relaxed his grip and Ognam opened his hand and gave him the glowing jewel.

'What can I say to make amends for the distress I must have caused you?'

'Nothing. I knew it was you.'

'How so?'

'Who else? Neither Gambal nor Alwald would have use for it. Whatever else The Mage may be, he is not a thief, so that left you. Besides, I could guess your reason since you had told me of the beautiful captive. Tell me, did the magic of the jewel perform the task you set it?'

Ognam nodded.

'Good, but it is best that I know nothing more so that by accident or sorcery I cannot betray your secret.' He smiled. 'Love makes fools of us all . . . and sometimes it is good to be a fool.'

'Master Krispin, will you tell—'

'Tell what? That you came to bid me goodnight?'

'Then goodnight. This will not be forgotten.'

Ognam turned and left the chamber.

'We are all fools, Ognam,' Krispin whispered to himself and pulled the fur over his shoulder.

*　　*　　*

Although he had rested for many hours, The Mage looked so frail when he entered the feast hall that Gambal muttered to Alwald that it would not be long before he was entertaining the Dark Maid.

'As long as we get the chart, I care not,' he replied. 'I am heart sick of gramarye.'

All looked at The Mage expectantly as he carefully seated himself in his high-backed chair.

'This is the last time we shall dine thus, you and I,' he said in a voice little more than a whisper. 'Choose your courses well so this farewell meal will be a pleasant memory when viands are less appetising or plentiful.'

'We are more interested in the course to be followed than to be eaten,' murmured Ognam.

The globes swirled about the long table and a variety of foods materialised on the platters before the guests, but their appetites faltered when The Mage said, 'I have no map that will lead you to the Princess Livia. She is hidden in the Shadow Realm and that is uncharted.'

'But . . . ' began Alwald.

The Mage raised his hand. 'Fear not. You shall have the means to reach the end of your quest.'

From his gown he extracted a small box of ivory and taking off the lid showed them that it contained a pointer mounted on a pivot so it could revolve freely.

'The needle was cast from a fragment of the Lodestone that rises from the ocean at the world's end,' he told them. 'In its natural form it has the property of always pointing to the rock from which

159

it was taken, but this was bespelled at The Enchantment always to point to where Livia lies. All you need to do is follow its direction until you reach your destination. Guard it with your lives if you would brave the Shadow Realm.'

'This realm, is it then so dangerous?' asked Ognam.

'It is not only parlous but . . . *strange*,' said The Mage. 'The Princess lies bespelled there because it is far from the known world and ringed by perils. It was said that its very nature was warped by The Enchantment.'

'Tell us about The Enchantment, Mesire Mage,' said Alwald. 'It is a word oft used but little understood. Why was Princess Livia stolen away and entranced?'

'It is something you will learn only if you complete the quest,' said The Mage in a voice that was suddenly cold. Then he added in a milder tone, 'The weight of the years has dimmed much of my memory. It is not for me to tell of the past, for though I be a mage, my mind remains mortal.' He raised his wine to his lips.

Aware that the old man would say nothing further on the subject, Alwald asked the question that had been hanging over them all.

'Although we shall have the means of finding our way, how shall we travel it?'

A rare glint of humour crept into The Mage's expression. 'It is your quest. Why do you ask me? In return for the Jewel from the Stars I agreed to provide a means for you to find the Princess, not a means to get there.'

'But what use is the Lodestone if we have no way of leaving this islet?' Alwald exclaimed.

'What indeed?'

There was a long silence.

'Then, with respect, Mesire, there is no point in our trading the Esav,' said Krispin quietly.

'Your words come close to impudence,' said The Mage. 'You talk of trading, yet it seems you are in a poor position to bargain. If I but said one word, the Esav could be in my hand and you . . . ' He did not need to finish the sentence.

'It is true, Mesire Mage, that we are not proof against sorcery,' said Gambal, 'but mayhap the Esav itself would not be complaisant if it were to be obtained by such means from him who rightfully owns it. Master Krispin owns it by right of finding, for in the City Without a Name no men have dwelt for centuries as you told us.'

A sound like a rill gurgling over stones came from The Mage. For a moment they feared he was choking but to their relief they realised he was actually laughing.

'You have a cunning wit,' he said to Gambal. 'No wonder you were a revel master, but I would guess that in Danaak your wit was too cunning for your own good.'

Gambal gave a slight bow from his seat.

'As far as being able to continue your quest from here, you are in luck,' The Mage continued. 'On the landward side of my island there is a tiny harbour, sheltered somewhat from the tempests that sweep the Cold Sea, and in that harbour lies a sound vessel, the *Amber Star*. she is well-named,

161

for her master brought her to these climes to seek the amber cast ashore by the waves. She had the misfortune to be attacked by corsairs and in the chase most of the crew were killed. At the last moment the shipmaster was able to sail into one of the banks of fog which come with the summer season and his luck brought him through the skerries to my islet. And here he has remained for he has none who can man the ship.'

'He is alone?' asked Krispin who, like his companions, tried to hide his elation at the thought of quitting the islet.

'He has with him his steersman, who was wounded ill by the corsairs, and an old amber-seeker but no crew – until now. The *Amber Star* will take you to the Shadow Realm, for today I have agreed a reward for such service and Shipmaster Danya knows the penalty of breaking an agreement with a mage.'

'As the one who was entrusted to lead the quest, I give you heartfelt thanks on behalf of us all, Lord Mage,' said Alwald. 'And now let us complete the trade – the Esav for the Lodestone.'

The Mage looked slowly from face to face of the companions.

'First, is there aught else you would ask?'

'Yes, Mesire Mage,' said Krispin. 'In Danaak, when we were told to seek you as the only one who knew the secret of the Princess, it was also said that you could tell us the manner by which she might be wakened.'

'A very important question,' said The Mage. 'It would profit you naught to reach your destination and then have to leave the lady in her slumber. Alas, the method is not that told of in traditional tales – the kiss of a handsome prince.'

Again The Mage laughed and the others smiled politely.

'Nor will it be necessary for a magical rite to be performed. There is only one element that has the power to rouse her from such strong sorcery. She must be bathed with water from the Wells of Ythan.'

'But,' said Gambal remembering scraps of conversation overheard in the Citadel, 'since The Enchantment, no man knows where they lie. Or if they were no more than a legend from the olden time.'

'They were no legend,' said The Mage. 'They were outside the laws of both nature and gramarye, and it was said that not only were their waters the waters of life but that truth lay in their depths. But it is true that their secret was lost with The Enchantment.'

'Serene Mother!' exclaimed Alwald in sudden anger. 'This quest is like a midsummer dance – for every two paces forward there is one step back. Must we now quest for the Wells before we seek the Princess?'

'I doubt if even your errant skills could lead you to them,' said The Mage. 'But if you look at that chest in the corner you will see on it a flacon of blue glass.'

Their eyes turned towards a large long-necked vessel.

'It is my parting gift,' continued The Mage. 'It

was filled with water from the Wells before The Enchantment. Guard it with your lives and do not dare pour forth its content until the moment for Livia's awakening has arrived. You would do better to die of thirst than remove that seal for your own purpose, for it is the mighty seal of Ysldon.

'Tomorrow, when it is light, you will take supplies from the kitchens down to the harbour, victual the *Amber Star* and meet her master who will set forth immediately. By then I shall have returned to that long slumber from which your presence roused me, so this is our farewell.

'I have done what I can to help you on your quest. How it turns out depends on your luck and your luck depends on your own efforts and courage. Now, let us trade.'

Krispin withdrew his purse and passed it to The Mage whose near transparent fingers trembled as he removed the heart-shaped crystal. It threw a spectrum of vibrant colours across his age-worn lineaments, and it seemed to the onlookers that his eyes shone with a brief semblance of youth as they reflected the unearthly light.

Still gazing at the Esav, he pushed the box containing the Lodestone across the table to Alwald.

'Now the Jewel from the Stars is mine,' he said. 'I wonder if you will ever realise what you have sacrificed for your quest. Even so, remember that I have treated you fair.'

'Indeed, Lord Mage,' said Alwald.

Krispin turned away. It piqued him that it was the young noble who should have been given the

Lodestone when it was he who had gained the Esav in the City Without a Name, but a deeper feeling was one of loss. Close to his heart he had carried that beautiful, magical crystal across the vast kingdom from the Land of Blight to the Cold Sea. All that time he had been aware of its latent power – indeed, he believed that it was the influence of the Esav that had animated the stone giants in the Desert of Akea.

And for what had he given up the most beautiful thing he had ever seen? More hardship, more imperilment!

The Mage rose amid a swirl of golden globes.

'One word of warning I shall give you,' he said. 'On your voyage stay clear of Haven.'

'Haven?' began Gambal, but The Mage merely raised his arm as though in benediction and turned away.

Krispin seized a halyard to keep his balance as the *Amber Star* reared to meet the sea surge. Chilling spray fountained over the bows, wind shrieked through the rigging and the shipmaster shouted oathfully at his lubberly crew to trim the cracking sail.

Like his companions, Krispin's experience of sailing had been confined to rivers – none had seen the sea until the griffins brought them to The Mage's tower – and they gazed with apprehension at the smoking ridges of grey water rushing past the twin pillars of natural rock that marked the harbour entrance.

That morning Alwald, Krispin and Gambal had

165

been woken early by deferential globes who chanted, 'Arise, good guest, resume your quest.'

They hurried to the kitchens where they found that Ognam, the bells of his motley jingling merrily, was already at work carrying sacks of provisions and water kegs down the steep stepped path to the tiny harbour where the *Amber Star* was moored.

'The fool is in a fever to be off,' said Gambal. 'I have never known him so eager for work.'

'Did you rise with the dawn?'

Ognam seemed strangely embarrassed by the grins of his companions and muttered as he turned back to his task, 'I could not sleep so I left the tower when it was light.'

'He was already here when I came to the ship,' declared the bearded shipmaster Danya. He greeted them with the politeness due to guests of The Mage combined with scepticism as to their ability to do the work of mariners. He was broadly built, in his middle years with hair bleached by sea salt and a face tanned by years of sun and wind.

The companions were heartened to see that the *Amber Star* was a well-built vessel with massive timbers designed to withstand the buffeting of the Cold Sea. Like others who ran the gamut of corsairs to this remote coast, she was armed with a metal-sheathed ram beneath her two dragon-visaged figureheads and a mangonel mounted on her high stern. Beside it stood the steersman who, having lost both his hands to the corsairs, had hooks attached to his wrists. These he rested on the helm whose grotesque decoration suddenly took Krispin's mind back to Toyheim and Father Tammas' carved pump handle.

After the newcomers had stowed their packs in the tiny forecastle cabins allotted to them, they hoisted the striped sail under the direction of the shipmaster and the *Amber Star* moved from the quay as though eager to be away from the harbour that had imprisoned her for so long.

As The Mage's tower fell behind them, Krispin looked astern and like the others had the illusion, perhaps born of morbid fancy, that the grey cloud rolling above its topmost turrets momentarily coalesced into a vast semblance of human features expressing ironic mockery: the face of The Mage.

Then the cloud was rent by a new onslaught of dark wind, cordage thrummed and the *Amber Star* swung towards the skerries that stood between her and the open sea.

Book Two

Only the most desperate mariner seeking rich amber and the scented sickness of the whale dare venture to the Cold Sea, and then not beyond land sight, for the waste of water is made perilous by floating islands of ice and kraken, who of the creatures created by the All Father are most gigantean and fearsome. Also there be isles that are the bane of seafarers, and whirlpools, and great currents which wash a frozen land told by fable to be the home of giants, and past the Lodestone which riseth from the oceanstream like a pinnacle to the clouds, and so to the world's end. If the amber-seeker hath the fortune to return from this desolation he will perforce follow the coast on his steerboard for several days if the wind be steady until he sees that said coast is no longer bare rock but hath trees upon its heights. This be the portent for the navigator that he quitteth the Cold Sea into better climes. After passing the light-tower of Haven, the currents will speed him past fair land with goodly ports which is Ythan. Should he continue the length of this country he

171

will behold a mighty range of mountains: the
Mountains of the Moon beyond whose peaks lies
the Shadow Realm which being uncharted and
without virtue is shunned by honest travellers.

– extract from *Geographis*
by the Sage Omgarth.

ONE

The Skerries

The wind that filled the sail of the *Amber Star* drove spindrift across the face of the sea so it appeared to the travellers they were moving over a plain of flowing mist. Behind them The Mage's tower shrank to a grim finger raised against cloud wrack; to the steerboard lay the foam-fringed cliffs of the mainland.

'Ahead of us lie the skerries,' said Shipmaster Danya who stood in the bows with Alwald and Krispin. 'Keep a watch for them, lads, and be ready to drop the sail as soon as you spy them. You and your friends must be ready to man the sweeps.'

'Skerries?' asked Krispin, embarrassed by his lack of knowledge of anything pertaining to the sea.

'Rocks, lad. Wicked, black, hull-ripping rocks. It is shallow hereabouts and a maze of them rises from the seabed and circles The Mage's islet. Once we are through them we will be in open sea and away from that tower. Not that I am saying anything against The Mage, mind,' he added

173

hurriedly. 'He treated me fair when I found harbour there but I never felt easy. Too much magic, nothing seemed real somehow . . . Now I must return to Gled. We will get acquainted when we clear the skerries.'

The sturdy shipmaster hurried back to the high poop where the steersman steadied the tiller with the hooks which replaced his hands.

'I know exactly what he means,' said Alwald. 'If it were not for this,' he took the ivory box containing the Lodestone from the pocket of his tunic, 'I would not be sure of what was dream and what was real. Something happened that I cannot get out of my mind.'

'Yes?'

Alwald paused, not sure whether to continue but the desire to confide was irresistible.

'I went through a magic casement.'

'And where did you find yourself?' Krispin asked with sudden interest.

'Mabalon.'

'Mabalon! Did you see the Lady Demara, and Margan?'

Alwald nodded. 'Again there was something of a dream about it. I saw people there we knew – Mistress Earth and the landlord of the Rose and Vine, and all the others – yet when I spoke they heard me not, and when I reached out to touch them it was as though I was a spectre.'

'I, too—' Krispin began.

'The Lady Demara was delivered of a son. She called him Grim, after my father. Praise the Mother, she was well.'

'But has it happened yet? By my reckoning it is not yet the time for her birthing. Perhaps what you saw still lies ahead, yet when I stepped through my casement I went back in time.'

'You may be right. I think the casements are doorways to what we desire to see, but we are left more sadly than when we entered.'

'At least you know that the birth of your half-brother was – or will be – without hurt to Demara. But what of Margan?'

'Margan . . . ' For a moment Alwald wondered whether he should tell Krispin that she was with child. Was there a point when he was so far from the Vale of Mabalon and unlikely ever to return there? On the other hand . . .

'Skerries!'

Krispin gestured beyond the twin figureheads of the *Amber Star* to where rocks rose out of the spume like black fangs so numerous that it seemed impossible for a vessel to be piloted through them.

The shipmaster shouted orders and Krispin and Alwald hurried to the waist of the vessel to help Gambal and Ognam to lower the square sail with its star emblem. Their efforts were clumsy, ropes burned the palms of their hands but under a hail of instructions from the stern they finally succeeded and the *Amber Star* slowed and then drifted with the current towards the skerries.

'Out sweeps,' commanded Danya. They ran out a heavy oar either side and then with Gambal and Ognam heaving on one and Krispin and Alwald the other, the *Amber Star* regained her steerage.

'I would not wager on our chance of getting

175

through, Gled,' the shipmaster muttered. 'What we see are bad enough but the Mother knows what lurks beneath the surface to tear us.'

The steersman responded with a bitter oath. 'The Dark Maid haunts this voyage.'

'Follow my signals,' said Danya and he hurried to the bows to seek a passage among the rocks. Suddenly a huge fish leaped high in the air ahead of him and then fell back with a resounding splash. Its back, crested with a triangular fin, gleamed black, its underside gold and white; and, to the shipmaster, its eye glittered with intelligence that he had never before observed in a sea creature.

Again it leaped and for a second appeared to balance on the tip of its tail as though endeavouring to win the shipmaster's attention, then it fell back and began to circle just ahead of the *Amber Star*'s ram.

'He would be our pilot,' shouted Danya in amazement. 'Follow him, Gled. And you on the oars, row your hearts out!'

The fish ceased his circling and swam towards the skerries with the *Amber Star* following. The crew winced as he leaped between two fearsome rocks which stood so close together that it seemed the vessel would be caught in a jagged vice, but Danya roared at the steersman to follow and, with the sweep blades grating on the shell-crusted pillars, the *Amber Star* swung between them.

Despite the chill wind, sweat soaked the rowers as they fought to keep the vessel in the wake of their guide who swerved and twisted in search of a passage. Often the heavy oaken hull groaned as cataracts of white water churning through the skerries thrust it against rocks, several times the ship reeled as random currents merged to trap her in whirlpools.

From time to time the fish made a tremendous leap, turning its body in the air as though to make sure that the *Amber Star* was following.

'That is no ordinary fish, but I care not what it be if he leads us clear of these demon teeth,' Danya declared.

'I would not die of astonishment if I learned that The Mage had something to do with it,' muttered Ognam as he pulled on the oar. 'Though he could as easily work a spell and make the rocks vanish.'

'They give his harbour protection,' said Krispin.

'Protection from what?' Alwald demanded. 'Who but the witless would come to this desolation!'

The last group of rocks raced towards them, so closely ranked it seemed impossible for the vessel to escape their clutch. The fish swerved and swam along them in search of an opening. The *Amber Star* followed, rolling alarmingly as she swung broadside to the wind. The four companions were hurled across the deck, bruising themselves against the bulwarks. As they struggled to get control of the sweeps again, their pilot lunged towards a gap. Gled swung the tiller over; a powerful surge caught the vessel and hurled it forward.

Krispin was aware of his sweep splintering as the *Amber Star* grazed a pyramid-shaped rock and cannoned into another. For a moment the vessel tilted over so steeply saltwater cascaded over the deck, then she trembled like a living creature and swung free with a screech of gouged timbers. The last of the skerries whirled past and then they were clear, with nothing but open sea undulating ahead of them.

The fish made a farewell leap and vanished in a fountain of spray.

'Up sail,' shouted the shipmaster and as his new crew hauled it into position it cracked in the wind, then filled, and even the taciturn steersman grinned as the *Amber Star* raced with a glittering bow wave tumbling on either side of her wicked ram. The skerries shrunk to black specks behind them.

On the steerboard side of the craft stretched a forbidding line of basalt cliffs over which grey vapour flowed like a gloomy aerial river, but on the seaward side shafts of light suddenly pierced the cloud banks as though to celebrate the escape of the *Amber Star*. Caught in one of these celestial rays a distant object flashed with diamond brilliance.

'Ice,' commented Danya. 'Even in the summer season the Cold Sea is never free from bergs which remain from when it was a frozen plain during winter.'

'You mean to say this is the *good* season?' muttered Ognam. 'I am frozen to my gizzard already.'

'You will find warm seamen's cloaks in your cabins,' said Danya. 'Thanks to the corsairs, my crew will never again have need of them.'

As he spoke, a bent old man with wildly flowing locks and the longest nose the travellers had ever seen emerged from the deck cabin.

'So we are clear at last,' he said in an impatient voice.

'This is Nomis, our amber-seeker,' said Danya. 'He is the best in his guild.'

'With a nose like that he must smell the stuff,' whispered Ognam to the others.

'There is none there,' declared the old man, nodding to the desolate coast. 'Sail west to the Thule islands if you want amber. The current casts it ashore in abundance but no ships go there.'

'Why is that?' asked Gambal.

'Kraken,' said the old man. The word had a vaguely familiar ring to it, a word used by Mesire Florizan in the Domain of Olam.

The shipmaster began to introduce them but Nomis returned a perfunctory nod and scuttled back into his cabin, complaining about the cold.

'Heed not his manners,' laughed Danya. 'He is an irritable old body but thanks to him I have amber enough to ensure that I never have to sail these Mother-cursed seas again, provided the Regent's tax-gatherers do not steal it all. And now, Lord Alwald, tell me what course you want me to set. I came to an agreement with The Mage and will fulfil it by taking you where you will.'

Alwald produced the box in which the Lodestone was mounted and explained that the steersman merely had to follow the direction it indicated.

'More gramarye,' said Danya watching its slight

179

movement with fascination. 'We must divide into watches so that there are always two of you on deck, and Gled and I will take turns at the tiller. Master Nomis is too old and, like all amber-seekers, too proud to work the ship.'

Because Gambal had little regard for Ognam, it was tacitly agreed that the jongleur would share the nightwatch with Krispin. Then Ognam left them in the bows with the excuse that he wanted to rest. Out of the corner of his eye Krispin saw him disappear below deck instead of to his cabin, but a moment later his attention returned to the shipmaster who was explaining the workings of a windlass.

For the first time that Krispin could remember, the sky above the Cold Sea was clear, allowing the moon to flood the world with his cold radiance. To the toymaker, perched on the cramped lookout platform just below the masthead, the sea ahead appeared like a sheet of beaten pewter. Around him rigging creaked as the *Amber Star* raced before the cold north wind, called the Moon Wind by the shipmaster because of the sailors' belief that it actually blew from the moon. Below, a large lantern spread a circle of light over the poop deck where Danya leaned against the tiller to keep the vessel on her headlong course. Ognam was in the galley warming broth for their midnight meal.

Once he had become accustomed to the swaying of the mast, Krispin enjoyed his solitary perch. Not only was the speed of the ship exhilarating but he felt a great sense of release now that The Mage's tower was below the horizon. Like the others, he had been oppressed by its arcanal atmosphere, but now as he swung between sea and sky his spirits soared. Surely this was the last stage of the quest. He had no reason to doubt that the Lodestone would lead them to the resting place of Princess Livia and then he would be free to return to the High Wald where he would find Jennet safe in the Peak Tower and – the Mother willing! – restored to her right mind.

Again he recalled his experience of going through the magic casement and watching the child that he had been wandering in the forest with little Jennet. If only he could elicit some hint of the truth from the words they had said to each other but they remained merely the words of children trying to hold back their fear of the unknown.

By the time the quest was concluded, the Lady Eloira would have doubtless kept her side of their agreement to discover who they really were, and if he and Jennet were able to marry he would find a peaceful place remote from the evil of the world, build a cottage and return to his craft. He imagined Jennet watching him carving at his bench in her dear familiar dress of blue ninon. Then a treacherous thought intruded . . .

Margan!

Alwald, in talking of his passage through the magic casement, had merely said that he had seen her tending Demara and that she looked as pretty as ever. Unsought memory returned, sharpened by a qualm of guilt, of the sweetness of their night together before he left the Vale of Mabalon. There was a stirring in his loins at the thought of her caresses . . .

There was something far ahead on the shining surface of the sea. Krispin wiped his wind-watered eyes and peered more intently. It was not a ship. Dreading corsairs, Danya had warned him to watch for sails but this was more like a white column rising above the water.

He shouted to the shipmaster who ordered Ognam to hold the tiller while he climbed the rigging to Krispin's perch.

'Kraken!' he said and added an exclamation that was both an oath and a prayer. 'Do you know what a kraken is, lad?'

'Some sort of sea creature.'

'*The* sea creature, lad. Dragons, basilisks, simurgs are nothing to the kraken. That is only its neck you can see, think on that! Probably it has a mate hereabouts. Keep watch.'

He slid down a rope to the deck and seizing the tiller changed the course of the *Amber Star* while Ognam ran to waken the others. As the vessel heeled over, Krispin kept his eyes on the kraken. It seemed so far away that he could not share the shipmaster's alarm. The strong wind would surely bear them away from the creature. Then across the face of the waters came a mournful lowing sound, the cry of the kraken, which to the alarmed crew carried the very essence of doom.

'Not many a mariner has heard that sound and lived to tell of it,' muttered Gled coming into the lantern light.

'What do we do?' asked Ognam anxiously.

'Run for it,' retorted the shipmaster. 'Get ready to trim the sail. Keep your eyes sharp, Master Krispin.'

The kraken moved at tremendous speed towards the *Amber Star*. Waves parted from its neck like the bow wave of a ship, and Krispin soon made out its triangular head. He remembered the terrible waterhorse he had done battle with in the subterranean river beneath the Domain of Olam, but at least that had been the size of a horse. The neck of this monster rose to the height of a ship's mast and he dared not speculate on the size of the body beneath the surface.

All aboard carried arms against the appearance of corsairs and as Krispin reached for the comforting grip of Woundflame he felt a familiar tingle run up his arm.

Again came the long-drawn wailing. It was answered by a blast of sound so loud and close that Krispin almost fell from his precarious platform. Turning, he saw the head of the kraken's mate level with his own.

It was structured from the stuff of nightmares. It was a nightmare made flesh.

Rearing out of a foaming maelstrom, the towering neck was covered with corrugated skin as white and dead as that of drowned sailors; filaments of seaweed clung to it, as did crab-like creatures ever eager for scraps from the creature's victims. The huge head was infinitely more repulsive. Beneath wide bony ridges, a pair of immense globular eyes appeared to Krispin's

183

fearful gaze like two moons. below these were a series of nostrils from which wisps of vapour flowed down to gigantic saurian jaws. As these opened, Krispin saw they were lined with rows of fangs, each longer than a sword blade, and capable of rending the side of the stoutest ship.

From the kraken's tunnel throat came a gust of breath hot and foul; Krispin choked on the fetor of dead whale flesh rotting in the monstrous bowels. But worse, far worse, was the tongue. It slithered like a thick slime-glistening serpent across the ivory palisades of the creature's jaws and wavered towards Krispin. There was a curious delicacy about the motion as though the kraken wanted to caress its prey before devouring it.

On deck all except Ognam looked up aghast at the terrifying head looming over the masthead; the jongleur vanished down the hatchway.

The kraken had no difficulty in keeping alongside the *Amber Star*. The forked tips of its tongue came closer and closer to Krispin's face as he clung to a stay, paralysed by fear. It was a burning sensation in his palm which brought him back to life – his hand still clenched Woundflame's grip. He wrenched the sword from its scabbard. Though usually dull, the blade now flashed as it must have done when it first came from the forge of Wayland the Swordsmith, generations ago.

Balancing himself on the platform, Krispin swung the blade in a glittering curve. A jet of dark ichor splashed about him and rained on the deck, and the kraken dived beneath the surface with a bubbling lament.

TWO

The Watchman

Seen against the dark green of the forest, the white walls of River Garde shone in the early summer sun. Its appearance had changed little from the days when its master had been the Hereditary Lord of the River March, Grimwald VII, though a traveller returning to the Wald from a long journey would be struck by the fact that the traditional pennants which used to flutter above the ramparts were replaced with wolf skulls mounted on spears. And instead of armoured sentinels at attention in the crenels, there were lounging nomads armed with long-hafted axes worn across their shoulders.

Most of all, the traveller would have been surprised by the makeshift bridge which spanned the sombre water of the aptly-named River of Night. This slow-moving river with its treacherous undercurrents was the natural frontier between the Outlands – the endless plains whose long grasses rippled like waves under the everlasting wind – and the Wald with its wooded hills climbing gradually to distant snow-crowned mountains. The fragile bridge was the only link between the two worlds and over it pressed a stream of leather-canopied wagons and squat plainsmen leading their horses.

Alas for the Wald, no travellers returned to River Garde.

Dressed in wolfskins and with the mask of a huge wolf worn as a headdress, the Wolf King sat enthroned in what had once been the castle's audience hall. About him were his captains who preferred to sit cross-legged on mats of auroch leather rather than use the carved chairs which lined the hall; before him stood a shackled Waldman in filthy clothing, half his face covered with congealed blood which, at a distance, gave the appearance of a carnival mask.

'My wolflings tells me . . . you fought boldly,' said the King, his tongue clumsy with the speech of Ythan. 'That is good . . . we honour foes of spirit.'

'Honour!' muttered the forester through his bloodied mouth. 'What do beasts know of honour?'

The Wolf King smiled a terrible smile, reminding the captive of the rumour that he was a shape-changer.

'I want to know . . . who in the forest dares attack us?' he said. 'Who is the girl . . . you follow? Why you follow a girl?'

'She is the Wish Maiden,' replied the forester throwing back his head with desperate pride. 'She may be a forest girl but there is that within her which will free the Wald from your creatures. She is the messenger of the woodland spirit and she gives new courage to those who feared all was lost. Each day more fugitives join us.'

'She your shaman?' demanded the Wolf King. 'You tell . . . where we find her. You show path to her . . . you go free.'

'I would die before I would betray her,' retorted the prisoner. 'And it is she has given me the heart to say that.'

The Wolf King looked at the swaying man thoughtfully.

'Very brave but you no die . . . you will do what I want . . . soon. Soon.' He nodded to the nomads who stood behind the captive. 'The pit.'

The shouts of the forester became fainter and fainter as he was taken to the castle's cellars. Then there was a stir of interest as the Wolf King's herald ushered in a man who stood a head taller than the nomads and whose bearing was one of easy confidence.

'Greetings, Watchman Affleck,' said the Wolf King and his company laughed appreciatively for this was the watchman, a spy for the Regent, who had opened the gates of River Garde to them.

'Greetings, Wolf Lord,' replied Affleck. 'I have returned from the pass between the White Virgins where I have learned much from a courier who brought a dispatch to the Companions of the Rose who keep vigil there.'

'Come . . . sit beside me . . . do you talk as Lord Regent's man?'

'I talk as my own man,' replied Affleck. 'Much has changed since the Regent sent men to teach you how to cross the River of Night and take the domain of his secret enemy Grimwald. They say that in Danaak the Regent has a distemper that leads to fits of madness. There are times when he can no longer make decisions.'

'I pray Wolf-in-the-Sky heal him,' said the Wolf King.

'You will be better served by praying the opposite. The other news is that the Regent lost a great army to the Red Death when it besieged the heretics of Thaan. Such is the fear of the plague in the city that the survivors were slain by arrow fire and avalanche in a gorge. The Commander of the Host is now starving to death in sight of the citizens.

'The time is right to cross the mountains and invade Ythan. You have been building up your men for weeks and could sweep down on the plains like a wolf on the fold.'

The Wolf King nodded his appreciation of the remark. 'You tell me why,' he said.

'Because you want conquest,' said Affleck. 'You came to the Wald for plunder but that is not enough. Your nomads are becoming restless. They are men of the Outlands, not the forest. They want to go forward or go back. And you, my lord – are you content with one castle and victory over charcoal burners and toymakers when you could lead your horde to the gates of Danaak itself? You could trust me to guide you as you trusted me to open the gates.'

'Then you Regent's man . . . now you would betray Regent?'

'Betrayal is my trade,' said Affleck with a grim

smile. 'It is a trade my masters taught me well in Danaak.'

'Some day . . . you betray me?'

'Not yet,' said Affleck with a laugh. 'Not if I get what I want.'

'What you want?'

'This.' The spy waved his arm in a circular motion. 'This castle. In return for my services I would be master of River Garde.'

'You want . . . much, Watchman.'

'It is nothing to what you will gain, Wolf Lord. The pass is open and Ythan is weak. Your wagons will groan taking spoils back to the Outlands, your men will feast amid the enemy dead. Silver, wine and Ythan maids will be theirs. And you will earn fame that will be told a score of generations from now and the Wolf-in-the-Sky will be worshipped in Ythan while the shrines of the Mother burn.'

'Ah, that would be a holy thing,' murmured the nomad. 'But,' he continued after a long pause, 'we know nothing of the land beyond the Wald.'

'Follow me,' said Affleck, 'and you will set your wolf skulls upon the pinnacles of the Citadel.'

'So be it, Watchman.'

Both Mordan and Jennet were exhausted.

All through the long day they had wandered in the clammy vapour protecting the Peak Tower until both were so tired they sank on soft leaf mould with their backs against mossy tree trunks. From his scrip the Witchfinder took a piece of travellers' bread which, along with the knife he

189

had used on the old man, he had taken from the castle kitchen. He broke it and handed a piece to the young woman who childishly cradled her doll in her arm.

'Are you sure you can find the way to Kris?' she asked.

He made some reply but before he had finished, her head had fallen forward in sleep, her bread untasted in her hand.

Mordan still suffered from the effects of his wounds and added to this he felt an alien among the mist-shrouded trees. Had it not been for the austere training he had undergone at his seminary he would have given way to fear, especially when he saw distant lights moving like fire-flies through the mist. Perhaps they were nothing more than will-o'-the-wisps, or perhaps they were the lanterns of the Fey who, Mordan had learned while at the castle, were the survivors of an ancient and magical race dwelling in the deepest parts of the forest.

He remembered that the Lady Eloira had told him that it was one of the Fey who had brought him to the Peak Tower so he need have no fear of them . . . unless they had learned of Jennet's abduction. He consoled himself with the thought that while the mist that had been laid by sorcery made it impossible for enemies to find their way to the Peak Tower, it did not mean that one could not find a way out of it. Once the sun came up he would see enough to find a trail and follow it until they were clear. He would make for the pass between the White Virgins which were guarded by soldiers under the command of a couple of Companions of the Rose.

When Mordan awoke he saw patches of blue sky through the milky vapour and knew that they must be close to the periphery of the protecting cloud.

He roused Jennet who kissed her doll good morning and then ate the crust that was still in her hand.

'Hurry,' said Mordan. 'We still have a long way to go.'

She nodded, climbed to her feet and brushed brittle leaves from her cloak. Mordan took her by the hand, thankful for her acquiescence. In his scrip he carried a length of cord to bind her if necessary but so far she had behaved like a child obedient to an adult who obviously knew best, and this was how he found himself regarding her, full grown and beautiful though she was. Her mental condition could not have suited his plans better. With her incredible likeness to the portraits of Princess Livia, the Regent, if he so wished, would be able to present her as the daughter of King Johan XXXIII, resurrected from her entrancement but simple-minded – mad even! – and that would end The Enchantment myth and the Pilgrims' questing for ever. On the other hand he could marry her as Livia and change from Regent to King by starting a new royal line. Whatever the Regent decided, there could be no doubt that the loyal Witchfinder who had made it possible would be justly rewarded, with promotion to the upper hierarchy of his guild at least.

'Tell me a story,' Jennet said as they set off between boles of trees that rose about them like the pillars of a shrine. 'Tell me about the woodcutter's daughter and the wicked wolf.'

'Not now, my dear. We must keep very quiet.'

'Why?'

'Because . . . because there is a wicked wolf about.'

'Just like the story?'

'Hush. We do not want him to hear us.'

Jennet giggled.

Soon they walked out of the mist bank and began to follow a deer trail which climbed up steeply wooded slopes in the direction of the White Virgins. Every few minutes Mordan would halt and strain his ears for a sound that might warn them of enemies but all he heard was the distant note of a bellbird or chuckle of a mountain beck.

Being a girl of the High Wald, Jennet was more used to wandering in steep terrain than the young man and at times he had to summon all his self-discipline to keep going while she ran ahead to pick wildflowers. In mid-afternoon they left the trees behind them and crossed slopes of coarse mountain grass that followed the contours of the mountain range just below its snowline. To the south-east lay the sea of cloud that hid the Peak Tower, but by looking over the forest that carpeted the slopes and valleys to the west they could see a sinuous gleam marking the River of Night. The wind that blew endlessly from the

Outlands beyond plucked at their hair and made their eyes water. High above, an eagle drifted on its flow.

'We will not find Kris up here,' said Jennet suddenly. 'Why have you brought me to this place?'

'We have to go through the pass,' said Mordan reassuringly. He pointed to the twin summits of the White Virgins glittering magnificently against the blue-washed sky. 'He lives on the other side.'

'Then let us hurry.'

The sun was low on her path to the western horizon when they came to the lip of a scarp overlooking the entrance of the defile which wound between the peaks. Mordan was thankful to see Ythan's plain yellow gonfalon fluttering above the small camp set up before it. A number of troops lounged in the shelter of black rocks, obviously bored with guard duty in this windswept frontier post. The Witchfinder was further reassured to see a pavilion on which was emblazoned the black rose insignia of the Regent's elite guards. Once he had explained the importance and urgency of his mission to them, they would ensure that he and his precious captive were escorted to Danaak with all possible speed.

He was about to lead Jennet down the incline when some instinct – perhaps an alien sound mingled with the rush of the wind – made him glance down the track snaking away from the pass to the High Wald where it continued for a dozen leagues through forest and valley to River Garde. Through a gap in a belt of pines came a group of horsemen led by a man dressed in wolf fur. In his left hand he held a short pole sceptre-like on which was mounted a wolf skull painted crimson. Beside him rode Affleck the Regent's spy; behind them emerged a seemingly endless cavalcade of nomads.

Instinctively Mordan pulled Jennet down out of sight. Wearing clothing supplied to him in the Peak Tower, he knew he was likely to be taken for an enemy by the wolfmen and transfixed by an arrow before he had the opportunity to prove his identity. A few moments later the soldiers below caught sight of the leading horsemen and jumped to attention. A trumpet sounded and more troops ran from the tents, hastily buttoning their uniforms. Out of the pavilion appeared two Companions of the Rose. One advanced in front of the guards and raised his arm in salute.

'Welcome, Wolf Lord, and you, Master Affleck,' he said. 'Would that you had warned us of your visit so we could have had refreshment prepared. But tell us why we are honoured with this unexpected visit, and why you have so many riders.'

'We go . . . through pass,' said the Wolf King.

'What do you mean?'

'He means,' said Affleck with a grim smile, 'that he is going to lead his army through the pass.'

'But that is forbidden by the Lord Regent. The agreement was for the Wolf Horde to hold the Wald but come no further.'

'We go . . . through pass.'

'Never. Stand to, men.'

The Wolf King turned to the riders who had reined up behind him.

'Kill,' he said.

As the nomads unslung the long-hafted axes worn across their backs a heart-chilling howl burst from their throats.

'Treachery!' shouted the Companion. 'Take word, Karik.'

The other Companion was already climbing into the saddle of a horse tethered by the pavilion.

Prone on the edge of the scarp, Mordan saw the nomads spur their horses forward with their axes held high while the Wolf King watched impassively. The troops raised spears and halberds to meet the onslaught but it was so quick they did not have time to lock their shields into the shieldwall which would have blocked the pass.

The baying wolfmen rode them down. Axes fell and rose bloody. A horse impaled on a spear screamed. Several nomads fell from their saddles but the terrible axes continued to sweep down on the footmen.

Behind the mêlée, Affleck saw that the Companion named Karik was urging his frightened mount into the pass. He shouted to the Wolf King who waved more riders forward.

'He must not get through,' he commanded in his own tongue.

Seeing the slaughter about him, the other Companion withdrew into the narrow opening of the defile where he stood, sword raised, to give Karik a chance to get clear. Here it was only wide enough for one rider at a time to reach him. The first to swing at him with an axe he ran through the body and there was confusion as the nomad's horse reared in terror and its dead master toppled over its rump.

Another wolfman spurred forward but his horse stumbled over the prone body and he pitched forward onto the Companion's ready sword.

The Wolf King shouted commands. The riders backed away; several dismounted and ran forward on foot to engage the lone defender of the pass. An axe blow sent him reeling backwards but he recovered his balance and continued to use his sword to bitter effect. When two more nomads were sprawled before him, the rest withdrew.

'Your treachery will be your bane, Affleck,' he panted as he leaned on his sword.

'Be that as it may,' Affleck shouted back, 'it will be your death unless you surrender.'

'Until I die I hold the pass.'

In the lurid rays of the westering sun the Companion was a terrifying figure as he stood over the tangled bodies of his victims, one of whom was alive and clawing at a gaping belly wound. The Companion's surcoat glistened redly and a rivulet of blood trickled down his left arm, but with his right he lifted his sword high in defiance. The wolfmen stood awed and silent, each waiting for another to lead the next attack.

'Guard this, Watchman,' cried the Wolf King. He tossed his skull sceptre to Affleck and swung down from his saddle. Then, with a harsh ululation, he raced towards the entrance to the pass.

From his vantage point Mordan could hardly

believe his eyes. As he ran the Wolf King appeared to crouch lower and lower until he gave the illusion of bounding on all fours, then he launched himself in a flying leap at the Companion.

The man swung his sword in a gesture of defence but there was something in the appearance of the Wolf King that unsteadied him. The blow was wild. The Wolf King bore him backwards to the ground. For a moment the two writhed almost like lovers, arms locked, heads together. Then the Companion gave a bubbling cry and his assailant slowly climbed to his feet, and it seemed to the watching Witchfinder that he was not seeing the face of a man but the bloodied muzzle of a wolf.

THREE

The Kraken

Krispin climbed down to the deck of the *Amber Star* with Woundflame in his hand. He felt as though he had been stung by firewort where the ichor from the kraken's severed tongue had spattered his flesh. On the poop deck the steersman threw all his weight onto the tiller while Shipmaster Danya shouted to his novice crew to trim the sail for the new course.

'You did mighty well with your sword, Master Krispin, but that sea dragon will surface soon enough,' he cried. 'Our only hope is to run with the wind.'

As Krispin hauled on the unfamiliar ropes he looked astern to where the first kraken was throwing up sheets of spray with the speed of its pursuit.

'Where is that potton turd of a jongleur?' panted Gambal when the struggle to set the sail was completed. 'Trust him to vanish when there is work to be done. Why in the name of the demon Omad did I not leave him to the dungeon rats!'

At that moment Ognam appeared out of the hatchway.

'You cursed coward!' hissed Gambal moving towards him threateningly. 'Your only thought was to save your own pox'd skin when the kraken appeared.'

'I had to go below,' retorted Ognam.

Gambal muttered a fitting obscenity.

'Besides, what could I do against a kraken?'

'You could have told it one of your jokes,' said Krispin to ease the tension between the two men.

'That would not have been fair even to a kraken,' added Alwald.

Their attempts at humour had no effect on Gambal. He bunched his fist and was about to deliver Ognam a blow when Danya uttered a yell of warning. A couple of hundred paces from the steerboard side of the vessel they beheld the head of the second monster emerge into the brilliant moonlight from a welter of foam. Up and up reared the great neck, the head turned towards them with its globe-like eyes aglow. The moment it saw the *Amber Star* it uttered the heart-sinking cry of its kind, which was answered by its mate half a league away.

With threads of ichor streaming from its mouth, the kraken turned its enormous and faintly phosphorescent body towards the ship.

'If we can keep ahead until morning light there might be a chance for us,' Danya muttered. 'Meanwhile there is something else I can try.'

He disappeared into the deckhouse and reappeared carrying a long brassbound case. This he opened in the light of the ship's lanthorn and brought out a crossbow and several bolts, each individually wrapped in oiled spider silk.

'Surely a bolt would be no more than a thornprick to that beast,' said Krispin.

'If it were an ordinary bolt, that would be so,' answered Danya unwrapping one with extreme care. Its point was protected with a sheath of soft leather which he did not remove. 'But this is no ordinary missile.'

'Not more gramarye!'

The shipmaster shook his head and glanced up anxiously at a ragged cloud racing towards the moon.

'Only the highest magic would prevail against the kraken,' he said as he fitted the bolt onto the crossbow. 'Like the cockatrice, it has some inward power that protects it from ordinary sorcery. But these bolts are tipped with the most noxious of all poisons. It is distilled from Upas sap. Ships that come to the Cold Sea for fur and amber carry them for protection against sea dragons.'

With the crossbow loaded, he took up position in the bows of the ship, signalling Gled to steer the *Amber Star* in a way that would allow the leading kraken to swim within range. Closer and closer it came with its huge mouth agape. Danya squinted along his weapon, praying to the Serene Mother of the Sea that he might be successful in his aim and send his bolt between the creature's swordlike teeth into its gullet.

He was about to fire when the cloud crossed the face of the moon and darkness fell over the Cold Sea.

Wary of the sheathed tip of the bolt, Danya lowered the crossbow. The light from the lanthorn failed to reach the kraken though they could hear the surge of its body close at hand.

'Mayhap I can help,' Krispin called.

In his tiny cabin in the forecastle he unbuckled his pack and extracted the leather tube containing the light wand he had taken from the armoured hand of the eidolon in the City Without a Name.

Those who had not seen it before were amazed at the intensity of the cold light that radiated from the tip of the black rod when Krispin withdrew it. Not only was the vessel brilliantly illuminated by the wand, but a great circle of the sea was too. The light shone on the pallid neck of the kraken and reflected in its bulging eyes.

Danya released the crossbow's trigger but the rolling of the *Amber Star* marred his aim and the bolt whistled harmlessly above the kraken's bone-crested skull. As though aware of the new danger, the creature slowed and continued the chase from a safer distance.

'Old mariners tell that krakens have more understanding than any other creature in the sea,' said Danya as he tensioned the bow again. 'It would be folly to waste bolts on it now but I shall keep the weapon ready for when it comes within range. Do not handle it. A touch of the toxin on the point is enough to summon the Dark Maid.'

'At least we have a weapon against them,' said Alwald.

'But only effective if the bolt strikes the eye or enters the mouth. The skin of the neck is too tough for bolts and arrows to penetrate.' Danya turned to Krispin. 'But your sword did it enough injury to save us. It must be a special blade for it flashed like lightning.'

'I was lucky that I caught its tongue,' said Krispin quietly. He avoided looking at Alwald for he sensed that the question of Woundflame's ownership still rankled with the young noble who had given it to him without realising the power latent in its tarnished metal.

Meanwhile the *Amber Star* plunged before the wind that sang shrill in the rigging and blew spindrift from the crests of the waves rolling eastwards. Astern, the two krakens continued their inexorable pursuit without any lessening of speed. From time to time their forlorn cries reached the ears of the crew, filling each with a sense of dread which he sought to conceal from the others. Several times Ognam slunk below deck under the scornful gaze of Gambal.

Dawn began as a silver edging along the horizon. To the travellers watching for it over the twin figureheads of the *Amber Star*, the pale streak of light was a reassuring sign.

'You said that we might have a chance if we saw daylight,' said Gambal to the weary shipmaster who had just relinquished the tiller to Gled. 'Is that so, or was it to give us heart when we needed it?'

'There is a chance after sunrise, but I shall say no more because hope can be a bitter draught if it turns out to be false.'

The light increased, dimming the wand in

contrast so that Krispin stowed it away once more. It was now easy to see the kraken following just out of range of boltshot.

'When I hunted in the Wald I never gave a thought to the quarry,' said Alwald. 'This morning I know what it feels like to be a deer with the hounds in cry.'

The sun climbed over the edge of the world and her wan beams gave both cloud and wavecrest the sickly pallor which the travellers had seen so often through the lancet windows of The Mage's tower. With the sunrise came a shift in the wind. Danya glanced anxiously at the masthead vane and led his ill-assorted crew in trimming the sail. They were drenched when a sheet of spray exploded over bows as the *Amber Star* changed course. Behind, the kraken swerved to follow their wake.

'I fear me the wind may not hold,' said Danya quietly to Nomis.

The old amber-seeker sniffed the air. 'And I fear me you are right,' he answered testily.

Within minutes the others were aware of the change. The wind no longer blew steadily and there were moments when the sail half crumpled before filling again. Danya gave an order for the spare set of sweeps to be made ready and though he was obeyed without question all knew of the impossibility of keeping ahead of the krakens by rowing.

Suddenly Gambal called out from the bows that there was an island ahead. The others ran to him and followed his outstretched arm with their eyes to a black pyramid shape silhouetted against the cold glare of the sun.

'We have come far into the sea so it could be one of the Thule islands,' said Nomis. 'What a chance to hunt for amber! Head for it, Shipmaster.'

Danya actually laughed. 'I shall steer for the island for refuge rather than amber. Do not forget, old man, there are two astern who are hunting us.'

Nomis muttered against fate which brought him so close to an unimaginable store of the precious resin but allowed him little likelihood of his getting his fingers on it.

'Can krakens walk on land?' Ognam asked.

'That is something we will find out soon enough – if the wind holds,' replied Danya.

But the wind did not hold. The *Amber Star* was close enough to the island for the travellers to make out details of its rock-strewn shore and steep cliffs when the sail flapped limply against the mast and the soughing in the rigging died away. The vessel lost speed and soon merely drifted with the ocean swell.

Without a word Danya took up his crossbow. Alwald and Krispin unsheathed their swords and the others looked around for what weapons they could find, which turned out to be axes and a harpoon. Yet again Ognam went below, muttering that he would be back in a moment.

The krakens approached rapidly, parting to right and left so that they would be able to attack both sides of the vessel simultaneously. The noise of their calls to each other filled the air with heavy thunder.

As soon as the first came within range, Danya fired the crossbow but the pitching of the *Amber Star* made accurate aiming impossible and the poison bolt whistled harmlessly past it. Quickly he reloaded and fired again but with no better result. A moment later the creature was rearing above them.

Krispin gripped Woundflame with both hands and watched as the kraken's head swooped towards the deck. Huge splinters of wood flew in all directions as its teeth tore at the bulwark; timbers snapped like twigs and decking was wrenched away. Aiming for the kraken's eyes the crew swung their weapons at the horrendous head, but only Woundflame made any impact by cutting a groove across the monster's leathery snout.

The creature reared away with broken planks and cordage falling from its jaws. Danya raised his crossbow but before he could fire, the *Amber Star* rocked as the other kraken attacked from the opposite side. The yardarm snapped as its head swung down, its jaws closing on the body of the helmsman. The head soared again and those on the deck saw Gled's hooks waving frantically as he sought to free himself. Blood rained on the planking and it seemed his scream would never end. The kraken drew away to savour the squirming morsel.

Beseeching the Mother for a steady hand, Danya raised the crossbow again and this time his aim was true. The bolt struck Gled and mercifully his scream ended the same instant.

Those below turned away in horror as the jaws of the kraken began to work and the bones of the dead steersman cracked in its mouth.

The other kraken, jealous that her mate had won the first tidbit, circled to gather speed and raced towards the *Amber Star*, her bulk rising from the seething water as though to destroy it by sheer weight. The vessel reeled under the impact. Krispin found himself flung to the tilting deck. There were shouts of dismay and oaths of anger from the others who were toppled like peg pins in a children's ball game. A spar crashed and a tangle of ropes netted Krispin as he tried to pull himself to his feet. And again the noisome breath of the creature sickened him. Looking up through the rope tangle he saw it looming above him, the scaled body half out of the water, its forelimbs resting on the stern.

Serene Mother, into your hands . . .

The prayer, remembered from childhood, formed in the minds of all as the ship tilted until seawater cascaded through the gap in the bulwark. To add to the horror, the second kraken returned with bloodied jaws to add its strength to capsizing the ship.

So ends the quest! thought Alwald bitterly. It was not the first time that such an idea had come into his head on the long journey from the Wald, but this time it seemed that fate would not be cheated.

Gambal cursed, and then laughed, as he saw Ognam crawling up the wildly sloping deck to the hatchway.

The mental orisons continued. *Serene Mother, into your hands . . .*

A deep roaring filled the air.

The *Amber Star* shuddered as the kraken's weight slid from her stern and she rolled to right herself.

The roaring increased, lion-like and terrible.

Krispin used Woundflame to free himself from the entanglement and staggered to his feet. The others were climbing to vantage points and cheering like boys at a kick-bladder game. And then Krispin saw why.

The krakens had turned from the *Amber Star* and were fleeing westward – yes, fleeing! – leaving long sparkling wakes behind them.

Over the mast of the ship hurtled six flying figures, golden wings outstretched, beaked mouths wide to emit their deep hunting roar.

'Griffins!' shouted Krispin in delight.

'Aye, lad,' cried Danya. 'It was my hope that some would sight the krakens after sun up. Griffins fly to the Cold Sea in the summer season to hunt them.'

'So Mesire Florizan told us,' said Alwald. 'How fast they go, how magnificent. I swear it is they who bore us to The Mage's tower.'

'I recognise the one that carried me,' cried Gambal. 'Look, the attack begins.'

One after another the griffins left their goose-like formation and dived with their viciously-clawed feet outstretched.

'They go for the krakens' eyes,' Danya said, his voice high with excitement.

207

Bellows of pain rolled across the water.

Now the griffins circled the two creatures in bewildering streaks of gold. The eyeless krakens dived but they could only stay submerged for a short period and as soon as they surfaced again the circling griffins plummeted upon them. Blindly the sea monsters clashed their jaws and turned their bodies this way and that, but their panicked frenzy had no effect on the griffins. Again and again they flew at the bleeding heads, their beaks and claws merciless.

One of the tall necks began to bend. For a moment it was almost graceful like the drooping of a long-stemmed flower, then there was a tremendous splash as the head struck the surface. The vast body wallowed in the crimson swell, the feeble movement of its limbs showing that it still held life.

The second kraken threw back its head and from the depths of its being a cry of wild lamentation soared to the grey sky, then it too collapsed and drifted beside its mate.

Roaring in triumph, the griffins spiralled above their prey and then flew straight towards the *Amber Star*.

Fearing that they were about to attack the ship, Danya seized his crossbow but Alwald tore the bolt from it.

'No need!' he shouted.

A moment later the griffins slowed and began to circle the *Amber Star* with slow wingbeats and a noise like the purring of a thousand cats. The travellers waved and shouted their gratitude and the griffins inclined their heads as though in acknowledgement, then flew back to land on the vast carcasses to begin their feast.

'It is as though they knew you,' said Danya wonderingly.

The others said nothing. Their bodies were drained of energy and they peered about the damaged ship like drunken men, but behind their blank expressions they were savouring the fact that they were still drawing the salt air into their lungs.

'Alas, that I killed my friend,' muttered Danya at last.

'It was a great act of friendship,' said Nomis with unexpected gentleness.

'There was nothing else I could do and yet I feel have done him murder.'

The others turned away as tears began to course down the shipmaster's wind-tanned cheeks.

Ognam slowly got to his feet and began to walk across the littered deck in the direction of the hatchway but before he was halfway there, the slender figure of a girl emerged wrapped in a spider-silk cloak patterned in squares of silver and black. Her face was without colour apart from her eyes and lips, and her hair was as black as the breast of a raven.

Slowly she looked about her.

'Who . . .?' began Gambal.

Ognam drew himself up to his full height, the bells of his motley giving an incongruous tinkle.

'This is Tana,' he announced.

'The beautiful prisoner . . .?' said Krispin.

'Quite. She had the misfortune to be held captive by The Mage. I had the honour to help her escape—'

'And smuggle her aboard my craft,' said Danya.

Ognam nodded. 'I did it while you went to collect supplies from the kitchens,' he said simply. 'I could not leave her to spend the rest of her life alone beneath the tower.'

Gambal made the Circle of the Mother. 'Accursed fool!' he shouted. 'Did you not consider the vengeance The Mage will wreak upon us for such a soft-headed deed!'

FOUR

Earthquake
Weather

The village stood beside the road which meandered across the plain for many leagues towards the ranges that made the horizon ragged. In the olden days of Ythan it had been a busy highway to the Wald which lay beyond the mountains but now, apart from a few merchants who journeyed once a year to buy toys from the craftsmen of Toyheim, the road was deserted. Grass waved between its cracked pavings, drifts of soil hid it in places and weeks might pass without a traveller being seen.

The village, too, had seen better days. Paint on cottage doors peeled like diseased skin, cracked walls begged for plaster, and fences sagged. The only brightness was the brightness of the sky reflected in pools of stagnant water in a square whose cobbles, once set in fine geometric patterns, sank neglected into the sour earth. Like the road, the village had once been a symbol of prosperity, but those days had become a folktale. Now the dispirited inhabitants eked a meagre living from the surrounding fields.

Since there was no longer a priest to take services in the shrine, there was little to mark one week from another. Day followed identical day with the menfolk grumbling over apple ale in the evenings while their exhausted womenfolk cooked their miserable suppers. But early this summer morning the monotonous tenor of their lives was shattered when a cavalcade of drongs trotted into the square and soldiers of the Tempest Legion swung down from their high saddles to take up positions throughout the village with bored efficiency. Only two men remained mounted, the veteran captain of the troop and a cowled figure whose black robe had the symbol of the Mother embroidered over the heart in silver thread: the abhorred badge of the Witchfinders.

The blast of a herald's trumpet summoned the womenfolk and children from the cottages and the men from the fields. They gathered uneasily in the square, the adults scowling to hide their apprehension, the youths conscious of the contrast between the strangers' well-cut uniforms and their own patched smocks, the children fascinated by the drongs picketed in an obedient line.

From long experience, the captain knew the effect of silence, and silent he remained until feet shuffled nervously and hands were drawn across dry lips. Finally he spoke in an official tone from which all humanity had been leached.

'It has been reported by the tax-gatherer of this district that this village has defaulted in the payment of its dues by the sum of fifty crowns. As a representative of the Lord Regent I am authorised to collect that amount and a similar sum as a penalty for the wanton withholding of the aforesaid fifty crowns.'

Whispers filled the square. *A hundred crowns . . . a hundred crowns!*

A middle-aged man with an iron-grey beard stepped out in front of the captain. 'Your honour, there must be a mistake. We paid the taxer all the coin we could but we explained that such a great sum was impossible—'

'Who are you, fellow?' interjected the captain.

'If you please, your honour, I am Ketch. The good folk here made me their mayor . . .'

There was laughter from the soldiers stationed about the square at the idea of these miserable peasants presuming to have such an official.

'Well, *Mayor* Ketch, you had better find those missing crowns,' said the captain. 'I suggest your folk may have forgotten those they once put safe under thatch, and sewed in mattresses, and buried under doorsteps.'

'Your honour, I swear— '

'One moment, Captain.' it was the sepulchral voice of the Witchfinder. From beneath his black cowl his eyes had been raking the square and now he goaded his drong to the dilapidated shrine at the far end. Reaching out, he plucked a doll figure made of twisted straw from the lintel and returned holding it high above his head.

'Why was this abomination placed on the House of the Mother?' he demanded.

'Why, Master Witchfinder, it be no harm,' said Ketch. 'Crops were so poor last season — as I told the taxer, your honour — that some thought a harvest queen might bring luck to the next reaping.'

'Apostasy!' declared the Witchfinder. 'You know the penalty for that?'

'I do not rightly know what the word means, your honour.'

'You will learn. Captain, this village is fined fifty crowns.'

A cry of despair rose from the square.

'We have no money,' said Ketch steadfastly. ''Tis madness to ask for crowns from them who has hardly any copper or to punish us for apo . . . apos . . . for having put up a lucky charm like all country folk do.'

'If you have no coin then we must collect in kind.'

On cue the soldiers drew their weapons with a threatening clash.

The captain's gaze rested on a young woman. 'She might fetch twenty crowns in Danaak. And how many cattle do you have, Mayor Ketch?'

'Why not tap our blood and take it to your pox'd Regent — they say he drinks it!' someone shouted.

There was a sudden movement and a cobblestone hurtled close to the captain's head. Several members of the crowd bent to wrench similar missiles from the ground.

'This district needs an example of discipline and you will provide it,' the captain shouted above the

214

clamour of the villagers. He pointed to a cottage. 'Trooper, do your duty.'

The soldier nearest the cottage was ready with his tinder box and a torch of tarred rope. Almost before the villagers realised what was happening he fired the thatch. Wisps of smoke curled from under the eaves, then the dry straw bundles of the roof exploded into flame. Charred fragments floated like black snowflakes upon the villagers as they backed away from the sudden heat. There was a roar as a column of fire danced above a second cottage.

The flames and the weapons of the troopers were too daunting for the villagers. As they cowered away, the captain ordered some of his men to search the rest of the cottages for hidden coins and objects of value while others rounded up cattle.

'Then we shall see how many slaves are needed to make up the quota,' he said to the Witchfinder who observed the conflagration with pious satisfaction and then hurled the straw doll into the flames.

The far end of the square was now obscured by a curtain of smoke and through this appeared a phantom-like figure. As it emerged from the swirling cloud, the captain stiffened – on the man's bloodied surcoat was a black rose emblem.

He urged his drong forward and saluted the reeling stranger.

Ignoring the pillage going on about him, Karik, the Companion of the Rose, said, 'Captain, my horse died under me two leagues back. I need the fastest drong you have to take word to Danaak that by treachery the Wolf Horde now holds the Pass of the White Virgins. Barbarians are pouring through by the thousand. It will take an army to contain them.'

The captain did not allow the impact of these words to show on his face or in his speech. He said with professional calm, 'I shall give you an escort. Are you wounded badly?'

'Not as badly as those I left behind,' he replied grimly. 'You, Captain, fall back immediately to the first fortified town and stand siege there until reinforcements arrive.'

'As you command.' The captain turned to the herald. 'Sound the assembly – these wretches can count themselves lucky.'

'Until the werewolves come,' said Karik.

The plump merchant Umer intoned a monologue detailing his own astuteness as he rode at the head of the caravan on a specially upholstered drong saddle over which a beaded canopy protected him from the sun. Beside him in less comfort rode the captain of the caravan and the pilot. The two men had found early on that part of their employment consisted of listening to Umer recounting tales of his past successes and reminding them of their luck in working for a fellow as fine as he was.

The pilot looked ahead, hoping that some quirk of the landscape would give him an excuse to ride forward; the captain glanced over his shoulder at the column of panniered drongs hoping for an excuse to ride back. But the old trade route led arrow-straight across a plain of coarse grass and magenta sage and the caravan proceeded in perfect order with its hired guards flanking it. Both men sighed and reminded themselves that within a fortnight they would be signing off in Danaak's great caravanserai.

Umer guffawed at one of his self-congratulatory jokes. His laughter died and he frowned. 'You have nothing to say, Master Guide,' chided the merchant, meaning that the pilot had not joined in the laughter and such omissions would be remembered when it came to calculating the end-of-journey bonus.

'There is something in the air that gives me unease,' replied the pilot. 'It puts me in mind of earthquake weather.'

'What earthquake weather?' demanded Umer. 'Earthquakes never happen here.'

'That is true,' said the pilot, 'but they do in the Sabbah region where I was raised. And some time before the earth shook there was a strangeness that descended upon the land; everything became hushed, not a leaf stirred, no bird sang and a shadow fell across men's hearts. It was as though nature was holding her breath and we were on the brink of something unknown but stupendous. We called it earthquake weather.'

'And you feel this now?'

'I have the same feeling, Master Umer, as I did as a boy when there was earthquake weather – a feeling of forebodement.'

The merchant laughed and slapped his stout thigh. 'You are getting too old for this work, pilot,' he teased. 'Look about you. What is there to fear on this empty plain? Your fancy runs wild like those foolish fellows who swore they saw a winged man flying through the sky when they rode ahead to prepare camp.'

'It seems to me this plain is not quite empty,' said the captain and he pointed to the west where a grey line appeared along the horizon.

'It is not cloud, the sky is cloudless,' said the pilot. 'And the air is unusually still.'

The drongs continued their steady walk but all eyes turned to the west and the line which seemed to move towards them like a solitary wave rolling across a flat expanse of ocean. After a few minutes, a cloud of dust was visible drifting behind it.

The pilot halted his drong, lowered himself from the saddle and put his ear to the ground.

'Do you hear the rumble of your earthquake?' said the merchant.

'No, Master Umer, I hear the rumble of horses' hoofs.'

'It cannot be. It would take hundreds of horsemen to make up such a line.'

The pilot shrugged and climbed back into the saddle.

The captain turned and urged his mount along the column, shouting orders.

Within minutes it was obvious to the caravaneers that an army of horsemen was sweeping towards them. As it drew closer they saw that each rider wore a wolf helmet, and the terrible truth struck them. Men leading strings of pack drongs dropped the snaffle lines and goaded their mounts into action; the hired guards broke formation and fled while the merchant howled at them to protect his goods.

On their small steppe horses, the nomads surged round the caravan, shouting in amazement at the sight of the drongs which were unknown in the Outlands. There was a roar of laughter as an axe smashed open a cloth-covered cage carried by one of these strange animals and a fountain of rainbow-feathered birds – living curiosities from the Arkad Woodlands – soared to freedom.

The pillage was over in a matter of minutes and the caravaneers lay dead on the plain. The captain and the pilot died honourably, sword in hand, in defence of the merchant who had hired them. He was overtaken and disembowelled with the sweep of an axe.

Then the Wolf Horde spurred forward again.

Dawn appeared in streaks of carmine and saffron behind the peaks of the White Virgins. In a bed of fern, Jennet stirred and looked straight into the placid face of her doll. For a moment she smiled back at the porcelain features, then memories came flooding back. She was lying on the edge of an incline and looking down at fur-garbed men with animal skulls leering above the black hair that fringed their foreheads. They began to fight and there was blood and she knew that she had seen the men and the blood and the axes before.

And though Mordan pushed her out of sight, it did not stop her hearing the howls of the animal men and the shrieks of their victims. She had heard that before, too. And then they were running down the mountainside. Mordan pulled her by the hand, jerking her to her feet when she fell, and yet she never let go of Dolly's hand because they could not stop if she let her fall. When they finally reached the trees, both she and Mordan collapsed with their chests heaving.

At last Mordan sat up and drank from a flask. He passed it to Jennet and as she held it to her lips she recognised the taste of wine. Then it felt as though something inside her broke and she gave a cry and her body shook with sobbing that went on and on. The tears continued to stream down her face until Mordan slapped her. But she could not tell him that the tears were not only for what she had just seen but for the time before also.

'We will sleep in the forest tonight,' Mordan said more to himself than her. 'With the nomads holding the pass, we will have to find our own way over the ranges tomorrow.'

He gave her travellers' bread and made her a bed of fern fronds. She pretended to go to sleep but the tears still welled from under her eyelids. Mordan spent the night with his back against a tree and the long kitchen knife in his hand.

Now the sun was rising and shooting beams between the tree trunks on her and Dolly, and through leaf clusters above her head the sky was changing from pearl to cornflower.

'I hope you feel better, little girl,' said Mordan with an attempt at cheerfulness. 'We will get far away from the bad men today.'

Why call me that? she wondered.

Aloud she said, 'Krispin?'

'I told you, I am taking you to him. He lives a long way away and you must be patient.'

'I am glad Dolly is with us,' said Jennet and returned the porcelain smile.

FIVE

The Amber Isle

For long moments the only sound was the slap of waves against the rolling hull of the *Amber Star*. So much had happened – the tears for the death of his steersman were still wet on the face of the shipmaster – that it was only Ognam and Gambal who could feel deep and differing concern over the appearance of the beautiful stowaway.

'She must be returned to The Mage's tower,' Gambal declared finally. 'And soon, for who can say what form his anger will take when he realises how we have repaid his hospitality.'

Again there was a long silence.

Krispin, who alone knew Ognam's story of finding the captive beyond the subterranean lake, looked with interest at Tana who as yet had not uttered a word. Her perfect features, which reflected the pallor of her long imprisonment, showed no sign of dismay at Gambal's angry words. There was a calmness within her which was in contrast to the exhausted men about her on the bloodied deck, and Krispin could imagine many being lost to the challenge of unattainability that surrounded her like an aura at this moment.

Danya rose to his feet. 'I am shipmaster,' he said, 'and it is I who must make decisions concerning my ship. Master Gambal fears that in bringing this stow . . . this lady aboard the *Amber Star*, Master Ognam will have aroused the wrath of The Mage. Before I make any comment, I will heed what each of you has to say. First let us hear Master Ognam's words upon what he has done.'

Ognam, a ludicrous figure in his motley, looked about him as though for once in his career he was at a loss for speech. From his belt he took out his short jester's staff and this he clasped as though to draw inspiration from it.

'I – I can only repeat what I have just said,' he began. 'It was impossible for me to leave her captive . . .'

Then his voice took on a more positive note.

'And I shall tell you why. In my life I have seen the inside of prison cells many times, usually for being a strolling player which, in the minds of Witchfinders and village elders fawning to the Regent's rule, is a crime. It is a crime for no other reason than strolling players, like other artists, exist outside the established order, and in Ythan all must bow to the order established by the Regent. There was a time before The Enchantment when those of my guild were welcomed with garlands and there were more minstrels than beggars in the land.'

Gambal muttered impatiently but Danya gestured the jongleur to continue.

'For mocking the Regent in – if I may say so with

due modesty – one of my best performances, albeit for a yokel audience, I have also seen the interior of the Citadel's dungeons, as have you, Lord Alwald and Master Krispin, and very terrifying it was for one who in truth has little heroism in his heart. Although Master Gambal sees fit to revile me, I shall always owe him a debt of gratitude for allowing me to go with those he delivered from the Witchfinders.

'I tell this because you must know that although I may seem a comic character to you, a mountebank trading in nothing more than tunes and tricks, I worship at the shrine of liberty. I know no greater prize than freedom. Thus when I found this lady, imprisoned for no other crime than her name, it was impossible for me not to try and release her from her bondage.

'You three, Lord Alwald, Krispin and Gambal, are Pilgrims; you are on a quest which, if you succeed, will restore freedom to Ythan, and therefore I have the hope that you will agree the importance of liberty for a single person as well as for a kingdom.

'I ask your pardon if I have offended you by the way I have gone about this, but I saw no other path while in the tower, and I beg you in the name of her for whom you quest that Tana may continue aboard this ship.'

Tana gave a slight enigmatic smile as Ognam, now emptied of words, leaned wearily against the bulwark.

The old amber-seeker spoke up unexpectedly. 'Well put. Well put.'

'Let us hear you, Master Gambal, for it seems you most fear the presence of this lady aboard the *Amber Star*,' said Danya.

'It is not her presence, it is the vengeance of The Mage that I fear,' Gambal said in a calmer voice and in the style that he used when he was the Regent's Revel Master. 'The use of words is the craft of the jongleur, and Master Ognam has made a pretty speech about freedom. It is a word for many occasions. The Witchfinders claim to give the people freedom from the threat of heresy and sorcery! Master Ognam talks glib about the quest for Ythan's freedom, so I ask him if he would hazard the return of the Princess for the escape of one prisoner. We do not know why The Mage saw fit to make a captive of the lady, but we do know that he is strange in his ways and his magical powers are formidable and must be more so now he holds the Esav. To enspell us would be but a matter of a moment to him even though we may be over the horizon. For the sake of the quest I say we return to the tower and make our peace with him.'

'And the lady?' asked Danya quietly.

Gambal smiled. 'The lady, dressed in spider silk, hardly looks like those wretches one saw in Danaak's dungeons. Her hands do not bear the marks of toil or her face the aspect of ill-treatment; indeed she has retained her beauty and I wonder if it is not that beauty which inspired such noble sentiments in the jester's breast.'

Suddenly his voice hardened.

'We have come hundreds of leagues along the

Pilgrim Path, beheld a city fall and braved journeys never before undertaken, and I have no wish to see that effort wasted when we are on the final stage of the quest. Return to The Mage's tower, I say.'

The shipmaster looked at the others and nodded to Alwald.

'It seems to me that if The Mage was likely to punish us for Ognam's action he would have done so by now. But remember, the night before we set sail he resumed that sleep such as we found him in, so it may be months before he awakens and finds the lady gone, by which time we will be a thousand leagues from his tower and scattered. More than that, I believe from what I saw that he does not have his full wits and his memory oft fails him. It is likely that he does not even remember the lady if, like everything else in the tower, her captivity was regulated by gramarye. As to the lady herself, one can see immediately that she has the bearing of noble blood and my honour would never allow her to be delivered back into the power of a deranged old man. Let us sail on, Shipmaster.'

'And you?' Danya said to Krispin.

'When I was a little boy in Toyheim I got into trouble for releasing robins from their cages so I understood Ognam's words, but I also understand how Gambal does not want the quest endangered. But to me Alwald spoke the most sense, and I agree with him. Let us sail on.'

Alwald bestowed a smile on Krispin in recognition of his good sense.

'What are your feelings, Nomis?' Danya inquired.

'If The Mage does not know of the lady's escape, we would be moon mad to sail back and make him aware of it. For myself, I never want to behold The Mage's tower again even though I make no complaint of his treatment of us. Besides, fate has led us to this distal isle and there, I swear, will be amber for the picking up.'

'So far the lady has not said a word,' said Danya.

'My wish must be obvious after so long from the real world,' said Tana quietly. 'I shall not try to persuade you with words but abide with what you decide is right. Tell us your view, Shipmaster.'

'When I took my commission from The Mage I was told that while I was to be in full command as far as the sailing of my ship was concerned, I should heed your wishes in other respects. Therefore I suggest you vote quickly and we then get on with repairing the *Amber Star*.'

'Voting is not necessary,' said Gambal. 'There is no agreement with me and that I accept, and with that acceptance may I say I had no personal ill will towards the lady. My concern was purely for the success of the quest, and I pray the Mother that no evil will come from your decision.'

While Tana's future had been under discussion, the current had steadily borne the *Amber Star* towards the isle of black rock which rose steeply ahead of them.

'We can moor there while we make repairs,' said Danya.

'And collect amber,' added Nomis.

Under the shipmaster's direction, a sweep was

fitted on either side of the craft and the travellers pulled on them to give her steerage.

'No doubt after hiding in the hold you will want to refresh and rest privily,' Danya said to Tana. 'I must take the helm now poor Gled is no more, but Nomis will show you to our best cabin beneath the poop deck. Do you need food or drink?'

Tana shook her head. 'All I require is a soft bed to rest on. For the other things, Master Ognam kept me well supplied – and with comfort when those sea dragons threatened us.'

She smiled at Ognam heaving on one of the oars and then followed Nomis to the stern.

With Danya steering, the *Amber Star* drew closer to the shore until the crew could hear the hiss of small waves creaming over its black sand. As the sand rounded a sheer cliff, Danya was relieved to see a small natural harbour. A few minutes later they edged safely into it and the anchor chain clattered through the hawsehole. When the sweeps were shipped, preparations were begun to repair the shattered woodwork and replace the rigging which had been torn from the mast. As the travellers inspected the gashes in the planking caused by the teeth of the kraken, their gratitude to the griffins increased.

Danya, busy unpacking a chest of tools, called Krispin to him.

'Old Nomis insists on going ashore to seek amber,' he said. 'This isle looks barren and deserted but there is nothing in these climes that I trust so I would take it kindly if you would go with him.

After seeing you use your sword on the kraken I reckon you are best armed for the purpose.'

'I shall go willingly,' replied Krispin to whom the idea of strolling on the island was far more pleasant than toiling aboard ship.

A few minutes later the keel of the *Amber Star*'s skiff furrowed the coarse sand of the beach and the two stepped ashore. After the boat was hauled beyond the highwater mark, Nomis led the way round a large rock outcrop which hid the anchored ship from view.

'Know anything about amber, my boy?' he demanded as they trudged towards a bank composed of stones which had been rounded like slingshot by the action of the waves. Beyond it a fall of massive boulders marked the end of the bay.

'Only that it gets a very high price in the jewellers' marts.'

'And yet it is not a jewel,' said the old man with a laugh. 'It is the tears of ancient trees that fell into the sea and which, down the centuries, have been carried north by the currents that flow to the Cold Sea and on to the world's end.'

'And you find the amber pieces washed up on beaches here?'

'That is right. I have the gift of knowing where to look, and I can tell you that there will be amber among those stones ahead. I can smell it.' He tapped the side of his preposterous nose.

Krispin was alarmed at the eagerness with which Nomis hurried over the shingle, expecting him to stumble at any minute, but the thought of amber seemed to renew his vitality. With a cackle of triumph, he stooped and then held up a translucent brown lump.

Krispin was disappointed by its appearance.

'It has to be polished,' Nomis explained. 'It may look nothing to you but someday in Danaak a nobleman will pay a ransom for this to grace his lady's breast. Look, there is more. I wager we are the first amber-hunters to visit this spot.'

'Why do not other ships come here?'

'Their masters hate to take them out of sight of land. Such is the nature of the Cold Sea, the only sure passage is to follow the coastline, and mariners fear the islands because of strange tales told about them along the seaways, though apart from being a griffins' eyrie this isle seems safe enough.'

'What sort of tales?' Krispin asked.

Nomis shrugged. 'I take little notice of seamen's stories and what I have heard I have forgotten.'

I wonder, thought Krispin. *It would suit him to forget if he thought there was a chance of finding amber in these islands.*

'You do not need to mount guard over me,' Nomis continued. 'Climb up the cliff and see if there is another beach like this beyond the rockfall.'

Krispin looked doubtfully at the natural path which wound up the cliff face. Though it did not appear particularly steep or dangerous, Krispin had an aversion to heights – he remembered with a shudder his climb up the chasm wall to reach the Domain of Olam – but pride did not allow him to refuse.

'Shout if you need me,' he said.

The going was not as bad as he had expected and within a few minutes he reached the top to find himself looking over a windswept plateau on which black rocks reared above coarse grass like natural megaliths – or were they natural? Their shape put Krispin in mind of the forbidden stone circle he had visited secretly as a child in the High Wald, to Jennet's satisfactory terror and admiration when he later boasted to her about it.

They must be natural, he told himself. *They are too haphazard to have been put up by men, and who is there here on this unknown isle to have done such work?*

He walked past several of the rocks to reach a point where he could look down beyond the rockfall. Nomis would be disappointed. There was no shore, only a cliff falling sheer into the sea. The dark heads of some plump sea creatures appeared in the swell that washed against it and Krispin, to whom the sea was a new and wondrous world, stretched out to watch their playful antics.

He suddenly remembered Nomis and climbed to his feet, guilty that more time must have elapsed than he intended. Turning from the sea, he walked quickly through the shadows cast by the standing stones. And then he heard it, the sonorous tolling of a great bell.

SIX

Holy Fire

In the Peak Tower's taper-lit shrine the murdered watchman lay in his coffin while by ancient tradition a silver bell chimed once a minute, one chime for every year of his long life. With each clear note a chill ran through those who heard it; the serving women could not stifle their sobs nor the men their imprecations against the killer who had been brought into the castle out of compassion and had repaid it by spilling old Dodkin's lifeblood. There was no doubt of his identity. When the watchman had been found he had muttered, 'No-Name – why?' just before the Dark Maid led his spirit from his body.

In her solar, the Lady Eloira, dressed in a mourning gown of white samite, felt the remorseless chimes were driving her mad, and to escape them she went to an attic chamber situated beneath the steep roof of the main tower. Here silence reigned and she sank thankfully into a dusty chair and gazed at a collection of toymakers' work which had built up over the years as a result of the Choosing ceremony.

When the persecuted members of the Guild of Toymakers had arrived in the High Wald during the chaos which followed The Enchantment, the Lady Eloira's grandsire had permitted them to build the village they named Toyheim in return for the finest example of work produced by the apprentices each year. This custom became enshrined in the ritualistic ceremony known as the Choosing, and Eloira, as Reeve of the High Wald, had forgotten how many of the exhibits she had chosen.

Each had been the pride of some young man who, having had his work chosen, set out to spend a year and a day in the outside world as a journeyman before returning to be welcomed into the guild. There were a great many rocking horses, but what caught her eye was the figure of a dancer – an automaton that actually danced – which she had chosen only a few months earlier.

'Ah Krispin, I have failed you,' she cried aloud. 'I swore to protect your Jennet and now . . . ' Her words failed.

What increased her anguish was the fact that Krispin's dancer had been modelled on Jennet.

There was a discreet tap at the door and her steward entered.

'My lady, the bell has ceased. It is time to attend the shrine.'

'Thank you. I shall be down directly.'

Left alone again, the Lady Eloira summoned up her reserves of strength and dignity. Was she not the Reeve of the High Wald, the descendant of a remarkable line that went back to the warrior Rusthal who took the mountainous land by right

233

of conquest? Old she might be, heart-broken she might be, but she would not allow this to affect her last farewell to a retainer who had served her faithfully all his life.

Her resolve was firmed when, on the way to the shrine, she paused in her solar and drank a goblet of the sparkling green-tinged wine which she referred to as her 'greatest indulgence'. Her cat gazed at her from his place by the herb-scented fire with censorious eyes.

'Smoke,' she said, 'if she lives we will get her back. No matter the cost, Jennet must be found.'

In the shrine, taper flames became haloes as the sweet smoke of incense rose about them. The Lady Eloira intoned the ritual words, after which the life achievements of the departed were recited: he had loved his wife, fathered two children, been a kind friend, had grown the finest climbing roses in the castle . . .

Finally, quavering voices sang the Hymn of the Dead and the coffin was borne away to the catacomb reserved for the castle's retainers.

As Eloira reclimbed the stone staircase to her solar, she paused as the voices of two maidservants discussing the murder floated up.

'He was no forester, that No-Name,' said one. 'Right from the start I knew that. I had to take food to his chamber while he was ill and I got a good look at his hands. Soft as a lady's, they were.'

The Reeve continued to her solar with questions crowding her mind, but the one that remained uppermost was why had he abducted Jennet? Surely, with such dangers surrounding them since the invasion of the Wolf Horde, he had not risked leaving the safety of the tower with her just to satisfy some perverted lust. In his eyes, the urgency of his action had warranted murder so . . .

Suddenly Eloira's inward eye returned to the attic and the dancer that had been made by Krispin Tammasson in the likeness of his sister Jennet. At the Choosing she had signalled it as the winning exhibit not only for its excellent craftsmanship but because it resembled a miniature of Princess Livia. And when she actually saw Jennet she was amazed at the resemblance. Few in Ythan had any idea of Livia's appearance, yet did the stranger have some knowledge of it and plan to profit by Jennet's similarity to the entranced Princess?

In the solar, Eloira trembled as though with the ague at the possibilities this line of thought presented. It could threaten the whole concept of the Pilgrim Path.

'What shall I do, what shall I do?' she cried aloud. It was one of the very few occasions when she felt old and bewildered. Her fingers trembled as she poured another goblet of chilled wine in which strings of minute bubbles rose gracefully to the surface.

The effect of the wine – brought at great expense from a vineyard on the far side of Ythan – calmed her panic. She repeated to the dozing cat, 'Jennet must be found, and for that I will have to look to the past.'

Leaving the solar, she hurried through the castle

235

to a door which she unlocked with a key of ancient design. In the chamber beyond, light shone through casement panes of rose-tinted glass shelves onto shelves of hide-bound books and lines of scroll jars. It was the library in which generations of her ancestors had followed the family pursuit of arcane knowledge, and where Eloira, at first under the tutorage of her father, had spent some of her happiest hours poring over old manuscripts and even older tablets.

As she entered the room, the odour of vellum was like a beloved perfume, and her self-assurance returned as she moved along the shelves in search of certain works which had been written by her scholarly forebears. She placed several on a table marbled by ancient ink spills and, as she prepared to read, she remembered her meeting with Jennet when Krispin had brought her from the village whose sacking had shocked her mind back to childhood. She had given her a doll with the words, 'She has given me comfort more years ago than I can recall – I hope she still has the power to do the same for you.'

Wherever Jennet is, she will have the doll, thought the Reeve and untied the ribbon of the first scroll.

The hot night hung heavy over the Wald. Apart from the sighing of trees, the only sounds were the occasional cry of a wolf deep in the forest and the chuckling of water among the reeds on the banks of the River of Night. The moon threw silver arabesques on its oily surface and some of these shifting patterns were briefly obscured as a small boat moved silently from the shore.

In the stern, Brindal the burly riverman paddled with slow strokes; in the bows, the Wish Maiden and Wode gazed downstream to where River Garde cast streaks of light across the water.

'I remember hot nights like this in my village,' murmured the Wish Maiden. 'We had music and lamps in the apple trees, and dancing on the courtyard of the inn. What an empty-head I must have been then, for all I thought of was dresses and fairings, and which of the lads I might marry.' She sighed.

'Was there a special one?' asked Wode softly.

'I flirted with them all but not one did I love. I am called the Wish Maiden – and it is true. I am a maiden yet and will remain so.'

'You sound very sure of that.'

'Of course. It is my strength.'

Brindal let the boat drift with the current. He too had memories of happier days, when he lived in a cottage close to the river where each day he tossed a copper coin as tribute to the pikemaids before lowering his nets. Now all was gone, only a square of ash told where his home had stood. His consolation was that, thanks to the Wish Maiden, he had been able to fight back against the nomads.

'Where does your strength to inspire men come from if you were only a simple village girl?' asked Wode after a while.

'I can only say it is something that entered me – a spirit. Somehow I know what to say, how to act – and with your experience as a soldier to guide us, the folk of the Wald are learning that it is possible to resist the wolfmen.'

'We need to do more than ambush small parties,' said Wode.

'Is that not why we are in this boat?'

Instead of answering directly, he said, 'I think you are acting too much, Maiden. Inspire men with your words and leave the danger to them. Your work would come to naught if you were killed – or, worse, captured.'

'You are wrong for once, Wode, and I fear you think more of my safety than the cause. Men will join us and follow me as long as I share battle with them like a shield maid of ancient times. That is why I am with you tonight. If your plan works, the news will spread beyond the territory the Wolf King rules that the Wish Maid halted the barbarians coming to invade Ythan.'

'Sadly, it will not be for long but, the Mother willing, it will be a gesture,' said Wode. 'I have in my mind a more ambitious plan, but enough. From now on we must stay silent.'

For many minutes the dark boat, its occupants swathed in dark cloaks, drifted with the current towards River Garde, with Brindal only occasionally risking the splash of his paddle to keep it on course. Then, almost before they were ready, they were opposite the castle. The slender bridge that was the only link between the Wald and the Outlands loomed above them on its fragile-seeming piles. Brindal leaned out and caught one with an outstretched arm and managed to hold the boat to it so that the bows chafed against the opposite support.

Without a word, Wode stood up and the Wish Maiden gasped as the boat rocked alarmingly. Reaching for a crosspiece, he hauled himself up and sat astride it just beneath the planking. Still without a word, the Maiden handed him small kegs wrapped in oil-soaked blankets which deadened the sound as he hung them on the timbers with lengths of chain. Wode knew from secret observation that nomad sentries guarded the bridge at either end, which made silence imperative. He endeavoured to calm his racing pulse with the thought that while the wolfmen were demonic when the battle lust was upon them, they did not have the discipline necessary for routine duties.

When the last keg was in place and a length of oiled hemp hung down, he lowered himself back into the boat, but at the vital moment an eddy swung it slightly and he dropped straight into the black water. His hand grasped the side of the boat and his head rose close to that of the Wish Maiden bending over in alarm.

'My tinder is useless,' he whispered. 'Use the spare box.'

She nodded and he waited in the water, the current plucking at him. He heard her blow the tinder into life.

'It is alight,' she whispered.

Brindal freed his aching arm and dug his paddle into the water so that the boat, with Wode clinging to its gunwale, raced downstream. Looking back

Wode saw a spark travel up the hemp to the kegs. They were several hundred paces from the bridge when the oily blankets caught fire, followed by a gush of yellow flame as the kegs ignited.

The supports above the water began to blaze and flames danced along the planking. Shouts and curses came from either side but there was nothing the guards could do; the bridge became an inferno, its glare lighting the walls and turrets of the castle. The castle gong, which Wode remembered so well from the time when it signalled the changing of the guard, boomed the alarm but before its echoes had died away, several of the flaming stilt-like bridge supports twisted and the whole structure began to cant.

This curiously lifelike movement made Wode think of a gigantic insect outlined in fire; then the insect toppled and was lost in hissing steam.

Brindal headed for a dark spit of land and as soon as Wode felt his legs dragging along the bottom he stood up and took his place in the boat. Smuts drifted about them and the smell of wet charcoal was heavy in the air. On the spit, Brindal planted a pikestaff on which was mounted a lock of the Maiden's hair so that in the morning light all would know who had dared to fire the bridge.

'I never thought it would blaze up so quickly,' she said as they continued downriver.

'Sulphur, naphtha and pitch. It is a mixture used in casks that are hurled by mangonels,' Wode told her. 'We called it Holy Fire, and I have heard tell that it will burn underwater and so is used in sea battles.'

'You must be cold after your ducking.'

He felt her warm hand rest on his.

'In days to come you and I will be known as the Bane of the Wolf King,' she said.

'For that we will have to do more than burn down a bridge,' he said.

'What was the plan you had in mind?'

'It would take more men than we have at the moment.'

'I shall get you men enough, Wode. After tonight, more outcast foresters and rivermen will want to join the Wish Maiden.'

'Now the nomads are going to fight on the other side of the ranges, River Garde will be merely a garrison. I believe we could capture and hold it.'

SEVEN

Shath

The shipmaster watched approvingly as Ognam and Gambal set to work clearing the deck of the *Amber Star*. Although everyone felt exhausted after the night encounter with the krakens, there was an unspoken wish to make essential repairs and set sail from the island. Something about its barren appearance caused unspoken misgiving; unspoken because there was nothing specific that anyone could describe. True, the dark cliffs looked forlorn and the shores of black sand dismal, but that was nothing different to the mainland coastline. To the travellers, everything they had seen since reaching the Cold Sea suggested desolation. Their apprehension arose from something more subtle; some psychic tremor in the air or a kind of prescience that had developed within them since following the quest.

Tana, who had changed her spider silk for a cloak of black-dyed wool, emerged from the galley where she had cooked thick broth over the charcoal stove, and even Gambal nodded appreciatively when he took a steaming bowl from her slender hands.

'Lady, I would talk with you,' said Danya.

She inclined her head.

'First, may I say that however unexpected your appearance was, you are welcome aboard the *Amber Star* – especially if you can provide such meals as this.'

She inclined her head again.

'But I must warn you that we are on no ordinary voyage.'

'That I know from what Master Ognam told me.'

Gambal looked about to say something then checked himself.

'If it were a matter of sailing to Ythan to trade our amber, it would be possible to take you to some safe port and arrange for you to return to your home, but I swore an oath to take these four directly south to a land which The Mage called the Shadow Realm and which, I do confess, is unknown to me. Thus you will have to sail with us until my commission is discharged, after which I shall see you safely on your journey.'

'I have no objection to sharing your voyage,' said Tana with a slight smile. 'And afterwards, I know not.'

'Where is your home?'

'From here I know not where it lies for I was snatched from it by sorcery and, time and memory being so queer in The Mage's tower, I fear it may have changed much since I dwelt there. In my cavern I had no way of counting days, many years may have passed and yet through the gramarye of the place I remained unchanged. I no longer know my age and mayhap if I could trace my way back to my home I might find those I knew long gone and strangers feasting in my father's hall. I do not know, but at this moment I am content enough with freedom.'

'Can you recall much of your home?'

'Oh yes. My father's palace stood on the edge of a lake. There was woodland all round, and behind it rose hills rent with great ravines. When one wandered among them there was always the murmur of waterfalls and vistas of land covered with vineyards and orchards, and here and there hamlets with smoke rising from them.

'But it is the palace I remember best. While I was a captive I spent much time revisiting it in memory. Particularly do I remember the view of it from the lake. A broad marble staircase curved from the quay to the terrace which ran in front of the main building. I can see that staircase now with its double row of urns from which flowering creepers spilled over the carved balustrades. At night it was lit by lamps of violet-tinted glass, and from the casements above came sweet music . . .'

And smiling at recollections summoned by her words, Tana went on to describe the palace in great detail.

'And the lake on which it stood?' asked Danya.

'It was a vast lake yet so calm that the image of the palace it held hardly wavered, while at night the lamps set along the terrace reflected on it so brightly that none could tell which were real and which mirrored.'

'What was its name?' asked Alwald who, moved by her description, remembered how the lights of River Garde threw streaks of gold across the River of Night.

'Taloon. The Lake of Taloon.'

'I am sure that I once heard that name in a poem,' said Ognam. 'Long ago, when as a young man I had some pretensions to versifying. But, as I recall, it was written before The Enchantment.'

'The Enchantment?' said Tana. 'What was that?'

'Too long a story to tell now,' he said quickly and picked up a hammer. 'Back to work.'

The jongleur, having had experience in assembling stage sets, was the most skilled with tools. He nailed planks across the gap in the bulwarks while Alwald and Gambal hoisted a spare yardarm into position under Danya's direction, too busy to wonder further.

'The old man calls you,' said Tana, pausing on her way to the galley. The hammer blows stopped and all went to the side to see the amber-seeker standing on the beach where the ship's skiff was drawn up.

'What is it, Nomis?' shouted the shipmaster.

The old man's words came faintly across the water.

'What does he say?' asked Alwald.

'It seems he sent your friend Krispin to spy out a beach and he has not returned,' Danya replied. 'We had better—'

His words died as the deep tolling of a bell reached their ears.

*　　*　　*

245

The brazen notes of the unseen bell seemed to reverberate within Krispin's head; he paused and looked about him but all he could see was the black stones dotted across the plateau and the restless marram grass that covered it. To his right the ground rose in a gentle swell to a rocky elevation, above which towered granite pinnacles reminiscent of a castle's towers and which he guessed provided the summer home of the griffins. It was from this direction that it seemed the slow tolling of the bell reached him, and without a second thought he set off in that direction.

A few minutes later he had climbed the slope and here he saw the bell, a great bell of verdigrised bronze as large as Grand Johan in Danaak's chief shrine. It hung beneath an arch which long ago had been cut high in a massive rock pillar. The mystery was that no person was visible to ring it, yet the clapper continued to swing, the sound spreading like gigantic ripples over the island.

For some minutes Krispin stood as though spellbound, his hand resting on the hilt of Woundflame. He felt there was something about the sound that he ought to recognise – a warning perhaps – but whatever it was, it remained beyond the edge of his consciousness. Indeed, the more he listened, the harder he found it to think. It was as though the metallic notes dulled his intelligence.

The tolling ceased. The resonance of the bell became a hum growing fainter and fainter.

Krispin remembered Nomis.

He was supposed to be guarding him. He must return to the shore . . .

Ayyyyyyyyyyyyyyyyyyyyyyyyyyyyyyyyyyyyy

The sound was soft, a sigh lasting longer than a mortal sigh, and it seemed to Krispin that he was not hearing it with his ears but that it was somehow within his skull. Perhaps it was the effect of having listened so close to the bell. He took a step forward.

Shhhhhhhhhhhhhhhhhhhhhhhhhhhhhhhhh

The sigh, sibilant and sad, halted him.

Ayyyyyyyyyyyyyy   ammmmmmmmm Shhhhhhathhhh

It was a voice now, a voice that was like the wind soughing through a forest but with enough humanity for Krispin to distinguish the words. He gazed about him in wonder but the bell now hanging motionless, was the only sign of humankind, if indeed it was humankind that had placed it in its rough-hewn belfry. Nothing stirred but the restless grass.

Ayyyy ammm Shath

It was a voice from nowhere. Krispin suddenly had the thought that it might be a voice that had waited long for some living person to hear.

'What do you want?' he demanded aloud.

Youuuuuuuu

There was something about the long-drawn word that made Krispin shudder, yet he found it impossible to move from the spot. His fingers tightened on Woundflame's grip, and then he realised that even such a sword could offer him no protection against a sound.

247

'I do not understand.'

Lisssssssten . . . my name is Shath . . . long ago I was a Sea King . . . my black ships made the ocean my kingdom . . . none could withstand them . . . ports paid tribute . . . I sailed up rivers and sacked cities . . . I exulted over my enemies . . . all except one . . .

The words faded. Krispin remained standing for a full minute, held by some perverse curiosity that he could not break.

Shhhhhhhhhhhhhhhhhhhhhhhhhhhhhhhhhh

The sighing returned as if the voice had received new strength.

Ayyyyyy won all a conqueror could win except one thing . . . I relished glory so much I wanted lasting life . . . my slavers brought me the consort of a great sorcerer captured from her river barge . . . beautiful she was . . . so beautiful . . . her ransom was a spell to free me from my destined span . . . he agreed for she held his heart . . . the spell was cast and I returned her . . . but she had found love in my arms . . . and when he found her faithless he banished me by magic to this isle . . .

Again the voice trailed away, gathered strength and resumed.

The spell he did not undo and yet he cheated me . . . my spirit was freed from death's shadow but my body . . . my body wasted with the years until I was naught but a voice upon the wind . . . waiting . . . waiting to regain flesh from some stranger who would brave the bell . . .

'The bell?'

The bell was placed there by the sorcerer . . . its

248

periodic tolling was to keep mariners away but none strayed thus far on the Cold Sea . . . so long ago its message was forgot though still it knells . . .

Krispin tried physically to shake himself out of this waking dream that had fallen upon him. He attempted to walk away but the inner voice continued.

In your strong body the Sea King shall return to the world . . . together we will share the joys of conquest . . . look out to sea . . .

Unable to resist, Krispin turned his head and saw a number of black ships sailing in sickle formation against a line of war vessels with various banners fluttering from their mastheads. As he watched, the two fleets engaged, hulls caved in under the impact of the black ships' rams, tar barrels hurled by mangonels left smoky trails over mastheads, ships blossomed into flame, weapons of boarding parties reflected fire, the cries of the wounded were borne on the salt air. In triumph the black craft cruised past the wreckage of the defeated fleet.

Nothing could withstand me . . . so it will be again . . . see what I offer you . . .

The scene changed and instead of the sea, Krispin saw a broad river flowing between banks of vivid reeds. Towards him came a gilded barge with two banks of oars rising and dipping in perfect time. On a throne set high in the stern sat a young woman whose beauty was so perfect it had an unearthly quality about it. Although she was surrounded by retainers in gorgeous costumes she wore a simple robe of virginal white. Her only ornament was a silver band round her forehead. On a little platform beside the deck, a slave in an eyeless mask kept a fringed fan in motion above her head.

The barge flashing in the sunlight and the lady seated like a queen above it created a scene of richness and beauty the like of which Krispin had never imagined. Then, from a bend in the river, he saw a black dragonship emerge and overtake the barge despite the frantic efforts of its rowers. Laughing men in outlandish helmets climbed aboard with axes swinging. Blood ran down the white oars and stained the ivory deck, and through the carnage strode a warrior in glittering mail and a helmet surmounted by a crown. Ignoring the dying huddled at the stern, he seized the lady and held her high like a hunter flaunting his quarry.

Seeeeeeeeeeeeeeeee . . . wealth, beauty and power . . . all will fall to me again . . .

The vision melted away. Krispin, left with the thought that what he had witnessed must have happened long ago, now saw nothing but the leaden sea. Again he made an effort to leave.

You have a fine sword . . . you will return to your ship . . . you will slay the crew . . . we shall sail south to gather men who would be sea rovers . . .

'No!' shouted Krispin. 'No! You are nothing, a voice . . . I shall leave you here.'

Again, the long drawn sigh.

You cannot . . . I am within you . . . go now to the ship

Like a somnambulist Krispin walked down the

slope to the plateau between its upright rocks. The wind had begun to blow again, to ruffle the grass and carry Krispin's name.

They seek you . . . hurry to them with your sword . . .

Krispin's hand tightened on Woundflame's grip.

EIGHT

The Progress

I was the Commander of the Host and as such I shall meet my fate with dignity.

The phrase ran through Mandal's mind like a litany as he lay on the bars of the Cage. The idea of dignity was all that he had to hold on to; his greatest fear was that his body might betray him into pleading for mercy, especially as hunger pains were writhing in his belly.

Serene Mother, let me give no satisfaction to the Regent in the manner of my passing.

He climbed to his feet and with difficulty paced across the lattice floor to stand beneath the gargoyle from whence rust-dyed water dripped steadily. For a long time he held his open mouth.

'You do right, dearie,' mumbled his fellow prisoner who lay curled up in the opposite corner. 'If you keep filling yourself up with water you might last longer but it does not feel so bad.'

Mandal tore a piece of cloth from his tunic, soaked it and carried it to the old woman.

'Here you are, gammer,' he said. She opened her toothless mouth in a way that reminded him

252

of a baby bird waiting to be fed on the nest. He squeezed the cloth and she smiled up in gratitude.

In normal times the thought of even talking to a beldame like her would have been repellent to him, but these were not normal times. She had aroused a protective instinct such as he had never experienced before.

'My wits have gone withershins – I cannot remember how many days I have been here,' she said, her voice more clear now that her throat was moist again.

Remembering her wish to survive for a fortnight in the Cage, he answered, 'This must be your thirteenth day. Hold out until tomorrow and you will have proved yourself.'

She nodded solemnly like a child; indeed he realised there was much of the child hidden behind her hag-like features.

'They are quiet down there – not like yesterday,' she said.

Yesterday a huge crowd had assembled in the square below, hurling abuse and ineffectual missiles at the Cage. Word had spread among the citizens of Danaak of the destruction of the army and that its disgraced Commander was on public display. All day long their chanted insults had risen about him and only in the evening when a bonfire had been lit below the Cage did the guards clear the square.

But today Mandal saw that apart from several beggars playing toup with copper coins, the place was deserted.

For a long time he gazed over the city, remembering the times he had led a triumphant army down the main thoroughfare to the Citadel to receive public thanks from the Regent.

'You got a family, dearie?'

He turned back to the old woman. 'Dead,' he said, thinking of his army.

'A blessing. It would be sad for them to see how you have ended.'

'And you, gammer?'

'Only Grimalkin, and she ran away when the Witchfinders came. She knew when it was time to leave, did Grimalkin.'

'How did you become a witch?' he asked, more for the sake of talking than curiosity.

'One day when I was young I went into the woods to pick mushrooms and I met a man dressed all in grey. He took me by the hand and, well . . . afterwards . . . he asked me if I wanted powers and, being tired of being a kitchen drab, I answered why not, and then he said he was the King of the Coven and he would teach me its secrets. To tell the truth, dearie, it was more fun than magic but I learnt enough and I had a better life as a witch than if I had stayed a scullion.'

'Until now.'

'Until now.'

Mandal returned to his corner and continued to look over the city. It was a fine summer day and its very brightness seemed to mock those who lay in the shadow of approaching death. The verse of a minstrel's lay came into his mind and he repeated it with trembling lips.

Up looms the dark, dim future and it holds
With steel-bound fingers all my destiny.
No human eye or heart upon this earth
Will ever see inside its mystery.
   It is calling,
   Sadly calling,
Time is come, you are no longer free.

Distant music roused him from his reverie. Opening his eyes he looked down to where the Green River emerged from beneath the Citadel. Its banks were lined with guards in bronze armour and behind their gleaming ranks jostled a restless crowd ranging from the well-to-do in their carriages down through the gamut of Danaak's society to the strumpets and cut-purses who saw profit in such occasions.

As the music grew louder, a barge moved into Mandal's view, a gaily painted vessel in which musicians played. It was followed by a long craft, its deck lined with men whose faces were hidden by visors. The black rose emblem on the gonfalon fluttering above proclaimed that they were the Regent's elite bodyguard. A magnificent galley followed, with the plain yellow banner of Ythan floating above it.

'The Regent's galley,' Mandal murmured aloud.

'What was that, dearie?'

'The Regent is leaving Danaak by the Green River.'

After the galley came a line of barges carrying soldiers, horses, bales and barrels – all the necessities for a progress royal, except that it was

255

not undertaken by a member of the royal house. A century had passed since a king had set out thus in Ythan.

When the boats were clear of the Citadel the musicians ceased playing, as tradition dictated, and their rondos were replaced by the thudding boom of a drum mounted on one of the vessels. The oars began to ply in time to its rhythmic beat, the speed of the procession increased and was soon lost to Mandal's sight though the sound of the drum continued to reach him for some time, a regretful reminder of the great drum by which his army had drilled and fought.

'It is unusual for him to make a progress,' he said to the old woman as he went to the gargoyle.

'Mayhap he seeks a cure,' she said. 'It is said he has an affliction that cannot be healed by priest or physician – nor by all the blood an alchemist can distil.'

Once the line of boats had passed the spectators lining the banks of the Green River, the Regent, who had been acknowledging his subjects with a studied smile that suggested a benign but authoritative ruler, entered his cabin and sank onto a couch. The smile had gone from his features which were white beneath the dusting of rouge he now used on occasions when he was viewed at a distance by the people. Sweat trickled from beneath the glossy black hair which was cut straight above his heavy eyebrows and he would have had the appearance of a raddled invalid if it

256

were not for the cold determination in his adamantine eyes.

The two female pages who stood at the head and foot of the couch exchanged glances of alarm. Urwen waved them out of the cabin and then knelt beside the Regent. She gently removed the cloak of maroon velvet which he had worn to hide his bandaged arm and then handed him a cup of dark Ronimar wine.

'The unguent will bring ease, my lord,' she said as she unwound the dressing.

'It feels aflame,' he muttered.

When the swollen hand with its thick talons was exposed, she calmly took it between hers and began to massage an aromatic lotion into the livid flesh with her fingertips. As she bent over it her red tresses fell forward and while she worked thus the Regent watched her with the ghost of an ironic smile on his lips.

'Thanks to you it pains less,' he said when she bandaged his arm with fresh thyme-scented linen. 'Now wipe this powder from my face – I must appear like a brothel youth.'

She did as she was bidden and then poured more wine for both him and herself. Through the curtains of loosely woven spider silk which hung across the cabin's casements they had an impression of verdant banks and groves of fruit-bearing trees gliding past. Only the steady thud of the rowers' drum disturbed the tranquil atmosphere.

'It is a long time since I made a journey out of Danaak,' said the Regent. 'In the past I feared the mice might become too playful without the cat to watch over them.'

'And now, my lord?'

'I rather hope the mice will play.'

'But is there not danger in this, especially as rumours of your malady abound?'

'Those rumours will encourage the mice to venture out of their holes. Since Odo's capture and punishment for trying to poison me, conspiratorial mice have not dared squeak yet their whiskers still quiver at the thought of treason. While I am on my so-called progress, they may become overbold so that when the cat returns he will know where to pounce. The Lady Mandraga will keep watch and ward while I am gone and none could do it with more guile.'

'That I can believe.'

The Regent gave a rare laugh. 'The time of change is upon Ythan,' he said in a graver tone. 'It was predicted and I shall ensure that it will be for ever in my favour.'

'How so, my lord?'

'Urwen, I have it in mind to become King.'

For a moment she looked at him with a wide-eyed mixture of admiration and astonishment, then said, 'But a king must have royal blood, and while the legend of Princess Livia lingers . . .'

'As to the Sleeping Princess, I do believe the quest may soon be accomplished by a tiny band of Pilgrims who, to give them their due, have survived great hazards to get so far on their journey. They think that by finding Livia, Ythan will be returned to some mythical golden age.

What they do not know is that they are doing my work for me and when they reach their goal the last of Ythan's royal line will cease to be a threat. It has always been my policy to permit my enemies to carry out my plans unbeknown.'

'Like the Wolf Horde in the Wald.'

'Or when Archpriest Gregon, no friend to me, was assassinated by Odo's supporters. Thus, when it can be proved that Ythan's royal line is extinct, I shall be free to mount the empty throne.'

'But, my lord—'

'It will be simply done. It is a century since The Enchantment and mayhap the Lore Mistress will discover old documents of ancient law proclaiming that after such a time the throne of Ythan may remain no longer empty. Or it might benefit the new Archpriest to announce he has been granted a miraculous vision in which it was made known that it is the divine will that Ythan, so long deprived of a monarch, should have a new royal house. And who better to found a new dynasty than the Regent who has served Ythan so well? As for the people – they have a need for royalty, and they will forget grievances in the excitement of the coronation and the free wine and meat that goes with it.

'You may smile, Urwen, but I tell you that while the peasantry would not hesitate to hang the Regent if they could, they would fight to kiss his hem once the crown was on his head. An anointed king has a mystic power over his subjects, and that I shall have – provided the Wells make me whole again.'

'You believe we will find them?'

'A fool I would be to make this journey if I doubted. According to the scroll brought from Thaan, my cure lies beyond the Mountains of the Moon.' The Regent drained his wine cup. 'And, Urwen, there is one more thing for me to ponder on – a king needs must have a queen.'

Urwen lowered her head and said nothing.

Mandal awoke shivering in the cool night air.

He was immediately assailed by hunger cramps and the pain inflicted upon his flesh by the lattice on which he lay. In her corner the old woman muttered incoherently in feverish sleep. Struggling to his feet and thankful for the light of the moon which hung low over the steep roofs of Danaak, he edged his way towards the gargoyle. One misplaced step and, as had happened several times already, his leg would plunge between the iron bars as far as his thigh and more skin would be lost as he forced it free again.

It was something that had greatly amused the spectators when it happened after they returned to the square from watching the Regent's departure. Embittered veterans had mimicked phrases which officers had used on them such as 'Lift your legs, you whoreson!' or 'Are you a cripple or a soldier?'

The abuse had floated about him until the sun went down and the crowd dispersed to the wineshops. The silence that followed was like a blessing, and as the Constellation of the griffin began to glitter in the northern sky, he fell into merciful sleep.

Now as he leaned against the wall with his mouth open to catch the water, he sought in his mind for some way of escape. He knew that physical escape was impossible. His weakening fingers were useless on the iron bars, though he had tugged at them hard enough, but there might be escape for the spirit. He had no instrument with which he could wound himself mortally, and though he had thought of striking his head against the wall, he realised that he would probably only knock himself unconscious and awaken to even greater pain. It was ironic that for a man whose career had been the business of death, he could not devise his own. Yet if only his head would clear, he was sure he would find the answer.

A scratching sound made him look up the wall. High above, light shone from the small window where on several occasions he had glimpsed the head of the man with white hair. In the shadow below the window he was sure he could see a movement, and as he strained his eyes he made out a vague shape that was slowly descending the wall towards him. At first he thought it was a small pale animal, such as the human-shaped beasts captured for pets by his soldiers manning remote outposts. Then it moved into the moonlight and Mandal heard himself give a cry of disgust.

The nude female creature was the size of a child, and was climbing down the wall by inserting the horny nails of her hands and feet in the cracks between the stone blocks. Her skin, on which no hair grew, was pallid and her hands and feet were too large in proportion to the size of her body.

261

When she reached the top of the Cage and squatted on the bars, he found himself looking up into a broad face with bulbous eyes and a gash-like mouth. Her pendulous breasts hung down to her belly and, adding to the impression of incomplete anatomy, were without nipples, yet despite her grotesque appearance she exuded an aura of primal strength.

Mandal had seen much that was horrific in his career but the sight of this debased parody of the human form made him cower back. The creature now lay full length on the bars and reached towards him with her hand. For a moment he thought she was trying to attack him, and then he saw that she was offering him a small bundle.

He straightened and the moment his fingers closed on it she leapt up and climbed towards the window where she vanished inside.

His heart still racing, he opened the rolled-up cloth. Inside he found a piece of folded parchment covered with neat writing, and a large crust of bread. His first impulse was to cram the bread into his mouth; instead he held it under the dripping water for a few moments and then stepped carefully over to the huddled form in the corner.

'Gammar,' he whispered. 'I have something for you.'

NINE

The Lady
of the Lake

Soft fingers caressed Krispin's forehead.

He opened his eyes painfully and, from the way the room was rocking, concluded he had drunk too much apple ale the night before at the Jack-in-the-Box tavern. But this was not his room in Toyheim. It was far too small. And it was not Jennet but another girl sitting patiently beside him. Noises, too, were strange – an endless creaking and a banshee keening.

He was on a ship, of course. He had been returning to a ship with his sword unsheathed as the voice had told him. The voice?

He sat bolt upright with a cry of horror.

Where was Shath – the disembodied Shath who had entered his being?

'Lie down, you are safe now,' came the soothing voice of Tana. 'Your friends are working the ship so I have watched over you.'

At any other time he might have appreciated the cold beauty of the girl, but grim memory was

263

returning. He lay back on the bunk with a groan.

'What happened?' he asked. 'Tell me true – did I bring harm to anyone?'

'Mayhap to yourself. You were found lying on the grass beneath a great stone. They thought you might have fallen against it, or possibly the blood of the kraken that spilled upon you had some dire effect. I think it was neither of those things – you muttered strangely while I waited beside you.'

'No, not a fall nor kraken blood.'

'Who is Shath?' asked Tana. 'You cried the name in fear.'

'Someone – *something* – from long ago.'

'Would you like water or wine? No? Then I shall tell your friends you have revived.'

'Tell me, Tana, are we far from the isle?'

'Many leagues.'

A look of relief crossed his face.

Alone, he mentally retraced his footsteps after he had heard the tolling of the great bell. When Shath's voice ordered him to return to the *Amber Star* and put his friends to the sword, he had tried to reach inside his jerkin to grasp the Disk of Livia he wore in the hope it would give him protection, but the voice mocked him and said that no talisman made by man could save him from the power of the undying Shath. With Woundflame in his hand, he began a slow march across the plateau, struggling to halt each step he took and not able even to pause. And all the time the abominable voice of Shath hissed in his head.

He had almost reached the edge of the plateau

when he saw the figure of an old man in the shadow of one of the natural monoliths. He wore a dark cloak and held a long staff, and under his broad-brimmed hat his features were a combination of age and authority. He raised his hand palm out and Krispin found that he was able to obey the gesture.

'Stay, accursed Shath,' he commanded. 'He is not for you. You have had your day and here you will remain to trouble the innocent no more. In the names of Succoth-benoth, Nergal and Ashima I order you to quit him.'

The shriek that tore through Krispin's head was too terrible for mortal mind to bear and he fell to the ground unconscious.

Now Krispin wiped his forehead with the edge of his blanket and wondered who the old man was and why he had saved him. It was probable he would never learn the answer. So many strange things had befallen him since he had set out from the High Wald that he had begun to accept the marvellous as merely an element of the quest. What he mostly felt was gratitude to the deity for what seemed a miraculous intervention.

Danya and Alwald entered the narrow cabin.

'You certainly gave us a turn, Master Krispin,' said the shipmaster.

'I might have given you something more than that,' Krispin replied grimly.

'Were you taken ill?' asked Alwald.

'I was possessed,' said Krispin and he endeavoured to give an account of what had befallen him.

'No wonder all but the desperate or foolhardy shun the Cold Sea,' Danya said when the account was concluded. 'I blame myself for your ordeal for I had heard that there are isles in these waters that no man should set foot on, yet when I saw a harbour that would shelter us while we made repairs I never thought of danger.'

'It was not the place that was evil but what haunted it,' said Krispin.

'We are sailing south with a good wind and, bless the Mother, I have enough amber aboard to ensure that I shall never have to return to this forlorn clime,' the shipmaster continued. 'Thanks to Lord Alwald's magic needle we do not need to keep within sight of the coast which twists like a serpent but can venture across the open sea. Master Gambal is at the helm and it is time I relieved him. Stay abed as long as you need. An exhausted man is little use on deck.'

'I shall rest awhile,' said Krispin. 'I have been drained of my strength.'

When Danya left, Alwald said, 'I trust that this may be the last peril to be faced on the quest. There has been too much misadventure but now, if The Mage be right, the Lodestone will lead us directly to the Princess and then we can return to our people.'

'Have you not thought as to what will happen if and when we find the Princess and release her from her trance?'

'Our task will be done, surely, when we deliver her to followers of the Pilgrim Path who will present her to the people of Ythan.'

'The Regent may have something to say about that.'

'Such is the hatred for him that his words will count for nothing when the throne is no longer empty. Krispin, I must confess that when I stepped through that magic casement and saw my Lady Demara – whether in a dream of the future or through some magical illusion I care not – I knew that my duty lies in . . . in protecting her for the sake of my father. I weary of this travelling.'

'May it soon be over,' agreed Krispin.

'I must go and read the Lodestone,' muttered Alwald with a feeling that he had said more than he intended. 'I dare not risk it out of my hands.'

Some time later Ognam came with a bowl of pottage which he announced proudly had been prepared by Tana.

'It is amazing that one high-born can cook so well,' he said. 'To think of those slender fingers handling pots and ladles.'

'She probably finds it a pleasure after having her food provided by the tower's gramarye for so long,' said Krispin, and he thought: *He really has lost his heart to her, poor Ognam.*

Late that night Alwald stood alone at the helm holding the Lodestone in the light of the ship's lanthorn.

'It is a dismal watch,' said Tana appearing from the main deck with a cup of posset for him. 'What do you think about during the night hours?'

'Past times,' Alwald replied.

'That I can understand. During my captivity

there were masques that I relived a hundred times.'

'My father held masques at River Garde,' Alwald said. 'For the spring festival the castle was decked with green boughs from the woods and we were all attired in the garb of foresters. The peasants would elect the most beautiful girl as their Spring Queen and she would be crowned upon my father's throne. And the wine flowed in torrents.'

'It is a pleasure to talk to one who has such memories,' sighed Tana. 'As soon as I saw you I guessed that your station was different from the others.'

'We are an ill-assorted band. A toymaker, a one-time slaughterman and a jester, but we have survived much hardship together, and you have reason to be grateful to the latter.'

'Ognam? Oh yes, he served me as well as a prince in a folktale, only . . .'

' . . . only he is not a prince,' laughed Alwald. Tana joined his laughter.

'At my father's palace my favourite festivity was the celebration in honour of our lake which was held on midsummer's eve,' she said. 'A great floating platform was moored some distance from the shore. It was lit by flambeaux and on it musicians played soft airs and tables groaned beneath their burden of delicacies. In the palace we masked ourselves and donned whatever costumes our fancy took, and when the moon rose, a fleet of gondolas ferried us across the water to the raft, and there we danced until the dawn when a ritual gift was made to the lake.'

268

'A gift to a lake?'

'Yes. We sang the Taloon paean while casks of scented oil were poured on the waters. As the oil spread across the surface, it carried the most delicious odour. It might be musk or myrrh, attar or heliotrope; it was different every year and the scent lingered for days afterwards.'

'And in what disguise did you attend the dancing?'

'Cannot you guess, Lord Alwald?'

He laughed again and shook his head. 'For one like you there could be so many characters renowned for beauty.'

'I always went as the same one – the Lady of the Lake.'

And so they talked until the lanthorn light was dimmed by the coming of the day.

For several days and nights the *Amber Star* sailed steadily south out of sight of land, a speck on an empty sea beneath an empty sky. The only break in the monotonous seascape was the flash of a distant iceberg or the veils of coloured light which sometimes festooned the northern sky at night, a sight which made Danya mutter with a sailor's superstition.

Being young and not inflicted with too much imagination, Krispin soon recovered his strength and spirits. He enjoyed working the ship and volunteered to keep watch at the masthead for the twin hazards of corsairs and ice. He savoured the sensation of being alone with the wind singing in the rigging around him. Alwald spent much of his time on the poop deck with the Lodestone in his hand to keep whoever was steering in the right direction, a difficult task at times when fierce currents caught the ship and swirled her off course until the shipmaster managed to sail her out of their grip.

'If we were disabled and drifting, those ocean streams would carry us north, far past The Mage's tower, to a whirlpool that spins at the world's end so huge it swallows ships as a drain swallows straws,' he said. 'In the end all the ocean's wrecks, and those drowned in them, are engulfed by it.'

One morning the crew of the *Amber Star* found they were once more within sight of land, a low coastline whose covering of firs reassured them that they had indeed sailed a long way south, for in the region of The Mage's tower the only vegetation had been drifts of sepia wrack that the endless storms wrenched from the seabed.

From his vantage point on the mast Krispin saw that the land was a monotonous wilderness. The trees lay over it like a dark green carpet and no shrine spire or any other work of man broke their line.

It was noon when a dirty white column of smoke rose from a small bay and, slitting his eyelids against the glare of the sea, Krispin saw that it was billowing from a ship. At his shout the travellers crowded the rail and Danya, taking the helm from Gambal, headed for the stricken vessel.

'Look about you,' Danya shouted to Krispin. 'She may be a corsair's victim, and he may be hove-to.'

Krispin scanned the sea in every direction.

'I see nothing,' he reported.

As the *Amber Star* drew closer to the ship its crew saw a number of people, many of them in women's clothing, outlined against the smoke as they waved desperately from the bulwarks.

'Help us, for the love of the Mother.' Their piteous cries floated faintly across the intervening water.

'What can we do?' cried Ognam who like the others felt keen distress at the plight of their fellow seafarers.

'There is only one thing, we must take them off,' Danya answered. 'Get ready to lower the sail when we go alongside. Gambal, stand by to throw them a line.'

'It is strange there are no flames,' Tana remarked. 'Could they not row themselves ashore?'

'There will be fire enough below,' Nomis told her. 'And men lose their wits when a ship burns.'

'We must be quick,' shouted Alwald as he took up his position at the foot of the mast. 'That poor woman is holding a child.'

he pointed to where a mother held her baby over the side of the ship in an attempt to keep it clear of the smoke.

As Danya expertly piloted them towards the stricken vessel the cries of those aboard became jubilant.

'May the Mother bless you, may the Mother bless you!'

The *Amber Star* drew alongside and Alwald and Ognam prepared to lower the sail while Gambal and Krispin threw lines to seamen on the opposite deck.

A resounding cheer rent the smoky air . . . and then everything seemed to go mad. The mother dropped her baby into the sea and the women ripped away their gowns – the baby was merely a swaddled doll. Freed from their female clothing, bewigged men seized hidden axes and grappling hooks while other corsairs tossed bales of smouldering cloth over the side.

TEN

The Summoning

As the spires and turrets of Danaak emerged from the shadows with the coming of the dawn, Mandal unfolded the parchment that had been passed to him by the creature who had climbed down to the Cage, but it was not until the sun rose that he was able to read its message.

Greetings,

Like you I am cut off from the world, like you a victim of He who Rewards old Loyalties with Shameful Death. For myself suffice it to say that I must languish amid my experiments until my small store of food be consumed when perchance I shall have the courage to summon the Dark Maid with a merciful elixir. As for you, Commander, I recognised you from long ago when you were thrust into the Cage, and I have a proposition for you. It is possible I can help you to remove from your present indignity to my chamber where, with your resource and strength (alas lacking in one of my years) you may find a way to freedom. If so I shall expect you, on your soldier's honour, to

*take me with you. Should you find such escape
impossible, at least you will have the consolation
of avoiding the necessity of spending your last
hours as a public spectacle. My idea is thus . . .*

There followed a detailed plan which caused
Mandal to nod in agreement while his stomach
pains eased at the possibilities it suggested. The
missive concluded:

*Should this be agreeable to you, merely wave
when you see me at my window. And fear not the
appearance of the one who brought this message
to you, she may not be of our race but to me she
is as loyal as a child to its father.   Leodore*

Leodore?
There was something familiar about the name.
Mandal thought back to the days when he had
been stationed in the Citadel and had heard
whispers about a wonder-worker or magician
whom the Regent shielded from the Witchfinders
for some purpose of his own.
The thought that Leodore might provide him
with a means of escape renewed Mandal's failing
strength, and he waited impatiently for him to
appear at the window.

The Lady Eloira gazed over the parapet which
surrounded the flat roof of the Peak Tower. Purple
dusk fell over the distant mountains and the lake
of cloud which lay between them and the castle.
It thickened the air about the statues of the

274

Reeve's ancestors and the curious bronze device mounted on a plinth in the centre of the terrace. In appearance it resembled an astrolabe, and beside it stood a tall tripod supporting a venerable tome with wooden covers. In front of these instruments, a geometric design – a seven-pointed star within a double circle – had been traced on the marble paving in charcoal.

With an obvious effort Eloira, her eyes reddened from reading through the previous night and all this day, turned from the vaporous panorama and walked to the tripod with the aid of a carved staff. Her steward, a dignified figure in his olive robe of office, rose from a marble bench and stood beside her.

'I have deep doubts about what you are going to do, my lady,' he said. 'Please understand that it is your well-being which emboldens me to say so.'

'That I do understand, faithful Hans,' she answered, 'but I owe it to Krispin to do all that is within my power to help Jennet.'

'Within your power, yes. But conjuration is something else and can have fateful penalties.'

'My mind is made up. I shall invoke the last spell bequeathed to me. So say not another word but light the thurible.'

Shaking his snowy head, Hans produced tinder and bent to light incense in a silver vessel which, when white smoke curled from it, he swung to and fro on a chain.

Eloira removed the stopper from a jar of peacock blue porcelain and extracted a piece of black cord the length of a man's arm. Several kinks indicated where knots had been previously undone, and one remained tied tightly near the end. Was it a trick of the fading light or did the cord twist in her fingers of its own accord as she sought to unpick the knot?

The more she tried to loosen it, the more difficult the task became until Hans put down the thurible.

'Let me do it,' he cried impatiently. Obediently she surrendered the magical cord to him, and watched with equal impatience as his efforts appeared to be no more effective than hers.

'Hurry, Hans, or we will lose the light. Surely you can do better.'

'I am trying my best,' he retorted. 'Accursed gramarye! I am a fool to have aught to do with it.'

At that moment he had the sensation of the cord unravelling itself and a moment later he held it up unknotted. Eloira snatched it from him and threw it into the centre of the seven-pointed star where it squirmed like a thin black serpent. She turned to the book supported on the tripod and began reading an incantation in Old Ythan while Hans swung the censer. Aromatic smoke swirled about them.

For a while the only sound was the sonorous sentences which Eloira pronounced with surprising power, then from afar came a roll of thunder. The old steward looked up to see if it were about to rain, then with a shiver realised it was a preternatural accompaniment to his mistress's words.

As the ritual continued, the cord in the centre of the pentangle continued to coil until the dusk above it lightened. At first it was merely a paleness without a form, a shadow in reverse; then it slowly assumed the shape of a cone which stood above the star to the height of a man.

'It comes!' Hans exclaimed.

Eloira ignored him. With her finger she traced the lines of black script before her and chanted as loud as her old throat would allow.

Silver motes filled the cone and the light they generated shone on the intent faces of the two old people. Out of this radiant dust a figure materialised, a boy with golden hair framing a face of infinite beauty. Indeed, it was so well-formed that it transgressed the normal concept of beauty and the words 'terrible beauty' formed in Eloira's mind as she gazed at the being she had raised.

Thunder rumbled and incense smoke streamed as though caught by a wind, though neither Eloira nor Hans felt movement in the air.

'You summoned – I have come.'

The words, spoken in Old Ythan, sounded too deep for a boy and this added to the awesomeness of the spectacle.

'Why have you drawn me from so far? Do you not fear the consequence, not just to your body but your spirit, of beholding one such as I?'

From between the pages of the grimoire Eloira extracted a piece of parchment on which – not trusting her memory in such circumstances – she had written a number of sentences.

'I have summoned you, Tartak, because of your

277

obligation to my ancestor that was sealed by a knot. That knot is undone and I demand your aid.'

Amid the minute floating lights, the boyish apparition smiled a smile of menace.

'Demand? Demand? You dare to make a *demand* of one of the Children of Yth who roamed the world before your kind made a footstep? Do you not know that I have to sing but one note and you would be naught but a pile of ashes? Or, worse, I need but show you my other appearance.'

'Be that as it may,' answered the Lady Eloira, 'but in the formulary it states the word to be used is "demand". As for appearances, your beauty is such that you would do yourself injustice if you do not stay exactly as you are.'

Within the shimmering cone the boy laughed and it was a boyish laugh.

'Say on, old woman. What boon do you *demand*? Some years of youth regained? Be careful of that one, it never works out as is hoped. Speech with one whom the Maid took with words left unsaid? Not silver, surely? No, my guess is that you would treasure wisdom above all else, but do you not know that commodity is to be found in the depths of a well?'

'I want naught for myself,' said Eloira.

'That makes a change for a mortal,' chuckled the boy. 'Wealth, personal beauty, requited love, revenge . . . those are common aspirations of your kind and, if I may say so, very tedious they are.'

'Tartak, this is what I want,' said Eloira firmly, and from her parchment she read a carefully composed request couched in archaic terms.

When she concluded, the boy was hugging himself.

'You summoned a Child of Yth for that?' he laughed. 'Ho! Ho! I like your audacity. In return for that which the knot was tied I shall briefly quicken the stock.'

'So be it,' returned Eloira ritually.

The voice of the boy resumed its menacing depth. 'And thus ends the obligation.'

'So be it.'

The motes of light swirled like a miniature snowstorm round the radiant figure. It became indistinct, then vanished as the light faded. Thunder muttered and died far in the distance and the incense smoke rose straight.

The steward dropped the thurible and caught his mistress as she collapsed.

The sky was rapidly changing from mauve to purple when Jennet was allowed to sit with her back against a stone outcrop. All day she had obediently trekked after Mordan as he sought a way over the ranges but each trail they followed had ended at impassable snow banks or under the frowning faces of precipes.

'Tomorrow we will find the way,' he reassured her as he passed her travellers' bread and dried fruits.

She nodded without conviction.

'You want to see your precious Krispin again, do you not?'

Again she nodded, this time with conviction.

From this high point the view was magnificent.

Rock-strewn slopes fell away to the High Wald covered by unbroken forest. In the distance the cloud surrounding the Peak Tower became a sheet of gold as the sun cast her final rays upon it; further still the River of Night was transmuted for a few moments into a river of light, a gleaming thread beyond which the Outlands were already under the shadow of approaching night. Far away there was a growl of summer thunder among the peaks.

Jennet placed her doll on a piece of rock that formed a natural seat.

'That is just the right size for you, Dolly,' she said in a voice loud enough for Mordan to hear. 'Rest now. We are all very, very tired.'

But not only was she weary, she was confused. Through the day there were times when she was a child and others when she felt completely different, when half-formed memories swam into her head and she had the sensation that if only she could make a great effort of will everything would become clear. And like a frightening accompaniment to these thoughts was the remembrance of the nomads with wolf skull helmets killing men in the pass . . . and not only in the pass but somewhere else where women shrieked and cottages burgeoned into flame. Oh, how much happier she was as a child!

'Dolly,' she said. 'It will be cold up here tonight so I shall wrap you cosy in my shawl.'

And at her words the doll's head turned and the rosebud mouth smiled.

*   *   *

The witch woman in the corner was dying. She looked vacantly into Mandal's face when he squeezed water into her parched mouth but uttered no word, and when he took her clawlike hand he was shocked at the heat radiating from it.

'Poor gammer,' he muttered as he resumed his seat in the corner and waited for the moon to set. It was already half a disk made jagged by the gambrel roofs of the sleeping city. Below, the watchman's fire flared yellow and its smoke drifted up through the Cage. The woodsmoke took him back to his happy boyhood in the woodlands where his father was a hunter and where he would have followed his calling had he not been caught by a recruiting squad – 'A crown for every likely lad, men!' – to become a soldier in the Regent's army.

The roof teeth devoured the moon and darkness engulfed Danaak. Above him Leodore must have been waiting with equal impatience, for within a couple of minutes Mandal heard the scratch of talons on the wall and he made out the bizarre shape of the old man's messenger against the faint starshine. When she reached the bars above him she pushed through another rolled bundle of cloth and climbed out of sight. Having read Leodore's detailed instructions several times during the day, he knew what to expect as he carefully unfastened it.

His fingers closed on a piece of bread from Leodore's dwindling store that the alchemist had sent to renew his strength, and there was also a small flask of wine. Next he came to a file, and a

281

bottle of oil that would ease the work ahead and soften the sound of metal upon metal.

Standing upright, Mandal worked on one of the overhead bars close to the wall. Metal filings dusted his face as his arms rose and fell, but soon he was panting with exhaustion and his starved limbs felt like lead. It was the wine that enabled him to continue, urged on by the thought that he must cut through three bars before dawn began to lighten the eastern sky.

An hour later he felt the third bar part and then he had to summon up what remained of his strength to force a gap large enough to haul his thickset body through. But before he attempted this he unrolled the rest of the bundle which was made up of an old blanket, breeches and a tunic. Careful not to let anything fall through the floor lattice, he changed into the new clothing and then stuffed his own garments with the blankets to create a crude dummy. This he laid in a curled position in the corner of the Cage so that when the crowd stared up in the morning they would think that he was either dead or lying in a stupor. And as corpses were never removed from the Cage it might be a while before the deception was discovered.

Having completed these preparations he crossed to the old woman whose breath rasped ominously.

'Farewell, gammer,' he muttered, and as he turned away he realised he had felt closer to the old witch than any other person in his adult life, perhaps because in doing what he could for her it was the first time that he felt needed by a fellow human.

'Wait.'

He spun round and leaned over her.

Making a supreme effort to form her words, she gasped, 'Because I confessed . . . I . . . was not searched. I want you . . . to have . . . this . . . dearie.'

Her palsied hand sought his and he felt a coiled chain and a metal disk placed in it.

Probably a witch charm, he thought and hung it round his neck. Aloud he said, 'I shall ever keep it, gammer.' She made no reply; her breathing reminded him of the panting of a hunted animal that can run no more.

Mandal drained the flask, pulled himself up through the aperture and squatted on the bars to bend those that he parted back into position. Then his hand encountered a rope, made out of plaited strips of cloth, which hung from the window above.

'Serene Mother, give me enough strength,' he prayed.

The Companion of the Rose, his surcoat rent and bloody, rocked with fatigue as he was led by one of his fellow guards up a staircase in a remote part of the Citadel.

'It is evil luck, Karik, that after such a rough journey you reach Danaak to learn our master is on a progress,' said the guide. 'Something must have decided him on the spur of the moment, and he took half the guard with him under Bors. All very odd, if you ask me, but these are strange days. Some reckon it might be the Red Death that helped

283

him make up his mind, but none of the troops returning from the Thaan campaign survived the Raven Pass so the city is not endangered.'

The two Companions halted at a door and Karik leaned against the wall while the other rapped a special signal on the carved wood. A servant opened the door and, being without speech, nodded for Karik to enter.

'Good luck with the Hag,' the Companion muttered. 'And keep a good watch on yourself – it can be a riskful time in the Citadel when he is away.'

Karik nodded and was shown into the presence of the Lady Mandraga who sat on a throne-like chair with her skeletal fingers resting on the crosspiece of her crutch.

'Wine for the Companion,' she ordered. 'You may sit for I see you are wounded and have travelled far.'

'I have ridden from the High Wald with dire news for my Lord Regent,' he said, lowering himself onto a tabouret.

'The Lord Regent is gone three days and three nights down the Green River,' said the Lore Mistress. 'In his absence you must confide in me.'

'It is simply that the Wolf King has broken his agreement, my lady,' he said. 'Our men guarding the only pass that leads into the Wald were treacherously massacred. I fled to bring word and as I looked back they were already pouring through it.'

Mandraga gestured to him to drink the wine the mute had proffered and then she questioned him in detail. Finally she said, 'What do you believe these barbarians seek?'

'Danaak,' he replied sombrely.

'You have done well to bring word to me, Companion,' she said. 'But do not make mention of it outside this room. Go, have a chirurgeon dress your wounds and then take the rest you need. When you are refreshed we will talk again.'

When he had gone, Mandraga closed her eyes in thought. In her vivid inner vision she could picture a vast array of wolfmen riding across the plains, clouds of dust rolling behind them, the light of holy fanaticism in their eyes as they sought to do the will of their Wolf-in-the-Sky.

Throughout Ythan there were military forces capable of countering raids by loot-hungry reivers or putting down revolts, but the army capable of meeting such an invasion had been lost to the Red Death. It would take a commander of outstanding ability to get a suitable force into the field at short notice, and there was only one that came to her mind.

'Mandal,' she said aloud.

ELEVEN

The Spirit of Mercy

'Corsairs!'

The shipmaster's furious cry echoed over the deck of the *Amber Star*. He was answered with jeers as the men on the opposite ship hauled on the ropes to bring their victim within boarding distance.

Krispin ran into his cabin and tugged Woundflame from its scabbard. Its blade was not only gleaming but beaded with what appeared to be minute droplets of blood – the Death Dew which warned that conflict was at hand. A moment later he was back on deck and saw that the gap between the two vessels was almost narrow enough for the enemy to leap across.

A giant of a man, still wearing the lavender cloak of a fashionable lady, jumped , his heavy, sickle-bladed axe poised to strike. He landed on the deck with the ease of a cat and aimed a blow at Gambal who was endeavouring to release the line he had flung out as a merciful gesture a few moments earlier. He drew his body back so that the glittering blade missed his chest by a hand's breadth, and at that moment Krispin lunged with Woundflame.

The bedewed sword appeared to vanish into the corsair's mail shirt; the man opened his mouth to scream but only bloody froth passed his lips, then he thudded to the deck. Biting his lip with revulsion, Krispin had to put his foot on the convulsed body in order to withdraw the blade.

A roar of fury greeted the downfall of the champion. Pirates climbed onto their ship's bulwark to spring over and avenge him but there was something berserk about Krispin as he raced along the deck severing both the mooring ropes and grapple lines with his reddened weapon that made them hesitate.

'Up sail! Up sail!' Danya shouted from the poop and the others heaved on the halyards to hoist the yardarm back into position.

Another corsair reached the deck but while he tried to gain his balance Woundflame dealt him a gaping chest wound.

At that moment the sail of the *Amber Star* caught the wind and billowed so taut its sheets creaked under the strain. Danya swung the tiller and she rolled away from the corsair. Several men who had flung themselves across the widening gap plummeted into the sea. One managed to hang by his fingers from the rail – until Gambal brought a belaying pin down on them with all his strength.

On the deck of the corsair, men struggled to raise the sail and sweeps were run out to give her extra speed. Archers took up position in the bows.

'Keep down,' shouted Danya throwing himself flat as the first volley of arrows embedded themselves in woodwork or smacked impotently against the yielding sail. He remained on his back with only his arm upraised to keep the helm in position until the *Amber Star* raced out of range.

When he stood up again he saw that the corsair – the name *Spirit of Mercy* was painted in gold beneath her bows – was in pursuit.

'Over the side with the bodies,' he shouted with his seaman's regard for orderliness. 'And sluice the deck. Lord Alwald, I want you to take charge of the mangonel.'

The two corpses were pushed over the bulwark while Krispin leaned wearily against the mast and wiped clean Woundflame's blade which had now returned to its usual dull state.

'Are you all right?' Ognam asked as he washed away the bloodstains.

Krispin nodded. 'The trouble with killing is that it gets easier each time.'

On the poop deck Alwald removed the canvas cover from the mangonel and looked it over with a professional eye. There had been several of these engines mounted on the ramparts of River Garde and he had often joined the men-at-arms in practise firings. Meanwhile Gambal and old Nomis struggled up the hatchway with casks of pitch in their arms.

'Let them see that we have some teeth,' said Danya.

'Willingly,' Alwald answered, 'though with the ship plunging as she is I cannot promise success. The trick will be to fire at the moment we are poised on the brow of a swell.'

He loaded a cask in the mangonel, removed its circular lid and squinted along the sighting mechanism. After making adjustments he nodded to Gambal who thrust a blazing torch into the mixture of tar and naphtha the cask contained. Flame spurted upwards and a moment later, when the *Amber Star* hung on the back of a ridge-like wave, Alwald tugged the release lever and the blazing missile hurtled towards the *Spirit of Mercy* like a comet with a tail of smoke. It fell a dozen paces in front of the corsair and threw up a geyser of steam.

'Good, they will know what to expect at closer quarters,' declared Danya.

'Except that their bowmen will be able to rake the deck,' said Alwald gloomily.

'Perhaps they will grow tired of the chase if we can keep ahead of them long enough,' said Tana who, wrapped in her black cloak, gazed at the pursuing vessel.

'Not they!' Nomis asserted. 'They know that coming from the Cold Sea we must have amber aboard, and they would follow us to the world's end for that.'

Through the afternoon the chase continued and as the wind lessened the *Spirit of Mercy*, having the advantage of two banks of oars, began to overhaul the *Amber Star*.

'When we were attacked before, I managed to escape into a bank of fog,' muttered Danya. 'I cannot expect such luck a second time,'

Nomis disappeared down the hatchway and returned carrying a locked bronze-bound chest which he deposited carefully in the bows. He then brought up several more and threaded a length of robe through their handles. This he lashed to the anchor so that, if released from its chain by knocking out the shackle bolt, it would pull the boxes into the depths.

'Our amber,' said Danya. 'The old fellow will sink it rather than let it fall into corsair hands.'

'Mayhap we could bargain with it,' said Ognam, his face unusually anxious when he glanced at Tana.

The shipmaster was about to make a retort and then, as the girl was in earshot, thought better of it and merely said, 'Mayhap, Master Jester, mayhap.'

The wind seemed intent on tantalising them. As the *Spirit of Mercy* drew closer it freshened and sent them surging ahead only to drop again. With her sail flapping listlessly, the *Amber Star* wallowed. She was almost within arrow range of the corsair when a gust blew spindrift from the wave crests and the next moment a stiff breeze moaned across the sea and sent her leaping forward once more.

'Often I think that whoever it is who rules our destinies is a joker,' said Ognam sometime later as the wind became erratic again. 'A joker who likes to play tricks on us petty mortals. As long as we provide amusement by having our hopes blighted just when we believe all will be well, we are permitted to survive – until the next divine jest. But once the joker gets bored with our antics we are cast into the dark like discarded toys, for there are always fresh playthings for the joker to set up and knock down.'

'That sounds like blasphemy,' said Nomis, 'and I doubt not that you are right.'

'Philosophy from the Fool,' muttered Gambal. 'I believe a man can make his own luck . . .'

He stopped dead as he remembered such a conversation with his lost love Lorelle who had wanted desperately to believe that she was mistress of her destiny. Now she lay beneath a simple monument in the Domain of Olam, and Gambal realised his desire of avenging her someday had displaced the memory of her as a person . . .

Strange that such thoughts should occur to him when his own death might be less than an hour away. But everyone's thoughts were interrupted by a shout from Krispin high on the lookout platform. They ran to the bows and could just discern a thin white column rising above the shore several leagues ahead.

'A light-tower,' cried Danya. They who had not been to sea before turned to him questioningly.

'At night, or in a storm, it shows a great light to guide vessels to port. If we can reach it we shall be safe because no corsair would dare follow us into a protected harbour.'

'Can you be sure that it is protected?' asked Ognam.

'Where there are corsairs, all harbours are protected.'

'Pray the Mother the wind holds,' said Nomis, 'and mayhap we will get the amber to market after all.'

A slender symbol of hope, the tower lifted their spirits and Alwald and Gambal returned to the mangonel to send several more blazing casks astern as a gesture of new-found defiance. The tower was also visible to the corsairs and had the effect of making them redouble their efforts, for not only was the thought of plunder sweet but they burned to avenge their comrades who had fallen to Woundflame. The men at the sweeps forgot their fatigue as they pulled to the beat of the oarmaster's tabor.

The chase continued and the tower became clearer, as did the harbour behind it lined with the roofs of venerable buildings. The masts of a couple of moored vessels rose above its mole. But most reassuring was the huge trebuchet at the base of the light-tower which was being hastily manned. Such engines were designed to hurl boulders into besieged cities. When the captain of the *Spirit of Mercy* saw his quarry sail within range of this mighty weapon he sheered away to search the sea for a more likely victim. All cursed but not one of the corsairs would have willingly approached the harbour.

On the breakwater, spectators cheered as the *Amber Star* swept past the light-tower and into the harbour. The sail dropped and the sweeps manoeuvred her to a quay where eager hands caught her mooring lines. Laughing with relief, the companions looked about them. Tall timber-framed houses and taverns with steeply gabled roofs lined the stone-flagged waterfront on which were piled barrels and bales of merchandise. More gambrel roofs were visible on the steep hill rising behind, as were the turrets of the high defensive wall which protected the town. Here and there banners displaying heraldic beasts floated from gilded flagpoles.

No sooner had the lines been made fast to iron mooring rings than a group of richly dressed folk made their way through the crowd to the quay. The most richly dressed of all stood on the edge and raised his hand in welcome.

'As burgomaster I am happy to offer you sanctuary and to say how grateful we are for your deliverance from the accursed corsairs,' he said with a warm smile. 'As you are in need of rest – and later entertainment, no doubt – I will provide watchmen for your craft so you can all come ashore as guests of our town.'

A matronly woman with a merry smile stepped beside him.

'And I invite you to be guests at my inn the Marlin,' she said. 'You will find the beds soft, the ale strong and the food . . . ' Here she kissed her fingers to suggest its excellence.

'Would you tell us the name of this haven?' said Danya from the poop. 'Though I have sailed to the Cold Sea several times I do not know this stretch of coast.'

'You have already said it,' laughed the burgomaster. 'It is Haven.'

TWELVE
The Gala Night

'There is nothing so good as being snug in a port after riding out a storm – or having been chased by corsairs,' declared Danya, raising his tankard in the Marlin inn. The rest of the company were seated round a highly polished table with wine or ale in front of them according to taste. The drinks had been paid for by the friendly folk who packed the inn and who, when thanked, merely grinned and toasted them. Most had witnessed the dramatic arrival of the *Amber Star* and welcomed those who sailed in her as heroes.

'It is good to be in a normal town amid normal people at last,' said Ognam. 'No gramarye, no monsters, no pirates! Such a pretty place and what a cosy inn. Haven! It could not be better named.'

'I seem to remember hearing The Mage mention that name,' Alwald mused.

'I think he meant that we should not come here as it would be off our route,' said Danya. 'But after meeting the *Mercy* I followed the coast in the hope that we would find such a place as this or, if the worst came to the worst, beach the *Star* after

294

nightfall and hide in the forest. I have no doubt that when we set out again, Lord Alwald's Lodestone will soon set us back upon our proper course.'

'How does it feel to be in the company of men and women again after being shut away from the world?' Gambal asked Tana who, in her black and silver gown, was the focus of all eyes. Her animated expression was an answer in itself.

The merry landlady arrived at the table with two serving wenches carrying trays on which soup bowls gave off delicious steam.

'First course,' she announced. 'Eat well and then enjoy the celebration.'

'Celebration?'

'Tonight is gala night in Haven. Soon you will hear the music, and the square will be lit for dancing.'

She looked boldly at Danya. 'You seem a likely man and one of my age, Shipmaster. Shall we show the young ones how to step a reel tonight?'

'That we will,' laughed Danya.

When the meal was over, the companions retired to change their garments for the evening and Krispin sought the bath house where he lay soaking in a great tub of hot water. Although no blood had splashed him in his fight with the corsairs, he had an overwhelming need to cleanse himself. He had begun to doze with his chin just above the water when Alwald crossed the puddled tiles.

'It is carnival and you snore in the bath!' he cried cheerfully. 'Climb out and come with us for it is high time we forgot the quest for one night and had some enjoyment. The Mother knows it has been a scarce commodity of late.'

Thus encouraged Krispin surfaced and hurried to his room where he donned his best breeches and jerkin and a silken shirt of dark green, costly apparel which had been given him by Mesire Florizan in the Domain of Olam. When he joined the party he saw that Gambal and Alwald were equally attired. Ognam, as ever, retained his red and green motley.

When the landlady, who was known as Dame Floris, led them along the brightly lit quay from the Marlin many townsfolk turned to stare at the well-dressed strangers.

Lanterns with glass of many different colours were strung along the waterfront and here and there flambeaux threw capering shadows; music was in the air and silken banners billowed and drooped as warm airs wafted fitfully from the sea. Revellers promenaded wearing an assortment of masks ranging from the beautiful to the grotesque.

Soon they reached a square with one side opening on to the harbour where the mast of the *Amber Star* was silhouetted against the reflected lights, and here they seated themselves at one of the tables ranged round it. Immediately a smiling girl brought them a jug of dark wine and when Alwald felt for one of his few coins to pay, she shook her head and explained that during gala night liquor was free. On a platform overlooking the square, musicians tuned their instruments in preparation for the dancing.

Laughter rose all around them. A fire-eater stood in the centre of the square and from his mouth sent streamers of orange flame leaping to incredible heights. When his act was completed, the crowd, having noticed Ognam's costume, called loudly upon him to entertain them. He smiled and waved his hand to suggest that on this night he was merely a spectator like themselves but as tankards continued to crash on tables, and the chanted word 'Jongleur! Jongleur!' rose higher and higher, he stood up with a foolish grimace. Krispin noticed a frown cross Tana's face as with a comical cry he leaped into the square and then to the surprise of his companions performed a series of somersaults to land neatly on his feet.

'Lords and ladies of Haven,' he declaimed. 'Strolling players such as I are creatures of conceits and fancies, purveyors of laughter and dreams, tellers of tales, mountebanks perhaps, and yet beneath the motley I – we – are children who still see the world with eyes of wonder, who sigh for beauty and . . . ' here he looked to the table where his party sat '. . . who can lose our hearts.'

His tone suddenly changed, became brisk. 'Lords and ladies, my fellow voyagers and I thank you for your welcome and for a few minutes I shall repay such bountiful hospitality with some tricks and ditties which, I say in all humility, affected the great Regent of Ythan so much that I was rewarded with free board and lodging in his palace.'

The jongleur flapped his arms, crowed like a cockerel and holding to his lips his jester's staff, which was holed like a flute, began to play a tune so rollicking and fast that within seconds the revellers were tapping and clapping. As he played he skipped so wildly that his knees almost touched his chin in quick succession and his head wagged from side to side.

This was followed by bawdy jokes, a comic song, more pipe music and then a love song sung with surprising sweetness which brought a hush to the square. The moment it was completed he changed the mood again by a tumbling act, after which he bowed amid cheers. A woman in the crowd threw a flower which he caught deftly, pressed it to his lips with a flourish and then returned to his table.

His moonface was glistening with sweat as he seated himself and with a shy smile presented the red rose to Tana who accepted it graciously and laid it beside her goblet.

'A token, a mere token.' Ognam said quickly. 'Ah, it was good to have an audience again.'

The musicians struck up and the dancing began. Dame Floris seized Danya by the arm and whirled him into the throng; a young woman wearing a gilded mask took Alwald by the hand; and Gambal, with a formal bow, asked Tana if she would do him the honour. Nomis, to his own amazement, was invited to dance by another masked lady and thus Ognam and Krispin were left alone at the table, the carnival on one side and the still water of the harbour on the other.

'You seem rather glum for such an occasion,' remarked the jongleur pouring wine for them both. 'Is there aught wrong?'

'It seems strange that some hours ago I was

298

killing men and now I am in the middle of a gala,' replied Krispin. 'At the time we were all so intent on saving ourselves that I gave the matter little thought, but now it comes back to me.'

'Yet if it had not been for you and your remarkable sword we might be performing a saraband on the seabed,' said Ognam raising his cup.

'That is true and yet I do not feel right about it,' said Krispin, following his example. 'The truth is, my friend, I am still a toymaker at heart. Quests and adventures are very well for such as Alwald, but I would be more happy to be at my bench with good sharp tools than wandering the world in search of someone else's dream.'

'I understand,' said Ognam with a sigh. 'Yet fate – or the Mother – does not let us choose our wyrds. It was not your intention to be other than a maker of wooden soldiers and rocking horses yet you now follow a quest because your bench was burned and Toyheim is no more.'

'It is a bitter thought,' said Krispin gloomily, and he raised his cup. 'Looking back, my life in the High Wald was like paradise but, fool that I was, I did not know it then.'

'You are not alone,' said Ognam. 'As a youth I burned to be a poet, to write lines that would fill men's hearts with glorious fire – and you have just seen the outcome of that.'

Krispin nodded with the solemnity of one who, while not drunk, has enjoyed several cups of wine.

'And yet,' continued Ognam, 'mayhap not all youthful ambition is lost. To my own surprise I find the poetic urge returning after all these barren years.' He glanced to where the carmine rose lay on the table. 'It is a question of inspiration, Krispin, a question of inspiration.'

'Tana.'

The jongleur nodded and the bells sewn to his motley tinkled incongruously. 'I feel poems rising within me like bubbles rising in wine. What curiosities we mortals be – to be elated by the sight of another.'

'It was you who behaved like an errant knight,' said Krispin whose words had begun to slur slightly. 'You rescued her from captivity like . . . like an errant knight.'

'I fear that she may no longer see me in that light.'

He turned to look at the dancing crowd and, catching sight of Tana laughing as she showed Gambal the movements of a galliard, sighed deeply.

A pox on Gambal, thought Krispin. Aloud he said, 'You must expect her to be merry after so long beneath The Mage's tower.'

'That I understand. And who am I to—'

'A poet,' interjected Krispin. 'You have the spirit of a poet.'

At that moment a masquerader appeared at the table. She was dressed in a black gown that did nothing to obscure the voluptuous line of her figure but her face was hidden by a beautiful silver mask on which the lineaments of a goddess were drawn. Above the forehead, lacy fretwork decorated with black arabesques suggested a headdress. The only sign of humanity was the two eyes shining behind black-rimmed slits.

'You should not sit staring into your wine when all the world is dancing,' said a light-hearted voice. 'Not often is it gala night in Haven so when music plays all must tread its measure.'

The festive lanterns threw glints of colour onto the mask.

'My name is Gayl,' continued the warm voice behind it, 'and as this is the gala night I must be obeyed, so come dance with me.' When the girl stretched out her hands to Krispin he took them and rose to his feet. The goddess-mask turned towards Ognam.

'Forgive me, Sir Jester, if I deprive you of your companion for a little while.'

Ognam laughed. 'You do not know it but you do me a favour. Phrases jostle in my brain, demanding I give them life.'

As the couple vanished among the merrymakers he produced a piece of parchment and an inkstick from his scrip and began to write quickly as though afraid of losing the words before he captured them in his florid lettering.

When, with remarkably few corrections, his verses were complete, he read them through, raising his winecup with every line. Then he folded the parchment, wrote Tana's name upon it and laid it beside the rose, after which he stood up a little unsteadily and strolled along the quay.

As Krispin danced with the girl in the goddess-mask, for a while his gloom receded – until he remembered the last time he danced had been with Jennet at her name-day feast in Toyheim's ornately carved hall. Despite the music and laughter about them, his partner immediately sensed his change of mood and led him from the throng to the table overlooking the dark water, where she poured him a cup of wine.

'I am sorry your heart is not light on this night of all nights,' she said.

'And I apologise that it needs to be lightened,' he answered. 'Not that many hours have passed since I was wiping blood from my sword . . .'

'Then let us walk and mayhap if you talk to a masked stranger you will feel eased.'

He nodded.

'Your old companion seems not to share your gloom,' she said, pointing to the dancers. Krispin looked in the direction she indicated and was amazed to see Nomis dancing like a man of half his years. His usual irascible expression was replaced with a delighted grin as he cavorted opposite the dominoed lady who had drawn him into the square.

'For once his mind is on something other than amber,' said Krispin. 'Tonight he is regaining his youth.'

'Come,' said the girl. 'Let us walk along the harbour away from the noise.' And hand in gloved hand they followed the lights which hung like glowing fruit along the quay.

A few minutes later Gambal and Tana returned to the table, out of breath and laughing and thirsty for wine. As she sat down she held up the rose to catch its scent and then, noticing the folded parchment, picked it up and scanned the lines which read:

Come, my belov'd, and drink the dark red wine
While gala laughter fills the evening air.
A carmine rose shall be my fortune's sign
That new content shall banish old despair.

The sleepy sea shall murmur its slow rhyme
And stars put harbour lights to shame –
Then shall this jester tell of ancient time
And lovers who caressed their way to fame?

Or is there need to speak a prosey word
If beside me you will walk this night?
Old loves can keep their tales unheard –
'Tis you, lov'd friend, who are my Heart's Delight.

'A love letter from Master Jongleur?' said Gambal.

Tana made no reply but folding the parchment she placed it in the bosom of her gown.

In his room at the inn Krispin lay on the bed, his mind maudlin with wine, and watched the girl whose silver mask gleamed in a shaft of moonlight slanting through the small dormer window.

'I would like to see you without your mask,' he said.

'I can do better than that,' she answered. She removed her gloves and then with a supple movement let her gown slip slowly to the floor to reveal her naked in the moonlight.

'Gayl, you are beautiful,' Krispin said simply as

he gazed upon her ivory skin. Though her figure was slender, her breasts were full like ripe fruits and in his hazy state he wanted no more than to lay his face upon them and forget the world.

She sat on the bed beside him, her warm fingers slid beneath his shirt and caressed his chest, and then moved down his body.

'You are beautiful,' he repeated and raised his hands to her shoulders only to let them glide to her breasts which he grasped with a surge of excitement, making her exclaim behind the black lips of her mask.

'Gently, Krispin, gently, my love. Lips are softer than hands.'

For long minutes they held each other while waves of increasing desire swept Krispin, but each time she hushed him so that his urgency built up and up until the only thing that mattered in the world was to find sanctuary in her smooth body.

Then Krispin found himself gazing down on the silver mask while her warmth teased him, then her indrawn breath echoed his relief as he entered her. Together they were swept away by a night tide of pleasure until nerve and muscle could no longer stand the tension. Gayl voiced her satisfaction with a shuddering cry as he felt his very essence flow into her to be replaced with a sense of dawning serenity.

For a long time they lay still part of each other, their bodies held by a sheen of sweat while the surge of their pulses gradually lessened to the throb of a distant drum. At length they parted like spent combatants and lay in strangely formal attitudes side by side. The effects of release and wine pressed heavy upon Krispin and he fought to prevent his eyelids closing.

'Krispin, my love, why leave Haven?' Gayl spoke in a voice that seemed to come from a great distance rather than from behind the mask that still remained in place. 'Why not stay with me and rest from the tribulations that have beset you? Haven is a fair place where you will be content as my master . . . always . . .'

He made a great effort against the black sleep that was descending upon him.

'Gayl, you are beautiful – even more now that we know each other thus – and I would not be a man if your words did not tempt me, yet I cannot.'

'Krispin, there is rest here, and forgetfulness from the pain of the world. Your companions will be sure to stay, so why travel on alone and lonely?'

'I made a promise . . .'

'Say you will stay and I shall show you my face and in all the world you will not find its like. I shall be yours for ever, loving you, and yours to use as you will. Say you will stay, Krispin, and we shall explore pleasures such as you have only had inkling of in dreams. Stay in Haven, my love. Only *declare* that you will stay . . .'

But Krispin's eyelids closed and he heard no more.

When Krispin awoke he believed he was still in the grip of some bewildering nightmare. He was alone and instead of lying on a comfortable inn bed he was on the cracked floor of a ruin. He shivered as a salty breeze whined through a gaping hole in what might once have been a window.

'Gayl,' he called but the only response was the desolate cry of a gull.

Shocked into full wakefulness he stood up painfully and gazed out expecting to see the houses of Haven dreaming over their reflections in the harbour. Instead he saw only unroofed walls crumbling into rubble, the harbour mole subsiding under the sea's relentless attack and a light-tower that some long-ago catastrophe had rent from crown to base.

Book Three

Beyond the Mountains of the Moon
The Sleeping Beauty dreams.
Take a candle to her couch
And see her in its beams.

Prince or pauper, for her sake,
Kiss her quick and let her wake!

Long ago she was bespelled
And hidden out of sight.
She has slept a hundred years
In what seems a night.

Knight or jester, best beware,
You are in a witch's lair!

Kiss her rosy lips so red,
Stroke her lovely breast –
Sleeping Beauty will be yours
When you break her rest.

Smith or sailor, be not shy,
Kiss her quick or she will die!

Treasure all around her lies
In her cavern cold . . .
And if you want a happy life
Leave her for the gold.

– words from Ythan children's rhyming game.

ONE

High Wind
over Ythan

Krispin looked about the decayed walls of the
Marlin in fearful bewilderment, his mind haunted
by an alarming childhood tale of a man who had
gone to sleep in an enchanted forest to awaken
after a century had passed. The sight of his pack
gave him solace; no rot or mildew suggested that
it had been lying beside him for an unnatural
length of time. He slung one of its straps over his
shoulder, seized Woundflame and hurried down
lichened steps to the great room where – or so it
seemed – he and his companions had drunk and
dined the night before. It was equally empty and
dilapidated.

'Serene Mother be praised!' cried Danya
catching sight of him. 'Lad, I know not whether
I am mad or dreaming – but if it is a dream, at
least we share it.'

'I wish it was a dream,' Krispin said. 'Then we
would awake and find things as they were.'

'It is more like a jest played by evil spirits,' said

Danya. 'Or is it the same as happened to you on the Amber Isle.'

'No. There it was just a voice within my head. Here everything was real. The people at the gala were flesh and blood.'

'No doubt of that, and none more than Dame Floris . . . ' His voice trailed away, and they looked at each other as memory of willing arms returned.

'I never even saw her face,' Krispin muttered as a wave of sadness eclipsed his shock. 'And yet she asked me to remain in Haven.'

'And so it was with me,' said Danya. 'Floris wanted me to stay and share the inn with her. The mellowing of drink made it seem a fair prospect but I told her I was under oath to complete this voyage. Still she begged me to declare that I would stay, and I felt mean-hearted when I gainsaid her.' An expression of intense regret creased his weathered face as he continued gruffly, 'Let us see the state of our ship – if indeed we still have one.'

Outside the derelict inn they found Alwald, Gambal, Ognam and Tana gazing at the ruinous harbour in disbelief. What had been neat paving beneath their feet the night before was now shattered and partly covered with drifts of sand; the tall half-timbered houses of yesterday were empty shells with caving roofs, but to their relief the *Amber Star*, moored further along the sagging quay, appeared unaffected.

'Speculation can come later,' said Alwald. 'Let us begone from this hexed place.'

The others needed no encouragement and they set off with many a sideways glance at the ruins.

'I cannot believe that here I had an audience,' said Ognam as they crossed the square that the night before had been aswirl with dancers beneath the glow of coloured lanterns. 'Afterwards, when I took a stroll through the streets, the burgomaster followed and pressed me hard to stay as resident jongleur.'

'Why did you resist such an offer?' asked Gambal sourly.

Ognam glanced at Tana and then said, 'Having come so far upon the quest I want to see it to the end.'

'I, too . . . ' began Alwald and then muttered, 'At least the wine was real enough last night.'

'Where is Master Nomis?' asked Krispin.

'He must be aboard the ship, keeping an eye upon the amber,' Danya replied. 'He thinks of little else.'

'His mind was on other things last night,' said Tana. 'I did not believe he could be so merry until that dame snatched him into the dance.'

On reaching the ship they found everything aboard as they had left it, but the heavy mooring rings to which she had been tied were now rusted bangle thin.

'Get ready to cast off,' said Danya. 'Ho, Nomis, show yourself, old man.'

There was no response and a quick search proved that the amber-seeker was not aboard.

'Lady Tana, you stay on the ship in case he turns up while we seek him,' Danya said.

On the quay they set out in different directions, the shipmaster saying that the first to bring the

313

amber-seeker back to the *Amber Star* should sound the ship's gong to recall the others. But the gong never sounded and after an hour they returned, voices hoarse from calling the old man's name.

'I entered every ruin where he could be lying but I saw not a sign of him,' said Alwald who was the last to return.

'Yet we cannot sail without knowledge of his fate,' said Krispin.

'I think I know the answer,' said Danya, and he climbed down the hatchway to return a moment later looking more sombre than before.

'Untie the lines,' he said. 'We will not see Nomis again. Last night he must have agreed to stay in Haven.'

'Can you be sure?' asked Alwald.

'The chest that held his rightful share of amber is gone.'

'Mayhap it was stolen.'

'Thieves would have taken all.'

No one spoke. At a sign from the shipmaster, Krispin and Gambal climbed back onto the quay to release the mooring ropes. A minute later the *Amber Star* moved across the harbour as the crew pulled on her sweeps.

Alwald nodded in the direction of the two ships they had seen tied up the previous afternoon; now all that remained of them were two rotting hulks.

Once past the eroded light-tower, the sail was raised and as the ship surged forward with new life, all except Danya felt their spirits soar. Never had the sight of empty ocean been so welcome.

Whatever Haven was or had been, its mystery was behind them. But Danya, alone at the helm, could only brood upon the thought that, with the disappearance of Nomis, he was the last of the *Amber Star*'s company who had undertaken the voyage to the Cold Sea.

The twin figureheads of the ship gave the impression of leaping forward, their dragon jaws agape, as the ocean wind whistled through her cordage and sent her racing across the froth-capped swell. When the shattered top of Haven's light-tower was finally lost to sight it seemed to symbolise deliverance from the dangers and discomfort of the Cold Sea. Instead of being shadowed by grey wind-harried cloud, the sky was a warm blue, and this was reflected on the undulating face of the ocean. The air, too, lost its bone-chilling coldness and the crew discarded their heavy seamen's cloaks.

Ahead of the ship's metal-sheathed ramp, flying fish glided in glittering shoals, lazy-winged seabirds followed the bubbling wake and on several occasions distant pillars of vapour marked the presence of whales. And all the time the wind remained constant so that the *Amber Star* followed the course indicated by the Lodestone with no slackening of speed.

After their adventures together the travellers tended to relish their own company when possible. With a following wind, there was little need to trim the sail; Krispin resumed his watch at the masthead, Gambal lay brooding on his bunk, and Ognam found a spot in the bows where he gazed with unseeing eyes over the grotesquely carved prow. Alwald spent most of his time on the poop deck with the Lodestone needle pointing steadily ahead while Danya, thankful to have returned to more tranquil seas, leaned easily on the helm lost, like the others, in his own thoughts.

Only Tana seemed free from this languid state of mind. She busied herself in the galley and was continually bringing tasty dishes and warming drinks to the men whose appetites, thanks to the freshness of the salt air, remained remarkably keen. When she took a steaming bowl to Ognam, he would thank her politely and she would smile at him but there was an awkwardness between them and he would resume his horizon-gazing without a word. In contrast, when she climbed the poop ladder to take food to Alwald and Danya they talked easily and their windborne laughter taunted the jongleur.

At night the lanthorn threw its yellow light over the helmsman, and with just one other member of the crew on watch the *Amber Star* sped on with a phosphorescent trail glowing behind her. On occasion, distant lights showed that they were not alone on the ocean, and once Krispin turned his gaze to steerboard and beheld an enormous black vessel silhouetted against the moon.

At his shout Danya swung the tiller so that the *Amber Star* veered away in the opposite direction, and when Krispin, thinking he might be needed on deck, reached him he was surprised to see an expression of disquiet on the shipmaster's face that was out of character.

316

'What is it?' asked Krispin.

'The great black ship,' answered Danya.

'She certainly seems big.'

'None bigger sails the seas, lad.'

Krispin watched over the stern as the vessel swept on her way under a vast press of dark sail. 'You mistrust her,' he said turning back to the shipmaster.

'Aye. No mariner is at ease with the black ship in sight.'

'Is she a corsair?'

Danya shook his head. 'None can say for sure what she is, though you will hear a score of rumours in waterside taverns. None know of any port where she puts in. Some think she carries cargo that would be baneful to ordinary mortals, others that she is a slaver, but most believe she belongs to the Regent of Ythan and her mission is best left a mystery.'

'At least she takes no interest in us,' said Krispin. 'This wind bears her fast away to the west.'

'Thanks be to the Mother for the high wind. And may it keep our sail stretched.'

The high wind that filled the sail of the *Amber Star* began its journey over a thousand leagues away in an unknown region beyond the Outlands which the nomads knew only as the Home of the Winds. Few had ever glimpsed its mountainous terrain, for it lay far to the west of the vast plain over which in normal times the wolf-worshipping barbarians wandered in their leather-canopied wagons in search of auroch herds. Their shamans told it was in that distant place that the earth spirit breathed forth the wind which sighed day and night across their vast steppe, making its tall grass ripple like waves across the face of a drab green ocean.

This restless grassland ended where the River of Night ruled a natural frontier between the Outlands and the forested Wald, but the west wind knew nothing of frontiers. Once it had whip-cracked the black pennants which streamed above the turrets of River Garde; now there was only one banner for it to tease. Fluttering from the flagpole mounted on the central tower was a huge sheet of cloth on which was daubed the outline of a wolf standing on a pathway of stars.

This crude emblem of the nomads' Wolf-in-the-Sky deity had been raised to the accompaniment of shamans' drumming when the nomad army set out beyond the mountains that enclosed the Wald; what had begun as a raid across the River of Night had become a crusade in the mind of the Wolf King who vowed to fly a similar banner from Danaak's highest spire. The castle was guarded by men of the Wolf Horde whose luck had run against them when the lots were drawn for garrison duty. They felt ill at ease in buildings of stone and on patrol along the narrow trails that led among the alien trees, especially since some fugitive Waldmen had banded together to fight back.

The wind, carrying the smell of steppe grass, was a reminder of lost freedom to a small group of nomads following a forest path in the direction of the White Virgins. Rounding the bole of a huge oak they raised both their voices and axes at the sight of a man and a girl on the trail ahead. At their harsh cries the girl gave a shriek; abandoning her to the paralysis of terror, the man broke into a limping run.

Here was sport. The nomads' spurs urged their horses into a gallop – then the leading rank disappeared as the ground beneath it collapsed. Unable to rein up, the rest of the riders plunged into the deep pit that had been concealed by fowler's nets covered with leaf mould. The air was rent by screams of men and horses impaled on scores of stakes whose sharpened ends had been hardened by fire. The two decoys ran back hand in hand and looked down on the scene of carnage with expressions of grim satisfaction while from the trees appeared a motley band of Waldmen carrying bows and laughing at the success of their ruse.

'Shall we finish them off?' asked one.

'Do not let the horses suffer,' said the Wish Maiden.

'But leave the other beasts to squirm in their pit,' ordered Wode. 'It will give their comrades something to think on when they find them.'

The moans of the dying were soon lost in the endless sighing of the trees as the indifferent wind ruffled the forest, stirred the ashes of Toyheim and swept on to the Peak Tower. Here its wailing was a fitting obligato to the muted words of the castle's retainers as they expressed their anxiety and foreboding. Their beloved mistress the Lady Eloira lay in a stupor beneath a rose-coloured coverlet on her four-poster bed. The evening before, Hans the steward had carried her there in a swoon from the roof and now the chirurgeon shook his head, cursing his inability to restore her while the old servants pondered on their own fates should the Dark Maid be reaching for the frail hand of their mistress.

Outside the castle the wind stirred the lake of mist protecting it and then howled round the snow-capped ranges, tugging at two figures on a dizzy path that crossed the face of an ice-bound precipice. With each step the man in the lead turned to look back at the girl inching behind him, one hand gripping the cord that linked them and the other holding a large doll by the arm.

'Not much further,' he kept repeating. 'Once we reach the other side we will be well on the way to finding your brother.'

Having whistled through the jagged peaks, the wind swooped down to the plain beyond and then flowed over great tracts of grassland and shallow river valleys famous for their vineyards. To the south it snatched smoke from the cooking fires of the Wolf Horde encamped before a walled town that straddled the highway to Danaak, heedless of the terror of its townsfolk as they waited for the barbarian army to attack. Far away to the north it drove wavelets up a lakeshore to soak into white sand leaving a lather of froth. It made the weeping branches of willows dance to its song and played with the silver mane of a horsemaid who sat outside a rough shelter that had been constructed of branches and reeds the night before.

'We stay here awhile,' she said as she raised a handful of berries to her mouth. 'From Olam it has been a long journey. And hard. Here it is beautiful. We have enough to eat. We have each other. You need rest. Wings tired.'

The man sitting opposite smiled at her fondly. 'At this moment I feel I would be happy to stay here for ever.'

There was little about his appearance to suggest that until recently his back had been so hunched that he was known as the Hump; the membranous wings that had finally burst from what he had always believed to be a deformity folded so neatly between his shoulders that under a cloak they would be unlikely to attract notice.

'Then let us stay. For ever,' she said with a laugh.

'Silvermane, I promised I would take you back to your homeland and now we are very near.'

'You sure?'

He nodded. 'I remember the *feel* of the country from the time I was pilot of Azrul's caravan which brought you from the Arkad Woodlands to Danaak.'

Silvermane looked reflective. 'You were so kind to me then,' she said. 'I think I would have died if it had not been for you.'

'Yet you always seemed so self-assured.'

'That the strength of pride. Not the heart.'

'And I wondered that you could see anything in me – a moody crouchback whose only virtue was that he could find the way where others could not – a creature of the wilderness.'

'What they think now – if they could see you?'

'Who?'

'Our companions. Lord Alwald, Krispin.'

'Probably think I was even more of a freak.'

'Never say that word.'

'I am sorry. You see, my beloved, my body changed very quickly and my mind has not yet caught up with it.'

'That I know. But you will learn.'

'At least I have learned to use my wings. At first I could only flap and I soon got exhausted but now I am beginning to float on the air like the eagles I used to envy.' He glanced up at the small clouds scudding across the sky. 'The wind is good. It will lift us high and then we can glide a great distance.'

'We go then?'

'We may as well make use of the high wind.'

She rose and her small hoofs left dainty prints in the sand as she collected their few possessions. As she put them in a bag that hung from her shoulder she said, 'I wonder where they are, those companions. If they still live? If they finish quest?'

'I think of them, too. I pray them good luck on the Pilgrim Path but I suppose we will never know the outcome. Thank the Mother the affairs of Ythan and its cursed Regent are no longer our concern.'

He stood up and his graceful wings unfolded and moved gently to keep him balanced. Silvermane came and stood with her back to him, turning her head over her shoulder to kiss him on the mouth. For the sake of safety he buckled her girdle through his belt and then put his muscular arms through hers and clasped his hands beneath her breasts.

'Comfortable?' he asked.

'Yes. And happy.'

His wings became taut and began to rise and fall. As their speed increased, it seemed to Silvermane that her body became lighter. For a few moments they hovered a pace or so above the ground and then they rose above the threshing willows. The wind pressed her long skirt against her equine limbs; for a moment she felt whirled like a feather in a gale, then everything steadied and they soared until the Hump was satisfied with their height. With his pinions constantly flexing to enable him to rest on the current he turned his gaze to the north where a ragged-edged expanse of green told him that his instinct had been correct.

He straightened his body and with his arms still supporting Silvermane he glided swiftly towards the woodlands that were the home of the horsemaid and her kind. But as his keen eyesight roved over the distant treetops, he was puzzled by smudges of smoke that billowed above them to be swept away by the wind. As they flew nearer, Silvermane gave a cry of surprise and alarm – vast swathes had been cut through the forest.

'It is the work of men,' she cried.

Her words were soon proved. With his wings drawn back, the Hump glided in a steep descent towards the nearest of the long clearings, and as it appeared to rise towards them he saw the details of the desecration. On every side trees were being felled by axmen, the sound of their rhythmic blows

323

reaching his ears like a continuous tapping. Gangs of chained men hauled the heavy trunks to enormous fuming pits, lines of burdened drongs plodded through the smoke and confusion, and everywhere guards watched the work with naked weapons.

'They kill the woodland,' cried Silvermane. 'Why? Why?'

'A slave colony,' he answered. 'They make charcoal for Danaak.'

He had been so shocked by the sight of the destruction that for a moment he had not thought of personal danger. Then he saw the guards pointing towards them and his wings beat frantically to lift them to safety as the first flight of arrows flew towards them.

TWO

The Mountains
of the Moon

Day after day the *Amber Star* sped south over
calm seas with a clean fresh breeze filling her sail.
Her crew relished the warmer weather after the
rigours of the Cold Sea. Most of the time they
sailed out of sight of land, and when the needle
of the Lodestone led them closer to the coast they
merely saw distant lines of cliffs shining white in
the sunlight. On one occasion they saw a cone-
shaped mountain rising behind the shoreline with
a thread of white smoke flowing from its summit.

'Fire Mountain,' cried Danya. 'I know that old
landmark well, I have seen it spewing flame and
burning rocks into the night sky from some demon
region below the earth. It tells me that we are
about thirty leagues from Gysbon.'

'And what is Gysbon?' asked Alwald who stood
on the poop deck beside him.

'It is Ythan's greatest trading port,' the
shipmaster replied. 'And it may be the answer to
something that has been troubling me.'

325

'And what might that be?'

'In a word — crew. When you leave me I shall have no one to work the ship, but in Gysbon I could probably find two or three seamen.'

Alwald frowned. 'I seem to remember The Mage saying we must not deviate from the Lodestone's course, and I must confess that I would be uneasy in a place where there will be Witchfinders and spies who might take too much interest in the *Amber Star.*' He sighed. 'I can understand your need, Shipmaster, but . . . ' His words died away but his expression remained worried.

'We will be opposite Gysbon after nightfall,' said Danya. 'We can anchor in the harbour and I shall row the skiff to the Mermaid Quay — that's where mariners in need of work wait in the taverns. It will not take me long to find the lads I need.'

'I feel uneasy about anyone else joining us,' Alwald said to Krispin later. 'How can we be sure of them? After all, we are on a secret quest, not a potton-cursed trading voyage.'

Krispin raised his shoulders and let them fall. 'All we can do is be vigilant.' He sounded as worried as Alwald.

Some hours later, after night had descended upon the ocean, a tiny cluster of lights appeared on the steerboard.

Danya grunted with satisfaction. 'Gysbon.'

In the glow of the ship's lanthorn Alwald watched the Lodestone needle swing to the left as Danya pulled on the helm so that the twin figureheads of the *Amber Star* turned in the direction of the distant port.

Suddenly there was a shout from Ognam who was sitting in his favourite position in the bows. 'I can see something against the lights,' he called.

'Drop the sail,' ordered the shipmaster. 'There is a boat drifting ahead of us.'

The yardarm was lowered, the ship slowed and then wallowed in the swell beside a small rowing boat. In the yellow light of the lanthorn the travellers made out two figures inside it, one lying prone and one sitting hunched in the stern. Even in this dejected position the latter appeared to be a giant of a man, and as he lifted his head up they saw that he had once been handsome. Now his features were ravaged by privation and a deeper expression of despair.

'Water,' he muttered. 'He is dying.' And he nodded to his companion.

'We will get you aboard and then you can have all the food and water you want,' said Danya. 'Catch this rope if you can. Are you two the only survivors?'

'We are not wrecked, Shipmaster,' said the big man wearily. 'We are . . .' And he held up his right arm. From a ring welded round his wrist, a short length of chain gleamed as it swung in the light. 'You know the penalty for aiding such as we. For the love of the Mother just give us some water and a crust and leave us.'

'I know the penalty,' agreed Danya. 'And I know the reward for returning escaped slaves, and I care for neither. You are coming aboard.'

A few minutes later the big man, who said that his name was Dikon, was sitting with his back against the mast with a bowl of broth in his trembling hands. In the cabin which had been used by Nomis, Tana spooned water into the parched mouth of his companion who lay unconscious on the bunk. The sail had been raised and the *Amber Star* was back on her proper course with the faraway lights of Gysbon slipping past them.

'Mayhap fate has sent me the answer to the problem of crewing,' muttered Danya to Alwald. He went and stood over Dikon.

'You will be treated fair if you treat us fair,' he said. 'When you get your strength back you will help to work the ship. In return, when our voyage is completed, I shall put you ashore in some place where you will be safe.'

'You will find me willing,' replied Dikon in his deep voice.

'And your companion – what is his name?'

'That I do not know, his tongue has been split. We were brought to Gysbon to be shipped to work in the mines on the Sulphur Isles, but while we were waiting in the slave cells I managed to break our chains one night and we . . . escaped to the quays where we took a boat. Our plan was to sail down the coast to a remote region where I have heard outcasts can live beyond the law of the Regent, but currents carried us out to sea where we drifted for several days until you found us.'

'Your story is your own,' said Danya. 'Aboard the *Amber Star* you will be judged only on the manner of your behaviour. I know that in Ythan a man does not have to be a criminal to have the brand.'

Dikon looked down at the back of his left hand

where a half-healed scar in the shape of a crude flower showed where a red-hot iron had inflicted his slave mark.

'I was not a criminal, Shipmaster,' he said. 'Let us say I fell from grace. As for my companion, I know not whether he was a cut-purse or a cut-throat but if he cheats the Dark Maid I promise he will give you no trouble.'

During the next two days Dikon quickly regained his great strength and insisted upon doing his share of work. In his thirties, he stood a head taller than Alwald who up until then had been the tallest aboard the *Amber Star*, and beneath his cropped black hair his features were strong and held the suggestion that once they had been imperious. When not on deck with his watch he spent his time tending his fellow slave whose recovery was much slower. He was a small man with dark eyes set in a narrow pointed face, giving him an unfortunate rodent-like aspect. Although he was unable to form words as a result of the torture he had undergone, he could still scream, and on several occasions the shrill echo of his nightmares brought everyone on deck. Then Dikon would apologise on his behalf and blame his outcries on his past suffering.

To the travellers the curious thing about the big man was his lack of curiosity. Although he was almost formally polite, he never asked them about themselves or even inquired of Danya the object of the voyage. It seemed that his escape from captivity was enough to content him.

It was during the third day after the two slaves

had been rescued that Krispin shouted from the masthead and pointed to the horizon where, appearing to float above a bank of low cloud, a line of ethereal white-edged ranges was visible against a pale blue sky.

'The Mountains of the Moon,' said Danya. 'They mark the final frontier of Ythan.'

Alwald glanced down at the ivory box containing the Lodestone. It still pointed ahead.

'We sail on past them, Master Danya,' he said.

'Few have done that, for the word is that the coast is wild and there is naught of value to be found. At least by braving the Cold Sea one may find amber, but yonder there is nothing.'

'Except the Shadow Realm,' said Dikon quietly.

'What do you know of that?' demanded Alwald.

Dikon shrugged his massive shoulders. 'It is just that I used to listen to travellers' tales,' he said and went back to filing his gyve. Although he had spent many hours working on it so far he had only a shallow groove in the metal to show for his efforts. In Ythan, once a bracelet of a special alchemic alloy was welded round a slave's wrist, it was there for life.

The sight of the mountains, which appeared as delicate as a moon in an afternoon sky, lifted the languor that had lain upon the travellers since they had left Haven. To Krispin and Alwald they indicated that they must be finally nearing the end of the quest. Somewhere ahead lay the mysterious Shadow Realm and there – if The Mage had spoken true – the splinter of Lodestone would point the way to Princess Livia's resting place.

330

That night the ranges, looking even more illusory by moonlight, fell astern of the *Amber Star*. Krispin watched them dwindle and then went to his cabin, confident that the voyage was almost over. He was sitting on his bunk, making up his mind to slip off his clothes and at the same time pondering lazily on what the next day might bring, when the door opened to allow a shaft of moonlight into the cabin.

'Tana,' Krispin exclaimed.

'Hush, Krispin,' she said. 'I would have a quiet word with you.'

The door closed again and she sat beside him on the bunk. Outside the only sounds were the creak of the ship's timbers, the thrum of taut rigging and the endless swish of the ship's ram cutting through the waves.

'And what is this quiet word?' he asked. He was aware of perfume in the air and though they did not touch he could sense the soft suppleness of her body beneath her black and silver gown.

'I need to talk about Ognam.'

'Why to me, Tana? It seems that you have more in common with Alwald, or Gambal for that matter.'

'You sound jealous.' She said it with a laugh.

In the heavy darkness he shrugged. Tonight he found her irritating – and at the same time, he had to admit, exciting.

'I can talk easy with Alwald because there is much we hold in common.'

'Both palace-bred,' said Krispin.

'I think Alwald is castle rather than palace, but

it is near enough. As for Gambal – he has a certain quality that men may not recognise but women do.'

'Yet he was the one who wanted to deliver you back to The Mage.'

'Yes,' said Tana. 'That is part of it.'

She was silent for a moment and then continued: 'But you, Krispin, I believe have the most heart, and you have been a good friend to Ognam. He told me how he took the Esav from you and that you forgave him.'

'I think,' said Krispin slowly, 'that it would be better to talk to Ognam rather than about him.'

'But I do not know what to say, Krispin. He has fallen in love with me and it hurts me to see him miserable.'

'I have not had much experience of love except to know its strength when it is returned,' said Krispin, 'but it would seem that you have no such feeling for him.'

'For a jongleur?'

'For a jongleur who freed you.'

'I am grateful, Krispin. But you cannot love someone out of gratitude.'

'I suppose not. And yet, when he first crossed the lake . . .'

'I was overjoyed to see him. Imagine if you had been alone down there for longer than you could remember, would you not feel delight in seeing a fellow being?'

Krispin said nothing.

'Do not think badly of me, Krispin.' She laid her hand on his arm; he was aware of her breath on his cheek.

'So what do you want of me?' he asked gruffly.

'I want your advice. Tell me how I can explain to Ognam that I do not feel as he does without hurting him.'

'That would be impossible.'

She sighed. 'Life can make one seem cruel. Oh, why did you not come across the lake and find me! There would be no difficulty with my heart then.'

'I do not think a toymaker has more to offer than a jongleur. On the contrary . . .'

'Krispin, are you being stupid on purpose? You may have learned the toymaker's craft but you are much more than a craftsman now. Surely you must realise that. The very fact that you undertook the quest proves that. And with my own eyes I have seen you handle your sword like a warrior out of a saga. Krispin, do you not understand?'

He made no reply, telling himself that it was she who did not understand, and yet he would have been less than human if he had not felt flattered by her words.

Suddenly he felt the sweet warmth of her lips on his, her arms were about him, the scent of her hair filled his nostrils and in the dark he responded without thought, his arms tightening round her exquisite body.

'Krispin . . .'

The door opened and in the moonlight which flooded into the cabin Ognam saw them embracing.

333

THREE
Twilight

Krispin, perched on the lookout platform, was out of favour with himself. Again and again his mind returned to the events of the previous evening and he felt both anger and a sense of guilt. Ognam was the last person he would have wanted to hurt, and he cursed himself for having responded to Tana at the wrong moment.

Ognam had said nothing. He had merely closed the cabin door. When Krispin had risen from the bunk to go after him, Tana had taken his arm and said, 'Stay. It is best this way. Mayhap he will understand now.' But he had shaken her arm off and gone out onto the deck to try and explain to Ognam, but there was no sign of the jongleur and Krispin guessed he had bolted himself inside his tiny cabin. For a moment Krispin was tempted to go and knock on his door, demand that Ognam listen to him – and then he shrugged and, not wishing to return to Tana, climbed to the masthead. He realised there was nothing he could say to Ognam who had been obviously brooding over Tana since the voyage began; he had found them embracing in the dark and whatever was said could not alter the fact.

When dawn lightened the eastern sky Krispin looked down on the deck and saw that Ognam had taken his usual solitary place in the bows, and it seemed to Krispin he could feel the jester's heartache. What infuriated him was the thought that he was innocent; and then an inner voice asked what might have happened if they had not been disturbed. His reply was an uncharacteristic flood of anger. Was it his fault if Ognam had chosen to make a fool of himself over Tana! Surely he should have realised that she had seen in him a means of escape – and who could blame her! And so on.

But when Krispin gazed down on the hunched figure in red and green motley, holding his jester's staff almost as a child would clutch a toy, his anger subsided.

It was with relief that he heard Alwald call to Danya at the helm that the Lodestone needle was turning. A moment later he felt the *Amber Star* change course. This surely meant that they were sailing towards land and the voyage would soon be over. New journeying lay ahead and he welcomed the thought. There would be no Tana to cause misunderstanding; once more they would be the four Pilgrims who had set out from Danaak together and together reached The Mage's tower on the backs of the great golden-feathered griffins.

Scanning the sea ahead, Krispin was puzzled. Although the sun had risen, and its rays sparkled on the spray cascading on either side of the bows, the sky above the horizon was strangely dark. At first he thought it might be the result of storm clouds but, remembering stormy skies from the Wald, he realised there was a difference here. It was as though the air itself was tinged with twilight.

By midmorning he shouted to those on the deck that he could see land – a dark strip that separated the water from the darker sky above it. By now the sea itself had changed. The waves had flattened to a leaden-hued swell on which banks of livid weed undulated, and spray was replaced by scribbles of lather.

The shipmaster continually sniffed the air.

'I mistrust this sea,' he said to Gambal who, like Tana, had climbed to the poop deck to watch for the coastline. 'I have the feeling that a storm is due, yet there is not a cloud in the sky and the water is lifeless.'

'The sky behind us is bright still,' said Tana. 'But ahead it is like the gloaming which came over the Lake of Taloon at even.'

'I do not envy you going ashore here,' said Danya. 'And though I shall be sorry to part with you, for we have adventured together as good seamates, I shall be relieved to return to known waters.'

'The Mage told us that we were to go to a region known as the Shadow Realm,' said Gambal. 'And here we are. It is exactly as it says – a land covered by shadow.'

'But shadows must be cast and what casts this?' muttered Dikon.

No one answered but Danya unconsciously made the Circle of the Mother.

Towards noon the *Amber Star* was close to the flat coastline whose long stretches of shore appeared dismal beneath the dusky sky. A maze of sandbanks lay ahead. Alwald noticed that the Lodestone was in continuous movement.

'It will guide us through the shoals,' he told the anxious shipmaster. 'Just as The Mage said, it will guide us all the way to our goal.'

'I pray you are right,' said Danya. 'To run aground here is the last thing we need.'

Alwald was right. Standing with his ivory box in his hand he shouted directions to the shipmaster while Gambal stood by to trim the sail as the vessel turned and twisted among the banks. To give her more manoeuvrability, the two sweeps were run out and the rest of the crew hauled on them. Krispin found himself with his hands on the oar next to Ognam but neither spoke or looked at each other.

The other sweep was pulled by Dikon and the small slave with whom he had been rescued, and who, because of his affliction, was named Mute by the others. Thanks to Tana's ministrations he had recovered enough to stand on deck. He was still weakly, but his lack of strength was compensated by Dikon whose strokes were equal to those of both Krispin and Ognam.

After an hour of delicate navigation the *Amber Star* cornered a low headland and the travellers saw a wide estuary stretching before them. With the sandbars shielding it from the open sea, its water was as smooth as that of an inland lake.

'Upriver, Master Danya,' cried Alwald. Although, like the others, he found the gloom that hung over the bare landscape depressing, he was excited that they had made landfall at last.

'As you say,' replied the shipmaster and shifted his weight on the curiously carved tiller. Soon the sail flapped idly as the wind that had blown them so far and so steadily was deflected by the estuary's banks. When it was lowered and the crew were about to heave on the oars again Tana, having obeyed a whispered command from Danya, appeared with a tray of brimming winecups.

'Ease off for a minute, lads,' the shipmaster called. 'This slow current will not bear us far while we drink a toast to the end of your voyage.'

'And to you, Shipmaster, for bringing us safely through the perils of the deep,' cried Alwald raising his cup.

With the wine came laughter except for Ognam, who turned away and gazed moodily over the horns of the figureheads, and for Danya who gazed into his cup and thought of those who had ventured with him to the Cold Sea, never to return.

'And what does your future hold?' Krispin asked him.

'With the help of Master Dikon and Master Mute I shall sail to a quiet port where they and Lady Tana may go as they will, and where I shall sell my amber,' he said, bringing his thoughts back to the present. 'I have it in mind to give up the sea and buy a harbourside inn, and in memory of you travellers I shall call it the Quest.'

'Then I hope that someday I shall stay at the Quest.'

As more wine was poured, Krispin raised his cup and cried, 'To the Quest!'

Thinking that he meant the Pilgrim Path, Alwald and Gambal responded enthusiastically. When Krispin tried to explain, Danya laughed and said, 'No matter. All of life is a quest. It begins in our cradles and we follow it until the Dark Maid tells us that it has ended. Some quests are noble such as you and your companions follow, some are for love which is perhaps the hardest of all, and some are merely for an end to fear.' He laughed ruefully. 'For me it was nothing more than amber.'

'I think it was more that which amber could bring,' said Krispin.

'Mayhap, mayhap. It is time to get back to the oars, for the voyage is not over yet. I promised The Mage that I would take you as far as I could by water.'

Through the long afternoon the *Amber Star* moved up the estuary under her creaking sweeps. As she went further inland her crew saw that the banks became covered with the tangled trunks of stunted and sere-leafed trees, some of whose roots writhed serpent-like into the water. Above, the sun was a white disk in the dark sky, yet the air about them was warm and humid. Apart from themselves, the only living creatures were funereal birds who watched their progress with onyx eyes from mudbanks fringed with olive-brown reeds.

'Although it is different in appearance, the atmosphere of this place reminds me of somewhere we passed through early on the quest,' said Alwald to Krispin who was taking his rest turn from the sweeps.

'I know,' he said. 'The Shallows. Let us hope it is not similarly haunted.'

'It is probably just the effect of this gloom. I have only known anything like it once before when I was a boy. For half an hour the moon passed in front of the sun and threw a shadow over the Wald.'

'I remember that. In Toyheim we children thought the end of the world was coming. I remember Father Tammas telling Jennet and me not to be afraid because that happened at least once in everyone's lifetime. But it did seem strange to be in twilight at noontime. And now the further we go the darker it becomes.'

'The land is well-named Shadow Realm. And seeing no natural cause for the dusk I cannot help but wonder what gramarye lies behind it. If Princess Livia is hidden somewhere here, it is likely that powerful bewitchment was laid to guard the secret.'

'The same thought has crossed my mind,' said Krispin. 'Remember the folktale of Sleeping Beauty.'

'I remember the rhyme about her that we used to play a game to as children,' said Alwald with a smile. 'If you were lucky you kissed one of the girls. Now I am a man I am learning it is possible that there are threads of truth in folktales.'

'Mayhap this quest will be told as such a tale someday,' said Krispin thoughtfully.

'Only if we succeed.'

'Master Krispin, back to your sweep,' shouted Danya from the poop. 'Master Ognam looks ready to drop.'

'He looks more like to throw himself over the side,' muttered Alwald. 'Did something upset him last night?'

Krispin merely nodded and walked away to grasp the sweat-polished oar.

The sun, which seemed little more than a silver crown in the unnatural gloaming, was sinking towards the west when the crew of the *Amber Star* saw that the estuary was narrowing to the width of a river. Another apparent change was in the vegetation covering the banks. Creepers and streamers of tree moss hung from trees many times taller than those that sprawled half in the water further down the estuary, and though all flora was pallid it possessed a sickly vigour like that of plants struggling towards the grating in a darkened cellar.

As the banks drew closer together their towering walls of foliage caused the dim light to become even dimmer, and to the travellers it seemed they were moving into a world of eternal evening.

'I hope this river will take us closer to our destination,' said Alwald peering anxiously at the Lodestone. 'I like not the thought of having to make our way through those trees on foot. It is not like the honest forest that I knew in the Wald.'

'As I said, I shall take you as far—'

Danya's words were cut off as a bone-tipped

341

spear clattered on the deck in front of him. It was the signal for attack.

From the left bank came a volley of missiles – slingstones, flint-headed darts, arrows with fire-hardened points. As they clattered on the deck and against the hull, the crew threw themselves below the bulwarks and only Danya remained upright at the tiller to see scores of half-naked men and women emerging from the trees to hurl crude weapons and shriek hatred.

A stone opened his cheek and an arrow caught him on the shoulder, but he hardly felt the pain as he realised that the sluggish current was bearing the *Amber Stone* slowly but remorselessly towards the left-hand shore.

'Row!' he shouted. 'Row!'

Dikon was first on his feet. Seizing one of the oars in his huge hands he heaved on it with such strength that it almost snapped. Danya felt the ship straighten and when the others threw their weight on the sweeps she surged forward.

The attackers followed but were impeded by tree trunks and tangles of vines. To avoid these, some ventured on to the muddy margins at the water's edge and within seconds were floundering waist deep. But missiles continued to fall on the deck from others stationed along the bank. Gambal slumped to his knees with blood streaming from his temple.

Ognam let go his oar and began to haul on the halyard. Realising what he was about, Krispin joined him and between them they raised the yardarm high enough for the sail, which had been stowed lengthways, to give some shelter from their enemies' missiles. As the two men made fast the ropes, their eyes met. Krispin opened his mouth to speak but Ognam turned away and a moment later was rowing.

High on the poop a new vista spread before Danya as the *Amber Star* followed a curve in the river and he saw that it entered a broad lake. Once through the narrows that led into it they would be safely out of range and he tried to shout encouragement to the oarsmen above the enemy's ululation but the missiles thudding against the canvas sail were encouragement enough and the ship continued to surge against the current.

They were only a hundred paces from where the river entered the lake when the shipmaster saw two tall trees that stood like sentinels on either side of the passage begin to teeter towards each other. The enemy might be tattered and armed only with primitive weapons but they were not deficient in cunning; axmen had prepared a trap for their victim. Within seconds the great tree trunks would topple and trap the ship in the channel or actually crash down upon it.

Danya roared at the crew to row faster. The two trees swayed over the water, the cracking of timber louder than the cries of the enemy or the curses of the shipmaster.

Looking up, Krispin saw one of the trees falling towards him and he closed his eyes and braced himself for the fatal impact. Instead he was drenched by a deluge of muddy water as the trunk struck the river a few paces from the stern of the

343

Amber Star. His relief was cut short by the sight of the second tree descending. The ship's momentum carried her out of the tree's path – but only just. A massive branch sheered off the lanthorn which was mounted over the helm. Another wave bearing a mess of twigs and shattered wood foamed over the deck, and then they were gliding over the still dark waters of the lake.

Even though their breath was rasping in their throats, the crew continued rowing until the *Amber Star* was safely in the centre of the water. Danya, bloodied and covered with leaves, released the anchor, and they collapsed with heaving chests.

When their pulses no longer drummed in their ears and they could breathe without pain they looked to each other's hurts. Most had suffered some wounds but because the attackers were without metal weapons, none was dangerous. The worst affected were Gambal, who was laid on his bunk after his head had been bandaged, and Danya who had an arrow shaft protruding from his shoulder.

Working on the principle that because he had made toys and therefore must have a delicate touch, Krispin was elected to remove it. The shipmaster sat stoically by the helm as Krispin approached nervously. Tana appeared with the strongest wine in the biggest cup the galley could provide. Danya took a long drink as Krispin placed one hand on his shoulder and seized the arrow with the other.

'It seems we are all on your quest now,' Danya said bitterly. 'With those trees across the river we will never . . .'

He broke off as Krispin pulled the glistening shaft free.

' . . . be able to return to the sea.'

FOUR

The Colossus

'They are outcasts,' said Dikon in answer to Tana. 'To think it was my plan to escape to such as these.' He gave a bitter laugh. 'They may have been ordinary refugees from the Regent once, but they have reverted to savagery. Did you see that many had decorated their faces with stripes of coloured clay?'

The *Amber Star* lay peacefully at anchor in the centre of the shallow lake. Now that night was falling the deep dusk that lay upon the water seemed more natural to the travellers than the unearthly daytime twilight that gave the Shadow Realm its name. Wounds had been dressed and preparations made against further attack. Danya had brought out his crossbow whose deadly bolts were the mariners' only protection against the kraken of the Cold Sea; Alwald and Krispin wore their swords while the others kept axes or harpoons close to hand. And though it was an unlikely weapon against an elusive enemy such as the forest people, the mangonel had been loaded and tensioned. Danya had organised guard duty for the night and now the travellers took their rest with bowls of stew scorching their fingers.

'Mayhap it is only as savages that one can survive here,' said Danya thoughtfully. 'They lack the implements of civilisation.'

At the last word Dikon touched the half-healed slave brand on his hand and gave an ironical smile.

'Luckily you are right,' he said. 'Imagine your wound had it been made with a barbed iron arrowhead instead of a wooden point.'

'I can see what the ship must mean to the outcasts,' said Danya. 'They must hunger for its metal to make weapons, for the provisions they have not tasted the like of in years. Why, if they have seamen or mutineers among them they could go a-pirating in her. They will not allow such a prize to escape them easily.'

'We will not let them take her easily,' said Alwald. 'Do not despair, Shipmaster, there is always hope until you feel the touch of the Dark Maid. Trees cannot lie across a river for ever, and I think we were in greater danger from the krakens and the corsairs than we are from these runaway folk. All we can do is travel on tomorrow and see what fate awaits us.'

'It was always thus on the quest,' added Krispin. 'Just when things seemed to be in our favour a new difficulty surprised us, yet we are still a-questing.'

Danya tried to smile and then winced at the pain it caused in his bandaged cheek. 'When we cannot go back we can only go forward,' he said.

Those who were not on guard soon retired to rest their exhausted bodies and, if their hurts would allow them, get enough sleep to prepare for the challenge that the next day would bring.

The night passed uneventfully, and when morning light filtered through the perpetual dusk the anchor was raised and the sweeps began to rise and fall.

Gambal now felt recovered enough to come on deck and take short turns on the oar but the steady progress of the *Amber Star* up the middle of the lake owed much to Dikon's strength. The others were surprised – and thankful – at the way in which he had got over the effects of being adrift. Perhaps inspired by the danger surrounding him, Mute staggered from his cabin and made signs that he was willing to row. Instead, Danya posted him as lookout, giving him a small gong to beat in case he needed to raise the alarm.

Ognam and Krispin did not share the same oar, much to the latter's irritation. The situation now struck him as absurd, especially under such circumstances, but soon there was something more urgent to occupy his mind. As the *Amber Star* moved steadily up the middle of the lake the crew saw that in places on its shores trees gave way to open glades, and across these straggled numbers of outcasts who were obviously keeping pace with the ship. The unspoken question was whether they would find the river that fed the lake blocked when they reached the far side.

As the morning wore on, the gloom about them lessened slightly and the air grew unpleasantly humid so that sweat trickled down the faces of the rowers and dampened their shirts. This attracted repulsive black flies which swarmed about them, bit their exposed flesh and crawled infuriatingly in their nostrils, ears and eyes. The ship resounded with the slapping of palms on skin and cries of disgust.

'It is times like this I yearn for sorcery,' muttered Alwald. 'An incantation, a puff of incense and there would not be one Mother-cursed fly left in the Shadow Realm.'

Overhearing him, Danya hurried to the galley and brought out a brazier. He took sulphur from the ship's stores and sprinkled it on the glowing charcoal. A cloud of whitish smoke enveloped the deck and while it repelled the flies, it set the crew coughing.

'Take your choice — being stung or choking,' said the shipmaster. The vessel continued with sulphur fumes trailing behind it.

After a couple of hours it became apparent that they were approaching the end of the lake. To their relief it did not narrow into a river over which obstacles could be placed, it merely merged into a vast tract of everglade dissected by meandering waterways that appeared wide and deep enough to take the *Amber Star*. They were lined with wan rushes and behind them straggling trees completed the dismal effect in the eerie half-light. Miasma bubbled from the sluggish waters.

Having checked with his Lodestone, Alwald signalled to the shipmaster who steered into one of the widest channels. As the ship entered it, Mute, perched high on the mast, pointed to where a band of outcasts followed like shadows through the drab vegetation.

As Alwald looked ahead he had a strange feeling that he had seen this dreary landscape before, yet the Shadow Realm was as new to him as to the others. He tried to coax his memory but his efforts were cut short by a scream that echoed from behind a wall of trees on the right bank. It was so unexpected that the oarsmen paused and ripples spreading from the *Amber Star* died among the rushes. The cry was followed by confused shouting and then screaming that seemed to go on and on in the ears of the startled crew, filling them with a sense of horror.

Then in a natural clearing opposite the *Amber Star* a dozen outcasts appeared in flight before a similar number of greyish figures armed with long spears. It was hard to make out details of the pursuers in the gloom but there was no mistaking their intention. One after another the outcasts fell to their broad-bladed spears until a solitary woman, barefoot in a tattered skirt, reached the bank of rushes and began to push her way through the stems to the muddy water.

'For the Mother's sake, save me,' she implored. Instinctively Krispin drew Woundflame from its scabbard but a moment later the pursuers dragged her away, pausing only to surround those outcasts lying on the rank grass who still showed signs of life. There was growling laughter as spears rose and fell in a way that reminded Krispin sickeningly of men using hoes. Then, without giving the ship a second glance, the victors vanished into the trees from whence cries of conflict still sounded.

'Row, for the sake of the Mother,' shouted Danya.

The crew needed no urging. The *Amber Star* picked up speed and soon the glade with its scatter of corpses was far astern.

'At least we will not have to worry about outcasts any more,' declared Dikon when lack of breath slowed their strokes. His words sounded cynical to the others and yet they had to admit that thanks to the grey strangers their own danger had lessened.

'I wonder what it was about?' said Krispin.

'Tribal warfare no doubt,' answered Dikon. 'Mayhap those who have always lived in these accursed parts resent the outcasts. Let us be thankful and may the Maid take them all.'

'Did you get a good look at those grey fellows?' Alwald asked Krispin as they swung backwards and forwards on the same oar.

'No. Being grey they seemed no more than shadows, but . . .'

'Yes?'

'Although they were man-shaped I got a feeling they were somehow different to humankind, at least as we know it. I think they were mostly naked but everything happened so fast they were like beings glimpsed in a nightmare.'

'They made me think of stories told in the Wald.'

'I know,' said Krispin. 'Pottons.'

The rest of the day was one of peace for the travellers apart from the visions of the massacre that returned to haunt them from time to time. Although the grey strangers had taken no notice of the *Amber Star*, it did not guarantee that the ship would be safe from them in the future.

'I think they are primitives,' said Dikon when someone mentioned this, 'and they would not have the same need to capture the ship as the outcasts who could greatly improve their lot with what we carry aboard. Primitives are fierce enough as you saw but they have little power of thought, and I should know.'

'How is that, Dikon?' asked Gambal.

'I was a soldier once,' the big man replied. 'A long time ago. My company was sent against primitives in the Bilarim Ranges to the north of the Arkad Woodlands, which shows how remote they are. An imperial caravan had been attacked and we were sent to teach them a lesson.' He grimaced at the memory.

Apart from a single heron, which would fly ahead of the *Amber Star* and then wait on a bank for the vessel to catch it up, only to flap ahead again, the landscape remained without life or movement.

When the gloaming finally became too thick for the ship to be steered any further, she was anchored midstream. The weary crew said little to each other as they ate their usual supper of bread and broth which Tana had prepared. And when the shipmaster, remembering Ognam's performance in Haven and unaware of the situation between him and Krispin, asked him to liven them with one of his songs, the jongleur spoke for all when he said, 'The dimpsy day lies heavy on my spirits. I regret that the twilight has seeped into my heart and if I were to sing my most comic ballad it would come forth like a dirge.'

When those not needed to keep watch retired to their cabins soon afterwards, Ognam went to the bows and took up his usual place behind the figureheads. Hearing a soft footstep he turned and in the feeble light of a lantern suspended from the rigging saw the outline of Alwald who seated himself on the bulwark.

'It is not only the twilight that has seeped into your heart, Master Jester,' he said.

'My heart is my affair, Lord Alwald.'

'And the quest is mine.'

'No one would deny that, but why this talk of quests and hearts?'

'I cannot help noticing that there is ill wind between you and Krispin.'

'Have you seen me strike him, have you heard me utter a curse upon him? I have said naught, I have done naught . . .'

' . . . but sulked.'

'I mean no disrespect, but there have been times, Alwald, when your manner has been far from joyous. And even in Ythan a sulk is not a crime – unless it coincides with mention of our Most Glorious Regent. But, say on what you must.'

'It is just this, Ognam. You may have joined the quest for different reasons than I, whose family was dedicated to Livia's return, or Krispin who made quester's vow, yet we have travelled far together along the Pilgrim Path and in doing so have come to trust each other as comrades. Now I sense that we are close to our destination and

353

I do not want that to be endangered by bad feeling. It is folly that you and the toymaker should avoid speech together.'

Ognam said nothing.

'I guess it is some foolishness over Tana.'

'Perhaps foolishness in your eyes, but not foolishness in the eyes of a Fool.'

'You used the word, Ognam. You could not have expected a girl of noble birth to favour a Fool.'

'She called me "beloved",' said Ognam softly. 'She promised I would be writing sublime verse again . . .'

'But what has that got to do with Krispin?'

'Perhaps what she promised him.'

'Krispin cannot be in love with her.'

'Then that makes it worse. My dreams meant naught.'

'Serene Mother! You are a man of the world, Ognam.'

'No, a fool of the world.'

Alwald raised his hands and let them fall, then walked away.

The next day was as dim and humid as the day it followed. Still escorted by the heron, the *Amber Star* continued its toilsome course through the everglades until noon, when emerging from between banks of moss-draped trees, the travellers saw that the terrain ahead of them was changing. Instead of swampland, a river snaked over a plain towards a barrier of rock above which snowy outlines of mountain peaks floated in the eternal dusk.

Alwald immediately brought out the Lodestone and was relieved to see that it pointed to the distant cliffs.

'Obviously the river is the way to where the Princess rests,' he said to Krispin.

'That is understandable. I wonder what we shall find when we get there. I never thought much about it before – it always seemed too far away, and I suppose I already had a picture in my mind from the Sleeping Beauty tale that Father Tammas used to tell us. But it might be utterly different.' He gave an uneasy laugh. 'All we might find is a skeleton.'

'We will know soon enough. But no wonder those who followed the Path before us never found her . . .' Alwald's voice trailed off and then he pointed over the bows. 'It is difficult to make things out at a distance in this cursed light but can you see a figure?'

'There is something standing over the river where it flows into that gap in the cliffs,' said Krispin after straining his eyes for a minute. 'It looks a bit like a statue but it must be many leagues away, so if it is one it must be taller than the stone giants of Olam.'

'Perhaps it is only a rock pillar,' said Alwald doubtfully. 'I shall ask the shipmaster. He has the best eyes of anyone aboard.'

He climbed up to the poop deck where he found Danya already gazing ahead. 'Is it a figure?'

'I think so,' said Danya in an awed voice. 'Only once before have I seen anything like it. The Island of Pearls has a harbour with a gigantic statue

355

standing astride its entrance. She acts as a light-tower, holding a torch aloft which burns at night. But why should such a colossus be erected in this Mother-forsaken wilderness? And who by?'

He looked over the empty plain which appeared devoid of all forms of life; indeed the only animate thing was the heron which continued its short flights in front of them.

As the *Amber Star* followed the river through the hot afternoon, the crew watched with amazement as the details of the figure became clearer, showing it to be an enormous statue of a man in antique armour holding a raised sword which Danya reckoned must be longer than the ship's mast. He was mounted on a base that had been cut in the rock overlooking the narrow channel in the natural ramparts that crossed the plain like a rough-hewn wall. As to what material he had been constructed of, it was hard to tell in the shadowed light.

It was late in the afternoon when they came close enough to see that the warrior was not a statue of stone but of bronze that had long lost its metallic appearance under a patina of greenish rust.

'I have a feeling that he is connected in some way with the Sleeping Princess,' said Gambal. 'Perhaps a symbolic guardian.'

'He might have been placed there to frighten the primitives from going any further up the river,' added Krispin. 'I like to think he tells us that we are on the right path.'

*   *   *

356

For a hundred years the colossus had stood with his great sword raised above his helmeted head. Behind his visor his eyes – mirrors of polished electrum that remained untarnished – gazed at the dark water flowing past his mighty feet. No earth tremor had displaced him and though verdigris had long stained his exterior, within he remained as he had been intended, a monument of patience in the twilight.

For a hundred years only the sluggish river had reflected in his eyes, but now an image began to cross them – a vessel seeming to crawl like a water beetle with sweeps like insectile legs. On its deck eight foreshortened figures gazed up in near-reverence not only at his magnitude but his heroic mien.

For a hundred years he had waited for such a shape to be thus mirrored and awaken the ancient magic that had been embodied in his parts. Now that magic came alive and released the hidden machineries that held the sword arm upright. There was a grating of monstrous cogs and axles, a groaning of ponderous weights, a screech of metal screeching on metal . . . and the sword of the colossus fell through the twilight and cleft the *Amber Star* in two.

FIVE

The Citadel

Mandal opened his eyes slowly and saw that he was in a chamber cluttered with objects of which he had no understanding. Retorts, crucibles, flasks and intricate instruments of brass and crystal stood in disarray on scarred benches; books with cracked spines were piled on carpets once priceless but now worthless through acid spills. And in a robe as old and stained as anything in this chaotic workshop the old man with the white hair sat by an empty fireplace.

'Good day to you, Commander,' he said when he saw Mandal stir slightly. 'I have waited long for you to awaken. The sleeping potion I gave you worked exceedingly well. Now I shall find something to wash its effects away.'

Mandal remembered now. In his weakened state the climb from the Cage had almost been too much for him. Several times he nearly fell back onto its bars, and when he finally reached the window the old man had hauled him over the sill, saying, 'You are spent, my friend. Sleep is all I can offer but it will renew you after your ordeal.'

He had passed him a cup filled with a bitter draught – 'Fear not, it is merely an elixir distilled from thyme, the favourite herb of the Fey' – and then Mandal had fallen on to a couch and into blissful slumber.

Now he sat up as the old man proffered him a goblet of wine.

'Wine I have, but little food,' he said, sitting down at a bench and raising a goblet himself. 'One of the Regent's mute servants used to bring me my meals every day so I had hardly any provisions when I fell from my master's favour – only scraps I had not bothered to eat. Mayhap there is still a crust or two . . .'

'Please, for the love of the Mother,' Mandal heard himself plead as his stomach pangs returned.

The old man went to a cupboard and brought out a wooden platter on which were several pieces of grey bread and a lump of cheese covered with mould. Mandal seized a crust and stuffed it into his mouth and when he found that it was too hard to bite he soaked it in his wine.

'Forgive my manners,' he muttered.

'I have observed that manners matter not in the Cage,' said the old man drily. 'While you break your prolonged fast I shall introduce myself. I am Leodore, and, until a few days ago, I was the Regent's alchemist, indeed since he saved me from the attentions of the Witchfinders who distinguish not between alchemy and sorcery. There was a price to be paid for that favour but at least I was able to continue experimenting in this lonely tower

359

and, though the world will never know of it, I achieved the alchemic dream.'

He gestured to a dark corner of the chamber and there Mandal saw the pallid creature who had brought him the means of his escape. She was curled like a sleeping animal in a large basket over the side of which drooped one of her huge taloned hands. There was something so unwholesome about it that Mandal had to force himself not to grimace with disgust. The monster might be an alchemist's dream but to him she was a nightmare.

To change the subject he said, 'I am sorry that I was unable to tell you my thanks last night.'

Leodore chuckled. 'The night before last. You have slept like the Princess.'

'Then the old woman who was in the cage must be dead.'

'I have seen the ravens fluttering round the bars.'

Mandal was filled with an unaccustomed feeling of loss. 'What sort of kingdom is it in which old women are starved to death for talking to their cats and mixing love potions for giglets?'

'One that you have supported very ably, Commander. More wine? Good. I still have a few more scraps of food but I think we should keep them for tomorrow. After that . . . ' He did not finish the sentence.

'In your missive you mentioned escape, Master Leodore. Have you aught in mind?'

'There is only one entrance to this tower, apart from my window. It is the doorway at the bottom of the stairs, and this was bricked by the Regent's order.'

'Could we break through it?'

'We would have to force our way through a massive iron-bound door to reach the brickwork, and then I have no doubt that if we could break through that we would emerge into the arms of a Companion of the Rose. I must confess, Commander, that although I have obviously given the question much thought, I have not had a single worthwhile idea, except flight.'

'Did you say flight?'

Leodore nodded.

'You can work magic then?'

'The laws of the alchemist are opposite to those of a magician, and the days of High Magic ended with The Enchantment. As a young man I used to be fascinated by the thought of flying, of making artificial wings that could be worked by pulleys so that one could rise like a bird. The idea came from the legend that occasionally men are born who in their maturity sprout wings, an old widows' tale doubtless but—'

'And did you attempt it?'

'Oh yes, I constructed wings but my attempts brought me to the attention of the Witchfinders. Watching the birds out of my window reminded me of my old pinions and I daydreamed about gliding through the air to freedom. Such are the fancies of the condemned!'

'And yet there might be something in such a fancy. I have used kites in warfare and if we could possibly fly one at night with a line to a roof or turret . . . but first let me see if I can think of something more feasible.'

'There may well be something that I overlooked,' said Leodore as Mandal finished his last wine-soaked crust. 'I am an old, unworldly philosopher while you are a proved man of resource and mayhap will see a means of escape that has eluded me.'

'For an old, unworldly philosopher you arranged my escape from the Cage remarkably well. But now let me see where you have been walled in.'

Carrying a candle lantern in one hand and leading the homunculus by the other, Leodore took Mandal to the bottom of the circular steps and held the light high for him to see the massive door. Mortar had flowed beneath it giving evidence of the barrier that had been raised on the other side.

'You are right, it would be time squandered to attempt to break through,' said Mandal. He looked about him in the pale light and then at the stone-flagged floor. 'What lies below, Master Alchemist?'

Leodore shrugged. 'I have no idea. Earth, I suppose, or rock.'

'Well, let us find out.'

After returning to the chamber above to take what implements he could find that might be of use, Mandal examined the paving.

'Thank the Mother it is not cemented together,' he said, and while Leodore held the lantern he inserted the end of a fire iron in a crevice between two stones and threw his weight upon it. At first nothing happened, then with frustrating slowness one of the slabs began to loosen.

'Help me lever it,' he cried to the old man. With extra weight applied, one end suddenly rose and

362

a gust of nauseous air hissed through the aperture. Holding his breath, Mandal curled his fingers under the raised edge, prised it up and then swung it to one side. Leodore raised the lantern and they saw that the paving had been set on stone corbels.

'These flagstones are also roofslabs for a passage or crypt below,' said Mandal.

'From the smell, it is most likely a sewer,' muttered Leodore through the edge of his gown which he held to his face.

'All sewers come out somewhere,' said Mandal. He picked up the lantern and lowered it into the square of darkness. 'It seems to be a passage – the Citadel must be riddled with such. Mayhap this one will lead us to freedom. Let us collect all we shall need and explore it.'

Soon afterwards Mandal – carrying a bag containing candles, flasks of wine and water, and Leodore's last crusts – lowered himself through the aperture. When his feet touched the floor of the passage he was thankful to find that he could just stand upright without having to bend his neck. He helped the old man down and then, fighting his revulsion, did the same for the homunculus.

'I shall carry her on my back,' said Leodore.

'And I shall lead the way.'

He picked up the lantern and cautiously set off between the narrow walls of roughly dressed stones. Lime formations glistened where damp had seeped through the mortar and filaments of nitre hung like white threads from the roof slabs. Much time had passed since mortal foot had trod that way.

The news that his master had departed on a progress was late reaching the custodian of his automata but when it did, the little man murmured a sad prayer of gratitude that he was free to carry out something that had weighed on his mind since the last visit of the Regent.

'Now, my dear one, we can show you the respect you deserve, oh yes, my poor love, dignity shall be yours,' he whispered aloud as he locked the door that led into the gallery – not that anyone was likely to disturb him now that the Regent was gone from the Citadel. He took a lamplighter's pole with a taper in its socket and went from chandelier to chandelier until the shadows were banished.

'*He* will find out and punish us when he returns but I care not,' he muttered as he tore the dust covers from the line of life-sized automatons that stood waiting for his touch to animate them. '*He* is mad, oh yes, crazed! How could he . . . ' His sibilant voice broke. 'How I wish the executioner had cut off his ugly hand and he had bled to death. Serve him right, oh yes, serve him right.'

When all the mechanical dolls had been uncovered, Prince spent a long time with each, setting clockwork in readiness for the complicated movements that they would soon be performing. The harper was the last. The custodian turned a pointer hidden under his cloak from the incised word 'dance' to 'dirge'.

Now a moment he had long dreaded. He went to the far end of the gallery where a coffin, draped with white samite, stood on silvern trestles. With a violent sob he drew the covering back and there lay the replica of the Lady Merlinda. Her head, with its realistic eyelids closed, lay on a pillow of the finest lace Prince could find in the Citadel; a scarf of similar material hid the damage made by the executioner's axe when she had been decapitated at the behest of the Regent.

With tears running down his sallow face, Prince leaned over and laid a bouquet of silken roses – there were no real flowers to be found in this remote part of the Citadel – on her hands which were chastely folded below her breasts.

'My darling, the time has come,' he murmured. Then he was flying along the line of automata, touching hidden levers, activating amazing mechanisms that clicked and ticked and whirred into life. The harper ran his metal fingers over the strings of his lyre and a chord of solemn beauty filled the gallery. The dolls – even the winged lion whose perpetual snarl the custodian detested – stepped forward, turned towards Merlinda's coffin and, led by a knight in full armour, began a slow procession to the lament of the harp. The only automaton excluded was the executioner. Since *that* night he had not been seen in the gallery.

Prince was unable to join the mechanical mourners. He was moving from one to the other, adjusting the speed of a footstep here, the angle of a neck movement there. The erotic dancer gave him the most trouble as she had a tendency to leave the procession and hoist her skirts in a way that made Prince want to scream.

The most difficult time came when the

procession reached the coffin. Although the movements of the mourners had been carefully set, there was still some confusion. The Mother-cursed lion kept on walking until his snarl collided with the wall, the knight suddenly froze as his clockwork ran down, and when the drummer blundered into him he began beating a retreat.

But soon the little man had restored order. Four of the male automatons stood with their hands clamped on the coffin handles; the rest stood two by two behind it.

'The time has come to bid goodbye to our beloved,' Prince said. 'Life without her will never be the same. Without her I . . .'

His voice broke. The words of farewell he had rehearsed remained unsaid. Again he touched levers, the men raised the coffin and the procession moved forward to a door that Prince had previously opened. Beyond it was a sloping passage lit by flambeaux which turned the cortège into a procession of flickering shadows on the ancient walls. The harper played sad music and step by measured step Merlinda was borne to her secret resting place.

Smoke drained slowly from the mirror and as Mandraga drew a silken veil across it she allowed her pale lips to form a smile of satisfaction. After locking the door of her mirror sanctum she limped with the aid of her crutch to a reception chamber where a tall man in a robe of pearl-grey gaberdine stood gazing through a casement at a vista of the city far below.

'The Lady Mandraga, Lore Mistress of Ythan,' announced the Companion of the Rose who stood on guard at the door.

The man turned and inclined his head the exact distance required by protocol. Mandraga seated herself in a high-backed chair of ivory, and the Companion ensured their privacy by softly closing the door.

'Archpriest Mattan, you are welcome,' she said. 'Do be seated.'

The Archpriest was a handsome man in his middle years, well-groomed, clean-shaven, and with piercing eyes set in a face whose straight nose and thin curving lips held a fraction too much pride for his ascetic calling, though he knew well how to disguise it in his manner. Now he looked at the chair the Lore Mistress indicated and seeing that it was lower than hers he smiled and said, 'Lady, mayhap I am old-fashioned but I grew up with the notion that it was unmannerly to be seated in the presence of the great.'

'As you will, but you are not before my Lord Regent, merely a very old woman whose only virtue is a memory packed with the lore of Ythan.'

Both smiled at the insincerity of this description.

'And how is the health of the Lord Regent?'

'He is well, otherwise he would not have undertaken this progress that has burdened me with responsibility, but have you a special reason for asking?'

'There have been rumours . . .'

'Rumours are more dangerous than serpents. Your lamented predecessor might now have been preparing the festival of the Summer Adoration if his assassin had not heeded rumours.'

'Ah yes, it was an ill wind . . . ' said the Archpriest. 'Following in the footsteps of such a one is a fraught task, yet it brings the realisation that one serves the state by serving the Mother, and not by seeking secular advantage. But I rejoice that the Lord Regent is able to leave Danaak as it must indicate that all is well with the kingdom.'

When the Lore Mistress said nothing he continued, 'May I enquire why you have given me the honour of this summons?'

'I felt that you, as spiritual head of Ythan, should be the first to be acquainted with a discovery I have made.'

'Yes, my lady?'

'As time weighs upon me my memory is not as fresh as it was of yesteryear, and sometimes I find it necessary to refer to past texts and chronicles in the preparation of ritual and ceremonies. Recently, in seeking a formula relating to the Empty Throne, I came across a document which was part of the royal testament of King Johan XXXIII, signed by his own hand and sealed with the royal seal.'

'A remarkable find, my lady.'

'Indeed, though I have no doubt that it was placed so that it would come to light at this time, for there was no reason for the tome I sought to be required until the centennial of The Enchantment.'

'And the burden of this testament?'

'King Johan stated that if his entranced

daughter was not found and awakened within a hundred years – or proved to be dead – a new king should be elected to establish a royal house for the well-being of the kingdom.'

'I am honoured that you confide a discovery of such magnitude to me. As a scholar I would be fascinated to see the document.'

'In the fullness of time,' said Mandraga.

In the fullness of time! he thought. *That means her forger has not yet completed it.* Aloud he said, 'As far as the shrines are concerned, there can be little doubt as to who should ascend the Empty Throne – especially after he has proclaimed his piety by stamping out the heresy of Thaan.'

'You are a man of wisdom and understanding, Archpriest,' said Mandraga. 'Should it fall to you to conduct an enthronement ceremony in the near future I shall be happy, as Lore Mistress, to advise you on the ancient ritual.'

'I shall be most honoured to be advised.' And again both smiled their insincerity.

SIX

Dark Journey

'The cursed Mage!' raved Alwald. 'Did he purposely not warn us about the colossus!'

'Mayhap he did not know about him,' said Krispin mildly. 'He never suggested he had been to the Shadow Realm but merely gave you the Lodestone to guide us. The blessing is that we are alive.'

It was the awesomeness of the great metal figure that had saved the crew of the *Amber Star*. Amazed at his size as he reared above the narrow river, all had been gazing up at him when his sword began to descend. They had just enough time to leap out of its path, some to the forecastle and some to the poop. The titanic blade caught the vessel amidships and severed her timbers in a shower of splinters. Water immediately filled her hull and those on the sundered deck felt it lurch wildly beneath them and braced themselves for an onrush of water as the ship foundered, but nothing happened. The shallowness of the river meant that the hull sank no deeper than an armspan before it rested on the bottom.

The *Amber Star*'s skiff remained undamaged and within minutes it had ferried the travellers to land, their anxiety to leave the ship being based on the fear that the colossus might raise his sword for a second stroke. But as they waited on the bank the huge blade remained embedded in the oaken keel of the vessel it had struck in half, and the figure looming in the eternal gloaming showed no further sign of movement.

Now that the initial shock was over, the companions discussed what they should do, and soon realised that they had little choice. It was out of the question to return to the coast on foot because of the danger posed by the outcasts and, as Alwald said, what would be the point of returning to the shore on the unknown sea upon which no vessels ventured?

'We must go on with the quest,' he declared. 'We have the Lodestone to guide us, and sooner or later we would have had to leave the *Amber Star.*'

'Easy for you to say, Lord Alwald,' muttered Danya gazing at the tilted wreck before them, 'but you have not just lost a ship. What ill fate brought me to this accursed land?'

'I can understand your anger, Shipmaster. The *Amber Star* brought us bravely through many dangers and we share your feeling of loss, but I vow that if the Princess Livia comes into her own you shall have a new vessel – or the worth thereof.'

At that moment the possibility of such recompense seemed so remote that Danya found it difficult to make a reply.

'You are right that we should continue, Alwald,' said Krispin quickly. 'For it seems to me that what has just befallen us is a proof that we are nearing our goal. If so much trouble was taken over the hiding of the Princess at the time of The Enchantment, it is likely that traps and hazards were placed to prevent her being found. That guardian that towers above us could only be the work of the most powerful sorcery.'

'I am sure you speak true,' said Gambal. 'We should view what has just happened as an auspicious sign.'

Danya muttered something under his breath that fortunately the others did not catch.

'In which direction does the Lodestone now point?' asked Krispin.

Alwald brought out the ivory box from the pocket of his tunic and looked at the needle mounted in it.

'It points along the river. And that means we may continue the journey in the skiff, for a while at least. Is that agreeable, Shipmaster?'

Danya shrugged and said with attempted resignation, 'There seems to be no other way.'

'Speaking for myself and Mute, may I say that while we are not part of your quest, Lord Alwald, we offer you our loyalty just as it was pledged to Shipmaster Danya when we were aboard the *Amber Star*,' said Dikon. 'It is a strange adventure that has befallen us, yet no matter what perils may lie ahead I will always thank the Mother that I am facing them rather than toiling in the sulphur mines where no man lasts longer than a season.'

Beside him Mute nodded his head in agreement.

'The gloaming will soon darken to night,' said Alwald. 'Let us get what is needful from the wreck and make camp here, and then in the morning we can continue in the boat.'

The *Amber Star* was no more than a dozen paces from the left bank to which the travellers had fled, and it did not take long to bring packs, provisions and blankets ashore. Danya ferried over a load of splintered decking.

'We will need a fire through the night and there are no trees on this accursed plain,' he said gruffly. 'Little did I think when we set out this morning that my ship would be of no use other than for kindling by nightfall.'

'Only the Mother knows what lies ahead,' said Dikon, 'and it is a blessing that she keeps it a secret for otherwise we would take to our beds and wait for life to pass us by.'

While the camp was being prepared, Danya returned to the *Amber Star* yet again and brought his boxes of amber ashore.

'A few of the finest pieces I shall carry with me,' he explained. 'The rest I shall bury in the manner that the corsairs hide their treasure. Will you help, Krispin and Dikon?'

They nodded and picked up the boxes while the shipmaster took a spade and led the way to a low bluff that he would be able to recognise in the future because of its resemblance to a beast stretched out as though in sleep. Here, between what might be fancifully thought of as the beast's paws, a pit was dug to hide the boxes of petrified sap for which Danya had lost his crew and indirectly his ship. An hour later the men tramped the sandy soil flat and returned to the others who were now eating cold food round a lively fire. In the darkness the enormous feet of the colossus were faintly visible on the opposite bank.

'We started the quest in a boat and it seems we may be ending it in one,' said Krispin as the travellers placed their belongings into the skiff next morning. No one responded to his remark as all felt an inner gloom that was a reflection of the purplish dusk about them. At least after nightfall they were in total dark and this was something to which they were accustomed; the twilight of the daytime inspired a sense of unreality, of deadness in the landscape.

When the skiff was loaded, Alwald cradled his pack on his knees when he took his place in the bows. It contained the flacon of water from the Wells of Ythan given to him by The Mage. He had wrapped it in a blanket for extra protection; his unspoken fear was that some accident might befall it and its wonder-working contents be lost on the final stage of the journey, and thus within seconds turn the possibility of triumph into disaster.

When Krispin accidently touched his shoulder as he settled himself in the boat Alwald rounded on him.

'You clumsy peasant!' he shouted before he could bite back the words.

Krispin said nothing. Like any young man of his age he was quick to be hurt by an insult but he appreciated his companion's nervousness. Ruefully remembering his resentment when The Mage gave Alwald the flacon in return for the Esav which he, Krispin, had won in the City Without a Name, he was now grateful he had escaped the responsibility of carrying it.

When all the party had embarked, their combined weight caused the gunwhale to sink to a hand's breadth above the water. Danya told Dikon and Krispin, who were taking the first shift as oarsmen, to row to the wrecked *Amber Star*. Here the shipmaster carefully climbed onto the sloping deck and vanished into the deckhouse. He was gone some time and the travellers looked at each other, puzzled. When he returned to the boat he merely nodded to the rowers to set off upstream and looked ahead with a set expression on his face. There was something about his manner that prevented comment or question, and the skiff proceeded silently for several minutes.

Suddenly there was a prolonged roar behind them. A gigantic tongue of orange fire leapt into the dusky air. Within seconds flames were licking hungrily over the deck and up the tilted mast.

'I lit the mangonel's casks of holy fire,' Danya said quietly. 'Somehow it seemed the right thing to do, rather than to leave her there to rot. Keep rowing, lads.'

They kept rowing, lit by the glow of the conflagration and with smuts whirling about them; no one spoke until all that remained of the *Amber Star* was a column of smoke far behind.

The cremation of the ship added to the

depression that affected all but Tana; perhaps after her mysterious captivity, freedom was something to be relished even in the Shadow Realm. She tried to make conversation with Dikon who was seated at the oars opposite her, the length of chain which hung from his manacle tinkling with every stroke, but he answered in monosyllables. She turned to see if any of the others would be more communicative but encountering Ognam's gaze she remained silent and watched the barren bank slipping past. To Krispin it seemed that everyone's nerves were becoming taut, yet this morning's journey was uneventful and they had not become so stressed in the past when threatened by danger.

It is something in this dark air, he thought. *There is an evil here that must have lingered from The Enchantment that may be of greater hazard to us than outcasts or metal guardians. It is something I must watch for but – Serene Mother! – I have become so weary of this quest. It is all right for the likes of Alwald . . .*

Alwald was thinking, *Mayhap I was short with the toymaker but while he has had his success with the sword I gave him, the responsibility falls on me. Serene Mother! How I shall welcome the day when we are free to go our own ways again . . .*

The river, having passed through the gap in the cliffs guarded by the titan, continued between rocky banks for a short while and then once more curved across a dim plain. It was as though the skiff had passed through a natural wall – or was it natural? Danya wondered. If the folklore stories of The Enchantment held any truth, stupendous magical forces had been involved, and it was possible that the land itself had been shaped to protect the secret resting place of the Sleeping Princess. The gap in the cliff wall meant that anyone seeking to go further into the Shadow Realm would pass beneath the sword that had brought destruction to his ship. There was something subtle but evil in the Shadow Realm that made the dangers of the Cold Sea straightforward in comparison.

Ognam thought less of the Shadow Realm than the others; in memory he crossed the lake beneath The Mage's tower to where Tana put her arms through the magical bars of her prison to greet him. With real pain in his heart he brooded on the contrast between the dream damsel he had talked to in the silvered cavern and the flirt sitting in the skiff.

I am in love with an ideal, with someone that only existed in my imagination, he told himself. *Curse Krispin! It was through him that I learned my folly and yet, knowing this, I still worship her. Would that I could escape this quest . . .*

As the long morning wore on, the travellers became even less talkative, and when some necessity caused them to speak they did so with little regard to their normal politeness.

By noon the scenery began to change. To the left the plain continued to stretch towards the darksome horizon but to the right it was replaced by more fertile ground in that it was covered with lacklustre clumps of spiky grass. It sloped gently towards foothills above which the white summits of the Mountains of the Moon appeared to float in the murk.

In the bows Alwald held up his arm. 'We can go no further by water,' he announced. 'The Lodestone has turned and our way lies towards the ranges.'

'You mean we have to walk?' demanded Tana with irritation in her voice for the first time.

'Unless you wish to remain with the boat.'

'Is there no way we could go a little further on the river?'

'See for yourself,' said Alwald impatiently and held out the ivory box containing the Lodestone.

'It means nothing to me,' said Tana with a shrug.

'I relish walking no more than anyone else, and I have had my share of it since Krispin and I left the Wald, but our way lies overland and that is all there is to it. I did not invent the quest, I am merely stupid enough to follow it.'

'There is no need to use that tone to Tana,' Ognam heard himself protest.

'A rebuke from the lovelorn,' Alwald jeered.

'For the Mother's sake, Alwald!' Krispin cried.

'Ah, the toymaker joins in. Mayhap if you had thought to lock your door—'

'Stop,' said Gambal. 'Have we come all this way only to fall out? You behave like children.'

Both Krispin and Alwald turned to face him but before angry words could leave their lips Danya said, 'Enough, enough. Get ready to land.'

He turned the tiller and the skiff nosed into the withered reeds lining the margin. Without speaking, they disembarked and buckled on their packs. Danya and Dikon drew the boat out of the water and turned it keel up. No one spoke. It was as though each member of the party was filled with resentment.

Alwald, Lodestone in hand, set off and the others straggled after him. The grass clumps grew as high as their knees and the tip of each blade was as sharp as a needle, as the travellers soon discovered when they brushed against them.

They trekked all through the dreary afternoon, resting briefly every hour, and were rewarded by more pleasant terrain as the ground rose. Softer sward replaced the grass clumps and, as the wan disk of the sun neared the western horizon, they saw groves of elegant trees ahead. Unlike the forest on the coast, these black-boled trees had healthy-looking foliage of dark green, and though their branches drooped in the manner of willows, there was nothing to suggest the lack of light had warped them.

The party pressed forward with renewed vigour in order to reach them before the twilight became night and make camp – if the mere laying of blankets on the ground could be called that. All were weary and as they ate their ship's biscuit and washed it down with a rationed measure of wine their eyelids became heavier and heavier. When they lay down on the soft dry leaf mould beneath the trees, which gave off a slight sweetish scent, an almost abnormal desire to slumber engulfed them. Alwald rolled himself in his blanket, laid his hand on the pack containing the flacon and plunged into oblivion. Krispin clasped the grip of Woundflame and followed suit. Tana breathed in the tree perfume and laid her cheek on her crossed hands in sleep.

In the darkness Ognam sat on his blanket, the sighing breath and snores of his companions telling him that he was the only one awake. Fighting the temptation to follow their·example, he climbed to his feet. The moon had risen, a lavender coin in the night sky, but it gave the jongleur enough light to hoist his pack and tiptoe away from the circle of sleepers with his jester's staff clasped in his hand.

The scent from the trees grew stronger as the night wore on and filled the nostrils of the travellers, but they were too deeply asleep to savour it – or feel the tendrils that slithered out of the mould and twined over their bodies.

SEVEN

Ognam Alone

Holding his jester's staff tightly, Ognam stole through the trees in whose grove his companions lay sleeping. The light from the moon was just enough to enable him to avoid their weeping branches and before long he felt the leaf mould beneath his feet change to soft grass. The night lay heavy on the Shadow Realm which, at that hour, could not have been more aptly named. Ognam was no more than a shadow among shadows and he sighed as he remembered the nights at the Domain of Olam when stars blazed in the clear desert air. What would he not give now to see the Constellation of the Griffin glittering like a familiar symbol of hope. Like many in Ythan he had wished upon the Griffin as a small boy – and occasionally as an adult, in the way that a childhood prayer comes unbidden to mind in a moment of crisis.

Here the shadow hid the stars and with them any idea of hope as far as Ognam was concerned. But at least he had carried out the first step of his plan – he had left his so-called comrades with their mockery and secret amusement at his unhappiness. And he had removed himself from the presence of Tana whose beauty had once filled him with wondering delight and which now was a taunt to his desire, and whose voice gave him a pang every time he heard her laughing with the others.

It was during the journey from the wrecked *Amber Star*, when everyone was becoming more and more ill-tempered, that he had decided to leave the quest. He sensed that he was on the edge of something terrible; one moment he felt like flinging himself on his knees before Tana and the next he was mentally cursing her for giving him false hope when she was a captive. A lot of the time he felt himself close to tears, and he loathed himself for this weakness. For a long time his livelihood had depended on his making a fool of himself but he had done it with dignity in his heart. Now he knew he was losing that.

During the day he had felt smouldering resentment against Krispin and Alwald, who spoke to him so crudely, and Gambal who never lost an opportunity to express his dislike of him. Yet later, when they settled in the grove, he remembered the hardship and adventure they had faced together and the times it had seemed there was a bond between them – when they had been like the brothers he had wished for during a lonely childhood.

Then, as he stole away, he thought how little the shared experience counted. If Krispin had any concern for him at all he would not have made love to Tana when he, like everyone else, knew Ognam's feelings for her. And the others would have sympathised with those feelings rather than sneer at them.

He would be far better off alone.

It was a step to regaining his tattered self-esteem. And, he hoped, his action would give Tana something to think about!

The problem was that having made the break, he did not know what to do next.

He was alone in an alien land that lay beyond the outermost boundary of Ythan. He could only think that if he travelled in the direction of the Mountains of the Moon and somehow managed to cross them, he might possibly reach an inhabited region.

What chance have I got of doing that? he asked himself. *I must have been mad to leave the others! Mad! Or was I? Better to perish in this no-man's land on my own terms than go on suffering. Serene Mother! I never believed that love could cause such agony. Only now do I understand poor Buffaloon!* – Buffaloon being a comic acrobat who had been in the same troupe as Ognam, and who one night hanged himself from his trapeze for the love of a wayward flowergirl.

With these thoughts in mind Ognam walked over the grass in what he thought was the direction of the Mountains of the Moon, and all the time the image of Tana – laughing Tana, pensive Tana, Tana with the loving smile – was before him. Tears filled his eyes with a sense of loss for something he'd never had.

It was in this state of mind that he suddenly felt

his feet sink into mud and he awoke to the fact that he was about to blunder into a small lake. He stepped back and sat on the firm ground. The water in front of him was almost as dark as the shadow about him, only the faintest reflection of faint moonbeams showed on its surface and that was tinged with amethyst rather than silver.

'We may as well wait here until morning,' Ognam said aloud to the carved head on his staff. 'Alas, how life has changed since you were presented to me by the guild at the end of my apprenticeship. High hopes then! We were going to bring merriment to a dreary world! We were going to fight the Regent with jokes! Instead we end up with nothing to show but patched motley and a heart breaking over a girl who could be no more interested in a jongleur like me than a stray cur.'

Perhaps Buffaloon had been right. Why suffer when a quick brave action would make it unnecessary? Here was a perfectly good lake. All he needed to do was wade into it and keep on wading until merciful oblivion overtook him. It was strange that this solution had only just come to him. Until he entered the Shadow Realm the idea of such easy relief would never have entered his head – he remembered swearing at the mottled corpse of Buffaloon for being a fool! – but now it seemed as though some mysterious inspiration had made him wiser.

Ognam stood up.

'Last performance!' he said to the head on his staff and stepped forward.

*   *   *

It was the sensation of being about to sneeze that wakened Gambal. There was a definite tickling in his nose, and he tried to raise his hand to rub it. But his hand remained at his side, and the young man almost dozed off again under the hazy idea that he was too sleep-sodden to make the effort. Then his nose tickled again. It felt as though a thread was moving within his nostril. This time he did make the effort and woke properly with the realisation that he was not able to move anything except his eyelids. A million filaments seemed to have wrapped themselves round his body – and now it seemed were probing it! He was reminded of cocooned flies he had seen dangling in cobwebs.

He fought to free himself. He tried to shake his body loose. He tried to open his arms wide to break the clutch of the threads, but he could do nothing except shout for help.

His cries were answered, not by cries of encouragement but by cries of panic and he realised that his companions were in similar bondage. And them, remembering a tale told in the Citadel by a merchant who supplied the Regent with costly woods, he knew that they were doomed.

They had gone to sleep in a Upas grove.

The water was cold.

As it rose up Ognam's calves his steps became slower and slower. For one moment the ludicrousness of the situation struck him and nearly made him laugh, and then his mind was filled with words and images that seemed to come from without. Pictures of a naked Tana moving frantically beneath an equally naked Krispin; Tana mimicking his lovelorn expression to make Alwald laugh, Tana flirting with Danya, Tana going into Gambal's cabin, Tana being fondled by Mute when she spooned broth into his mouth . . .

Where do they come from, these maddening pictures? Certainly not from his own mind or memory, for he had never seen Tana without her clothes or in such poses. He might be heart-broken by the fact that she could not return his love but Ognam knew enough of his own nature to be wary of what was passing before his inward eye. He turned abruptly and waded back until he felt short reeds brush his ankles and he threw himself down on the bank.

He lay for a long time, his heart hammering as though he had been involved in intense physical effort, tears of dismay coursing down his face. He felt that he was changing, passing the blurred border between sanity and madness.

Was I really going to drown myself? he wondered. *Surely I am too much of a coward for such a drastic step? Where is my sense of humour? I must have lost that when I lost my heart. Why in the name of Omad did I have to wander down those stairs, why was I such a fool to cross the lake, why was I fated to meet her?*

As usual with such questions no answers came and he sat for a long while with his legs drawn up and his chin on his knees.

When he first saw the light he thought it was the glint of a star that had broken through the shadow which hung over the landscape. It was like a spark in the darkness but he realised that it was not a star when he saw that it was moving. The observation of this mysterious pinpoint of light became all-absorbing, a rest from the questions and emotional shifts besieging him. For a while it seemed to Ognam that his whole future related to that will o' the wisp far out over the lake.

It began to shine more brightly, indicating that it was coming nearer and Ognam understood from its motion that it was flying. A minute later he saw that rays of different colours radiated from it.

And then it was suddenly close to him, a graceful bird that might have been sculptured from a glowing prism except that it had movement. Light emanating from it shone on the water below as with a slow wingbeat it circled and glided onto the surface of the lake. It folded its wings and bobbed on its own ripples, the head on its long swan-like neck turning towards the solitary man on the shore.

Ognam was enrapt as he gazed at the fabulous creature resting within a rainbow halo of its own making. The fact that since he had been in the Shadow Realm his sight had adjusted to the perpetual gloom now heightened the effect created by the bird.

It is as though it is made of crystal, he thought. *And to think I had the notion to end everything when this splendour was only a few minutes away!*

For the bird gave out something else besides light. Ognam felt some indefinable balm was entering him, that suddenly his spirit was freed from the bitterness that had been warping it. The sense of release both physical and mental seemed miraculous, and the jongleur continued to gaze at the bird with awestruck eyes. The only sadness that intruded into his new-found peace of mind was that sooner or later this wondrous creature would fly away.

For the moment it showed no sign of doing so. It appeared to be resting on the water like a normal bird, occasionally dabbing its beak in the water it had made iridescent. It was only later when his mind returned again and again to this mystic experience that Ognam realised that in one sense the bird was a real bird despite its unearthly splendour, and in another it was a visible symbol of something true and beautiful beyond human comprehension.

The passage of time meant nothing to Ognam. Whether it was hours or minutes that passed while he contemplated the bird he never knew; he was outside the dimensions of normal life and, under the influence of the bird, he saw aspects of his life with penetrating clarity. His weaknesses and equally his strengths came into clear focus and he was filled not only with self-awareness but a realisation of the amazing possibilities open to the human spirit. Tears again wet his face but this time they were not inspired by frustrated emotion but by gratitude for this inkling of something sublime beyond the bricks and mortar of the mundane world.

Ognam remained sitting with his knees drawn

up, his staff forgotten but still clasped in his hand, for a long time after the bird had risen from the lake and flown like a dying star in the direction of the Mountains of the Moon. He did not speculate on where the bird came from or even what it was – the fact that he had seen it and as a result his troubled heart had found serenity was enough. If a sage or a priest or a philosopher had suddenly appeared and offered an explanation, he would not have listened. A lily may be explained by dissecting petal, stamen and stem but you no longer have a lily.

At length the jongleur gave a sigh – partly satisfaction that the bird had come, partly regret that it had flown – and stood up, stretching his cramped limbs and mentally savouring the new concept he had gained. His plan of leaving his erstwhile companions had faded and he began to retrace his steps towards the groves.

They might not be aware of it, but in the realm of the shadow they needed him just as he needed them.

EIGHT

The Hermit

'I have heard it told that there are as many secret passages as there are ordinary corridors in the Citadel,' said Leodore as he rested with his back against the cold stone of the tunnel which he and Mandal had been following.

'That I can easily believe,' Mandal agreed. 'The place is so old, and has been added to so much over the centuries, I doubt if anyone knows it completely.'

'How long have we been following this passage?'

'I cannot judge in hour-glass time but long enough for one candle to burn down. When you are rested we will press on.'

Leodore nodded his white head. 'I think we have been going downward.'

From the stench it probably leads to the dungeons. Perhaps it was built as a channel for the noisome air, thought Mandal, *but there is no need to depress the old man before we know for certain. Anyway it is preferable to die hidden away than in the Cage.*

'Come along, Titi,' said Leodore climbing to his

feet and lifting the homunculus on to his back.

Titi! How can he give a ridiculous name like that to such a monstrosity? wondered Mandal. He shuddered as the creature made a whimpering sound and clung to her creator.

Soon the tunnel sloped and curved so sharply and continuously that Mandal guessed they were in a descending spiral. At times the air was so fetid that both gagged and held their hands over their mouths.

'I did not want to worry you before,' said Leodore after a long period, 'but I have a feeling that this must lead to the Netherworld – the dungeons which are hewn out of the rock on which the Citadel was built. The air is dungeon air if ever I had the misfortune to sniff it.'

'We may as well continue, having come – Serene Mother!'

In the light of the candle lantern a body dressed in ragged garments sprawled face down on the tunnel floor ahead of them.

They edged forward cautiously though there was nothing to suggest that life remained within its emaciated frame. Mandal leaned down and touched its shoulder. Immediately the body moved, not as though awakening but as one whose brittle flesh had been waiting for such a touch to turn it to dust. Its substance powdered away before their eyes until its tatters rested on bone.

'I would guess he was one of the few who ever escaped from the dungeons,' said Mandal as they carefully stepped round the remains. Nothing more was said. What they had just seen was a grim portent of their likely fate.

The passage ceased both its curving and downward angle, and Mandal shaded the lantern as they saw several luminous patches ahead of them.

'What are they?' whispered Mandal.

'Obviously you have not been incarcerated in a dungeon, Commander,' said Leodore in an equally low tone. 'But I have, and I can tell you that the light you see comes through the ceiling grilles of prisoners privileged enough to have a candle or rushlight – or unfortunate enough.'

'What do you mean?'

'Sometimes a light is necessary for a man or woman to be aware of the extremity of their situation. Sensitive people might be less conscious of the lice or rats or the dungeon litter spreading over their bodies if left in darkness. Others, of course, suffer more in the dark. All tastes are catered for in the Netherworld.'

They moved forward silently until they reached a grating set in the floor through which light filtered upwards as the alchemist had described. Mandal looked down into the cell below and bit back an oath.

'Not pretty!' Leodore murmured.

'How could they do that to her?'

The next grating showed what appeared to be an empty cell, but as both looked through the grating a face suddenly appeared on the other side of the bars. It was so unexpected that they leaped back in fright which caused gales of manic laughter to echo through the grille. They hurried on but Mandal could not rid his mind of the face with its staring eyes, diseased skin and grinning mouth of gaped teeth. It was how he imagined a demon would look.

No light showed through the next grille. The ammoniac reek that rose from it made their eyes stream and they were edging past when light from the lantern accidently shone upon the occupant below. Mandal gave a gasp of surprise.

'So that is what happened to him.'

'What do you mean?'

'Look.'

Leodore peered through the bars.

The dungeon below had a central pillar, and chained to it so that he could neither sit down nor stand upright was a prisoner who looked up with eyes unused to light. The skin of his face that was not hidden by a tangle of dirty beard had the pallor of the prison but he was still just recognisable.

'Lord Odo,' said Mandal. 'If we could but get him out of there he might be the key to the Regent's downfall.'

'How so? Alone in my tower and only visited by a mute servant or the Regent, I had little idea of what occurred in Danaak.'

'I heard that before Odo's mysterious disappearance he tried to usurp the Regent. There were many sympathetic to his cause and ready to act at the right moment, but on the Night of Election he vanished and no one dared to ask questions. If only we could restore him to his followers there might be a revolt after all.'

Leodore regarded the pathetic figure doubt-fully.

'I doubt if he remembers his name,' he muttered. 'And besides, we have not found a way out for ourselves. Your imagination runs ahead of reality, Commander.'

'It is something that I have a feeling about,' said Mandal. 'I used to get such moments in battle when I suddenly knew what was about to happen. These grilles are hinged so that they can be opened from above – I can guess the reason for that – so if we could find an exit it would be possible to come back for him.'

To prove his words he seized the corroded bars of the grille and raised it like a trapdoor, then he lowered his face to the aperture.

'Lord Odo,' he whispered.

'Lord Odo has gone,' came a faint voice accompanied by a jangle of chains. 'The rats have eaten Lord Odo.'

'Then who are you?'

'I am the phantom of Lord Odo, all that the rats left . . .'

His voice died as there came the sound of a key turning in a massive lock. Mandal immediately blew out the candle and waited as a strip of light appeared and widened at the end of the dungeon. A gaoler appeared in the doorway, brutish of face, clad in stained leather and metal boots to protect him from the rodents who lurked in the dungeon straw.

He carefully closed the door behind him and announced in a mock servile voice, 'Pottage, your lordship, the very best the chef could produce with his own hands, but I regret we are out of Ronimar wine.'

He hung his lamp on a bracket and approached the prisoner with a wooden bowl of slop.

'I do apologise for the utensil, my lord. The silver is being polished for the banquet you are holding tonight.'

Mandal sensed a sudden movement beside him and a second later he saw the pallid body of the homunculus fall upon the warder and her arms twine round his neck. The warder's cry stopped abruptly as her needle teeth closed on his throat seeking sustenance from his life blood.

'We are ready to set out, my lord. Your litter is prepared,' said Captain Bors as he entered the Regent's pavilion. The Regent lay on a damask-covered couch. Beside him stood Urwen dressed in a green riding habit which perfectly complemented her fiery hair.

'You have spoken to the scholars?' the Regent asked in the toneless voice of one who has passed a sleepless night.

'Yes, my lord. They have again been studying the manuscript in Old Ythan that they brought back from Thaan, and they assure me that since we left the river we have been approaching the Mountains of the Moon in the right direction. Apparently it is a matter of keeping three peaks aligned. Then, once we reach the ranges, it will be a question of following certain valleys.'

'Remind them that much relies on their accuracy

– including their lives,' said the Regent. 'And the caravan scryer?'

'She predicts a good day's journeying, though there may be some rain at midday.'

'Let us go then.' Under the attentive eyes of the Companion of the Rose and Urwen, the Regent climbed painfully to his feet. The young woman held a staff out to him but he shook his head impatiently.

'Let them see I can still walk on my own,' he muttered.

Nevertheless he allowed her to take his arm until he reached the curtained entrance, then he shrugged away her hand and walked out into the morning. Ranks of soldiers stiffened to attention while his herald saluted him ritualistically with an ivory clarion. In the background a line of loaded baggage drongs waited patiently and a number of Companions of the Rose, vivid in their red surcoats, sat astride their destriers with yellow pennants fluttering from their lances.

As the Regent walked slowly towards his drong litter, servants rushed forward to dismantle the pavilion in which he had passed the night. Towards the west the early sun played her rays upon the snow mantle covering the peaks of the Mountains of the Moon, giving them the effect of floating above the horizon.

'How soon should we reach the Wells?' the Regent asked as he reclined in the litter.

'The scholars say that if the way continues fair it should be no more than three days,' said Bors.

'It must be no longer,' said the Regent, wincing

396

as a slight movement by one of the drongs sent a spasm of pain along his arm. 'Now that the ranges are in sight we no longer need the services of the guide. Reward him so that he will not return to his village and tell of the direction of our journey.'

Captain Bors nodded, raised his arm and let it fall.

The shaggy guide, who had been engaged several days earlier, watched as the column formed up: Companions of the Rose in the vanguard followed by the litter, beside which Urwen rode on a white stallion; then men-at-arms marching to a muted drum, and finally a straggle of grunting drongs.

'Right, son,' said a Companion coming up to the guide. 'Your work is over. Time for payment, eh?'

The guide grinned his agreement.

'You can guess where that lot are heading, can you?'

The guide grinned again. 'They look for the Wells of Ythan. Old widows' tales say they are in the ranges but no one goes to the mountains from my village. All wilderness. The Regent must be very, very sick to come so far to search for wells that may be no more than legend.'

'You are a bright boy,' said the Companion.

The guide's grin became even broader at this praise. A sign was given. Two soldiers seized his arms and forced him to his knees, another twined his fingers in his long hair and pulled his head forward, a sword swept down and severed the outstretched neck.

Cursing the fact that they would have to hurry

397

to catch up the column, the soldiers began to dig a grave.

Until he hovered above the vast smoke-filled clearing in the Arkad Woodlands the Hump had never felt pain in his wings. Thus, when an arrow shot by one of the slave guards tore through the delicate membrane, he felt he was experiencing a spasm of agony that did not rightly belong to his body. But he had no time to reflect on the matter. Flights of arrows were hissing about him and Silvermane and his pinions beat frantically to lift them out of range.

As he soared upwards, smoke from the huge charcoal pits temporarily blinded him while the cries of both guards and slaves who were employed on the destruction of the forest rang madly in his ears. Then they were free of the smoke and almost out of arrow range. Several reached the high point of their arcing flight around him, remained motionless for a second and then fell away.

'We are clear,' he shouted to Silvermane whom he supported in his arms. In reply he felt her shudder and give a whimper that tore at his heart.

'Are you hurt?' he demanded stupidly.

'Higher. Go higher,' she answered.

He needed no urging. Despite the burning pain in his right wing, the couple continued to soar until the clearing was like a brown, smoking rent in a carpet of green, and they could see the smoke from other clearings. Now safe from arrowfire, he set his wings to rest on the wind that blew steadily from the west.

'My leg,' Silvermane said above the endless rush of air. 'Arrow hit it. Ill. I feel ill.'

Panic filled the Hump.

Riding the wind so high above the forest he was desperately aware of the trembling of her body. He knew he must find a place where it would be safe for them to descend, but then what could he do if she was badly hurt?

'Your people . . . ' he began.

She shook her head and the wind streamed her hair like silver flames.

'Fly on over woodland. Keep back to sun. Watch for hill with tower. Go there. Hermit's home. He help. He know horsefolk.'

The Hump's wings shifted and a moment later he was flying so fast that the trees directly below became a blur of variegated green. With Silverman's back pressed against him as he held her, he could sense the failing of her strength and with a surge of anguish he wondered if she were dying.

'Soon be there, soon be there,' he muttered in her ear as though to pacify a child though he had no idea how far they were from the spot she described. As he flew he kept increasing his height in order to get a better view of the terrain. After half an hour, when he felt his own strength ebbing, he saw on the horizon a small cone-like hill rising above the flat stretch of treetops. He prayed that it was what Silvermane had meant.

'Is that it?' he cried but she made no answer and despite the high wind, cold sweat broke out on his body.

Using everything he had learned since his wings had suddenly grown out of his back in the Desert of Akea, coupled with the instinct that had developed with them, he hurtled towards the distant landmark. Minutes later he was filled with relief when he saw that a tower rose from the summit of the hill. It reminded him of the Knights' Towers that he had known in the Wilderness of Gil. As he circled it, a cowled figure appeared on the flat roof and beckoned him.

The Hump swept over the tower's crenellated parapet and almost sprawled headlong as his feet touched the paved roof. Regaining his balance, he looked hopefully at the man who had watched his descent with a slight smile.

'Welcome, birdman,' he said. 'I am the Hermit.'

Dressed in a hooded robe of brown homespun belted with a piece of frayed rope, he reminded the Hump of some of the bare-footed mendicants he used to see trudging along the caravan routes until the Witchfinders, declaring their claims to be visionaries were heretical, put an end to such unofficial pilgrimage. In the shadow of his hood his face looked unexpectedly young despite a fringe of iron-grey hair. His brown eyes shone both with humour and intelligence.

'Silvermane . . . this horsemaid . . . has been hurt,' the Hump panted. 'She told me you might . . .'

The Hermit nodded. 'I am known to the horsefolk,' he said in a deep and melodious voice that made the Hump think of litanies he had heard when passing shrines. 'Bring her inside.'

He led the way down worn steps into a chamber whose furniture appeared to have been made from wood cut from trees about the tower. With relief the Hump laid Silvermane on a rustic couch and for the first time saw that the head of an arrow was embedded in her thigh. For a moment her eyelids fluttered open and she smiled at the Hump.

'You brought me safely,' she murmured. 'All will be well now.' Then her eyes closed again.

'Tell me what happened,' said the Hermit as he set a pannikin of water on a brazier.

The Hump gave a brief recital of what had passed after leaving the Domain of Olam.

'You will be able to cure her?' he said finally.

The Hermit shrugged. 'When I was a priest' – he smiled at the Hump's expression of surprise – 'I studied medicine – until I had theological problems and had to leave my order. I can remove the arrow with little difficulty. The trouble is, my friend, that the archers who guard the charcoal workings use poison-tipped shafts.'

'You mean that she will die?'

'Not immediately. The effect of the poison on her kind is to induce coma. She may last for weeks, even months, in an unconscious state.'

'There must be some antidote.'

'There is only one I can think of, an ancient panacea for human ills, but where it can be obtained I know not. Of course I will do all I can, for her people made me welcome when I came to the woodlands as an outcast.'

The Hump sat on a rough bench with his head in his hands. He felt there were sobs forming in

401

his chest and he did not know whether he would be able to hold them back.

'I noticed that you had been hurt, too, before you folded your wings,' said the Hermit. 'Let me see while I am waiting for this water to heat.'

Obediently the Hump unfolded his right wing and spread it so that the Hermit could examine the wound, saying, 'It is nothing. The shaft went right through the skin. It just felt strange . . .'

'I fear it is not that simple,' said the Hermit. 'Already the membrane round the hole is discoloured. That is a sign that your arrow was poisoned as well.'

'You mean that I too could fall into a sick slumber?'

'Yes, if I do not act quickly. The only way to stop the toxin spreading to your body is to remove the affected area. In other words I must cut off the tip of your wing. I wish I could treat your companion as easily.'

'You mentioned a cure – a panacea?'

'Put your faith in that, my friend. Fear not, I am sure there is a chance that you will still be able to fly. It will be a moment of agony, but you look like a man who can accept that. Unless I am mistaken, you have known pain in the past.'

As he spoke he placed the thin blade of a small knife in the glowing brazier.

'It is not for myself I ask but for her.'

'I was referring to the legendary Wells of Ythan. Water from the wells was supposed to hold the essence of life and could cure human ailments, and the ailments of those not fully human. I believe

402

the Wells did indeed exist but, like so much else since The Enchantment, their secret has been lost.'

'I shall find them,' muttered the Hump.

A few minutes later, after the arrow had been removed from Silvermane's flesh and healing herbs bandaged over the narrow wound, the Hermit removed the knife from the brazier. The blade glowed a dull red. The Hump flinched and hastily gulped the wine that he had been given.

'Lay your wing across the table,' said the Hermit. 'I am sorry there is not the time to get you dead drunk but the poison spreads fast and . . .'

Blood ran down the Hump's chin as he clamped his teeth on his lower lip to prevent himself screaming. A smell of singeing filled the chamber and the Hermit held up a piece of discoloured membrane resembling ancient parchment.

'I know nothing of such featherless wings,' he said. 'But I have no doubt it will heal soon.'

The Hump's wing moved violently as of its own accord, to the terror of a large owl that had been perched in a shadowed corner.

'My thanks,' murmured the Hump. He glanced over to the couch where Silvermane slept peacefully beneath a woollen coverlet. 'My only virtue is that I can always find the way. So, as soon as I can fly again, I shall seek the Wells of Ythan and – the Mother willing – bring back the cure while she still has life.'

NINE

The Upas Grove

Sickly light was filtering through the trees as Ognam neared the grove where he had left his sleeping companions. Having made up his mind to return to them after his vision of the crystal bird he hoped he would not have to explain his absence, or at least be able to dismiss it as having gone to answer a call of nature. The fact that his particoloured hose was stained with mud did not concern him, he could make a joke of having blundered into a bog. Yet he felt strangely nervous, guilty almost, at having decided to give up the quest during the night, and he hoped that this would not be betrayed in his manner when he found them.

Moving among the black-barked trees with their elegant weeping branches, he began to have a new worry – where were his companions? Only a few minutes earlier it had been dark. Surely they had not risen already and continued on their journey? He wondered whether to call out, but that might lead to embarrassing questions as to why he had lost them.

He entered a grove that looked vaguely familiar. It could have been the one in which they had all laid down in their blankets but there was no sign of life. There was only one thing to do. He would swallow his pride and shout.

'Krispin! Alwald! Gambal!'

The names faded forlornly among the trees.

When there was no reply he turned to walk on, and tripped over a soft mound that lay on the forest mould. It was composed of dark rootlets that sprouted from the ground beneath one of the large trees, and what startled – and then horrified – Ognam was its human form. It was like a corpse whose flesh had been gradually replaced by vegetation, which the jongleur had heard was a battlefield phenomenon.

Reluctantly he reached down with his hand and found that the mound was soft and moving slightly beneath the mass of fibres that bound it.

Next moment he was tearing at them with his hands but they were as strong as spider silk threads and he realised he had no hope of breaking them. For a moment he panicked and gazed about him helplessly. In the increasing light he saw that there were other mounds, and he was left in no doubt that he had found his comrades.

Fighting his fear and disgust, he forced himself to think clearly and from his scrip he withdrew his razor. He tried to remember where Krispin had laid himself down and hurried over to the cocoon in which he guessed the toymaker was trapped. Even with the razor it took him a seeming eternity to cut the filaments along the right side of the

405

mount. They squirmed as though possessed of independent life when the blade touched them. And the sap that bled from them!

It took all his resolution to keep sawing away but at last he felt the razor grate against something as hard as itself, and thrusting his hand into the gash he had cut in the palpitating fibres, he felt his fingers close on the cold grip of Woundflame.

With a cry of triumph he wrenched the sword free. If there was a match for these accursed strands it was this magical weapon. Holding it in both hands he drew the point over the mound that imprisoned Krispin. The myriad threads parted at its touch, threshing and hissing like a nest of serpents.

By the time the blade reached the foot of the mound, Krispin was struggling to sit up and tugging away rootlets that had squirmed into his mouth and nostrils. His ashen face was a reflection of the horror he had undergone.

'Ognam . . . ' he gasped but the jongleur had run to the next victim and Woundflame was scything through the cocoon to reveal Mute who, like Krispin, had a ghastly beard of filaments hanging from his face.

As Ognam raced from mound to mound with the sap-stained sword, a low moaning emanated from the trees whose roots he was mutilating.

Soon there were only two mounds left. The first opened to reveal Gambal who stared up at Ognam in silent astonishment; when the second was sundered, Ognam found himself gazing down upon the limp body of Tana.

For the last few minutes he had wondered what his reaction would be when he found her, if the insight and tranquillity bestowed upon him by the wondrous bird would survive the meeting with the one who had caused him such emotional distress. Now he knew that he felt – nothing. Nothing other than concern for a fellow human being who had been through a horrific experience.

Unlike the others, she was unable to sit up. Ognam knelt beside her to pull away the remaining rootlets. As he did so she opened her eyes and for a moment her face took on the ugly look of one about to scream as the horror of the night returned, then she saw the jongleur looking down upon her and her features relaxed.

'Ognam, I knew if anyone could save me it would be you.'

'It was just luck . . . that I did not get caught. Let me help you up.'

Throughout the grove the figures of the travellers moved as though performing some wild dance; in reality they were snatching root threads from their clothing and kicking away the strands that were still wound round their ankles. The beds of roots that marked where they had been trapped twitched impotently, and Ognam noticed that those still attached to the earth were withdrawing into it like worms. He was filled with an uncontrollable rage against them, and with Woundflame glittering in the morning twilight he began slashing the roots before they could disappear.

Sap spurted in all directions, the eerie lament

of the trees filled the grove and those that had just been freed watched in silence as the normally easy-going jester went berserk. When the floor of the grove was aquiver with dying fragments of root, he turned his attention to the trees, lopping off branches that oozed blood-coloured ichor. And each time one fell, the other branches trembled violently and a screech rent the air.

Suddenly Ognam was exhausted. He turned and held Woundflame to Krispin.

'Your sword,' he panted.

'And right good use you made of it,' said Krispin.

The others muttered their gratitude and Gambal said, 'If I have been harsh in the past, Master Jongleur, you have repaid it by saving my life.'

'Then the score is evened,' said Ognam, 'for I would have surely been thrown into the lime pit by now had you not saved me from the dungeons. But tell me, what . . .?'

'We are surrounded by Upas trees,' Gambal said. 'I have been told that at night they give off a perfume that dulls the senses of those who come near them, and when their victims slumber they enweb them so they can suck nourishment from them until they become husks.'

'Let us begone from this foul place,' said Alwald.

'How was it that you remained free?' Gambal asked as the travellers hastily collected their belongings.

'I felt restless and went for a walk.'

Gambal nodded. 'Thank the Mother for that! When I awoke I found that I could not move a fingerbreadth. Before long I could not even shout when the roots pressed my mouth . . .' At the recollection he hurried away to vomit his disgust.

A few minutes' walk later the party was clear of the deadly groves.

'It seems to me it may not have been by chance that the Upas trees flourished in a belt across these slopes,' said Krispin as they walked wearily over open grassland.

'You mean you think they are there to discourage wanderers from reaching Livia's resting place?' Alwald said.

'In the same way the colossus was set up to "discourage" any vessel that sailed upriver.'

'Then we must be on our guard for the next hazard.'

As the morning wore on, the travellers found themselves walking up gentle slopes towards the dim hills below the Mountains of the Moon which were silhouetted against a sky of dull lavender. Alwald was in the lead with the Lodestone in his hand. The others did not walk in a group but spread out, each wishing to keep his own company, for the terror of the night still weighed upon their spirits.

They saw no more Upas groves, the landscape having turned into smooth heath.

Ognam, walking in the rear, was thinking about his mystical sight of the crystal bird when Tana stood still so that he would catch up with her. Seeing this, he tried to move at an angle to avoid her – and was amazed at himself. A few hours ago he was ready to follow the example of poor Buffaloon on her account; now she was still the damsel he had rescued from the subterranean cavern but little else. Once her laugh would have pierced his heart, her figure excited hopeless daydreams, the smile she gave to others provoked shameful jealousy, but now he decided she was merely vain behind the mask of her beauty.

'Ognam,' she cried, crossing over to him. 'I could not thank you properly before because I was so upset. It was the second time you have been my knight errant.'

He mumbled that it was nothing.

'Ognam, I have long wanted to tell you that when you came into Krispin's cabin nothing happened. I mean, he did put his arms round me but it was just the gesture of a friend because I had been worried. Being a man you would not understand. But I was sorry that you misunderstood, and I was hurt by the way you sulked.'

Again Ognam mumbled.

'I want us always to be friends, but there is something strange about you,' she said. 'What has happened? Do you not have feelings for me any more?'

Ognam no longer mumbled. He looked at her, smiled slightly and walked on. For a long moment she stood looking after him, and then she too continued the trek.

By noon they had reached the beginning of the hills. The ground rose in a series of vast steps, some of which were covered with trees which, the travellers were relieved to see, bore no resemblance to the Upas groves. Having climbed up a steep slope to find themselves on a plateau stretching to the next step, they rested beneath a clump of firs and ate their simple midday meal.

'Did you do that on purpose?' Gambal demanded.

'What?' asked Dikon who had thrown himself down close by,

'You knocked my arm. My wine is spilt.'

'I never touched your arm, my friend.'

'I did not spill the last of my wine myself.'

'If I did then I am sorry.'

'Easy words. I suggest a better apology would be to fill my cup.'

'The pottons take your cup – and you!'

'Bold words for a slave.'

'You . . .!'

The big man leapt to his feet, his fists bunched, the chain that hung from his wrist jangling. Mute, alarmed at the unexpected flare-up of anger, seized it and pulled as though to draw Dikon away from the folly. In reply Dikon shook his arm and sent him reeling.

'Stop this,' cried Alwald. 'You are like two winesops brawling in a whorehouse.'

'Keep out of this, my lord,' said Gambal in a sneering tone. 'You may have been cock of the dungheap in River Garde but—'

'Speak not to my friend like this,' warned Krispin.

'Seal your mouth, Master Krispin, or you will make matters worse,' said Danya in a reasonable tone and he placed himself between Gambal and Krispin, with the result he received a cuff which had been intended for the latter.

'Pox on you! No one strikes me without repayment,' In swinging round Danya landed an accidental blow on Ognam.

'You are mad!' screamed Tana while Ognam, his face white with fury, climbed to his feet holding his staff like a mace.

Meanwhile Mute, having regained his feet, seized a clod of earth and hurled it at Dikon. It struck the side of his head and mistaking it as a blow from Gambal, who in his eyes was the cause of the trouble, Dikon flung him to the turf.

For a moment Gambal lay winded while everyone else shouted at each other.

Krispin did not know why Alwald, instead of appreciating that he had spoken in his defence, was swearing at him. 'This is the last straw, you overbearing potton turd,' he retorted and stepped forward.

'No,' pleaded Tana.

'Aside, harlot!' raved Alwald.

In reply to the insult she furrowed his cheek with her nails.

There was a pause in the abuse, and everyone saw Gambal slowly rise to his feet and draw a knife from his doublet.

'Kill the whoreson!' someone shouted.

Dikon advanced swinging his slave chain . . .

And then gentle music floated about them. Dikon paused and the hate-filled voices died, and slowly everyone turned to where Ognam stood on a log playing his flute-like staff just as he had played it to lead the children of Thaan into the Drakenfel.

The melody was simple but it had the effect of softening the anger that had been welling in each of the travellers. Pulses slowed. Gambal's knife disappeared. Tana looked with dismay at the bloody scratches on Alwald's cheek.

On and on went the music, becoming more lively and suggesting childish pleasures, and hands that had been fists began to beat time. Dikon found himself whistling to it.

Ognam jumped down from the log and began to walk forward with a skipping gait. The music seemed to invite everyone to dance and one after another they followed the jongleur. Gambal suddenly skipped in imitation of Ognam and was rewarded by a ripple of laughter. Mute wagged his narrow head in time to the piping. Danya suddenly broke into a sailor's dance. Tana whirled as she would have at a ball on the terrace overlooking Lake Taloon, and Alwald joined her.

Ognam continued playing and walking, and the others followed in a dancing line. It was like a folktale about enchanted dancers coming to life.

At last the jongleur had no more breath. He dropped on his bottom and threw his arms up with a comical expression. Laughing, the others collapsed round him.

Then, as the silence returned, they looked at each other in puzzlement. Had anger really flared a few minutes ago?

Ognam climbed to his feet and raised his staff to attract attention.

'My friends,' he said. 'My fellow questers, my companions in near-misfortune. A little while back

I could have broken this staff over the head of Shipmaster Danya and you all felt equally angry, even murderous, towards each other. Then I asked myself why a band of comrades such as we should act like this. Indeed, since we entered this land of accursed twilight, our tempers have been getting shorter and shorter with each other. We did not behave thus before, so why now? And it suddenly became clear to me that there is some malignity in the very air about us that is as dangerous to those who wander into this region as the bronze giant or the Upas trees – a malignity that turns friends into foes who will finally destroy each other. It is surely the effect of some spell cast over the land at the time of The Enchantment to prevent Princess Livia's resting place being found.'

There were murmurs of agreement.

'Let us be on our guard for such subtle deceits,' Ognam continued. 'Let us vow to ourselves not to be possessed by anger – or even thoughts of self-destruction.'

There were a few puzzled looks at his last words but Danya clapped him on the back. 'Without your music we might have been killing each other by now, Master Jongleur.'

'Music has its own magic,' Ognam replied.

TEN

The White Knight

'Travellers, go no further.'

The voice was imperious, as was the appearance of the speaker. Though his aquiline features showed great age, his eyes blazed beneath bushy eyebrows as white as his hair which hung in heavy braids from under a garland of oak leaves. His robe, too, was white and appeared to shine in the perpetual twilight of the Shadow Realm, and he reminded Alwald of a manuscript picture he had once seen in the library of River Garde of a pagan priest from the days before Ythan had been enlightened by the faith of the Serene Mother.

This figure stood above the travellers on steps that had been cut in the face of a low cliff. In his hand he held a staff which was topped with a garland similar to that bound about his brow.

'To have come so far is folly,' he intoned. 'To go further into the Shadow Realm will bring death to you all. There is no mercy in the Realm for those who trespass upon its secrets.'

The travellers moved uneasily before his piercing gaze, then several edged forward.

'You have been warned. I swear by my blasting rod that doom awaits you upon these forbidden step-lands. Turn away before it is too late.'

The figure raised its staff threateningly.

'Up your fundament with your blasting rod,' Ognam cried, 'and see what doom awaits you.'

There was muted laughter at this crudity. The figure shimmered and dissolved and the travellers mounted the steps.

'It seems to me that these apparitions are to test rather than harm,' said Krispin as he toiled behind Alwald. 'I doubt not the sorcerer who bespelled our path could have given them the power to destroy us if he had wished.'

'We have become used to such phantoms and can ignore them, but imagine the effect they would have on the lower . . . on humble folk such as outcasts or primitives,' said Alwald. 'I wonder whether the figure was really there or whether some lingering enchantment caused us to have the illusion of seeing him.'

'No matter,' said Gambal. 'To me such manifestations are portents that the end of the quest is near. In olden times did not magicians guard their treasure with tricks of gramarye? One would expect the most priceless treasure of all to be so guarded.'

Two days had passed since the travellers had left the Upas grove, and after Ognam had pacified them with his pipe music they had been remarkably courteous to each other. The Jongleur's suggestion that they were the victims

416

of maleficent forces hostile to intruders had soon been borne out by frightening phenomena.

The first of these had been a terrible voice that had rolled like thunder in the dark sky as it commanded them to abandon their journey. When they summoned up enough courage to ignore it, it had died like thunder fading in distant hills.

The next manifestation had been a band of spectral warriors but they too had faded when their threatening gestures were ignored. More alarming was a circle of standing stones which stood in the path indicated by the Lodestone. The companions saw that each megalith had a hint of humanity in its weathered shape, and as they approached they were conscious of sighing voices in the air.

'Once we were as you,' they seemed to be saying, 'but we did not heed the bane of the Shadow Realm. Turn back, travellers. To continue will mean that you become as us.'

For a moment their courage ebbed, then it was Ognam again who saved the hour. Raising his holed staff to his lips he played his lilting tune and marched on. The others followed and when they looked back there was no sign of the circle.

Now, with several manifestations passed, the travellers were close to the top of the foothills which lay beneath the Mountains of the Moon, the ranges that formed a mighty barrier between the Shadow Realm and the remotest areas of Ythan. While the light remained as dim as ever, the snow dusted peaks looming over them glimmered as though, being above the twilight, they caught the

417

rays of a higher sun. As they had gradually ascended from the humid plain, the air had become cooler and cooler until the companions regretted leaving their heavy mariners' cloaks behind in the wreck of the *Amber Star.*

'Do you realise that this stairway is the first true man-made work we have seen,' Alwald said as they neared the top of the cliff into which it had been cut.

'Apart from the colossus,' said Krispin as he climbed close behind his companion to protect the pack containing the precious flacon.

'I doubt me if that could have been the work of ordinary men. But this path was not formed by sorcery. You can see the marks of pick and mattock. I have a feeling that when we reach the top there will be something to surprise us.'

He was right. As each member breasted the lip of the cliff they beheld a changed landscape. A pleasant plateau ran to the Mountains of the Moon, guarded to the right and left by rocky ridges curving from the ranges to give the impression of a vast semicircular bowl. Here and there small hills rose from forest which covered much of its level floor, though grassland stretched like a broad avenue in front of the travellers towards the base of the mountains. What seemed so marvellous about it was the brilliance of its colours – the sky was azure, the grass beneath their feet emerald, the trees verdant . . . They had escaped from the twilight.

The last of their wine was brought out from their packs to celebrate their return to daylight and they

418

knocked their leather winecups together with great good will. There was laughter and handshaking, but as Tana was about to throw her arms about Ognam, he moved away as though unaware of her intention and she turned and embraced Danya instead.

When they were rested and their eyes accustomed to the pure light about them, Alwald consulted the Lodestone and pointed down the avenue which ran between tall forest walls to the mountains.

'Yonder our route,' he cried cheerfully. 'With luck we may reach journey's end by nightfall for I would wager my last crown that Livia must be hidden in a cavern at the foot of those peaks.'

With lightened hearts the travellers set forth towards the Mountains of the Moon. In the twilight of Shadow Realm they had tended to be solitary and morose but now they laughed together like old friends enjoying a pleasant outing. Even Mute grinned at the jokes being told.

After an hour Alwald paused. 'I cannot understand it but the Lodestone has turned,' he announced. 'It is pointing straight into the forest.'

'But ahead is the obvious way to the ranges,' said Ognam.

Gambal strode on for several hundred paces, then returned and said, 'Your Lodestone is intelligent, Lord Alwald. There is a deep ravine ahead which, without a bridge, would be impossible to cross. It is like an enormous crack running across the plateau.'

'Then let the Lodestone guide us – after all, it

brought us safe from the Cold Sea to the Shadow Realm,' said Danya, and hoisting his crossbow to his shoulder he followed Alwald into the tall trees growing on the righthand side of the avenue. To walk between their well-spaced trunks was another pleasure for the travellers. Here birds sang and there were the myriad tiny noises that rarely cease in woodland – the creak of branches, the whisper of leaves, the murmur of a rill, the stridor of insects – and they realised that not only had they passed through a land of shadow but a land of silence.

Holding the Lodestone box in his hand, Alwald led them on to a track, most probably a deer trail, that wound through the trees and which, being free from bracken and other undergrowth, made walking easier. Soon it widened and they stopped in surprise at the edge of a glade. At the far end they could see two massive pillars of rough-hewn wood supporting a dizzy rope bridge that crossed the ravine Gambal had seen earlier on. To one side of the glade was pitched a small pavilion beside which a richly caparisoned warhorse was tethered. A lance was set in the ground beside the tasselled entrance to the pavilion on which hung a white shield decorated with a black rose.

At the sight of this emblem Dikon uttered an oath of surprise. Krispin guessed that it reminded him unhappily of the Companions of the Rose, although the rose on the shield had an archaic look compared to the symbol used by the Regent's special guard.

A moment later the entrance curtains were

thrust aside and a figure, easily as tall as Dikon, emerged and walked to the middle of the glade. From his spurs to the plume on his visored helm he was arrayed in white armour, and his gauntlets were clamped on the double-handed grip of a massive broadsword.

'I am Pallus, Knight of the Bridge.'

The voice, issuing through visor slits, had a hollow timbre but nevertheless had the effect of filling the glade with menace. It was as though a cloud passed across the sun and the cheerful forest murmurings were silenced.

'While I stand, none may cross, and you challenge me at your peril,' the white knight continued. 'You have trespassed in a forbidden region and your time is short but it will be even shorter if you take a single step forward.'

'This is no apparition,' muttered Alwald.

'I fear not,' agreed Krispin. 'How do we get past him?'

'I must challenge him,' said Alwald. 'As a knight he will understand the code of chivalry.'

'But he is so much bigger than you,' protested Krispin.

'Let me try a bolt on him,' said Danya raising the crossbow he had carried from the *Amber Star*.

'He wears plate armour,' said Alwald. 'Even your bolts would hardly scratch it. This must be done in the accepted manner.'

'But you are without armour,' objected Danya.

'But I shall have Woundflame,' said Alwald. 'Give it to me, Krispin.'

421

'But I am used to Woundflame, mayhap it should be I—'

'That you have had some success in the past against odd creatures and common soldiers I shall not deny,' said Alwald in exasperation, 'but when it comes to knightly combat you have no experience or training, nor do you have the inherent tradition necessary for such passages of arms.'

'This is not a tournament,' retorted Krispin. 'We are not out to win glory but to get over that bridge.'

'Then give me my sword.'

'You did not want it when you passed it to me.'

'I want it now.'

'It is mine.'

'Serene Mother! Now I understand. You want to be the hero. You hate the idea of anyone else winning fame.'

'I give not a fart for fame!' Krispin protested. 'What use is fame to a toymaker! I just want to get this Mother-cursed quest over.'

'Then give me Woundflame.'

'Take it.'

He drew the sword from its scabbard and despite his anger he noticed that it retained its dull appearance.

'Alwald, the sword will not work for you,' he began but in a fury Alwald snatched it away.

'You know more about chisels than swords, I think.'

The others had watched this argument in bewilderment. Ognam raised his staff in case he needed to exorcise another spirit of hostility, but before anything more could be said Alwald marched forward and stood before the white knight.

'I, Alwald, son of Grimwald VII, Hereditary Lord of the River March, do hereby demand leave to pass over yonder bridge or if you gainsay my right of passage I do hereby challenge you, Pallus, Knight of the Bridge, to mortal combat,' he declared.

'Well phrased,' said the hollow voice from within the helmet. 'It pleases me to cross swords with one of noble lineage. Lord Alwald, I accept your challenge, and may the Mother have mercy on your spirit for I shall have none on your body.'

'I do not like this,' Dikon muttered.

'We should have tried to find another way over the ravine,' said Gambal.

'Should we not call him back?' asked Tana.

'His honour would not allow him to quit now,' said Krispin sourly.

'Commence!' shouted Pallus and swung his broadsword in a glittering arc. Alwald dodged easily and, unencumbered by armour, immediately lunged Woundflame's point at the knight's gorget. Pallus countered with an upward stroke that sent Woundflame spinning high in the air.

For a moment Alwald looked at his empty hands as though unable to believe he was weaponless, then he was aware of the white knight's upraised sword. He retreated backwards, ducking this way and that as the heavy blade swung at him.

Meanwhile Krispin darted forward to where Woundflame had come to earth and snatched it up.

'Alwald,' he shouted, and flung the sword hilt first in his direction.

At the sound of his name Alwald turned and managed to catch Woundflame by its grip, but the manoeuvre almost cost him his life. Turning back to face the white knight, he glimpsed his opponent's sword descending straight for his skull and he jerked his body backwards with such violence that he toppled full length onto the grass. Although the broadsword missed his head, its point left a bloody gash in his arm.

Pallus loomed above the prone youth.

'You have lost, Marcher Lord,' he intoned. 'You, and your companions.'

Again the knight's sword flashed as it swung downwards but Alwald – thankful that he was not weighted by armour – rolled to one side. A second later he was on his feet and with both hands gripping Woundflame he executed a sideways stroke that would have made his old fencing master at River Garde proud of him.

Pallus was still raising his heavy weapon when Woundflame's blade caught him on the exact spot where his helmet was laced to the collar of his breastplate. So strong was the blow that the helmet was shorn away. It struck the turf and rolled until it disappeared over the edge of the ravine. With a crash the armoured figure fell at Alwald's feet.

Tana gave a cry of horror at seeing the knight decapitated. The others craned forward, expecting to be sickened by blood flooding from the gap where the helmet had been. Instead they saw nothing. The breastplate was empty.

For a moment no one spoke, then Alwald muttered, 'More gramarye.'

He looked crestfallen that he had defeated nothing more than an empty suit of armour until Ognam cried, 'All the more honour to have won over sorcery.' He turned to the others. 'Lord Alwald's victory will become a minstrel's tale.'

When Alwald's wound had been bound and all were ready to cross the bridge, he held up Woundflame in front of Krispin.

'I misjudged its powers,' he said. 'Look at that tarnished blade. It is a blunt and chipped relic. And yet, when you have used it, I had the notion that it was bright and I thought there was magic melded in it. The white knight – or whatever it was animating the white armour – would not have sent my own sword spinning like that. Strange! You may as well have it back. It does not suit me.' He sighed and added quietly, 'Or mayhap I do not suit it.'

'Thank you, Alwald,' said Krispin and slid Woundflame into its scabbard.

Clinging desperately to the handrope, the travellers braved the swaying bridge one at a time. Krispin, terrified of heights but loathe to show it, was the last to step onto the jerking boards. Halfway across he paused to look back and was not at all surprised that the pavilion, warhorse and armour had vanished.

ELEVEN

Livia Found

The low sun cast a warm light over the Mountains of the Moon and even their snow-mantled peaks were briefly transmuted from silver to gold as the travellers walked wearily down the broad clearing that ran through the forest to the cliffs of reddish rock. Although their bodies were tired, their spirits soared when they beheld two gigantic statues carved in the cliff face ahead of them. From a distance they appeared to be identical, with the bodies of winged horses and the helmeted heads of men whose tightly curled beards flowed down to their massive chests.

As they drew nearer they saw that they were not quite the same. One held a bow and the other a lyre; one gazed with arrogant eyes towards the travellers, the other, equally haughty, looked down upon a paved square below. Set in a massive pylon between these fabulous creatures was a pair of doors, and the travellers had little doubt that they were approaching the entrance to Princess Livia's sanctum.

'Less than half a league to go,' exclaimed Alwald

who had finally put the Lodestone box away. 'I find it hard to believe after coming so far.'

'I wonder how many leagues we have travelled,' said Krispin who was marching beside him. 'It seems a lifetime ago since we set out from the Peak Tower and followed the River of Night to the Vale of Mabalon.'

'Mabalon!' echoed Alwald with a sigh.

'And we covered a goodly stretch of country travelling from the vale to Danaak, and then across the Wilderness of Gil with Gambal and Ognam to Thaan.'

'And from Thaan to the Domain of Olam along the underground river,' Alwald continued. 'And then – best of all – the flight to The Mage's tower. As long as I live I shall never forget soaring on the back of the griffin.'

'Never shall I.'

'I suppose our longest journey was coming down from the Cold Sea to the Shadow Realm in the *Amber Star*. I must ask Danya if he has any idea of the distance we sailed.'

'Thinking of the voyage, I often wonder about Haven,' said Krispin. 'Although it was passing strange, there was no evil there like some of the places we have known. The people were kindly and meant us no harm.'

'Except that they wanted us to stay. What should we have found if we had agreed as Nomis must have done?'

'Mayhap we will learn the story some day when the quest is over.'

'I cannot imagine the quest ending,' said Ognam.

'It has taken us on such a roundabout route, seeking clues, and it seems to have been going on for years.'

'Yet it is only a few months since we left the Wald,' Krispin said. 'It was early spring when the Wolf Horde crossed the River of Night and now it is high summer.'

'Those doors must be made of bronze,' said Alwald pointing ahead. 'They have gone green with age, like the door to the sepulchre in the Peak Tower. I must confess that I did not expect anything grand like this. I suppose I had an idea that she would lie in some hidden cave.'

'There is certainly nothing secret about that gateway,' said Krispin. 'It makes me wonder why no Pilgrims reached it in the past.'

'Perhaps they did,' said Ognam quietly.

'Of course, we may only be thinking wishfully,' Krispin continued. 'Just because there is a gateway in a cliff it does not mean that Princess Livia is on the other side of it. It may yet be another deceit. I shall believe we are at the end of the quest when we actually see Her Highness. And even then, if we awaken her, we will have to take her back to Ythan.'

'What is that peasant expression of yours – I shall worry about Moonday on Moonday,' said Alwald.

When they eventually reached the paved square beneath the two statues the travellers felt dwarfed by their size and by the huge pylon which was incised with strange patterns. A spiral of runes was carved on the stone lintel above the bronze doors which were three times the height of a man. Now that they were close, the companions saw that these were decorated with lines of bas-relief mouldings of humans and animals and some creatures that had characteristics of both animals and men.

Ognam in particular was fascinated by them.

'If one could learn to read their meaning I think they might tell the secret history of the world,' he declared. 'At least this knowledge escaped the Great Burnings of the Witchfinders.'

'I once said there was much more to you than just a clown,' said Tana.

'That seems a long time ago,' said Ognam without bitterness. 'In the daylight I returned to my true colours – red and green motley.'

'I confess that you are right but . . .'

'It is of no matter now.'

' . . . but since the Upas grove you seem to have changed again. You are as I imagined when I waited for you to cross the underground lake. It makes me glad, though I cannot explain the change.'

'I think a bird may have had something to do with it,' said Ognam with a gentle smile. 'But do not be deceived, I am nothing more than a jongleur.' And he walked closer to the doors to look at the lines of figures. Here a man lay as though dying with his hand raised in benediction, there two armies faced each other, here horned dancers pranced, there a couple were locked erotically . . .

'What a price those would fetch in Danaak,' said Gambal.

Outwardly he retained his usual self-assured calm, but behind this façade he felt as he had when, dressed in the pied garb of the dying Revel

Master Wilk, he had risked everything to present Silvermane to the Regent. His pulses throbbed and his fingers curled nervously round the mirror he carried in his doublet pocket.

''Tis a wonder without doubt,' said Danya to Dikon and Mute who stood close by with lingering deference to him as shipmaster. 'But I cannot see how we can enter. There is not even a keyhole in those metal doors.'

'Not even a keyhole!' muttered Alwald with suppressed anger. 'Why in the name of Omad did not The Mage tell us how we could enter?'

'Mayhap he did not know,' said Krispin yet again.

Alwald walked to the door and struck it impatiently.

'No one home,' said Ognam.

Krispin meanwhile was gazing at the rune spiral carved above the doors. It seemed very familiar and this was confirmed when he pulled out from his shirt the thin chain on which hung the Disk of Livia. As he held it up in the orange light of the sun that was about to sink below the gloom of the Shadow Realm, he saw that the runes and the way they were placed were identical.

As he continued to gaze at the arcane medallion a voice began to murmur in his inner ear. He was reminded of the day he had sought to find the black boat in the ruined shrine after they had saved the Lady Demara and Margan from the nomads in River Garde. And, as had happened then, he began to chant sonorous words that seemed to rise out of some forgotten recess of memory and which would only have meaning to those versed in Old Ythan.

430

The others fell silent while the incantation continued. Then, as the last words died away, they were replaced by a harsh grinding as the doors slowly swung inwards to reveal a passage leading into shadow.

'Where did you learn that?' asked Gambal.

'It must have been hidden in my mind by the Lady Eloira who set me upon the Pilgrim Path,' Krispin replied. 'She had a method of entrancement by which she planted knowledge in one's mind to lie forgotten until some sign or need would bring it forth.'

'I wonder how she knew the spell.'

Krispin gave his characteristic shrug and slipped the Disk of Livia back under his shirt.

The sun sent her beams horizontally along the passage as the travellers entered it but before long she dropped below the horizon and dusk gathered round them. Krispin produced the light wand from his pack and in its cold radiance they were able to continue without difficulty.

'It seems to run into the heart of the ranges,' said Alwald who walked beside Krispin.

Much of the companions' light-heartedness had evaporated; the awesome passage and the gravity of what lay ahead had induced a feeling of solemnity mixed with some apprehension of the unknown. At one point a metallic clang echoed between the passage walls, telling them that the doors which had magically opened to Krispin's incantation had closed against the oncoming night. Each felt an unexpressed uneasiness – would they be able to open them again?

431

At last they found they were descending steps into a hall that had been excavated from the living rock of the mountain. The wandlight reflected on objects of silver that were piled round the walls and was transformed into multicoloured sparks by gems heaped upon tables.

'We had best touch not a single jewel,' said Krispin. 'I believe they were left here as some sort of trap – a temptation that would beguile men from their purpose.'

'I remember a children's rhyme about the Sleeping Beauty,' said Ognam. 'That mentioned treasure but here there is so much sorcery in the air that if one took a handful of precious stones they would probably turn to dry leaves ere long.'

Careful to avoid the gleaming and glittering objects, they walked to the opposite end of the hall where they found their way blocked by a heavy door.

'I hope Master Krispin knows a spell to open that,' said Danya drily as he shifted his crossbow from one hand to the other.

'I think there is little need for spells,' said Krispin and turning a ring of wrought iron he pushed the door open. Air like that of long disused chambers, yet somehow heavy with rose perfume, met the travellers as they pressed forward to see if at last they had reached the chamber where the Princess had lain in a magical sleep since The Enchantment.

Holding the wand high, Krispin crossed the threshold and saw that several steps ran down to a floor of rare red porphyry tiles; the walls and pillars that rose to the vaulted ceiling were of white marble. In the centre of this chamber, which was about the size of a small shrine, lay a figure – the Princess Livia.

No one dared speak as they descended the steps and gazed at her in wonderment. At first it seemed that she lay on a slab of pale grey stone but as they looked closer they saw that it had movement, that it coiled within itself in the same way that colours had coiled within the Esav. It was not grey stone but grey smoke which held her as gently as the softest couch. She wore a robe of white samite which had yellowed with the passage of time, as had the pillow embroidered with lilies upon which her head rested. Her arms were folded across her breast and the expression on her face was one of serenity.

It was not just that they had finally reached the end of the Pilgrims' quest that kept the travellers speechless but the fact that they were looking upon the most beautiful woman they had ever seen.

'Jennet!' breathed Krispin.

To him Princess Livia was identical to the beloved sister he had left behind in the High Wald; her skin was naturally paler but her hair was the same spun gold and cascaded to the floor where it lay in profusion like the hair of Princess One-wish in the folktale. And Krispin had no doubt that when her eyelids opened he would see eyes of the same clear blue that held their own light. No wonder the Lady Eloira had been so struck by Jennet's appearance for she knew the features of the Princess through a portrait.

'At last,' said Alwald finally. 'Princess Livia,

daughter of King Johan XXXIII and heiress to the Empty Throne of Ythan.'

'Would that the Lady Eloira could be with us at this moment,' murmured Krispin.

'The Mother willing, she may see her someday,' said Alwald. 'But now let us not delay in recalling her to life.'

Bending over his pack he removed the precious flacon which he placed carefully on the floor.

'The Mage said that the only way she will awaken is to bathe her with water from the Wells of Ythan,' he said. 'It would be seemly if you were to do it, Tana.'

'There will be no need.'

Everyone had been gazing at the Princess but at the sound of an unfamiliar voice they looked about them in alarm.

'The quest ends here but not in the way you expected,' continued Mute. 'My name is Edom and I am a member of the Witchfinder's Guild, and I hereby charge you all with treason. Dikon is a Companion of the Rose and a champion of champions, and he will thrust his knife into the heart of the Princess should any of you make a move.'

The bewildered travellers saw the big man stand over the sleeper holding a knife with its point pressing into the samite over her bosom.

'Step back to the end of the chamber in orderly manner,' continued the Witchfinder. 'You, Shipmaster, will leave your crossbow on the floor.' For a moment they hesitated and Dikon pressed his blade further against the yielding flesh. They backed away.

434

'But how can you talk?' demanded Tana. 'You were dumb when I nursed you.'

'I was no more mute than Dikon was a slave.'

'But he has the brand.'

'He allowed himself to be branded to complete the deception. Such devotion to duty is to be expected in a Companion. We both starved ourselves before we were set adrift on the *Amber Star*'s course.'

'The black ship – the pox'd black ship!' cried Danya.

'Of course. With her tall masts it was easy to keep watch on you with her hull below the horizon.'

'But you had to know our whereabouts first.'

'We were given that information by the Regent.'

'The Regent? How could he know about us?'

'Because I informed him,' said Gambal.

Such was the impact of his words that no one spoke.

'That is so,' said the Witchfinder. 'When it was known that Lord Alwald and Master Krispin were on the Pilgrim's quest, and had a good chance of succeeding, the Lord Regent decided to allow them to continue it in the company of a trusted agent for he was as keen to find the Princess as any follower of the Pilgrim Path.'

'So that is why you arranged our escape from the Citadel,' said Krispin.

'Of course,' said Gambal. 'My task was to win your trust.'

'You did that,' Alwald agreed bitterly. 'But do you not have qualms over such treachery when we shared so much hardship together as comrades?

435

After all, if it had not been for Krispin you would have been killed by the dhrul in the Wilderness of Gil.'

'You speak of treachery but I was no traitor – I served my master. In law it is you who are traitors, for by seeking the Princess you conspire against the lawful Regent.'

'But how did you get word to Danaak?' asked Krispin. He still held the light wand in one hand, his other was inching towards his sword grip.

'The Lady Mandraga gave me a mirror,' said Gambal. He pulled it from his pocket and placed it on a narrow ledge that ran round the chamber. 'When I looked into it my face appeared in her ladyship's magical mirror. It is possible that she can see what is happening here at this moment. I hope so.'

An uncertain look passed over the Witchfinder's narrow face but he said nothing.

'And now?' said Alwald.

'The Regent's order is that the Princess must be revived and taken to him in secret.'

In that case they dare not harm her, thought Krispin, *and if so . . .*

His plan was aborted by the Witchfinder handing Danya's crossbow to Dikon who backed to the foot of the steps with the weapon pointed at the company from the opposite end of the chamber.

'A kraken bolt for the first to step forward,' he said.

'And what will happen to us?' asked Tana from where she stood beside Ognam.

'Although I would like to take you to Danaak for

436

fitting punishment, it will be enough to escort Her Highness through the Shadow Realm to the coast where our ship will be waiting. Therefore I have decided that you may remain locked in the sleeper's chamber for eternity. An appropriate ending after the effort you made to get here. Now, Master Gambal, it is time to revive the sleeper.'

Gambal picked up the flacon and stood beside the Companion of the Rose.

'Before I attempt to awaken the Princess there is something I would say,' he declared. 'And I hope that in faraway Danaak the Lady Mandraga will be watching her glass, for what it about to happen concerns her.' He bowed his head towards the mirror he had set up.

'Speak if you must, but hurry,' said the Witchfinder.

'My words will be few,' said Gambal, and he carefully set the flacon on a step. 'As you now know, my fellow questers, I travelled with you at the behest of my Lord Regent. You were strangers to me and why should I have cared about your fates – it was my fate that concerned me. And yet, as we travelled together and shared much, I must confess that for the first time in my life I began to understand comradeship.'

Danya sneered.

'And in Thaan I discovered something else I had not known before. Suffice it to say it was a gift brought to me by a heretical novice.'

Lorelle! thought Krispin.

'Fate decreed that the novice travelled with us to the Domain of Olam and there she died. Her death was the penalty for forbidden curiosity. She gazed into that mirror, and came face to face with the Lore Mistress of Ythan.'

'Enough,' said the Witchfinder. 'You can tell your tale some other time. Now is the time to bathe the Princess.'

'Of course, I have the water here,' Gambal said. 'But first, I want to be sure the Lady Mandraga will be able to witness the process.'

He glanced at the mirror and, putting his hand in his doublet, drew out a kerchief.

'One must have clean hands to touch a princess,' he said. Then, with a terrible change of tone, he cried: 'Mandraga, I know it was your witchery that brought about the death of Lorelle – of she who taught me love – and long have I waited for this moment to repay you.'

With a swift movement he turned and drove his kerchief-wrapped dagger straight into Dikon's heart.

The Companion of the Rose stumbled back, struggling to raise the crossbow but his strength was ebbing with his life, and the weapon was pointing at the floor when he fired.

Krispin saw the bolt strike the flacon, saw it shatter into brilliant blue shards, and felt a sob tear his throat as the sparkling water from the Wells of Ythan flowed over the tiles of porphyry, drained through the cracks between the tiles . . . and was lost . . .

For ever.